Rose

Rose Without a Thorn
(The Tudor Child Queen)

by
Anne Stevens

Tudor Crimes: Book XVII

Foreword

It is now the late Summer of 1541, and the Archbishop of Canterbury, Thomas Cranmer, is caught between his duty to his king, and the sacred trust of the Confessional.

Queen Catherine has told him, in the sacred secrecy he has foolishly granted her, that she has committed certain immoral acts with several diverse persons both before, and since, her marriage to Henry.

Archbishop Cranmer has stopped her from going into greater detail, and told no-one, save Mush Draper and Richard Cromwell, what has passed. Now, his lips are sealed, and he is sickened with the awful weight that has been placed upon his shoulders.

To reveal Catherine's secrets would ruin her, and might even lead to her death. The king is an unforgiving man, and cannot stand the idea of others having lain with his queen. The Archbishop of Canterbury must wrestle with his conscience.

Thomas Cromwell, posthumously trying to run England from the comfort of Miriam's Antwerp palace, is trying to limit the damage. His agents are watching Francis Dereham, the queen, and her household,

"That'll be Anne Boleyn," the little fellow replies, knowingly. "Back in the day, they say they were close. I dare say no one bothered telling Henry, or else Wyatt's head would have been taken with her brother's."

"It is a hard thing to do ... long for a love you can never have," Mush says. "Though I know, for certain that this poet never managed to quench his thirst at Queen Anne's well."

"Really?" The little man sniggers. "More fool him then. Getting all doe eyed over a woman who does not even let you touch her is a waste of time."

"*O Death, O Death, rock me asleep,*
Bring me to quiet rest;
Let pass my weary guiltless ghost
Out of my careful breast." Tom Wyatt intones, and someone blows a raspberry at the back of the room.

"If she was guiltless, then I am the pope," another mutters, and this gets a laugh all around. "Make it more cheerful, Sir Tom, and throw in some honest swiving."

"*Ring out my doleful knell;*
Thy sound my death abroad will tell,
For I must die,
There is no remedy.
My pains, my pains, who can express?

Alas, they are so strong!
My dolours will not suffer strength
My life for to prolong." Here, Tom Wyatt pauses, and throws his arms wide, as if he invites the audience to come into his bosom.

"Toll on, thou passing bell;
Ring out my doleful knell;
Thy sound my death abroad will tell,
For I must die,
There is no remedy..."

"There bloody well is," the landlord says. "Get off my table, sir, and stop going on about death and bleedin' disaster. It is bad enough with all this bloody plague going about. I lost six of my best customers just this last week. Either give us a good old one, or bugger off, and drink at the Black Boy Tavern instead."

"Have you no heart for a great love lost, sir?" the poet asks.

"Not when it is Anne Boleyn," the man replies. "Even mention of that woman can still get you locked up."

"Very well." Tom Wyatt sits down, and drinks off a good half of his tankard of ale. He has done as Mush asks, and his friend will be happy. The rumours about he and Anne Boleyn are still rife, and might yet get him *whilst Thomas Culpeper is spending time in the country, with Barnaby Fowler… a prisoner, although he does not yet realise it.*

Will Draper's fortunes continue to prosper, and as Summer gives way to Autumn, he is clearly amongst the king's best friends. This, however, can be a two edged sword, for Henry expects him to be able to solve every problem, and cure every ill.

Then the plague shows itself, striking down rich and poor alike. The outbreak sends those who can scurrying to hide in the countryside, whilst it lies over London, like a black raven of death.

Three months go by, and the colder weather seems to drive the cursed sickness away. Life can return to normal again, but what is normal now at court?

After the plague, there comes Henry; a king whose growing wrath threatens to bring England to its knees. His hatred for those who have misled him grows with each hour that passes, and Will Draper finds himself having to defend both the innocent, and the guilty.

1 Plague

"Sir Thomas Wyatt is in the Tap Room again, guv'nor." The landlord of the Swan Inn gives a huge sigh at this news, and goes off to nip any trouble in the bud. Of late, the poet has been coming in often, and causing uproar amongst his customers with his inflammatory verses, often aimed at the king.

He arrives just in time to find the room sitting in rapt silence, as the handsome versifier declaims about their most favourite theme; love, and love lost. They are a maudlin crowd, when in their cups, and any sad love tale will get them sighing with regret.

> *"Defiled is my name full sore*
> *Through cruel spite and false report,*
> *That I may say for evermore,*
> *Farewell, my joy! Adieu comfort!*
> *For wrongfully ye judge of me*
> *Unto my fame a mortal wound,*
> *Say what ye list, it will not be,*
> *Ye seek for that can not be found."*

"He speaks of a love lost because of false complaints against her," Mush Draper explains to the man beside him.

arrested, so Mush has a simple plan.

The Swan is notorious for being a haven for spies who work for Richard Rich and the Duke of Norfolk. By planting the story that the poet never managed to seduce Anne Boleyn, Mush hopes the news will get back to the king's ears, and so sooth his mistrust of his favourite poet.

Tom Wyatt considers where he is, and that the freehold of the tavern is held by the estate of the Duke of Norfolk. He taps a finger to his nose, and waves the sparse crowd in closer to listen.

"Here's a mucky one for you, lads," he says. "Gather round and listen well."

"Thank Gawd," the landlord mutters, and the poet launches into a scurrilous little piece he once wrote for the amusement of the king.

"There was an old man of Norfolk,
who could neither kiss, nor fuck,
When the girls did play,
He would run away,

and never chance his luck." the poet chants. "Or might you prefer this one, Master landlord?" Tom Wyatt raises a hand to his eyes, and makes out that he is gazing out to sea.

"Behold, a ship is hoving in,

*to make it to safe harbour,
the ship is Henry's own belaying pin,
and the quayside is his barber."*
or, alternatively,
*"The landlord's wife is full of joy,
and loves her bawbies kissed,
but he, poor soul, is often coy,
or simply just too bloody pissed."*

"Right, that's enough." The landlord begins to roll up his sleeves, as if about to administer a sound thrashing. "Out, the pair of you. I'm not being insulted by a failed poet and his hangers on anymore. Sup elsewhere, and moan about how you never swived Anne Boleyn to them, you drunken jack o' dandy. Go on... out of my pub!"

"Come, Sir Thomas," Mush says, rather theatrically. "Let us be on our way. I fear I have some odd lumps under my armpit, and must seek out a doctor."

"Sweet Jesus!" The landlord crosses himself, and hopes the Austin Friars man is jesting. The plague is abroad again, and it strikes without fear or favour. "Be gone, and may God protect this house."

"And your dear wife," Tom Wyatt calls back. "For you must ask yourself how I am so familiar with her un-kissed bawbies, Master Chesterton."

They are gone, and running down the nearest alley before the landlord can summon his thugs to hand out a thrashing. It is a good thing for them that they miss Wyatt and Mush, for the two men are in a boisterous mood, and are looking for trouble.

"Let us go to the palace, and try to seduce a couple of the waiting on girls," the poet says, but Mush shakes his head.

"Isabella," he says. "I cannot dishonour my wife, Tom. Let us think up another jape to pass the time. Damn all those who have fled London, just because of a little sickness."

"Then we must go to Lady Georgina's Bawdy House," Wyatt replies. "The girls there put on a fine show, and you need only watch as they *fal da riddle* with one another."

"Swiving without a pintle is beyond my ken," Mush replies. "It is like eating cheese without bread. Still, if it will keep us out of trouble…"

They make their way down the deserted streets that link the Swan's seedy environs towards the part of town where the better class of house can be found. Lady Georgina's establishment is close to Westminster Palace, and her exotic girls, some from as far away as France and Padua, are the most amenable in the city.

"I shall hire Ginny, the one who dances with her trained dog," the poet decides. "It makes me laugh so to see the little thing leaping about, and trying to nip her buttocks."

"How elegant a picture you do paint, old friend," Mush says to Wyatt. "Now, here we are and I ..." The words die on his tongue. There is a cart outside Lady Georgina's Bawdy House, and two men, their faces masked with linen, are busy loading it up with a human cargo.

"Dear Christ," Mush mutters. He recognises Lady Georgina, despite her bloated face, and swollen limbs. Two other bodies are already aboard the rough death cart; the dancing Ginny, and her little dog. The plague shows no favour.

"*Let us wait for the reaper's touch,*
his icy fingers are close by,
he seldom spares us over much,
once he's looked us in the eye." Tom Wyatt intones. "We might be better in the comfort of our own homes, Mush. Though I do not have one just now. I tend to sleep where I may... or where some kind lady dictates."

"Then come home with me." Mush is suddenly sober. "Isabella will be happy to see you, and we can repel this sickness with strong wine and locked doors."

"You speak good sense, my dear old friend," Tom Wyatt says, "but I will take my chances amongst those who have not yet fled London. We tempt fate, and court death as if it were a lover."

"The plague…"

"Will kill me, if it wishes, wherever I lay my head," Tom Wyatt says. "I shall seek out some willing lady, and spend my time trying to seduce her. It is a noble enough pastime for a poet. Farewell, old friend."

The poet is gone, and Mush is left to make his own way home. In truth, he would have liked to move Isabella out of London, but she is a fatalist, and believes that her future is already written. He will head for home, and hope that they are all spared. It seems odd to him that he can survive a dozen fierce battles, yet be open to the ravages of an invisible killer like the dreaded plague.

"Would that you had a solid form," he growls, "so that I might hack at you with my sword."

*

"God curse these lying time servers, Will," the king rants. His leg is paining him much more than usual, and his mind is turning to revenge. "First they trick me into letting them kill Tom Cromwell, and then they fail me at every turn. I curse the day I listened to their whining, mealy mouthed lies."

"Sire, not all those about you are such men," Will replies. He knows that the best course open to him is to placate the king, and try to ease the pain from his ulcerated leg wound. "Has not Sir Rafe Sadler served you well, whilst you were sheltering in the country?"

There is plague abroad, once more, and Henry has been staying in Suffolk and Norfolk, until it runs its natural course. For three long months, his court has been scattered far and wide, and any who showed even the mildest symptoms, have been banished to suffer alone.

Now, as the October cold weather arrives, the outbreak seems to have abated, with little loss of life, except amongst the very poorest, who have suffered in their many hundreds. Still, Henry thinks, that is their place in the scheme of things.

The many are there to serve the few, and God, in his infinite wisdom sees that the poor suffer in place of the rich and noble. In my father's house are many mansions, the king thinks, but he deserves the best one, because he is the representative of God's church in England, and equal, at least to the bastard Pope in Rome.

"Rafe Sadler is a political plodder, as is our own, dear Dick Cromwell," Henry complains to his General of Examiner. "I ask them something important, and what do they say? They beg a few days leave to ponder on the answer they will give me. Back in old Tom Cromwell's time, he would be here, forever whispering in my ear, and seeing everything was running smoothly. The man was a consummate fixer of things, and he acted promptly."

"Does this new advice then displease you, Your Majesty?" Will asks.

"Not at all… it is excellent too, but it comes to me with a day or two's delay, and it is that which irks me," Henry replies. "Would they were another Thomas Cromwell."

"The Earl of Essex was a unique man, Your Majesty," Will Draper replies, truthfully. His opinion of his old master, as a statesman, could not be any higher than it is, and as a man, he was also quite extraordinary. "We all miss him. Even his enemies lament his passing."

"How so, sir?" Henry thinks this is some kind of a jest, and in poor humour. Norfolk hates the very memory of the fellow, and could not do enough to harm him, when he lived.

"You'd ask Tom Cromwell 'what is the price of beef on the hoof', and he would say '4d a pound weight', without a pause. Now you ask the *Duke of Wherever you Wish* the same question, and he has to ask his manager, who speaks to his steward, who seeks out six different butchers, who all give differing answers. Then this duke, no friend of Cromwell, or England for that matter, comes to you, and says he thinks it might be about 5d a pound, and your tax revenues are lost. Am I right in this, My Lord?"

"Damn me, but you are, Will." Henry tries to stand, but his leg hurts him far too much. The ulcerations are deeply embedded, and beginning to suppurate with a dark green pus. "Where is Cully?"

"Cully, sire?"

"Thomas Culpeper, my good right hand," Henry replies. "I have not seen him for these five or six weeks. He disappeared, just before the plague struck in Stepney. He should be here, by his master's side."

"Perhaps he is dead, sire," Will says. He is on dangerous ground now, for he knows well enough where Thomas Culpeper is, and who it is who is keeping him there. "Though the plague did not much hurt your court, there were over a thousand deaths amongst the poorer commoners."

"Cully, dead?" Henry shakes his head in disbelief. The thousand dead are of little import, for they are peasants, and that is what peasants always do when the plague, or the sweating sickness calls on them… they die. "I do not believe it for a moment, sir. He is simply hiding from me… or the plague. I treated him rather unkindly, you see." The king's voice becomes maudlin, as it always does, when he wishes to be heaped with sympathy for something bad that he has actually caused to happen.

"The fellow is perhaps afraid to return to London, just now," Will Draper offers. "The plague has that effect on people. I sent Miriam and the children to Cambridge, and ordered the sick to be gathered up, and confined in one place, so as to try and lessen the spread of the sickness."

"You did?" Henry is suitably impressed by such forward planning, but he thinks it wasted on any, save the nobility. "There, you see, that is the sort of thing dear old Cromwell would have advocated."

In Antwerp, that is exactly what did happen, and Tom Cromwell also saw to it that good doctors and expensive medicines were shipped to London, using his adopted name of *Mijnheer Tomas Cornelis*. Miriam is there now, helping with the ordering of relief, for food will soon be in short supply.

"I try to always think like him, sire," Will ventures. "For never did a man love you so."

"Now I have lost dear Cully too… the most faithful of servants, bar your good self, dear General Draper."

"He will turn up." Will can offer no more, and hopes the king will let the matter drop now, but it is not to be. Henry grunts in pain, as he pulls himself up onto his feet, and sets his hands upon his hips, in a stance he thinks is noble.

"Sir, as General in Chief of my own King's Examiners, I expect nothing but the best from you. In return, I have raised you up high. Higher than your low birth might have suggested… for I have heard such tales about you… murdered priests, and the like, but no mind… and now I expect your undivided attention to my wishes."

"Of course, Your Majesty," Will says, and places his hand under the king's arm. "Pray be seated, sire. I do not want your wound to open again. See here what my wife has just received from the far off land of Cathay. Sit, and let me prepare some of this miraculous potion for you."

"Ah, the juice of magic flowers," Henry groans, and allows himself to be seated again. "Is there enough for my purpose, dear Will?"

"Alas, sire… never enough." Will's wife deals with traders the world over, and tries her hardest to buy up every drop of the juice she can. Even so, enough for but one man's use can cost her a thousand Venetian Ducati, and it comes onto the market in only tiny quantities. "Miriam buys all she can, and this must last out the month. Two drops taken in a glass of wine, when the pain becomes unbearable."

"Then prepare me a potion, my friend," the king demands. "For the agony is such that I else wise might throw myself into the Thames."

"Never that, sire,' Will says, playing up to the king's maudlin spirit. "I have never known a man stand up to pain as bravely as you, and this latest soreness will never overcome you."

"True, I am too heroic for mine own good, Will," Henry agrees. "Why, many the blow have I withstood in the lists… and some dealt by you, I recall."

"Sire, I recall battering at you with all my might, and it was as a humming bird pecking at an oak tree."

"Happy days, what?"

"Magnificent times, My Lord," Will tells the king. "Might I mention something my wife's learned doctors now employ in other countries?"

"Another potion?" Henry is all ears. "Pray tell me about it, sir."

"Maggots, sire."

"Maggots?" Henry shudders. The horrid things remind him of the grave. "I think not. Swallowing them would make me sick unto death."

"No, sire… one does not swallow them… one puts them on the festering sores. they eat the dead flesh, and leave the good flesh alone. Miriam says it is a wonder to behold."

"Modern medicine constantly astounds me," Henry admits. "What will they think of next?"

"Then might I order some to be shipped in, sire?"

"Have we none in England?" Henry complains. "We should buy English, where we can."

"They are the wrong kind, sire," Will explains. "My wife tells me that they must come from Arabian camel meat, left to rot for a month. Once it is turned and smelling, the meat becomes maggots."

"The meat turns into maggots?"

"So the wise men tell us, sire," Will says. "Meat always becomes maggoty… so I suppose they are right."

"Have it arranged," Henry decides. "Now, my potion?"

Will pours out the wine, and allows two drops to fall into the glass. He hands it to the king, who swallows it down in three long gulps.

"Damn me, but I feel it working, even as I drink, my dear fellow. Your wondrous wife must tender her account to my Royal Purse, and I shall see she is paid at once."

"The Draper Company willingly gifts it to you, sire, out of compassion, and self preservation," Will tells the king. "A strong king means we can trade around the world, with you as our overlord. As the king thrives, then so do we."

"Well said… now, will you do it, man… yes or no?" Henry asks.

"Sire, you have not asked anything of me," Will replies. "Though your royal wish is my command, of course."

"Then you will find him?" Henry says. "Find Thomas Culpeper, and bring him to me. I fear I misused him badly."

"How so, sire?" Will Draper asks the king. "The sure knowledge of what has happened might help my search for him."

"Oh, I see. Well, you see, I did try to twit him with a silly sort of a jest. It was nothing… nothing at all."

"Yet he has run away?" Will is confused at why the king thinks he is at fault. Courtiers are there to be dunned, and made into fools. It is their reason to exist, and they should take the odd kick up the arse as part of their job.

"I took his woman to my own bed, to make him think me the better man." Henry realises how lame this all sounds, for he is king, of course, and therefore better than any man in England, and he should not need to prove it. "I then banished her from my court, and spoke of her in a most vile way. The worst of it all was that I never did get to swive the damned woman. Somehow, she always seemed able to put me off. Such women are an offence against nature, Will." Henry can feel the drug working its magic, and he is ready to speak openly about anything now.

"The lady's name, sire?" Will uses his 'official' voice, and Henry actually casts down his eyes.

"Lady Jane... George Boleyn's widow."

"Damn, then she really *was* Cully's lover?" Will Draper sees now that Lady Jane is more involved than he first thought. In the past Thomas Culpeper had hinted at having bedded her, but his wilder claims had been made fun of. Why would a lady, related to the most noble families in England, want to take a mere squire to her bed?

"Does that help?" Henry asks. "The lady is no better than she should be, and bedded my own squire. The indignity of it all, sir. Can you find them?"

"Perhaps, Your Majesty. Culpeper might have gone to her. Find the lady, and we might well find the man. I doubt he has gone far from court. His family are not that well off, and he must be running short of funds."

"With the builders in Whitehall Palace, remodelling all the rooms to suit my dearest young wife... my *'rose without a thorn'*... courtiers are spread all about the city." Henry is happy now that his wishes are being attended to. Will Draper will find Cully, and return him to the king's side.

"I expect that is it, sire," Will agrees, but he knows that the time is coming when Thomas Culpeper must either re-appear, or disappear, for ever. If the queen's honour is to be saved, and Cromwell says it must be, then the courtier's future is looking bleaker by the hour."Let me look into things."

"Is that a duck smiling at me?"

"Sire?"

"Damn me, fellow… an Aylesbury duck, and he is grinning at me," Henry swears. Will Draper realises that this latest potion is too strong, and the king must spend a while conversing with smiling poultry.

"Calm yourself, sire," he says. "It will soon fly away. There is no harm in it, I assure you. Such creatures often appear as a sign of good luck."

"They do?" Henry asks.

"Yes, sire. I hear of one Milanese lord who was once approached by a unicorn. He tried to mount it, and found himself none the worse for wear, but in his own stable, sleeping in a loose box."

*

The red brick quadrangle that is Sutton Place, is a marvel of modern building, and not a day goes by without Thomas Culpeper enjoying its many comforts, and wondering how he came to be so lucky. It has been his home for five weeks now, and will remain so, according to Barnaby Fowler, until the moment comes when the foul tyrant, Henry Tudor, is finally toppled from his stolen throne.

"He is a common usurper," Cully mutters to himself, as he strolls around the inner courtyard. "His people are no better than mine… just luckier born. The father stole the crown, and the son is a second born, unfit for the position. Yes, that is it. A common thief. The grandchild of a mere Welsh hill bandit."

"What's that you are you saying, Master Culpeper?" Barnaby Fowler asks, as he emerges into the weak October daylight. "Who is this Welsh bandit you speak of, Master Cully?"

"Oh, nothing. I am rehearsing my first speech, for when I must rally my followers. I must rouse them, of course, but not too much. It is one thing to pull down a king because he is unfit, but quite another to ask them to place the crown upon my own head."

"That will never happen," Barnaby Fowler says, quite truthfully. "You are not of royal blood. Was not your grandfather a seller of faggots, and a sharpener of knives?"

"My greater grandfather was a son of the last King of Alba, and my mother's own aunt was married to one of the Kingmaker Warwick's clan. My grandfather served Warwick most nobly."

"The old duke's trusted Master of the Privy, I am told." The lawyer is enjoying his time with Cully, and has even developed a slight affection for the demented young fellow. "You cannot take the crown."

"I speak figuratively, of course," Cully tells his supposed follower. "The crown will go onto Catherine's head, as it should, by right. I shall stand by her side, and guide her through the long process of making England great again. In that true sense, I shall be king... though without a crown of my own, of course. Catherine will need my help, if we are to create a new Avalon in this land. The streets shall flow with milk and honey, and the poor shall become rich, as the rich shall become ... er... richer."

"What if people object to your great plan?" Barnaby asks. He knows all the answers, for he has heard them before from this young man, whom he begins to suspect is well addled. "What if they say they prefer moving right on to Edward. After all, he is next in line, according to the laws of primogeniture. Then, if he does not bring forth any issue, the princesses, Mary and Elizabeth are next."

"No! The baby Edward is too young, Mary is a Roman Catholic, and Elizabeth is named as a bastard… even by her very own father. Queen Catherine is the only sensible choice, and people will follow her, once Henry is dead, and they see that I am really in charge. They know I already rule the king, you see. Henry cannot manage without me, for I am a steady hand on the tiller of state. I wager he is suffering because of my long absence. When will it be, Barnaby?"

"When will what be?" the lawyer asks.

"When will you kill the king, of course?" Cully asks. "The man must die, before I can reveal my hand, and you are dragging your feet somewhat. When will you strike him down, sir?"

"Soon enough, my dearest friend, once this damned plague finally subsides," Fowler says. "Then what? Henry is dead, and England is without a monarch. Do we march on London?"

"No need," Cully replies, with a sly look on his face. "With Henry dead, the Duke of Norfolk will take London for me, and hold it against those few hundreds who might think to make a rebellion. Then, after a suitable period of time... a few weeks... dear Surrey will kill his father, and become Norfolk in his place. You see how simple it will all be? England is mine, because Surrey is my own creature."

"He is oath sworn to you?" Barnaby Fowler is a consummate lawyer, and knows that he must gather up every word the young man utters, so that it might be written down, and used as evidence in some future trial.

"I have his most noble word," Cully insists. "He supports me in everything, and wants his father gone."

"He has said so?"

"By looks, and casual inferences, I believe," Cully admits, "if not actually in writing. Harry Surrey is not the one for flowing words, when a glance and a nod will suffice. If looks could kill, the old man would be dead already."

"So, you think he is with you, because he has never said he is not?"

"Just so." Cully smiles, quite unable to see how ridiculous this sounds to a sensible mind.

"And what then becomes of Queen

Catherine?" Barnaby Fowler asks his deranged accomplice. "Will she accept your sudden usurpation of the throne?"

"Queen Catherine is mine," Cully says. "I have letters from her... loving epistles that show she desires me above all others. Francis Dereham used to bring them to me, but now I am in hiding... he does not come. It is odd, but I must suppose that he has succumbed to the plague. How bothersome."

"You have letters?" The lawyer sees how this might come in useful.

"Not here. They are, no doubt, safely hidden away," Cully confides. "Now Dereham does not hand them on to me."

"Perhaps he is too busy with the queen?" Fowler is asking those questions Cromwell would, were he able to be here. "Were they not once lovers of some sort?"

"That is unfair. She was but fourteen when Dereham plucked her maidenhead, and he is but a lowly servant now. When I become ... Regent of England... he shall be seen to."

"Killed?" Barnaby asks.

"If you like," Cully says, evasively. "Whose house is this, my friend?"

"Sir Richard Weston's," Barnaby tells him.

"Why does he let us use it?"

"He is dead, and cares not," the lawyer says. "It was his son, Francis, who was executed, for swiving the king's wife, Anne Boleyn. It is a heavy price to pay for a little pleasure."

"He was an utter fool," Cully decides. "If you swive a queen, you must do it for a purpose. Love is not a good enough reason. One must use the relationship to increase one's power over the entire realm. Henry is at my mercy, because the queen loves me, rather than the other way about. Kill Henry Tudor soon, and you will see how easy it is to win a royal crown."

"What will I be?" the lawyer asks. He knows that it is all make believe, but he is curious at how well he will be rewarded in the Kingdom of Far Away Cloud Cuckoo Land that is to come.

"Whatsoever you want," Cully replies with magnanimous ease. "How about becoming an earl, or the Lord Chancellor, or even Attorney General of all England?"

"Richard Rich will not like that, Master Cully," Barnaby Fowler guesses. "For it is a post he much enjoys filling."

"He is not for me," Cully says with some acuity. "I once sent him a gift of some fine bed linen, and he returned it, and spoke most rudely to me. Why, he actually asked if they were stolen. Imagine that? No, as soon as you have killed Henry, you must find Sir Richard Rich, and kill him too."

"And what of the rest?" Barnaby asks him. "Have you a conclusive list for me to study?"

"Norfolk, of course, and that sly dog, the Duke of Suffolk. He loves the king too well, you see. Then we must attend to Richard Cromwell, Sir John Russell, Rafe Sadler, Prince Edward, Princess Mary, Elizabeth, and Ned Seymour. There will be more, no doubt, as we go along. I am still unsure about General Draper, who is close to Henry, and might wish to save him."

"I shall be bathed in blood," Barnaby observes. "I thought this was to be a gentle usurpation."

"Better a dozen deaths now, than a hundred later," Cully tells him.

"And our supporters?"

"Norfolk, at first. Surrey, Tom Seymour, Bishop Gardiner, that little Spanish ambassador with the funny hats, General Draper and his troops… I could go on for ever, as most sensible folk are for me." Cully pauses and thinks for a moment. "I thought to cultivate the Pole family, once, but Henry saw to them well enough."

A few months before, Margaret Pole, Countess of Salisbury, and the implacable enemy of the king had finally gone to the block, along with most of her family. The bloodbath, ordered by the king, has put an end to the Plantagenet opposition for good.

"They would have opposed you," Barnaby says, just to see what the answer might be.

"I doubt it very much. Everyone loves me." Thomas Culpeper is quite convinced of this, and nothing will shake his belief in his own power. Barnaby Fowler sees now that he is suffering some kind of sickness in his head, and he thinks it better if the fellow was simply locked away in some safe place, where his madness can do no further harm.

He will report as much back to his true master, in Antwerp, but doubts it will do any good. The lad has gone a step too far, and Barnaby doubts he can be saved from himself. Culpeper may live in a world of fantasy, but he has crossed the line in sleeping with the queen, and to threaten the king, and the overthrow of the monarchy is something that cannot be ignored.

"Are you hungry, Cully?" Fowler asks, and he nods, like a little boy. "What would you like?"

"Everything," Thomas Culpeper replies. "I must get used to all this rich food, if I am to take my rightful place within the royal court."

"How will we style you, once you assume power?" Barnaby Fowler asks out of curiosity. For the man acknowledges that he cannot be the king.

"My Liege, I think," Cully replies, without hesitation. "Or, perhaps, like old Caesar… I will be *Imperator*."

"I doubt the commoners will take to such high blown titles, Cully," Barnaby says, quite truthfully. They are happy with the old ranks, such as king, earl and duke. "Perhaps you might wish to style yourself as '*Lord Protector*'?"

"Yes, that has a certain ring to it," Cully agrees. "For am I not the chosen one, the one to save England from all her woes?"

*

"Mad as a March hare, you say, Kel?" Thomas Cromwell sighs at the news, and shakes his head.

"Daft as a potter's glazer boy, sir," Kel Kelton tells his master. The sniffing of fumes from the glaze in a pottery is a sure way to losing one's mind. "Barnaby Fowler is no fool, and he insists the fellow is quite deranged. He speaks as though he is already our king, and seems to think the whole of England is in his thrall. The man is quite insistent that he will rule over us all."

"Then he must be kept closely confined, until we can sort out this unholy mess. England cannot stand another scandalous royal marriage. The French would laugh at us, and the king would be called such names as would drive *him* to the verge of madness."

"Master Fowler has him locked away, but the king wants to know where his squire has got to," Kel tells his master. "He has asked Will Draper to investigate the strange disappearance and produce either the man, or his body."

"Damnation," Tom Cromwell snaps, and bangs a fist down on his desk. "General Draper must keep things under control, until we can resolve matters to our own satisfaction."

"All the plans in the world will be to no avail, if Archbishop Cranmer informs the king of what the queen has told him." It is a simple fact that, a secret is best kept by not telling it, and too many people already know Catherine's.

The queen and the Archbishop of Canterbury have met, and Catherine had only to confirm her assumed chastity. Instead, Catherine, in her childlike innocence, has let the cat out of the bag, and confessed to having taken lovers. She thinks that the confessional is sacrosanct, and that Cranmer will remain silent. It is a foolish belief, and now, danger is all about them once again.

"Then we must stop him from telling the king." Cromwell wonders at how hard it is to think of some clever plot these days, and how his mind seems to move at a much slower pace. It is because I am dead, I suppose, he thinks. Once away from court, life became easier, and his will to involve himself in court politics lessened, but he must not weaken now. "Who best to speak some good sense to him, do you think?"

"I would silence the fellow without a moment's hesitation, Master Tom, but you forbid it." Kel Kelton is a man of action, rather than intrigue, and does not mind having the blood of a cleric on his hands. Thomas Cromwell, however, grows squeamish in his enforced retirement, and will not countenance any unnecessary blood letting. Kel offers an alternative. "Might we not have your nephew have a firm word?"

"Richard is just as like to strangle him," Cromwell replies. "No, we need a more subtle hand, Kel. Who actually *knows* about the queen's amorous digressions, save from her lovers?"

"You, me, Richard, Will Draper, Rafe Sadler, and Eustace Chapuys," Kel answers. "Though the list may not be a complete one, master. A broken secret travels even faster than an arrow."

"Then we must discount the first four names, for various reasons. Rafe is not the man for the task either, for he is too close to the king, and might let something slip, accidentally. That leaves only Eustace."

"You cannot expect Ambassador Chapuys to speak on your behalf," Kel objects. "He is the Emperor Charles' man, and will put his own master's cause before ours. I think he will refuse us."

"The emperor has an alliance with us, as Scotland does with our enemy, France. If England is weakened, then so is his alliance. Imagine this, Kel; what would happen if Henry's crown is threatened. Would not King James think the time is ripe to invade, and press his own claim to the throne?"

"Well... yes." Kel thinks it unlikely, but the chance does exist.

"And if England is torn apart into two camps; one for Henry, and one for the Howards... might he not sweep down, and defeat us?"

"Unlikely, but possible," Kel admits. "James is not strong enough to beat us."

"What if the French king steals Calais from us, and then sends King James military help?" Thomas Cromwell muses.

"Then we *may* be defeated."

"Leaving Charles to stand alone against the French and their allies?"

"That might come to pass."

"That is politics, Kel. The art of thinking what might be, and then using it to suit your own ends." Cromwell is shaking off the ennui which has been afflicting him, and thinks he can see a way forward. "We must use poor Chapuys, and hope the king never hears about his new wife's wickedness. As for her lovers, and all who are culpable ... I fear we must allow Richard to attend to them."

"He cannot do it alone, master." Kel Kelton says. "We might be talking about a dozen people whom she has corrupted, and whom she now bribes into silence. Even Richard cannot handle so many sudden deaths."

"Have him employ Mush, and see if

Ibrahim the Moor, and Edwin Tunnock, are available," Cromwell tells his devoted young servant. "They must be very clever about it. A couple of accidents, here and there. Perhaps a robbery gone wrong?"

"Leave it to me, sir," Kel says with a sly wink. "Between us, we will remove every danger. Though one name might make your nephew baulk at his duty."

"Lady Jane, you mean?" Thomas Cromwell knows the lady well, and owes her much. She was instrumental in ruining her husband, George Boleyn, and bringing down his sister, Anne. "It cannot be helped. She must be removed from England, or forever silenced."

"I shall advise her that she must move to Flanders, at once," Kel says, "or suffer the consequences."

"It must be as easy as possible," Cromwell tells him. "Promise her money, and bring her here to us at the *Palais de Juis*, if she will comply… otherwise… let her demise be as painless as possible."

"Of course, sir." Kel Kelton has to bite back the words. He wishes to explain that to bring Lady Jane to Flanders means risking Cromwell's own position. If the woman knows that Tom Cromwell is alive, it will give her power over his master. No, it is best that she dies, and as soon as possible. He will attend to her personally, and ensure she meets a swift and painless end.

*

Will Draper makes a great show of having his King's Examiners scour London and the surrounding shires, in the hope of finding Thomas Culpeper, and the king grows ever more irate at his failure to produce his much loved squire.

"Is the young fool actually hiding from me?" he raves over dinner that evening. "Am I such a malodorous monster, dearest Charles? Tell me true Wyatt, am I then so terrifying?"

"Perhaps the boy thinks he has upset you, Hal," Charles Brandon says, and shrugs his shoulders. "In his eyes, you must be like an angry father."

"Yes… an angry father," Henry says, with enthusiasm. "For he is like a son to me. Never has he ever done me any harm… and I would have him back by my side. Even the queen sees how missed he is, and says how she longs for his return to our court. You must find him, my dear Draper… and soon."

"I shall redouble our efforts, sire," Will tells the king. "Though I am beginning to think some mischief might be afoot. Either he is hiding because of some offence we do not understand, or he is in trouble. Does he owe money?"

"The lad is as honest as the day is long," Henry declares. "He does not gamble, and he seldom spends his hard earned coin in an unsuitable way."

"My agents report that he is a frequent visitor to the more expensive whore houses, sire," Will says.

"That is hardly cash spent badly," the Duke of Suffolk puts in, with a sly wink at the king. "Who here does not swive the occasional bawdy house girl?"

"Yes, but he might be deeply in debt," the King's Examiner replies, ingenuously. "Perhaps Madam Horton, or the Three Whistles hold his marker, and he lacks enough funds to cover his outlay." It is all a nonsense, of course, but Will has been told to delay for as long as he can, and so the wild stories must continue.

"Perhaps the Boggarts have stolen him away?" says Tom Wyatt, and the king gives him a black look.

"This is not a jesting matter, young Wyatt," he growls. "Besides, it is known that malevolent creatures cannot take the innocent."

"Just so, sire," Tom Wyatt replies. "I expect a howling night walker to come for me at any time."

"Night walker?" Henry's face drains of colour. He fears anything supernatural, and likes to think he knows of all the dangers, but this is new to him.

"They do say that a Night Walker is a fiend who walks ... by night, sire," Wyatt says. "It hides in its victim's shadows, and then leaps out and devours him."

"Sweet Christ!" Henry is shaken, and wonders how he will sleep that night.

"Are you sure?" Will asks. "Only, how does he walk at night, yet hide in your shadow?"

"How mean you, Will?" Henry asks, and Will waves a hand at the window.

"It would be dark, and shadows need sun, do they not?"

"What about candle light?" Wyatt asks, and the king shudders. There are dangers all about him, and now, he must see that he does not cast a shadow at bedtime.

"Tom, do shut up," the Duke of Suffolk tells the inebriated poet. "This ridiculous talk of dangerous demons and mischievous goblins quite disquiets the king."

*"The demon howls by pale moonlight
Its sorry work to do
Ask not the fiend's wicked aim
for it comes for me... or you."* The poet claps his hands at his own impromptu verse, and grins at the king. "Your Majesty is worried lest one of these night walkers slips into his disrobing chamber?"

"Not I, sir," Henry says. "I fear nothing. Now, find me Tom Culpeper within the week, or watch how I shall *night walk*."

The tumult of chatter around the long dining table remains good humoured, but Will Draper is not fooled. Something within the court has changed, and not for the better, he thinks. Though a casual enough remark, Henry has, for the first time in their relationship, employed a threat.

"I shall do as you wish, sire," Will says to the king. "If the man is alive, I shall bring him to you, and if he be dead…"

"No, not that," Henry moans. "The boy is too fine for this world, but I would not wish him out of it for all the gold in England!"

2 No Other Wish

Catherine Howard is, for the first time since she married the king, concerned for herself. She is still little more than a precocious child, and her recently adopted motto, '*No other wish than His*', she takes at face value. Henry must think himself the centre of her world, so that she might enjoy her life.

She wishes for nothing more than her high position, her jewels, fawning courtiers, and everything that goes with being queen, and she thinks that Henry is content, and everything is well.

Now this!

"Damn these bastard priests," she curses, and wonders what it is inside her that makes her fear them, and their ridiculous cant, so much? "That smelly old fool had best keep his bastard mouth shut, or else.'

"What smelly old fool?" Francis Dereham asks her. "His leg does stink of the grave somewhat. Is it then the king you speak of, my love?"

"No, my dear Hammy, but Henry is an old fool, isn't he?" Catherine says, spitefully. "Fat, old and stupid."

"Then who has upset your pretty little

head, my dearest little one?" Dereham asks of her. Since extorting his present position from her, he is becoming ever more affectionate with the queen. In many ways, it is just like the old days, save for that prating idiot, Thomas Culpeper, who seems to have quite vanished from court.

"Archbishop Cranmer," Catherine explains. "He asked me to confess, and I was a little too ardent. The fellow swore it is all to be a secret, and that anything I said was … sacro something."

"Sacrosanct," Francis Dereham says, helpfully. "Yes, that is so. A priest may not gossip about anything said to him within the confessional box. His lips are sealed. What did you tell him?"

"How you did swive me, as a child."

"Dear Christ!" Francis Dereham leaps up, like a scalded cat, and starts to pace the room. "You actually told him that, you stupid cow? How could you be so damned idiotic?"

"Why not?" Catherine says, taken aback by her lover's rebuke. "I was scarcely fourteen years old, and you treated me like I was your wife. You were the first, Hammy."

"But not the last," Francis Dereham replies, defensively. "I know, for a fact, that you frolicked with others, well before coming to court."

"I was young then," Catherine tells him. "Innocent of the world. Was I to blame for being so pretty? Did I invite Mary Lascelles into my bed?"

"You swived with Mary Lascelles?" Dereham is put out by this, as the woman was there at the same time as he. "She is over thirty!"

"Oh, Hammy, my dearest, do not be so foolish," Catherine says to him, with a knowing smile. "It does not count with another woman... not like it would with a man. I love you, second amongst all men."

"Second?" Dereham feels himself growing angry. "You mean behind that swine, Culpeper? Well, so much for him... for he is not to be found since the plague threatened. I wager he is dead in some charnel pit, or hiding in the country, like a cowardly dog."

"He will return," Catherine tells him. "Cully and I are sworn to one another. He is going to save me from the king's grasp, and then make me into a proper queen."

"You are already a queen, Catherine," Dereham replies. "Queen of England."

"No, a proper one. A queen who can rule in her own right." Catherine fingers the magnificent jewelled necklace hanging at her throat. "Cully has a wonderful plan, and will make me England's true queen."

"Tom Culpeper is a… a prating, spavined, dandycock!" Dereham shouts, and his voice cracks into a falsetto.

"Jealousy makes you seem rather ugly, sir," Catherine says, with a pert little smile. "Now, what do I do about this bastard priest, Hammy? I am sure he will tell my secrets, the moment he thinks he can. I should not have spoken as I did, but the wine loosened my tongue, and I was indiscreet."

"The Archbishop of Canterbury is no ordinary priest, my dearest one," Dereham explains. After Henry, Cranmer is one amongst a half dozen who can claim to be a true power in the land. "He is a great power, both political and religious, in of England."

"He is a mere man," the queen says, softly. "I believe he can bleed, like any other does… and he is not immortal. He might easily die of some sad accident."

"What are you asking of me, Catherine?" Francis Dereham begins to think he has made a terrible choice in coming to court. Catherine is unpredictable, and now, she talks of murder, in the most casual way.

"With Cully away, I am lonely in the night, my sweet love," Catherine says. "Even

Lady Jane has left me. Come at midnight, in stealth, and we will make the double backed beast, until dawn."

"You know I cannot resist you," Francis Dereham says, and allows his fingers to touch her shoulder. They are alone, and that in itself is a crime punishable by death. The queen must never be left alone with a man, save it be the king, or one of his very elderly cronies. "Midnight, my love. I can hardly wait for the hour to chime."

"And think on," Catherine warns. "I will have the old priest's mouth stopped, for good. You must think of a way that does not throw blame on us."

"I will see what can be done, my love," Dereham replies, and bows to her. He knows a few rough fellows who might do it for him, providing there is enough gold offered.

*

Lady Jane Boleyn, Viscountess of Rochford is feeding the pigs. Her estate in Dorset, a remnant of her late husband's holdings, comprises little more than a hundred and fifty acres, some livestock, and a rather ramshackle cottage. Her household is made up of Meg, an old woman who cooks and cleans, and her husband, Dan, who sees to the land. He is in his sixties, and finds the daily tasks too great for himself alone.

By the edge of her land, there is a hamlet, that is no more than a couple of extended families, and she sometimes exchanges food for their labour. Lady Jane cannot often afford to pay another labourer, so spends her days tending to the single plough horse, a half dozen pigs, and a small flock of sheep herself.

If she is careful, the revenue will keep her fed, and the small pension she still draws from the Cromwell estate will pay for the little luxuries, like a decent pair of shoes, and a couple of reasonable dresses. One day, she might return to court, and she must be able to present herself in a good light.

Her banishment, though imposed by the king, is something she has engineered, for her own safety. If the king ever discovers the truth about his new wife, she wishes to be out of sight and, hopefully, out of mind. If she can stay out of the way, she may yet live to a ripe old age.

"Mistress, there be a man here, asking after you," Old Meg says, as she comes into the yard. The old woman sees the look of fear cross her lady's face, and she hurries to calm her. "It isn't a king's man, ma'm. He says to tell you he is from Master Cromwell."

"Master Cromwell?" Lady Jane can only think that it is one of Richard's men, come to offer her some aid. "Have him wait inside, whilst I clean myself up. Do we have wine to offer?"

"Beer."

"Never mind."

She washes her hands at the pump, and splashes some water onto her face, then straightens her skirts, and goes inside to greet her visitor.

"Lady Jane Boleyn?" the man asks, and bows low.

"I am Jane, the Viscountess of Rochford," she replies, and the man smiles. She is dressed like a peasant woman, but has the grace of a fine lady.

"I am a confidential agent, madam," he says. "My name is Captain Amos Givens. I was once in the employ of Lady Miriam Draper, as a bodyguard, and lately, I work for Sir Richard Cromwell."

"You have news for me?"

"Only this, madam," Amos Givens tells her. "I am commanded to warn you that General Draper has been ordered to find a man called Thomas Culpeper, and that the search may reach as far as you. Sir Richard is minded of his past friendship with you, and thinks it best if you make haste to leave England."

"Leave… me?" Lady Jane frowns at this obvious warning. "I know not where Culpeper is, nor do I care, sir."

"Sir Richard understands this, ma'm," Amos Givens tells her, "but that will not stop them questioning you. If Culpeper is taken, he is to be brought to the king. Though there is no charge yet laid against the fellow, it is feared that his behaviour might throw a shadow over the queen. In this case, all who know him are in danger."

"I know nothing of his wild plotting," Lady Jane says. For all she knows, this fellow might be sent to trick her into flight, the better to make her seem guilty. "I shall stay here, and mind my own business."

"Madam, if I might be bold enough to say, that is a poor choice," Amos Givens tells her. "I can put you onto a cog owned by Lady Draper, this very afternoon, and you can live out your days in Ghent, or Bruges."

"On fresh air, sir?"

"Sir Richard bids me give you this purse," the man explains. "There are twenty pounds in it… enough to keep you in comfort for a few months. Then, every month, you will receive a like pension. There are only two provisos made. First, you must never return to England, and second… you must *never* visit Antwerp."

"Antwerp?" Lady Jane is bemused. "Why that far off place, sir? I would as soon stay here."

"If you insist on staying in England, then travel north,' Givens tells her. "The further away from court you are, the better."

"I am sure, sir. My dear Richard may think he is looking out for me, but I am safe enough here. Even if Culpeper is taken, I have nothing to hide."

"That will not matter," Amos Givens tells her. He only half understands the messages entrusted to him by Richard Cromwell, but he delivers them truthfully. "The king will have his revenge. My master cannot save you, if you do not wish to be saved."

"The silver is welcome," Lady Jane says. "Tell Richard I accept it, in memory of how it once was between us, but I am content here.'

"Very well. I have one final message from Sir Richard, and it is this, madam. Trust no-one, and admit nothing. My master will not desert you, but he cannot do the impossible." Amos Givens turns on his heel, and strides out to where his horse is tethered. He mounts, and rides away, without a backward glance. On the table is a bag of silver.

"Meg," Lady Jane says, "tonight, we eat well!"

Amos Givens rides to the top of a nearby hill, and sees another mounted man coming towards him. He waits, until the rider is within a few paces, and raises a hand in friendly salute.

"Why, young Master Kelton," he asks, "what business have you here?"

"I come to see if Lady Jane is keeping well," Kel says, brazenly.

"She is very well," Amos Givens replies, warily. "Your *Mijnheer* need not worry over her, my lad."

"Who sent you?"

"Who do you think?" Amos Givens says. "Is it then to be Cromwell against Cromwell, sir?"

"Have a care, Captain Givens," Kel says. "I have my orders."

"As do I." Givens says, and slips a hand to the pistol hanging on his saddle's pommel. "Must men who should be friends come to this?"

"You threaten me, sir?" Kel Kelton asks, and shifts in his own saddle.

"I warn you to common sense, boy," the older man snaps. "We are both adept at this business, and I doubt either would come off without hurt. Your dear Maisie would never forgive me, if I kill you. Though she would make a pretty enough widow, with all your money to play with."

Kel smiles at this, and lets his hand move away from his weapon. In truth, he thinks them to be equal with both gun and knife, and he has an even chance of finding a blade thrust into his gut.

"My dear Maisie is a shrew, Amos," he admits, "butI will not chance making either of my wives into a widow woman, just yet."

'Then it is true… you keep two wives?" Amos Givens nods his head, and half turns in his saddle. Kel Kelton goes for his concealed throwing knife, and finds himself staring down the yawning barrel of a heavy pistol.

"A three quarter inch lead ball, lad," he says. "Even if you reach your *miserere* and throw it, my finger will twitch. A ball this size, and at this range, will blow a hole through your rather pretty face."

"Peace, sir," Kel says, and raises his

hands to show himself disarmed.

"The woman is warned to silence, and watched by my agents, Master Kelton. You must stay your hand."

"She is a danger to us all, alive," Kel insists, but the gun does not waver from his face.

"Kill her, and Richard Cromwell will become your foe,' Amos Givens replies. "He will not let you live ... nor your family. Think, fellow…can you fight him… or even wish to?"

"Master Cromwell would understand the need." Kel says the words, but he has his doubts on the matter, and the younger Cromwell is an unstoppable force, when roused to anger. With two wives and four children to think about he cannot take the chance of making him into anenemy.

"Turn about, Kel," Amos Givens says. "You cannot win this one. Besides, See yonder trees?"

Kel Kelton glances to a nearby stand of trees, and sees that Givens has four men waiting, each armed with a musket, and each pointed at him. He bows to Givens, and turns his horse's head away.

"She lives… for now."

"She lives as long as Master Richard

sees fit," Givens says to his back. "Do not make the mistake of thinking that we are not watching, sir. The day you harm Lady Jane is the day that true misery visits your own kin."

*

The King's Royal Examiners make it their duty to know about the king's business, and how best to serve him. Their General in Chief, Sir Will Draper sees that they get to read every agent's report that comes in, and hear every piece of gossip that is spread.

Once the general makes it known that he wishes to find Lady Jane Rochford, it is only a matter of time before she is found. First, Will Draper hears the rumours, of how close she is to the queen, and then of her relationship with Thomas Culpeper. Finally, he is told of how one of Richard Cromwell's own men has been to visit her, and so fallen out with Kel Kelton.

"The damned great fool seeks to hide her away from the king," Will says, and Mush shakes his head in despair. The two men he loves most, after Cromwell, have not been close, ever since the affair of the King's Angels, when Richard Cromwell brought Will's honour into disrepute.

"Not so, brother in law," Mush says. "You think ill of him, because he once obeyed

Master Cromwell, rather than you. Richard does not seek to thwart the king, or even you, but save a woman he once loved deeply."

"By sending Amos Givens to warn her?" Will asks. "Does he think me such a monster? Does he think I would really hurt Lady Jane?"

"He thinks you would have no choice," Mush explains. "You seek her out, because the king wants Culpeper found. Yet you know we have the fellow locked away. What price honour now, Will? You lie to Henry, when you could quite easily produce Cully for him."

"And have his dalliance with Catherine come to light?" Will Draper curses court politics, and he curses how he must try to keep Henry from discovering the truth of things. "You know what will happen. He will have the queen arrested, and Culpeper put to the question. The man will break, and swear away as many poor souls as he can think of. Innocent men, and women, with go to the block, at his word."

"Worse still. Lady Jane must not be found. If questioned, she might implicate Richard, and then everyone associated with him… like you, your wife, and I. We must save Queen Catherine's reputation, if only to save ourselves, Will."

"The king will never think ill of me and mine." Will is sure of his position, and cannot think Henry would ever turn on him. "He needs me far too much."

"No?" Mush sighs. "The king will destroy Catherine, and then look to those around her. Her uncle, the Duke of Norfolk must come under suspicion, and the old man may well raise his troops if only to save his own soul. Then what? Shall we be plunged into another civil war?"

"Perhaps."

"Brother against brother," says Mush. "It does not bear thinking about."

"Let us pray that it does not," Will replies. "For it would drag on for years."

"Whose side will you join, my friend?" Mush asks of him, and Will sees the problem. The king will wish to safeguard himself, and that means he must remove any who might be used against him. "When Henry commands you to arrest Princess Mary, a Roman Catholic, what will you do? If he wants Elizabeth out of the way, to ensure Edward's place… what then?"

"The water is becoming muddied, Mush," Will Draper says. "We can only go with our hearts."

"Then we must try to keep Catherine's secret. Let us damn Culpeper for a fool, and see that Dereham is done for, but quietly. The master sends word from Antwerp, and wishes us to delay things, until Thomas Cranmer is spoken to."

"Archbishop Cranmer holds a terrible secret," Will says. "If he keeps it from Henry, and the king finds out, he will lose his head. Then again, if he reveals all, he risks being asked why he has not spoken sooner."

"Yes, but he hates Norfolk, and might use the information to help bring the duke down." Mush shrugs. "So many 'ifs', 'buts' and 'maybe's', old friend. Search slowly for Culpeper, and let us see what comes of it."

"Very well." Will Draper knows it is all he can do. His agents tell him that Lady Jane is staying put in Dorset, and that must remain his own secret, for now.

*

"How are things at court?" the Duke of Norfolk asks, and his son simply shrugs.

"How do you mean, father?" Surrey asks.

"Must I rip off your damned ear, boy?" Norfolk curses.

"You insult me, sir?"

"No, I *threaten* you," the Duke of

Norfolk replies. "When did the king get back?"

"Two weeks ago."

"And what of the plague?"

"Gone," says Surrey.

"Then Henry is content enough?" Norfolk asks.

"Not so," Surrey says. "It seems he has lost his little puppy dog, Thomas Culpeper."

"Your dearest friend?" Norfolk grins, and makes a rude gesture with his fingers to suggest that his son and Cully are much closer than mere friends,

"Hardly that, sir. You threw me into his company once, and told me to befriend him," Surrey complains. "He is a most dreadful little upstart. Always whining on about 'his rightful place' in the world, and dunning people down. He even said I should cast you down, and take your titles from you."

"Oh, that you might try," Norfolk snaps. "I would eat your stinking liver for breakfast, my boy."

"I did not pay him any heed, father." Surrey smiles, slyly. "You are the king's whipping boy, and it is not a job I relish. No, I would rather pass my days in pleasure, than trying to avoid having my head removed from my shoulders by an ever more dangerous king."

"You smile too much. What is it that you know, that I should know?" Norfolk asks his son.

"Only that the king is quite distraught. Cully has gone from court, and he wants him back. God knows why, for the wretched fellow was always saying how he would make a better king than fat old Henry."

"That is treason, boy." Norfolk looks about to see if anyone is listening in on them. Since Thomas Cromwell's death, he has had a strange feeling that he is being watched even more than is normal, as if from beyond the grave.

"Not mine, father." Young Surrey is enjoying himself, and baits Norfolk further. "They say he is overly friendly with Catherine too."

"God's Suffering teeth, are you mad?" Norfolk feels as though a knife is twisting in his vitals. "Not again. If the king hears of it, he will finish the girl, along with anyone stupid enough to be linked to her."

"Like you, sir?"

"Like *us*, sir," Norfolk replies. "Is there any proof of her actions?"

"Only if Cully returns to court,"

Surrey offers. "Someone might think to twist his arm. He would never be mad enough to confess, would he?"

"Richard Cromwell, or Will Draper, would torture the truth from him in a moment," Norfolk says. "Then they would implicate us, and Henry would have us killed in another moment. We must see that your friend, Tom Culpeper, never returns, and that anyone else who might be *in the know* vanishes."

"Who else could possibly know about it?" Surrey muses, then he smiles, and nods his head. "Lady Jane."

"George Boleyn's woman?"

"Yes, she is very close to Catherine," Surrey says. "I dare say she is privy to my cousin's wanton ways."

"Then find her, and see she is kept quiet," Norfolk tells his son.

"Why should I?"

"Because you are my son, and because… if I fall from grace, I will swear away your life to Henry. He will not take the father, and leave the son to survive him… I promise you that, you poor excuse for a living creature."

"You begin to frighten me, father." Surrey is not the cleverest of men, but it finally dawns on him that he is involved in something more than a silly political game. If Catherine falls from grace, then so will the Howards, and that fall will be a mighty bloody one. "Let us put aside our petty arguments, and work together, so that we might survive the coming storm, and keep our rightful places, by the king's side."

"Then find this pathetic Culpeper, and see he is swiftly silenced. Then look for Lady Jane Boleyn, and kill her too."

"Murder?" Henry Howard, Earl of Surrey sees a small problem in such an act. "Dick Cromwell will not like that, father. He protects the woman."

"How many times has a Cromwell humiliated you, boy?" Norfolk rasps. "Be damned to them all. It is about time we had a final reckoning. Let us see to Culpeper, and the Boleyn woman, and if needs be, we will rid the world of Richard Cromwell and his meddling friends too."

*

"You know Thomas Cranmer by sight?" Francis Dereham asks, and the big fellow, swathed in a long black cloak, nods his head. His face is partly obscured by a red scarf, but his eyes burn out like two red hot coals.

"I know him well enough," Abel Carter says. "He once preached a sermon in my town, all about loving my neighbour. He did not even know the man, or his wife. I marked him well then as a babbling old fool, and would know him again."

"Can you do what I want, fellow?" Dereham looks about him, but the other customers are all either drinking themselves into a stupor, or are already too drunk to care. The man slumped next to him is so drunk that he is snoring the night away.

"Of course. It is not that difficult to kill a man," Abel Carter replies. "The hard part is getting away with it, afterwards. The Archbishop of Canterbury will have many men about him. Armed men."

"Never more than two priests," Francis Dereham replies. "They are armed with daggers, and are there to ward off footpads alone."

"Then I will need six men."

"How much will it cost me?" The price of murder has risen steeply during the last couple of years; the cost driven by inflation in France, where a good assassin can command five Ducati for a simple stabbing. English killers, known as the best in Europe, now work abroad for the higher fees, and this drives up the prices at home.

"Five shillings for each fellow, and a pound for me,"

"What?" Dereham is shocked at the figure quoted. "Fifty shillings, for one little stabbing?"

"Take it, or leave it," Abel Carter says. "I can pick up ten bob a go putting an end to unwanted relatives for the gentry. The Seymour's have no end of poor cousins they can do without supporting."

"Very well, fifty shillings," Francis Dereham agrees, "though it must be done quickly."

"Pay me, and I will act at once."

"I need some time to get the money from … my principal."

"Oh, is that so?" Abel Carter grins then, and he displays a mouthful of broken teeth. "I see that you are the dog, rather than the master, sir."

"My mistress has the money," the queen's man replies. "You will have it by tomorrow evening."

"Then let me have the matter clear in my mind, Master Dereham," the hired assassin says. "Your mistress… Queen Catherine… wishes me to kill the Archbishop of Canterbury, for two pounds and ten shillings?"

"Just so."

"Do you have it in writing, sir?" the man asks, shrewdly. "What if the queen should decide to let you hang?"

"She cannot, for I own certain information that would ruin her." Dereham is proud of his own cunning in keeping back certain incriminating documents, but does not see that simply having them is as good as a sentence of death. "The queen is, effectively, my slave."

"I see, and you think it meet to discuss such things with a common murderer, Master Dereham?" Abel Carter rubs his stubbled chin, and drinks off a good half of his tankard of ale in one long swallow. "What if I decide against this perfidious act?"

"You are nothing but a common outlaw," Francis Dereham says. "You will obey me, and thus save your own worthless neck from the rope."

"Is that right, Abel Carter?" The incapable drunk next to Francis Dereham raises himself from the table top, and rubs his eyes open. "You are nought but a common criminal?"

"Not I, Captain Mush," the big man says. "I am a sergeant in the King's

Examiners, set to listen to this dog's wicked story. It is a good one, and no mistake. He wishes me to murder the Archbishop of Canterbury for him… and for the queen… whose name he takes in vain."

"What is this?" Francis Dereham steps back, as if slapped in the face. "You seek to trap me, sir?"

"You trap yourself," Mush Draper tells the horrified man. "Sergeant Carter, put this wicked villain in chains, and take him into custody."

"Very good, sir." Abel Carter is a big man, and his overbearing presence makes Francis Dereham cower in fear.

"I have done nothing here, save play a game of 'what if' gentlemen," he pleads. "I spoke idly."

"You spoke of murdering an archbishop," Mush replies, coldly. "Then you implicate the queen in your plot. Now you are taken, and you will spend this night in a damp cell within the Tower."

"Dear God, will I survive this night?" Dereham sees that he has been entrapped, and thinks his last moments are upon him. "I meant no harm to any soul, good sir."

"You have spoken treason, sir," Mush tells him. "I doubt you can live out the month, unless you tell me the truth of things."

"Then let me bargain with you, for my life, sir," he begs. "Let me live, and I will tell you something about the queen that will be of use to you."

"Sir, it is what you know about Her Majesty that will surely get you killed," Mush tells the courtier. "I suggest you keep silent, and die quietly, lest the king commands me to put you to the *question extraordinary*. It is not a pretty way to die. They do say that every bone is slowly broken; every muscle ripped asunder, and that after the hot pincers have done their work, the tongue is the last part to be sliced out."

'Oh, sweet Lord above," Francis Dereham gasps. "I am not a brave man, sir. Spare me these words."

"It is best you know how it might be for you," Mush tells him. "The torturer at the Tower can remove a man's pintle, and keep him alive, in the most exquisite pain for hours. I have seen a fellow beg to be strangled, rather than endure anymore agony."

"You have the wrong man. It is not I you should be taking," Dereham says, shaking now with fear. "Rather you should look to…"

The weighted leather cosh lands just behind Francis Dereham's left ear, and he collapses to the sawdust covered floor. The rest of the inn's patrons ignore the assault, and return to their ale, even as Abel Carter picks the inert body up, and slings it over his shoulder.

"Lock him up, Sergeant Carter," Mush orders of his man. "Allow no-one to hear his prating rubbish."

"As you command, sir." Carter frowns, then has a happy thought. "I could cut out his tongue, sir. That would stop his nonsense right enough."

"Perhaps we might resort to that later," Mush tells him. "For now, a gag will suffice, sergeant."

*

Kel Kelton enjoys his time spent in Antwerp, as it means he can visit with his two wives, and see his four young children. They are all boys, and Tom Cromwell treats them like his own, even the second child, who is Lucy's, and is as black as Ibrahim the Moor.

The girl is half Portuguese, and half African, and her children are of mixed race. The fourth child, called Thomas, for the master, is a quarter black, but has fair hair, and a soft white skin. Cromwell loves him well, and calls him 'my beautiful tow headed Moor'.

Because of this, Kel is as devoted to Tom Cromwell as any man alive, and spends his days rushing from one city to another, on his master's business. This means that he is party to his master's business, and able to offer the best advice.

"We have Thomas Culpeper locked away, Master Tom," he advises Cromwell, "and the other fellow is taken by Mush, and chained up in one of your nephew's cellars. Francis Dereham was taken whilst trying to arrange the murder of Archbishop Cranmer. He approached one of Mush's agents in his stupidity."

"Dear God!" Tom Cromwell closes the ledger he has been working on, and starts to pace his Antwerp study floor. "Such a thing has not been known since the days of the sainted Thomas à Becket's martyrdom by another Henry… the second of that name. How does Eustace Chapuys get on with the archbishop?"

"He dogs him hard, sir," Kel replies. "Since we asked for his help, he has called on Cranmer at every opportunity, and occupied his days with clever chatter, usually on points of obscure religious law. The one time Cranmer saw the king, Señor Chapuys went with him to court, and monopolised the conversation with a tirade about Armenian duck down, and its use as a finer padding for doublets."

"You jest, surely?" Cromwell cannot believe such a tale, but Kel assures him of its absolute truth. The pageboy is paid a shilling a week for such information, and reports it word for word to his master, Barnaby Fowler.

"Henry was fascinated, and poor old Cranmer just stood about, much bemused, and kept silent. Afterwards, the king demanded that his chamberlain obtained a dozen of these wonderful Armenian down pillows. As they are a figment of Chapuys' imagination, I doubt the fellow will have much luck."

"Have Lady Miriam purchase a dozen of the best pillows to be found in Antwerp, and send them to the chamberlain. I would not have him distressed looking for that which does not exist. Enclose a note, signed by Eustace, saying that these are the fabled pillows."

"You are too kindly, sir," Kel says. "It shall be done. Henry will have already forgotten about them though. That was but yesterday, and since then, the king has kept himself apart from the outer court, and does not know of Francis Dereham's rather naïve plot to kill the poor archbishop."

"That would take some explaining to Henry. Have we done enough to halt any other loose talk against the queen?"

"Catherine has employed servants from her past," Kel replies. "I think that her wantonness is known to them."

"I see." Thomas Cromwell is a much changed man, since his 'execution', and he is loath to make life and death decisions. "Will they keep silent?"

"I doubt it," Kel says, in his usual pragmatic way. "Is it not usual in these cases for the blackmailers to want more and more?"

"I suppose that is so, though they are not the blackmailers, but simply use their cunning to gain a job."

"They know."

"Yes." Cromwell cannot argue with the facts, and sees where Kel is heading.

"Then they must be silenced, as we discussed."

"How many?" Tom Cromwell asks of his faithful servant.

"Ten or twelve," Kel says, and Miriam, who is coming into the study with a tray of fresh bread and cheese is shocked at the cold manner of this discussion.

"So many to silence?" she asks, and Kel nods. He knows Miriam is sentimental at times, and he fears her interference now. "Can they not be simply... sent away?"

"Madam, you speak most compassionately, but such talk is foolish," the young man tells her, but for the benefit of them both, for Cromwell also wavers towards a show of mercy.

"But so many?" Miriam says.

"They must all die," Kel Kelton insists. "Let them live, and they will gossip, until even Henry must hear."

"Yes, I understand that," says Tom Cromwell, but he is not happy at so much murder being done at his command. "How many men will you require for this task, *if* I say yes?"

"No... you cannot," Miriam tells them. "These people have done nothing, save see their mistress behave in a lewd way. Murder is *not* the answer."

"Miriam, there is no other way I can think of," Cromwell tells her. "One word, and the queen is lost."

"And why not?" Miriam Draper argues. "Is she any more important than her many servants? Why must they all die, so that she remains with an unblemished character?"

"Lady Miriam," Kel Kelton says, sharply, " this is none of your business. I suggest you keep to victualing your ships for their new adventure." The rebuke stings Miriam into thought, and she suddenly sees that there might be a way out of this wicked mess, without blood being spilled.

"My new… but yes… I could put them on a ship to the New Found Land. The next expedition sails in a few weeks time. Can you take these people up, and have them delivered to the docks at Bristol, Kel?" she asks, excitedly.

"Why, I suppose so, but…" Kel says, and struggles for something to add to his lame 'but'. "Your husband can furnish me with a genuine arrest warrant, if I but ask it of him."

"Then do so, and I will indent them into my new colony. Each shall have a parcel of land, and enough help to start afresh."

"What if they refuse?" the young man asks. He looks for a reason to reject this new plan, which sounds too involved for his liking. Far better to slit their throats and bury the bodies in some lonely forest.

"Damn it, Kel," Thomas Cromwell puts in, impatiently. "When have you ever been refused? I suggest you bribe them to travel to Bristol, and then march them aboard the *Prince Edward* at sword point. Once at sea, they will see where their futures lie, or else, swim back to England. I doubt many will oblige by leaping overboard."

"It is much easier to just kill them," Kel mutters, but he will do as he is bid, and Miriam has saved a dozen souls from a wicked end. "What about our poor Thomas Culpeper… do I put him on a ship too, and let him rule your new colony?"

"That fellow wants to throw aside the lawful king," Miriam replies. "That is a different matter. I advise you to remove him, and Master Dereham, from this world, as soon as you can."

"Wise words, my dear girl," Tom Cromwell says. "Then the Queen of England is saved… save for the archbishop's own prickled conscience."

"Let me kill him," Kel asks, not for the first time. "He is an old man, and might succumb to a weak heart at any moment, master. Gomez tells me that a cushion over the face works within moments."

"He is the anointed… the chosen one… of Canterbury," Tom Cromwell says. "He is Henry's own man, and as loyal and decent as any in Christendom. I cannot give you the word. He is also an old friend."

"As was Thomas More, and you let him go."

"More died despite me... or to spite me, and would not let me save him from his folly. Cranmer is different... a weaker soul. More would have died rather than surrender the secrets of the confession.

"Then I shall..."

"Disobey me, Kel?" Cromwell asks of his devoted young man. Kelton's face reddens, and he shakes his head. If he is Cromwell's man, then he must keep faith with him in all things. He will obey his master, no matter what.

"Ambassador Chapuys cannot keep him away from the king for much longer," Kel Kelton explains. "Henry has only to ask the wrong question, and Cranmer will break down, and reveal all to him."

"Can we not prevail on Archbishop Cranmer to keep silent?" Miriam asks them. "What if he took an oath to hold his tongue?"

"God save us from such a thing," Cromwell curses. "It is oaths that have brought us to this pass. We swear an oath to the king, and another to our lord, and a third to our church. Before you know it, we are caught in a veritable tangle of word giving."

"But if he swears..."

"No, it will not do," Tom Cromwell tells Miriam. "He has sworn an oath of allegiance to the king, and that takes precedence over all others. Even if he swore on the bible, he could not keep his word. Let but the king ask if his wife is honest, and Cranmer must tell him the whole truth."

"Then Henry must not ask after the girl's virtue," Miriam says. "Might you not contrive to have the archbishop sent far away?"

"Of course, that is it," Cromwell says, and claps his hands in joy. "Were Cranmer to be abroad for some time, we could so order things as to make the queen's position safer."

"How so, sir?" Kel asks. He prefers the swift knife when solving problems, but he is not adverse to a little intrigue either.

"It must be done with some skill," Tom Cromwell tells them. "We must make it seem as if Cranmer himself wants to travel. Perhaps some interesting political news from Rome?"

"I can see to that part of things," Miriam says. "My agent in Rome can write to Henry, and advise him that the Bishop of Rome is ready to negotiate a favourable peace settlement."

"He will seek advice," Kel says.

"Yes, from my own nephew," Cromwell says. "Richard can advise Henry to send a 'high churchman' to Rome. Then, we can enlist Eustace Chapuys into our plot. He can write a letter to his emperor, hoping that Cranmer is not chosen, because he is so well fitted for the task, and would thus make Henry more powerful than Emperor Charles of the Holy Roman Empire."

"Of course,"Miriam smiles at the subtlety of it all. "The letter will be intercepted, and read, by our own people. Henry will see how Cranmer is feared abroad, and *insist* he goes to Rome. Richard can then write to the Bishop of Rome, and advise him of Canterbury's eventual coming."

"Speed is of the essence," Tom Cromwell tells them. "Henry must decide to send Cranmer within days, and the fellow must be despatched, without a final audience with the king."

"But it will take time for the letter to come from Rome," Miriam says.

"No matter. Rafe Sadler has a man who can forge one. As long as it matches that eventually sent, we are safe from discovery. We show Henry this copy, with the Papal seal I confiscated back in the day, and he will ask no further questions."

"A month to travel to Rome, three months waiting to see His Holiness, and another month back," Kel enumerates on his fingers. "I doubt poor Archbishop Cranmer will travel well, and we will not see him until the Summer of next year.'

"By which time the queen must be pregnant," says Miriam Draper, with great foresight. "With Tom Culpeper and Francis Dereham out of the way, and nobody here to dun the poor girl, Henry will be overjoyed at this proof of his continued manhood, and the prospect of siring another son."

"They say the king does not lie with the queen," Kel says. "She claims to suffer from sick headaches, and sleeps alone, in darkened rooms. Such behaviour seldom makes babies."

"Then she must be encouraged back to his bed," Thomas Cromwell replies. "No more of these sickly headaches for her, Kel. She must see that Cully can get her killed, and abandon her childish affection for him."

"Lady Jane Boleyn might help us there," says Miriam. "If only she can be brought back to court, without angering the king. I am sure she would act for us, and see the queen does her royal duty each night."

Kel Kelton blushes at this, and casts his eyes down to the floor. He has sought to silence the woman once, and failed. Now he sees that blind luck has saved his face.

"Thank God you did not ever act against her," Tom Cromwell says, and watches as his man turns a strange colour. He knows about the Amos Givens affair, from one of the man's own people, but has never laid it at Kel's door.

"Yes… thank God," Kel agrees.

"Yes… Lady Jane Boleyn." Thomas Cromwell nods his understanding of the worth of the idea. "Let my nephew seek her out, and ask her help with the king and his wayward wife."

"Perhaps she might respond better to another," Miriam guesses. "My husband knows her, and might…"

"No, let it be Richard," Cromwell decides. "He has never stopped loving the woman, and his honesty will shine through, and convince her to our cause."

"Let us hope so." Lady Miriam Draper has said all she can. Lives will be spared, and a royal marriage saved, if only they can get the king back into Queen Catherine's cold bed.

"If we fail, and Cranmer returns, he will tell all to the king," Kel says. "I wish she had confessed to a more malleable fellow."

"Great Christ, but that is a fine idea,"

Cromwell says. "With Cranmer away, Henry and the court will lack a father confessor. We must have Richard suggest a replacement."

"Who?" Miriam asks.

"Stephen Gardiner," Cromwell tells her, with a twinkle in his eye. "He shall be appointed, and then told to take the king's confession. It is always the same. How have you sinned, sire? I have thought ill of my inferiors, and did look upon a woman who is not my wife, Henry replies. Is that all… for you cannot repent your natural superiority, and looking is not acting. You are absolved of all sin, sire."

"Every time?" Kel asks, and chuckles.

"Every single time. Then Stephen must go to Catherine, and ask her to make a new confession. He will ask her but one question … if she is as faithful to King Henry *as one would expect*. Catherine will say that she is as faithful as any man would expect, and that is that."

"How will the king know about this though?" Kel asks.

"Bishop Gardiner will tell him. Oh, he will not break the confessional, of course, but he can, honestly, say that the queen's answers to him were most reassuring. The king will grin, and think it means what he wants it to mean… that his wife is honest to his bed."

"That will work," Miriam says to Cromwell. "It will put fire in his loins, as will the new potion I have for him. It is a Spanish concoction, which ensures a man's *fulness* for several hours. He will swive Catherine each night, and each morning, until the effect lessens…but by then she must be with child."

"Have you plenty of this wonderful stuff, Lady Miriam," Kel jests, "for I fear my two wives will become willing customers!"

Plans are discussed, and wine flows, until every detail is understood. Thomas Cromwell has but one reservation, and that is about Stephen Gardiner, the worldly Bishop of Winchester. His old friend is no fool, and he might well decline the part of willing confessor, for fear that it all goes wrong, and he ends up on the wrong side of the king.

"If not Stephen… then who?" he muses, and it is a problem that remains unsolved, even after a broken night's sleep.

3 Musical Chairs

The times when Thomas Cromwell can say *'make it so'*, and it is done, are long gone, and diplomacy must be conducted in an altogether different way, these days. The royal court is now like a game of musical chairs, where everyone dances around, hoping to find a place to sit down when the fiddle finally stops playing.

Barnaby Fowler must continue to be the friend, and gaoler, of Tom Culpeper, whilst the queen must be gently coaxed back to the king's arms.

Eustace Chapuys, Holy Roman Ambassador to the English throne, spends his days being Archbishop Thomas Cranmer's ardent friend, and sees that he is never once left alone with his king.

"I like the jaunty little fellow, of course," Cranmer tells Bishop Stephen Gardiner, "but he does not allow me time for my church duties. If he is not bringing me the most expensive books to borrow, he wants to discuss the various Canon Laws of the new Church of England. I think he wants to convert to our English church, and I am loath to reject him out of hand. Such a convert would please the king greatly, were I ever to see him again."

"Henry is in a most foul mood, these last few months," Bishop Gardiner tells Cranmer. "I think it better that you keep away from him, my dear Cranmer. Let sleeping dogs lie, eh?"

Then comes news of an unusual offer from Rome. The music stops, and Archbishop Cranmer finds himself without a chair. Henry thinks him to be the perfect choice as ambassador to the Bishop of Rome, and decides to send an expert diplomat with him.

"God's sainted bollocks," Tom Wyatt curses when he is told the news. "Rome, of all places. The last time I was there, the bastards tried to skewer me. Can not another fool go with him instead?"

"No, sir," Rafe Sadler tells him. "For no other fool is as trusted as you. It seems that the king thinks you to be perfect for the task."

"Then the king is..." Tom Wyatt halts, just short of treasonable talk.

"The king is... the king," Rafe concludes, and slaps him on the shoulder with hearty good humour. It is possible that the new embassy will never reach Rome, as Cranmer is an old man, and the road is a dangerous one to travel, even with Tom Wyatt and fifty King's Examiners as bodyguards.

"In a few months he will have forgotten he ever sent you. Just keep safe, and come back when things are more settled."

"Settled, by Jesus," Wyatt curses. "It is England you speak of, Rafe. This country has not been *settled* since the bloody Romans left our shores!"

*

Lady Jane Boleyn, the Dowager Viscountess of Rochford, is about to ring the neck of one of her precious chickens. The lack of money, despite the purse of silver so recently donated, is acute, and she must resort to eating her scrawny livestock, if they are not to starve. The chicken, whom she has foolishly named Ida, is about to die, when a horseman comes galloping into her yard.

"Good day, Lady Jane, might I water my poor horse at your trough?" Sir Richard Cromwell eases himself down from the big gelding, and lets it drink.

"Am I honoured by your visit, Richard… or should I be afraid?" Lady Jane asks her one time lover.

"You have nothing to fear from me, madam," Richard Cromwell tells her.

"Then you were merely passing?"

"You know that is not so," the big man replies. "I am here to make you an offer.

Come back to court with me."

"The king will not allow it."

"The king is a much changed man," Richard says. "He mopes about, lamenting the loss of his 'best boy'… the pathetic Thomas Culpeper. Come back, and he will think himself forgiven…at least, by you, madam."

"Forgiven?" Lady Jane is confused. "For what, sir?"

"He thinks his jest … in trying to bed you, has driven Cully away, and his remorse is real. Come back, madam, and serve your queen faithfully."

"Are you mad, Richard?" Lady Jane sees he is in earnest, and shakes her head in despair. "With Cully abroad, the queen is in mortal danger. The man is quite mad, and intent on bringing down Henry. He will ruin the queen, and destroy any who have been close to her."

"Not so. Cully is somewhere safe, and cannot plot any more," Richard explains. "The queen must be brought back to Henry's bed, and made with child. Once she is carrying his baby, her virtue is assured. Even an archbishop's words cannot harm her, and if the child is a boy, Henry will be doubly pleased."

"She hates him," Lady Jane says.

"That is why we need you... to convince her to her duty."

"I see." Lady Jane understands that she is, once more, back in favour, and her skills are needed. It will be no easy matter to talk Catherine back into Henry's bed, but she will try her best. "Very well, but I must have some assurances, sir."

"Pray, call me Richard, as you once did," the younger Cromwell tells her. "I recall a time when we were as one. Can you not remember the same?"

"I recall refusing your proposal."

"We were foolish then," Richard says. "Would that I could repeat my words, and would that you now accepted them."

"You would still marry me?"

"With all my heart."

"You are spoken for, sir."

"Then I shall take back my word for you," Richard tells her. "Come back to court, and give me a couple of months to extricate myself from my present involvement. Then I will make you into Lady Cromwell."

"Even though I refused you, once?"

"Do you love me, madam?"

"How does that matter now?"

"Do you love me?" Richard holds out his hands, and she comes to him.

"I do," she says, and they touch fingers, like two bashful youngsters.

"Then that is that," he says. "Have your servants pack your things, and we will return to London, as fast as we may."

"Where will I stay?"

"In my house," Richard Cromwell tells her. "Until we can find you chambers close to Queen Catherine's own. Once back in court you must convince Catherine to her duty."

"Duty, yes… it is that, and no mistake," Jane says. "The poor girl must close her eyes and use her imagination."

*

"How long must we carry on with this pretence, Will?" Colonel John Beckshaw asks his commander. They are at the head of fifty King's Examiner troopers, and have been galloping about the Berkshire countryside for three days.

"Until the king says we must stop," Will Draper replies. "He is adamant that we find his squire, Tom Culpeper. Since this is not possible, we might well be riding until the end of days. At the last trump, I must tell the king that we are unsuccessful in our quest."

"This is madness," Beckshaw complains. "The man is locked up with

Barnaby Fowler… and quite insane, if what we hear is true. Can we not just tell the king he has been deranged with fear of the plague?"

"And have the king demand to see him?" Will curses at how he is entangled in so twisted a plot. "As soon as he is brought before the king, the fool will call on all his 'friends' to rise up, and slay the evil king. Henry will be outraged, and he will listen to those names that Culpeper calls upon. He may name me, Richard Cromwell, all the great dukes and earls of England, and even you, if he recalls your name."

"The king would not believe it."

"The king would want to know why we have not taken him up sooner, and then, he would demand an investigation into those who seem to have supported dear Cully. Every man who has ever taken a present from him will be suspect, and the king's unwarranted obsessions will do the rest."

"Then Culpeper would go to the block," John Beckshaw says. "There is no proof against any other."

"No?" Will Draper shakes his head at his man's lack of acumen. "Do you recall a parade, some months ago, when Henry inspected us?"

"I do."

"Thomas Culpeper was with him, and afterwards, he sent a generous gift of money... from him, not the king. We used it to buy some silver plate for the mess, as I recall."

"That is so."

"The king will recall Cully sending a hefty bribe to his loyal troops, and wonder at it," Will explains. "He will think us guilty of something."

"I doubt it was five pounds," John Beckshaw says.

"Do you recall a man called George Cobb?" Will continues. "He was caught stealing a shilling chicken from the royal kitchens, last month. The king had him lowered into a cauldron of boiling water... for a damned shilling."

"Henry will not turn his hand against the Examiners."

"No. but he will promote me, and thus remove me from my command. He will put another in my place, and so take control of us. Politics, John. It is all politics."

"The men will not allow it."

"The men will do as their king commands."

"Then what can we do?" John

Beckshaw asks.

"Our duty, of course. Things are happening, as we speak, and a solution will be found." Will Draper slows his horse to a slow walk, as a rider approaches. The man is from London, and carries an urgent message.

"I am sent by my master, Sir Richard Rich," the man says, "and must speak with you alone, sir."

"Draw off a way, John, and let this fellow speak," Will Draper says. "I am intrigued as to why Rich might seek me out, for we are not friends by any count."

The young rider waits until they cannot be overheard, before delivering his message.

"The Attorney General of England sends greetings, sir, and bids me tell you this. It is his duty to maintain the laws of England, and ensure that the king's will be done. To this end, he advises you that a force has been raised to do deeds against the king's peace.'

"What force?" Will asks. "Do you mean an armed insurrection, or some even more wicked plot?"

"The Duke of Norfolk seeks to act against the king, secretly," the messenger says. "He and his son have gathered a force, intent on ridding England of certain people who stand in his way. My own master does not command enough men to stay Norfolk's hand, and begs your indulgence. He directs you, with all haste, to confront this armed force, and deter them from their avowed task.'

"How does Rich know this?"

"He was approached, by Surrey, but declined to act against the king.'

"And now, he fears for his skin, if Norfolk is successful," Will guesses. "I must know who he acts against."

"His men are looking for Tom Culpeper, so that they might silence him, and spare the queen. Then he intends removing all who know of his niece's misdemeanour."

"Speak plainly, fellow!"

"You, sir… your family, Richard Cromwell, and Lady Jane Boleyn." The rider takes a roll of parchment from his doublet, and hands it over to Will. "This is an arrest warrant, bearing the Attorney General's own seal, made out in the name of Norfolk. My master gives you this great power, to show his own devotion in this matter. He is for you, sir… and the king. If Norfolk gains power over you, he gains it over the king, and Sir Richard Rich will not suffer that to happen."

"He wants me to ruin Norfolk, and remove him from the game?"

Rose Without a Thorn

"I am but a messenger, sir," the man says. "Though even I can see how ruining the duke can benefit you both."

"Very well." Will sees that he must sup with the devil that is Rich if he is to overcome the devil that is Norfolk. It sits badly with him, but he cannot miss the chance to bring down one of his enemies. "Tell Rich that I will search Lord Norfolk out, and use his warrant, but only if the duke is breaking any of our laws."

*

Colonel Henry Black is a soldier of some repute. He is fresh from Ireland, where his skill as a fighting man, coupled with his natural brutality, has made him feared by the enemy and his own men alike. Now he is back in England, and commissioned to lead the Duke of Norfolk's best men, a company of tough dragoons.

These men, mounted infantry, armed with the latest '*dragon*' wheellock pistols are the best professional troops in England, and they are in the service of the Duke of Norfolk.

"My father should be here," Surrey complains to Colonel Black. "If anything goes wrong, he …"

"Nothing will go wrong, My Lord," Black says, almost sneering at the effeminate earl. He is half the man his father is, and Black sees how weak he is. "Your father commands me to seek out and destroy his enemies, and that is what I shall do. Your presence here is because My Lord Norfolk commands it. He thinks it might make a man out of you, to fight with us."

"Fight?" Surrey is aghast at the very idea. "There will be no fighting, sir. Your men will simply raid those places we have told you of, and kill all within."

"I fully understand that, my dear Lord Surrey," Black replies, coldly, "but this General Draper you speak of is no fool. He will have some troops at his disposal."

"Not if you strike fast," Surrey tells the mercenary officer. "Burn down Draper House, and kill him and all of his damned Jewish family. Then you can put paid to Lady Jane Boleyn, and Thomas Culpeper."

"We must find him first," Colonel Black says. "Then there is the king's first minister… Richard Cromwell… a giant of a fellow, I hear. You want him dead too?"

"Of course we do."

"The king will be displeased." Black has some grasp of court politics, and sees that there is a huge gamble being taken.

"Father is remaining behind, so that

he might protect the king with his household troops. There are several thousand of our men waiting outside the city, ready to enter, and seize key points. Once Henry is in our protective custody, we can rid England of all our enemies."

"You propose that we overthrow the king?" The colonel grins at the audacity of it all. "I have a hundred good fighting men, against how many?"

"My father's troops are already under orders," Surrey says. "Only Suffolk might fight, and he does not have enough men to stop us. We will hold London, and thus control the king."

"A fine madness, My Lord Surrey," Colonel Black says. "The headsman is going to be busy if we fail."

"Good sense," Surrey boasts. "If the king is ours, then England follows. I think Henry will be allowed to stay on the royal throne, providing he listens to the Duke of Norfolk's advice."

"Your audacious plot hinges on there being no one left to advise the king," the mercenary colonel says. "We must kill General Draper before he can raise his troops, kill Cromwell before he can aid the king, and kill this Boleyn woman because…?"

"Because she can ruin a queen," Surrey replies. "Catherine is a Howard, and will provide fine sons for Henry. Then, if anything happens to Edward…"

"By Christ, sir…you would murder the prince… why, you are as wicked a bastard as I, and no mistake. Let us get on, and start. I trust no one else knows of your plans?"

"Of course not," Surrey says. "Do you think me a fool?" The young earl neglects to mention that he has tried to enlist Richard Rich in the plot, and failed. It is of no matter, he thinks, after all, what could the man possibly do to halt him now?

*

Sir Richard Cromwell is seated on his huge gelding, and has Lady Jane Boleyn perched up behind him. She is holding on to his great girth, and nuzzling his neck with real affection. "I have often dreamed of this moment," she says into his broad back.

"We will be in London before dark," he says, as they gain the summit of the nearby hill. Six of his best men are waiting to escort them. He glances back at the farm, which is nestled in the valley, and his jaw drops in astonishment.

From the North, a swiftly travelling troop of horsemen, perhaps a hundred strong, sweep down the valley, and fan out into two lines abreast. Each man bears a long curved sabre, held upright and laid against the right shoulder. These are real soldiers, Richard thinks. They come on, relentlessly, and engulf the farm buildings. The servant, and those few peasants who live close by, run out to see what is afoot, and they are cut down, like dogs for their trouble.

The mounted men swirl about the farm, and then set about burning it to the ground. Lady Jane sobs in horror at the sight of her few faithful neighbours, murdered before her eyes, and Richard Cromwell spurs his mount into a trot.

"They told me that you would be spared," he growls. "Mush Draper swore it to me, and now… he sends military men to do bloody murder. By God, but I will gut him for this day's treachery, and that other treacherous bastard, Will Draper."

"You really think that?" Lady Jane says, into his back. "I thought them better men than that. Then, if it be so, I am a dead woman, Richard. For to send so great an army against one poor woman means they have not a care in the world. I am marked down for death, no matter what."

"I shall not let them get away with it,"

Richard snaps. He shakes with anger, and frustrated rage. Were either man to appear before him at that moment, he would snap his spine like a twig. "I'm finished with them."

"But to be so blatant can mean only one thing," she tells him. "They must have the king's blessing…or the king's person."

"What?" The younger Cromwell frowns, and tries to think quicker. Why would Mush use such a trick, when he could just have ridden up, one night, and cut Lady Jane's throat? Then again, the men were not King's Examiners. "Sweet Jesus, but I am slow witted, he says. "It is not the Draper hand in this, but someone else's. They seek to kill you with an army… which means they must have other victims in their sights."

"Listen to me, Richard," Lady Jane says. "I am a danger to the queen. I think they wanted me dead to keep her from harm. That means that a Howard hand is in all of this. The Duke of Norfolk is out of favour, and noble men wager on when he might end up on the block. So, why would he not act? If he can keep Catherine on the throne, and destroy his enemies… he might yet survive. Better still, with us dead, and Will Draper too, who would protect Henry from these accursed Howards?"

"The Examiners number eight

hundred men," Richard says. "Not enough to hold London. One pitched battle, and Norfolk will take Henry, and London, and all will be lost."

"We must reach London first, and try to raise enough men to fight him," Lady Jane says. "Send your men on ahead, to raise our people to action."

"He is a wily old bird," Richard Cromwell replies. "What if his hand is hidden from us, and these men are under another command?"

"His son?" Lady Jane guesses.

"Yes, and if he fails… the son goes to the Tower instead."

"I don't know," Jane says, "but for now, we must ride, my love."

My love, she says, and Richard Cromwell is enraptured. Jane is the only woman he has ever truly loved, and now, he will move heaven and earth to keep her safe, and by his side.

*

"Rome?" The Archbishop of Canterbury does not quite know what to say. A messenger, fresh from Richard Cromwell's office, has just delivered a sealed letter, instructing the elderly archbishop to prepare for a long trip. "What ever can His Holiness have to say to us at this late stage?"

"Who can tell," Eustace Chapuys says. He was 'just passing' once more, and seems eager to help Tom Cranmer. "My personal servant, Gomez, will happily help you pack. He is a rogue, of course, but are not they all?"

"Goodness … pack…?… but I must have a month, if I am to prepare properly,' Cranmer tells the little Savoyard. "These things cannot be rushed. Besides, I must see Henry, and take his personal instructions for any discussions I might have with the Bishop of Rome."

"I told you so," Alonso Gomez whispers into his master's ear. "He will try to get out of it, and even go whining to Henry about it. Let me cut his throat now, and save all the trouble to come."

"Enough, Gomez," Chapuys threatens. "He is a man of God, even if it is the wrong God he is the man of."

"Uh?" Alonso Gomez is confused at this. Once before, a Spaniard… also a bishop, sought to ruin his master, and Gomez was allowed, using the 'blind eye' approach, to smother him aboard his ship. "The man is a real danger. He knows … and he will tell what he knows."

"No. he will obey the king, and leave for Rome, with Sir Tom Wyatt to watch over his progress," Eustace Chapuys insists.

"I cannot go," Archbishop Cranmer says, with an air of finality. "My duty is here, with the king. There are momentous things to discuss with him; things that might change the face of England. If only I could get him alone for a half hour."

"See, he means to ruin the queen," Gomez says. He is Chapuys' servant, but he has been around the Austin Friars crowd for so long that he thinks of himself as an honorary member of the family. "Let me strangle him at once, master. He will feel little pain… more surprise than anything else."

"My dear Archbishop, this command is quite clear. You must leave for Rome within the week."

"Impossible!" Cranmer is beginning to grow worried. Such a strange command is quite unnerving him, and it is only six months ago that the king, for no obvious reason had him arrested for heresy, and locked up in the Tower of London. True, the chambers were very well appointed, with a comfortable bed, lots of books, and enough paper and ink for him to write a book of his own, but still he was made a prisoner. It lasted a week, before

Henry changed his mind, and released him without comment. Later, he was restored to his primacy, and even given wider powers.

"My servant will help us with all the preparations. We shall have you packed in two days, and on a boat by Sunday morning. I shall ask Lady Miriam Draper to lend us one of her faster cogs. They make regular trips across the Channel, and will have you in Bordeaux by next Tuesday."

"Bordeaux?" Cranmer groans at the very idea of setting foot on French soil. "We are about to go to war with the French."

"Of course. It would be a mistake to go via Paris, for the French king would only seek to delay you. He dare not interfere with a man of God, on his way to speak with the Pope. Land in Bordeaux, and then travel overland, towards Lombardy. Wyatt knows the way."

"But it all such an undertaking for a man of my years. I have never travelled so far before, not in all my life."

"I shall travel with you then, my dearest old friend." The words are out before Eustace Chapuys can think, and it seems to clinch the deal. The Archbishop of Canterbury's eyes fill with tears.

"You would do that just for me, my

friend?" Thomas Cranmer is deeply touched by such loyalty. "What of your political duties here in the city?"

"I will sail with you, as far as the French coast, then return on the next tide," Chapuys says. "But you must not dawdle, lest the king be angry with you."

"Of course. Yes, I must hurry," the archbishop says, but he has misgivings. The whole thing seems hurried, and he has yet to see a royal seal on any of his documents. How can one possibly visit a Pope without the right set of documents?

"What of the royal seal?" he asks.

"Wyatt will see to it," Eustace Chapuys lies. "We are looking for him, as we speak. I dare say he is in some low tavern, versing for his ale."

*

Will Draper is grateful that his wife and family are in Antwerp just now, and he can concentrate on the business in hand. Though being kept cleverly concealed, there is a plot afoot, against the king, and it is already well advanced.

Richard Rich suggests that Norfolk is the lynchpin, and that his arrest will nip the plot in the bud, but it is not that easy. Norfolk, it seems, is ensconced in Arundel, surrounded by a thousand men, whilst his idiot son is galloping around the countryside, burning down farms, and busily slaughtering the innocent populace.

Having missed Lady Jane, he is convinced she is hiding out with neighbours, and is intent on raising their homes to the ground. It is only on the second day that Colonel Henry Black finally persuades him to stop hanging women and children from trees, and return to the plan they have made.

"We must ride to London, and rid ourselves of this Draper fellow," Henry Black advises. "Then you must take charge of your father's soldiers within the city, and assume command. The king will be grateful to you, and place himself in your safe hands."

"What if he does not?"

"Then I will place him into your keeping, whether he likes it or not." Colonel Black is tiring of the fool, and sees he must be sterner. "You cannot ride about the countryside with an army at your back, unless you declare yourself, sir. You must claim you are for the king, and against his enemies. In this way, you may take London, and with it, all England. Lord Norfolk has six thousand troops camped outside London, ready to support their king. They will not make a move without your orders."

"But Will Draper is still at large."

"One man, with hardly eight hundred troopers," Colonel Black sneers. "He cannot match us, sir. Ride on London, now, and be damned to it. I will take care of Will Draper personally. His blood shall stain my sword's blade, and his men will swear to Norfolk."

"I have heard that before, Colonel Black," Surrey tells him. "Your hundred dragoons will not best him in a fight."

"No, but your six thousand will," Black says. "Once we have the king safe, he dare not move against us. Trust me, I know how to fight a battle, and will not fail like those he has bested before me."

"Yes, you are right," Surrey decides. "The time for action is now."

*

"Open up, in the king's name!"

Barnaby Fowler moves over to the platform above the portcullis, and looks down onto the half dozen men at the gate. They are mounted on excellent horses, and uniformed in the green and red of the new dragoon regiment.

"In Norfolk's name, more like," Barnaby mutters to himself. "You have a signed warrant, sir?"

"I have."

"Show it to me."

"Here, see?" The man holds up a scrap of paper, with a piece of green wax attached to it.

"No, I cannot see it from here," the lawyer replies. It is a ruse that has delayed matters in the past for him. "Let it be handed in at the gate, and I will study it at my leisure."

"Be damned to that," the sergeant shouts back. "I am commanded to bring forth the traitor, Thomas Culpeper, and take him into my charge. Open up, now!"

"He is in *my* charge, sergeant, and I outrank you," the lawyer calls back. "I see no reason to change the arrangement just yet."

"Admit us, now, sir... or we must resort to harsher tactics."

"Then do so," Barnaby Fowler tells the man. "Though I do not see any wings on your horses." The movement is so swift that the lawyer barely has time to draw back his head. The pistol ball passes where, but a moment earlier, his head would had been.

"That is not the act of a gentleman, sir," the lawyer says, and pushes the cannon ball he has perched on the parapet over the edge. It strikes one of the horsemen to the sergeant's left, squarely on his plumed helmet, and pushes his head into his shoulders with a sickening crunch of bone and flesh.

"Great Christ!" the sergeant cries, and pulls his horses head safely to one side. "Kill him, men."

The lifeless body slumps from its horse, and the other men all discharge their pistols. Lead rounds spatter against stone, making Barnaby retreat a pace, and the furious dragoons draw their short curved swords. Without a pause, they begin to scale the iron lattice work of the solid portcullis gate. It is not meant to repel invasion, and they make light work of gaining the parapet's lower shelf.

Barnaby pushes over another lead ball, as they climb, but it bounces away, harmlessly, and he is forced to resort to his hand weapons. As the first head appears at the summit of the gate, the lawyer levels his heavy saddle pistol, and fires at a range of less than two feet.

The dragoon's face explodes in a cloud of shredded flesh and blood, and he topples backwards. The next man gains a foot hold, and is almost onto the platform proper, when Barnaby Fowler hacks down with his own razor sharp sabre. The curved blade, a keepsake from the French campaign against the Malatesta priest, bites into sinew and muscle, opening a huge wound from neck to shoulder, and the man grunts once, as if in surprise, and dies. His blood gushes out, and makes the parapet slippy with gore.

The three remaining men pause, and consider how to continue. A sudden rush, onto the parapet, will do it, but they see that they will lose at least another man. The sergeant wishes to live, so decides on another tactic.

"Look, friend," he calls from the wrong side of the low stone wall. "We only want this Culpeper. Send him out to us, and save yourself."

"Too late," the lawyer tells them. "I know you will not believe me, so I must fight to the death of you all."

"Sir, I see that you are a learned gentleman, and not much used to telling untruths," the sergeant ventures. There is a way out, if only this madman will see it. "Tell me, and I will believe you."

"Very well. He left here this morning, with an escort made up of General Draper's best men. They are for London, and the king."

"Shit!" The sergeant, who is not of an academic mind, drops down to the ground, and runs to his horse. "Come on, you damned bastards… we may yet catch up with them on the open road!"

Barnaby Fowler watches them ride off, and climbs down into the carefully manicured quadrangle. He does not know if the man really believes him, or not, but it has saved a couple of lives, if nothing else.

"What was all that noise?"

"Oh, nothing," Barnaby Fowler says to his unknowing captive. "Just some passing folk. They are bound for London, I believe."

"Going to see the coronation, no doubt," Culpeper says. "I dare say that the people are waiting for me to be crowned. Catherine and I will make a pretty pair, and no mistake. Did you give them a shilling?"

"A shilling?"

"To keep them honest," Cully replies. "Tom Cromwell told me that, a little while before I had his head cut off."

"You had Thomas Cromwell's head cut off?" the lawyer asks. He knows it is just a romancer's tale, but he must listen, incase it contains some germ of truth that is important.

"Of course I did. Fat Henry does everything I tell him to." Cully grins, and taps a finger to his nose. "Though killing the old fellow was, I confess, a great mistake. He comes to me now, most nights, and tries to pull my ear, or tweak my nose. He is a wicked old fellow... jealous because I swived Catherine... and Anne Boleyn too."

"You ... and Anne Boleyn?"

'Yes, of course. I used one of Lady Miriam Draper's magic potions to disguise myself as her brother George, and did swive her silly."

"You are a walking marvel, sir, and no mistake." Barnaby Fowler will write all this nonsense down, and see that it reaches the right people, but he doubts that the poor fool will ever stand trial. His lunacy is so far advanced that he will be best off locked away in some safe place, such as is still maintained by the Church of England, or the benevolent Knights Hospitallers.

"I am the chosen one," Cully explains. "He has picked me, for my wit and my beauty. Men shall bow down to me, and..." He stops talking, as if suddenly realising that what he says is all some kind of madness.

"Rest yourself, Cully," Barnaby Fowler urges. He is sorry for the poor mad fool, and hopes he does not have to suffer too much. "It will be over... soon, now."

4 The King's Care

The kitchens at the *Palais de Juis* are second to none in Europe. Even the French royal kitchens cannot match them in either size, or modernity. There are the very latest brick lined ovens, crank handled spits, a charcoal grill, and a smoking pantry for the fish and meat.

The four huge fireplaces are tended, around the clock, by an army of eager youngsters, who prefer the honest hard work to sleeping on the streets. Food is cooked without halt, and entire roasted pigs and sheep are jointed and sent to Miriam Drapers' market stalls in Antwerp, London, and Ghent.

The ovens produce twenty-five scores of succulent meat pies each shift, and they too go to market, at a penny a piece. The whole business is overseen by Maisie Kelton, and brings in almost twelve pounds a week profit for Miriam.

"Business is very good," Tom Cromwell tells her. "The house alone produces enough profit to pay for itself, and the rest of your onshore business brings in three thousand Ducati a year."

"I make more from the cogs," she says. "I am worth almost as much as a decent sized country, and I spend my days waiting for my husband to show his face."

"Will has duties, my dear."

"His duty is to be with me, and the children," Miriam says. "I tire of all this intrigue, Master Tom. When will it all end?"

"When good men triumph," Tom Cromwell tells her. "Once Norfolk is brought down, and the king is safe."

"Safe to do what?" Miriam asks. "He is a monster. Once he is safe, he will start to look around for those he does not trust. Then blood will flow again. I think even Catherine will fall."

"No, he will not kill another queen," Cromwell tells her. "If he does, the world will judge him too badly, and he does not wish that."

"He cares not," Miriam says. "I want my husband away from him, lest he grows to be like him."

"Hush, Miriam," Cromwell says. "It will all turn out well, just you wait and see."

*

The Duke of Norfolk's pikemen are stretched out across the northern approach to the old city wall, and they advance at a steady pace. At any moment, they expect either cannon fire, or a sudden rush from the city, but all is quiet, and they approach without upset.

Colonel Henry Black sees that the nearest gate is unguarded, and he leads his dragoons in a wild charge at it. They surge into the city, unopposed, and find the bemused citizens going about their business, very much as usual.

"Playing at war, sir?" a small child asks of him. "Are you the king's men?"

"We are, lad," the colonel says to the boy, and flips a penny to him. "What is afoot?"

"Market day, sir," the small boy says. "I can gainsay the hot offal pies, for they are a wonder at a halfpenny a piece." The child is one of Austin Friars agents, and his task is to keep watch on the city gate and report on any untoward happenings. An army storming the city seems to fit that guideline.

"Have you seen any other soldiers this morning, lad?" Black asks, and the boy ponders for a moment.

"Only the guards on the gate, master," the boy replies. "They seldom stay around on a market day."

"Then they should be flogged," the mercenary pronounces. "Once I am in charge, such lapses will not go unpunished."

"As you say, sir," the lad agrees. "Fair shocking it is. Why, you rode in without a by your leave, and were left unchecked."

"Here, hold my horse's head for me, whilst I see how things stand."

"Am I then recruited, sir?" the boy asks, and Colonel Henry Black grins at his sheer bravado.

"You are my stableboy from now on," the colonel says. "Do well and I shall pay you a shilling a week and victuals, let me down, and I'll cut out your heart. Deal?"

"Deal," the boy says, and takes the big horse's bridle in his hands.

The local market is well under way, and the stall holders look at this sudden show of unadvertised military might with some surprise. No one has told them about any conflict in the shires, and they can only wonder at an army with no enemy. An alderman of the borough of Hackney village ventures to approach the massing troops, and asks whom they are for.

"For?" Black asks. "Why we are here to save the king."

"You are not the French, are you?" the man asks, somewhat confused. That the king is in need of saving is news to him. Surely, he thinks, it is us who needs the saving from him... and from his greedier tax gatherers.

"French? Damn me, no," Colonel Black replies, as his he pulls off the heavy leather riding gauntlets that he favours.

"Flemings?" the man guesses. It is the limit of his geographical knowledge, although he is aware that beyond the seas there are men who do not worship the same god, and who are of various colours.

"No, and be damned to you, fellow, we are all Englishmen!"

"Yet you invade our city, as if you expect a fight?" The man sniffs at this. "I doubt you will find us to be much opposition, sir. It is a pity that the King's Examiners are not here to greet you, and offer you a damned bloody nose."

"What of them?" Black demands. "Why are they not here?"

"Why, because they are ordered away," the alderman tells him.

"Where to, man?" The mercenary colonel feels a sickness, deep in the pit of his stomach. Something is very wrong, and he does not yet know what.

"Word is that they are ordered to take up residence in the Tower, sir."

"The Tower?"

"Of London," the man confirms.

"All of them?" Colonel Black sees that his quarry have all fled, and he is pleased that they have. "Run away to hide in the Tower, you say?"

"Hide, sir?" The man is confused by this. "No, sir. Not to hide. It is their duty, is it not?"

"What is it?" Harry Howard, the Earl of Surrey is there, and wanting answers. "Why are we not destroying the enemy, Colonel Black?"

"Gone, My Lord,' Henry Black tells him. "Run away to the Tower… to do their duty, according to this ignorant fellow."

"Their duty?' Surrey groans then, for he realises what Henry Black does not. "Pray God you are wrong, or we are done for, sir!"

*

"What is this, sir?" The king sees his throne being lifted, and carried from the chamber. "My bedroom hangings have been taken down too."

"We are moving Your Majesty to the Tower of London, sire." Sir Thomas Heanage says. "By the direct order of Sir Rafe Sadler, Your Majesty."

"Stop it, right now," Henry demands. "I am not a piece of old baggage, to be portered from place to place. Send Rafe Sadler to me, at once."

"There is not the time," Will Draper says, as he comes into the chamber. "The king must be placed in the Tower, without further delay. Sire, come along, if you value your crown."

"Never!" The king is outraged. "I see treason in this, Draper… and I smell some wicked plot. So, explain yourself, and without further delay."

"Of course, sire." Will Draper takes a vial from his doublet. "Miriam sends you this. She says you must take it with wine. It will cause your wicked pain to cease."

"My thanks," Henry says. "Now, why must I go to the Tower, General Draper? It is I who send people there."

Will Draper pours the potion into some wine, and hands it to the king.

"An army has entered London, sire," Will says, "and are intent on taking you captive.'

"Great Christ!" Henry downs his pain killer. "What proof have you of this, sir? Send for Norfolk and Suffolk. I must hold court and … and…"

"There is no time, Your Majesty," Will tells him. "Pray, sit down, for you grow faint. Men, support the king!"

Henry, double dosed with poppy juice, feels as if he has been struck on the head with a broadsword. He staggers, and starts to topple. Four strong Examiners take his weight, and ease him down onto his throne. Then they take a corner each of the huge ornate chair, and carry him out of the palace, and down to the river's edge.

They have him loaded onto a flat bottomed barge, lashed to the deck, and poled away from the shore, just as Colonel Black and fifty of his men arrive at the front gate of the unguarded palace. They will rage about, and search high and low for Henry, before coming to an inescapable conclusion. The king is gone, and out of their reach.

"Where?" Black demands, and one of the king's squires makes bold enough to step forward.

"You come here armed, sir," he complains. "That alone is treason. You must give up your sword within the palace."

"Very well, I surrender it to you, young man. The blade goes into the squire's chest, and strikes his backbone. The youth staggers back, astounded at finding himself so easily murdered, and falls down onto the marble floor. "Right which one of you damnable arse kissers is next? Lost your tongues have you?" A boy, normally busy building and lighting fires about the palace raises a hand.

"Begin' yer pardon, sir, but would there be a reward for me telling you?"

"I'll let you live," Black says. Then he laughs and opens his purse. "Clever lad, I jest. Let us say five shillings, if your information is useful to me."

"The king is for the Tower of London, by river, and he is already half way there." The lad, yet another of Austin Friars' well trained agents, is happy to oblige with this information, as it is five shillings earned for nothing. Henry is already a mile down river, and even the fastest craft cannot catch him. He holds out his hand and receives three shillings and four sixpenny pieces.

"Captain Ross, find us a boat. I want a dozen men, armed with muskets and giving chase at once."

"Yes, sir," says Ross. He knows it is a futile mission, but the mercenary colonel is in no mood to be contradicted. "At once!"

*

Thomas Howard, the 3rd Duke of Norfolk, covers the distance from Arundel to London in his coach, escorted by a thousand horsemen. Word has reached him that the city is in the hands of his son, and that no opposition has been met.

"Done something right, at last," he boasts to his steward. "The boy has finally come good."

"Yes, Your Lordship," the man says. "It seems that the enemy have fled, and left the field to you."

"As they should. With the king now in my care, I can see England back on the right road, once more. We must have arrest warrants drawn up for Henry to sign, as soon as I meet with him."

"Yes, sir." The steward beckons for a clerk to ride forward, with quill, ink and paper. "Might I have the names?"

"Charles Brandon in prime place," Norfolk replies. He is Henry's best friend, and therefore the most dangerous. "Then we must arrest General Draper, and his bloodthirsty brother in law. They will want to stand against us."

"Certainly, My Lord. What about the king's pet, Rafe Sadler, sir?" the steward asks, with a sly smile. "Is he not an old Thomas Cromwell man?"

"A small man," Norfolk says. "I think he will come over to us, when he sees the king is in our camp. Then we must see that Richard Cromwell is arrested."

"The Examiners will try to save their master."

"Then turn my troops onto them," Norfolk says. "We are saving the crown, and any who oppose us are traitors. Have they found Thomas Culpeper, and Lady Jane Boleyn yet?"

"No, My Lord, they have not, despite extensive searches." The steward reports only what he has been told by the lieutenant in charge of the hunt. "Both seem to have vanished into thin air."

"God's Holy bollocks," Norfolk sneers. "Can it be so hard? I need Culpeper silenced, and my niece's reputation protected. Re-double our efforts, Master Gilbert."

"Yes, sir. At once, Your Lordship." Gilbert bows and retreats. He is hitched to the duke's star, and must see that the old man triumphs. London is taken, on the word of Surrey, and over six thousand soldiers are in the city.

What could go wrong?

*

"Oh, my head hurts," the king moans as he tries to sit up.. "Have I been asleep?"

"Drugged, sire." Will Draper sees that

he must not lie to Henry at this stage. At least, not over the minor details. "By me."

"What?" Henry cannot begin to understand. "I thought you loved me like a father, General Draper."

"No man is more loyal," Will replies. "You were in danger at the palace, and I had to move you at once."

"Move me?" For the first time, Henry looks about him. "Why, where am I now?"

"The Tower of London, sire," Will Draper says. "It was the only safe place left in London. I have you surrounded by most of my loyal Examiners."

"Again I must ask the question of you… why so, sir?" Henry sounds deflated and hurt at Will's actions against him.

"The city is taken, Your Majesty," the Examiner explains. "Thousands of enemy troops are all about us."

"The French?" Henry is still befuddled by the massive dose of poppy juice, and thinks François has sailed over, and stolen his kingdom. "Those frog eating bastards have captured London from me?"

"No, sire… Norfolk."

"Norfolk?" Henry's eyes fill with tears. "Then he has taken my kingdom?"

"He thinks to take *you*, sire," Will

explains. "With you in his power, he would make himself the first man in England again."

"Then I am a prisoner in my own Tower?" Henry is fast becoming a wreck.

"No, sire. You are perfectly safe here, surrounded by your finest troops." Will beckons, and Mush steps from the shadows.

"Ah, the monkey," Henry says. "He is never far away from you, is he?"

"Speak, Mush," Will says.

"Companies of regular foot soldiers hold all the main gates to the city, sire," Mush says. "Patrols see that no boats move on the river, and the storehouses and docks have all been seized."

"Then we are under siege?" the king realises. "We are trapped within my strongest fortress, with but one regiment loyal to the crown."

"It would seem so, sire," Mush says to the king, "but Sir Richard Cromwell has a full report on our current status for you."

"Dick, is that you, my faithful friend?" Henry is touched that his best men are loyal to him, and he hugs the muscular giant to him. Richard holds him, and sees that the king's fabled strength is now but a shadow of its former self.

"It is truly I, Hal," he replies in his

most considerate voice. "I come to stand by your side, come what may."

"Sound fellow… do you recall how we twitted the French king over Algiers, and foiled *la Boleyns* many plots?" Henry is thinking of Thomas Cromwell, but the poppies are strong in his blood, and he struggles to keep his mind in order.

"That was when you were allied to my uncle, sire," Richard says.

"Was it? Then where is he now, for I have need of his… ah… I recall that he is dead, my boy. Sweet Christ… slain with the lies of lesser men than he."

"Yes, Your Majesty. Slain with lies whispered in to your ear by…"

"Norfolk." Henry shakes his head at this realisation. "Always, it is Norfolk. The man did beg me to put aside Queen Katherine, damned his own niece to death, and contrived Sir Thomas More's death on the block. It was he who forced me to condemn your uncle. I was for forgiving him, but Norfolk made that impossible, even for a king."

'Sire, I know the truth of it all, and I am still here." Richard Cromwell holds up a parchment to bring Henry back to the present. "We have enough food to last the garrison for three months, sire, and all of England's ordnance is within our walls. Two hundred cannon, of various calibre's, three thousand muskets, ten thousand pikestaffs, six thousand crossbows, and diverse swords and suits of armour."

"But only three months food?"

"It is enough, Your Majesty," the younger Cromwell replies. "As soon as word reaches your nobles that you are under attack, they will march against the rebels, and lift the siege."

"Or they will hang back, and let me lose my crown," Henry says, as his deep mistrust comes to the fore. "Who amongst them will be with me, lads?"

"Warwick loves you," Richard Cromwell says. "He alone has six thousand yeomen. Then Suffolk will come, as soon as he can raise his own yeomen."

"Dearest Charles… yes, I can see that," the king agrees. "The siege will collapse, and I will seek my revenge. You say that it is definitely Norfolk's doing?"

"It would seem so," Will says, carefully. It does not do to accuse a great lord openly, and he must hint carefully at the way of things. "My agents tell me that most of the men are his."

"He is in London then?"

"No."

"Then who directs the uprising against me?" Henry asks.

"I am not sure," Will confesses. "I think it might well be the son."

"Surrey?" Henry roars with laughter at this. "That callow youth does not have the nerve. He cannot direct his pintle into a willing maid, let alone run a siege, sir."

"Perhaps not," Mush says, "but there are six thousand soldiers outside, and they want to take you, sire. Does it matter who leads them?"

"Perhaps not," the king muses.

"Then we must fortify the Tower of London, and wait for help," Will decides. "Is that your wish, sire?"

"For now, yes." Henry frowns at how easily he has been drugged, and moved to the Tower of London, and he wonders at the motives of all those involved. Can he trust these few men, or is every hand now turned against him?

*

"We will camp outside the city tonight, and make our triumphal entry tomorrow, in time for lunch," Norfolk decides. "I shall meet with the king, and explain how we have his best interests at heart. He will sign the death warrants for me, and I can get on governing his realm."

There is a commotion, and Gilbert, Norfolk's steward, comes running towards the coach. He is quite breathless, and he is shaking with horror.

"My Lord!" He comes to a halt, and begs to speak with the duke alone.

"Get in," Norfolk says, "but try not to soil my seats. What is it?"

"Your son has taken London, sir…"

"I know."

"But not the king."

"What?" The duke's stomach twists into a knot of apprehension. "He does not have the king?"

"The King's Examiners have seized His Majesty, and have now retired within the Tower of London." Gilbert wipes the sweat from his brow. "Surrey sent a man to demand his release, and Will Draper told him to …"

"To what?"

"To '*piss off back to Norfolk, and bid him surrender his treacherous old hide*', My Lord." The blow comes from the shoulder, and Gilbert's nose crunches into a bloodied pulp. He slips from the seat, and starts to spit blood all over Norfolk's finest leather boots.

"My Lord… these are not my words,

I swear," he splutters. "Draper duns you in this way, and calls you 'traitor'."

"He lies!" Norfolk cries, and aims a boot at the cowering steward.

"He has the king, sir," Gilbert says, from the floor. "Henry listens to his Examiner, as in all things. If he says you are a traitor often enough... the king will listen."

"That spavined piece of festering chicken shit brained pus," Norfolk spits out.

"Draper, sir?"

"My son, you swiving turd!" the duke curses. "He has misled me. He says he has London, but does not mention that the king is fled from our grasp. I am undone. Henry will have my head for this day's work, and that is that."

"Sir?"

"Silence, you filth... I am trying to think. I might yet flee to France."

"They would send you back."

"Must I kick you to death, you worthless lump of pig's offal, or..."

"I have an idea."

"Does it involve me crawling on my knees to beg forgiveness from the king, after which he will simply cut my head off, rather than first rip out my guts?"

"It involves you being spared, and

even shown to be something of a hero in the king's eyes, My Lord."

"Really?" Norfolk helps the bleeding man to his feet. "If I like your plan, I will make you rich, Gilbert, and if not, I shall cut off your privates, and feed them to my hounds."

"Fair enough, sir," Gilbert replies, and mops at his crushed nose. It will mend, and he now stands the chance of becoming obscenely rich. "Prepare to make me wealthy, my dearest Lord Norfolk."

"What will it cost me?"

"Some of your foot soldiers… a few hundred or so… and then maybe, just maybe… your son."

"No real loss then," Norfolk replies, with callous ease. True, the Earl of Surrey is his heir, but Norfolk has a brother and nephews who can inherit and carry on the proud Howard line. "I suggest you proceed, sir… and save my arse for me."

"Excellent decision, My Lord. Listen carefully… for this is how it must be."

One hour later, Norfolk emerges from his carriage, and slaps Gilbert on the back.

"Would you were my son, old fellow, and not that festering boil of a mongrel dog who my wife foisted onto me. Let us get to it, and so save my life."

"As you command, sir," Gilbert says, and he contemplates the land and gold his lord will pour into his hands. "I will fetch your Colonel of Horse, at once."

"And ready my horse and armour," Norfolk tells him. "If this is to work, I must seem to lead my men into the charge."

"Yes, My Lord," Gilbert says, and hopes a stray bullet will find its mark, but not fatally. After all is said and done, he wants his reward for so brilliant an idea.

*

Will Draper stands on the high Bell Tower rampart of the Tower of London, and stares out in disbelief. Rank upon rank of heavily armed men are forming up beyond the walls.

"Are they mad, sir?" Henry is by his side, and insists on personally 'directing' the defence of his famous Tower. "What do they intend?"

"Why, to storm the Middle Tower, and then on to the Byward Tower, sire," Will explains. "It is the gamble of a madman, who does not care how many men he loses."

"Can we hold them?" the king asks. "Such a concentrated attack might see them inside our defences."

"We have cannon along the inner wall, sire," Mush says. "Our chain shot will flay their ranks raw."

"But will they still get in?"

"Yes. We cannot hold the outer wall with so few men," Richard Cromwell tells the king. "We will fall back, and kill them as they advance onto our guns. They might take the inner wall, but at the loss of two or three thousand of their men."

"Then are we done for?" Henry asks. "Must I seek to entreat with these rebels, whomsoever they might be?"

"Done for, Your Majesty? Hardly that," Will Draper says. "We must think of some strong point… somewhere to fall back on." The answer is blindingly obvious, of course, but it is better that the king thinks of it himself, so that his failing courage is bolstered. There can be no surrender.

"Some place?" Henry rubs his chin, and casts about him for an answer to the problem. Will is about to give him an obvious clue, when Henry suddenly gasps, and points across the well tended lawns. "There sir!' he shouts. "Is not the White Tower impregnable?"

"The White Tower, sire?" Will asks, and both Mush and Richard express their surprise at so clever an idea. "Why, that is a splendid notion, sire. Shall we prepare to withdraw within?"

"Of course," Henry tells them. "By the Gods, Sir Will, you are my General and should have thought of it before now. Have half your men fortify it, at once."

"Sire, will you take command of the White Tower for me?" Will says. "I must have a real fighting man inside the walls. See that the cannon are primed, and the men ready. I can lend Sir Mush to you, as second in command."

"It is an honour, sir!" Henry sees that he is to finally have that which he has always craved, a real battle. His knees are a little wobbly, but he believes that he will do his royal duty, even unto death. "I shall hold the tower, whilst you bring their main force into play. At the right moment, you must withdraw, and we will then close the tower to the enemy."

"Your military acumen does you proud, sire," Will says. "Let us get to it."

The king stumps off, all thought of his ulcerated leg gone for now, shouting orders to any who will listen. It is then that Richard Cromwell catches Mush by the arm, and draws him to one side. He bends, and whispers into the young man's ear.

"Take only one company with you, Mush. We will hold them, as long as we can," he says, "then fall back. If the king thinks we are retreating from the foe, he will panic and, in his utter fear, order that the White Tower's gate be closed on us."

"Yes, I know he will," Mush Draper says. "Not all men are cut out for bravery, Richard. I will not let him abandon you."

"He may order it be done."

"Let him," Mush says. "I will seem to obey him, but dawdle, and keep the gate open, until you are all safely inside, and damn him to Hell for his cowardice."

"Thank you, Mush. I regret the day I ever doubted you."

"You doubted me… when?" Mush asks, and Cromwell frowns, and shakes his head.

"I thought you had betrayed Lady Jane to the assassins."

"You truly thought that?'

"Love makes me blind, old friend," he replies. "The thought passed quick enough."

"No matter now, for I always sided with Will against you."

"You did?"

"Of course," Mush says. "It was a matter of family honour. Besides, in such matters, I always sided with the better looking one, and you are quite the ugliest bastard I have ever known."

"What?"

"Lady Jane told me of your doubts," Mush says, with a grin. "She did not wish it to come between us. She is a rare woman, Richard… but I fear for her, one way or another. Send her abroad."

"She will not go," Richard tells his friend. "Now, see… the king beckons for his monkey to come to him."

"Good luck, Master Bear."

"May God be with us all," Will says. "Now get to your places. They will soon be coming at us."

"Let them come," Mush says. "It is a good day to die, my friends."

"Protect the king," Will says, "even if you must close the White Tower's gate upon us."

"Of course," Mush replies, as he goes to the king. "I am not so sentimental as to risk the tower for a few beaten men."

*

"I am not the fighting sort, Colonel Black," the Earl of Surrey explains. In fact, he would have trouble in ever holding onto his sword. He has such a high regard for his own life, that he shakes in fear at the prospect of even the slightest danger. "You must advance without me."

"The men are about to storm the Tower of London for you," the colonel curses. "They will lose half their number, just to take the king for you, yet you would remain behind with the women?"

"And I have promised them double pay, and a share of any bounty we take from the Tower," Surrey reasons. "I really do not think I need flaunt myself at their head."

"They need a leader, sir."

"Then let it be you, sir," Surrey tells him. "I shall make you my commander of all the armies in England, Colonel Black, and raise you above all men."

"That is for your father to do, My Lord," Black replies. "You do not have the power, or the guts."

"If Norfolk dies this day, I will rule England in his place," Surrey says, slyly. "How often does a stray bullet, or a wayward crossbow bolt strike down the wrong man?"

"Like Richard the Lionheart?" Colonel Black says.

"Was he?" Surrey has little concept of

history, and wants only to attain his 'rightful' first place amongst the nobility.

"A crossbow bolt wound, that then went poisonous," Black persists. "It was a slow death. I imagine you want a quicker end for your father?"

"You put words in my mouth, sir," Surrey says, carefully.

"Then spit them out. Say the word, and I will do it... for half a kingdom. Give me Cornwall, and Wales, and I am your man, forever."

"Then yes, do it."

"Say the word, sir!"

"Kill him," Surrey whispers. "I want my father dead, and in the ground, this very day.'

"Then let me take the Tower of London for you, My Lord. In the confusion, all will die, save the king. Then summon Norfolk, saying you have the king. Take him into His Majesty, wearing his sword, and I will strike him down, and declare him to be a traitor. The king will not demur."

"Good fellow," Surrey says. "Then we must secure our kingdom."

"You mean Culpeper, and the queen?" Black grins. "It will cease to matter. The king will go into new quarters within the Tower, and the queen, for all I care, can join him."

"You are a black hearted rogue, sir." Surrey tells the man.

"Thank you, sir," Henry Black says. "Now, may I get on with stealing you the crown?"

"Yes, my friend," Surrey says. "I will not stay your hand. Lay on, and destroy our enemies."

The cowardly earl retires a hundred paces, and finds himself outside the *Lamb of Christ*, a rough drinking house, often used by Examiner men. He stoops slightly, and goes in through the low door. The floor is covered with rushes to soak up the spilled ale, and blood and the entire place is lit by no more than two tallow candles.

"What is this?" a voice bellows from the darkness. "A noble fellow, ready to rob and kill, I think."

"Dear Christ, good fellow, but I am but a worthless page, and not worth your effort." Surrey can feel his bowels loosening, even as he speaks.

"Oh, and I thought you to be that ignoble bastard, Hal Howard, who still owes me three pounds for a verse I wrote for him."

"Tom Wyatt, is that you sir?" Surrey sighs in relief. "Thank God. I will settle my bill at once, and buy you a flagon of the best wine in this place."

"Not your usual haunt, sir," Tom Wyatt says. "Though I see you come with a veritable army at your back."

"The king is in danger, and I am for saving him."

"Yes, I heard." The poet frowns at the earl's mendacity. "If Will Draper overcomes your force, he will have your head. Imagine the view from so high a spike, my friend."

"He cannot win this one," Surrey says. "Besides, I am not in charge. It seems that Colonel Henry Black leads this force."

"A mercenary?"

"Yes, bought and paid for…by I know not who, Tom. Here is your three pounds, with interest… and choose your wine, my friend."

"It will have to wait," Tom Wyatt tells the scurrilous earl. "I have to go out for a short while." Thomas Cromwell is wont to use an old adage, to the effect that if you wish to kill the snake, then cut off its head. If the poet can find this Henry Black, and kill him, the enemy army will fall into chaos.

He loosens his sword in its scabbard, and takes the small duelling pistol from his belt, and primes it. He is a man who has been well tested in battle, several times, but he has never come up against a man such as Colonel Henry Black.

The colonel has faced many men, and killed every one of them. He has no pity, and this makes him into a *machina diaboli*…a cold hearted killer … the devil's machine. Come what may, Colonel Henry Black is too good at his job to lose to an enthusiastic amateur like Tom Wyatt.

*

"Captain Lindsey, do you have the ladders?" Colonel Black asks, and the young captain snaps to attention.

"Yes, sir," he reports. "Two dozen of the best masons ladders, taken from the grand new church being built over in Stepney. Sturdy as any in London."

"Then take three hundred men, and move down the wall, to Legge's Mount. On my command, you will storm the wall there, and gain the outer wall with your ladders. Move back towards me then, and clear the first parapet of gunners. Once that is under way, I can lead the main force against the gates, without being flayed with their damned chain shot."

"Yes, sir." Lindsay sees that this is a masterful stroke, and will turn the enemy flank. They will have to fall back onto the White Tower, without artillery support. "And the cannon?"

"Swing them around, and point them at the great tower," Black says. He is a better soldier than any man there, and he out thinks even General Will Draper. "In this way, we will be able to threaten their stronghold, and gain an easy victory."

"You think they will give up the king, sir?" the younger man asks.

"Is that a worthwhile question, Captain Lindsay?" Henry Black asks.

"Sorry, sir. Forgive me for wasting your time." Captain Lindsay salutes, and moves off to carry out his task. The colonel is a hard man, with rules, and one of them is *never* ask a question, unless it confirms an order, or clarifies something not made clear. That the king will fall into their hands is a 'taken'.

*

"Will… there are ladders over at Legge's Mount," Richard Cromwell shouts, and Will sees at once that he has greatly underestimated his enemy.

"Be damned to it, where did they find so many? See there, he means to sweep down the parapet, and turn the cannon about." He thinks fast. "Richard, take a hundred men, and try to hold them back. I will stand my ground here."

The younger Cromwell details off a company of Examiners, and leads them down the length of the wall. The attackers are already on the ramparts, and they advance with pikes and swords at the ready. It is only their desire to remain in an orderly fashion that slows them. Had they rushed forward, the day would be won in a moment.

"Die hard, lads," Richard Cromwell says, and lunges forward. The parapet is only wide enough for three or four men abreast, and the cannon form an awkward barrier for both sides.

Captain Lindsay's men are promised great wealth, and are eager to get at it. So, they come on, pikes held forward. The Examiners hack at the thrusting lances, and try to get in return blows. A man overreaches, and a Surrey pike rips through his stomach. he screams and falls from the wall.

"Hold hard, boys," Cromwell shouts, and pushes into the front line. A pike comes at him, and he grasps it in his left hand, and pulls. The soldier is caught off guard, and stumbles forward, onto Cromwell's own blade. It goes in, is twisted hard, and then pulled clear.

Another Examiner is stabbed in the face, and he falls to his knees, with his hands over his ruined eyes. Richard swings his sword, two handed, and forces Surrey's men back a couple of paces. Then the hole is filled by Amos Givens, with Sergeant Carter but a single pace behind.

Captain Lindsay sees that these huge men are cowing his own men, and he lunges forward, into the front of the affray. He ducks under a wild swing, and darts his left hand forward. The sword sinks home, and Carter staggers back with blood smearing a wound to the stomach.

"Take him back," Richard orders, and goes for the officer who has so maimed his best man. He strikes, but another gets in his way with his pike. The sword clangs on the metal point, and knocks the shaft aside. Before the man can recover, Amos Givens flicks his heavy *Falcion* into his unguarded face, and bones are crushed to a bloody pulp.

The sword is an old sort of a weapon, with a curved cutting edge, and a heavy back shaft, not unlike a butchers cleaver. It is over a yard long, and deadly in close quarter fights. The man staggers away, and drops his pike to the ground.

Captain Lindsay sees that things are in the balance, and launches another foray against Cromwell. Richard sees the lunge, but just too late.

The knife blade, held left handed, goes through the thick goose down padding in Richard Cromwell's jerkin, and bites into flesh.

"God's teeth!" Cromwell feels the knife go in, under his arm, and roars his defiance. He grabs Lindsay's wrist, and pulls him backwards, from his own front rank, until they are apart from the general ruck.

Then, quite deliberately, he releases the fellow, and stoops to pick up the fallen pikestaff. Lindsay sees his chance and runs in to deliver the killing stroke. The pike's point takes him in the pit of his stomach, and sinks in a good eight inches.

Richard Cromwell tenses his muscles, and lifts. The pike, with the captain on it, goes up into the air, and Lindsay screams. The big man grunts, and walks his victim over to the edge of the wall.

Lindsay screams a second time, most pitiably, and tries to thrust home his dagger once more, but Richard Cromwell holds him high, and he cannot reach. Then the giant takes a final pace, and heaves his burden out into the void. The captain, disappears, with a terrified yell, followed by a sickening thud, as his body lands on the grey paving, far below.

"Next?" Richard roars.

Surrey's men fall back a few paces, and it seems that the Examiners have won this round, but a dozen men come forward, and raise their muskets.

Richard Cromwell can feel the blood soaking through his clothing, and he feels faint. He stretches out his arms, and commands his men to stand behind him, like he is a human wall.

"Let them all fire into me, my fine boys… then charge them. Spare no one, and win this day for England, and for Henry."

"Present your arms!" the sergeant says, with certainty. His men will blast the giant aside, and let his pikes finish the business. The front rank of Surrey's men kneel, holding out their pikes, and the musketeers behind use their comrades' steady shoulders to support their heavy guns.

Richard Cromwell understands that his own end is upon him, but will not step back. Instead, he advances onto the loaded guns, until he shields his own men with his vast breadth. Amos Givens is right behind him, ready to do murder on the enemy, as soon as they dare kill his master.

"Come on now, lads," Richard says to the armed men facing him. "I am a Cromwell, and you will be well paid for killing me." He looks up at the sky, and smiles. "A fine day to die. Who will give the order?"

"Yield, sir, and I will give you and your men quarter," the sergeant says. "I fought beside you once, in France, and have no stomach for this."

"Then you yield, fellow."

"I have taken my lord's shilling, Master Richard," the sergeant replies. "I beg of you… step aside, and let us pass."

"To take the king?" Richard shakes his head. "Never."

"Then so be it," the faceless sergeant says. Richard has fought alongside many men and cannot recall this one's features. "Musketeers', take aim!"

"I commend my soul to you, Almighty God," Richard says. "Let my sins be forgiven, and may I walk in your heavenly pastures, for eternity."

"Fuses lit?" Twelve men hold up their smouldering fuses, and show that they are all ready to give touch onto the pans, and fire. The sergeant nods, and sees that he must only say the word. He crosses himself, and then his eyes meet with Richard Cromwell's.

"You were with Thomas Wyatt's cannon, when we smashed the Baglione army in the *Calaisis*," the big man realises, with a start. It is meet that his executioner is an old comrade.

"I was, sir, and right proud of that day," the sergeant replies. "We cut down their heavy cavalry, and charged home like demons. I took a ten pound share that day. You were a fair man, and no mistake, your honour."

"I recall that you started to sing a song… about some saucy wench. One of Tom Wyatt's wicked ditties."

"The Milk Maid's Plight," the man says. "It was then we broke their cavalry."

"Good days, sergeant." Richard smiles at the memory of so much fighting.

"Yes, sir, they were. Now, I must beg of you… stand aside."

"No."

"Then damn me for it, but I must give the order. Men… prepare to fire!"

'Might I know your name, good fellow?" Richard asks.

"Blunt," the sergeant tells him. "Albert Blunt of Shrewsbury."

"No finer whores in England."

That is so. I said that very thing when you asked how I would spend my share of the spoils."

"Good times, Albert, now do your sworn duty, and be damned to this life!"

5 Tom Wyatt's Quest

Will Draper is bereft of his best men, with Mush keeping his eye on the king, and Richard busy trying to stem the flow of Surrey's men over the Tower's wall. He turns to John Beckshaw, and touches his sword to his head, in salute.

"Let us die bravely, if we must, Colonel Beckshaw… else make them pay a heavy price for taking the gates, and then withdraw into the White Tower."

"Richard Cromwell cannot join us, sir," Beckshaw says. He has served Will loyally for some years, and never spoken out, but now, he must. "I cannot abandon him to his fate. If the cannon are taken, we will soon lose the tower. I shall fight as hard as I can here, then… if God spares me… I will go to his aid, and die by my comrades' sides."

"You shame me, John," Will says to his second in command. "I mean only to save as many of my Examiners as I can, and have them live to fight another day. I too cannot abandon Richard Cromwell, and his few men."

"Hear this, boys?" John Beckshaw shouts, and the Examiners look over to him. "Who is for running away… and who for staying?"

"Stay!" This is from Tim Roland, the youngest of all the Examiners.

"Aye… stay," another says, and hefts his pike into the guard position. the feeling is unanimous, and it makes Will proud to be their leader.

One by one, Will's men line the inner wall, and wait for the rush. Will sees that the decision is made by all and his heart swells with pride at this mixture of loyalty and stubbornness. The Examiners are something apart, it says, and they do not run away. He moves from man to man and orders his crossbow men to gather in the centre.

"See the officers, lads? They are the fatter looking fellows, with the fancy feathered hats. Aim right for them, and kill every one of them," Will commands. "That will slow them up long enough for us to barricade the inner gate, and thrust through at them with our pikes. If they gain the courtyard, we must fan out, and present them with an unbroken line of pikes."

It is a flawed idea, he knows because, with an entire company of Examiners within the tower guarding the king, he lacks enough men to guard his own flanks. Surrey's men will surge to left and right, rather than attack head on, and then they will engulf his much smaller force. Will, and most of his men understand this, but they trust their commander to do his best for them. It is left to John Beckshaw to tell them the inevitable, and make it sound as though there is still some chance of victory.

"As they seek to outflank us, we must fall back onto Richard Cromwell's men, and form ourselves into a tight square, with crossbows in the centre," John Beckshaw tells them. "They cannot break a square of pikes, lads. It has never been done."

Save with cannon fire, Will thinks to himself. If Richard falls, they will turn the captured guns inwards, and flay his men with chain shot, until they cannot stand. It is a hard way to die, he thinks, but then again, is there an easy way?

"Tim Roland… here to me, boy." The fifteen year old advances, warily. "Run to the White Tower, and inform Colonel Mush of our plans."

"No sir."

"Must I flog you, lad?"

"Yes, sir… after the fight," the boy tells his commander. "I will stand by you, and either win, or die."

"Then I must let you," Will says to

the boy. It is useless to try and dissuade him, for his blood is up, and he will be shamed if he leaves now. "Your courage does you great credit."

"Bless you, General Will, I am fair shitting my pants, but is that not what bravery is… standing in your own stinking shit, and fighting anyway?"

"Yes. Know your fear, and face it down," Will says to the boy. "Stay by me and watch my left flank. I am weak on that side."

"Yes, sir… thank you." The young lad is inordinately pleased at such an honour, and he moves to protect his commander's left hand side.

"General Will, they come!" one of his crossbow wielding corporals calls, from the furthest crenellation. "Christ, but they are in their thousands!"

"John, pray take a half company of pikes down, and fortify the inner gate."

"Yes, sir," John Beckshaw replies, with a smart salute. "God be with you… and all our men." He signals to a sergeant, who gathers his half company, and troops off towards the inner gate.

"Let them come on at us, lads," Will Draper tells his crossbowmen. "Not a quarrel is to be fired, until they are within fifty paces."

"Officers only," Tim Roland reminds them, and he does a little jig. "Fancy that, lads, a chance to cut some big nobs down to size!" This quip tickles their fancies, and a ripple of laughter runs down the length of the wall. The oncoming enemy hear, and are astonished by the noise.

The Earl of Surrey's men are in three solid lines now, as they concentrate on the outer gate tower, and they advance, intent on battering it open. They will lose a good few men, of course, and some of the wilier officers have pulled the feathered plumes from their caps and their steel bonnets.

"Steady now, men" Colonel Black tells them, from his place in the rear rank. He is not the highest ranking officer there, but his military history makes him the obvious choice for leader. He hears his enemies laughter, and he wonders if he is pushing his own troops into a trap.

A quarrel is loosed ten yards early, and it hits a well dressed young lieutenant in the throat. He grasps at the shaft, and begins to dance about in a strange and grotesque parody of a jig. Such is the tensions of war that the defenders laugh again, this time at his antics, until he falls down onto the ground.

"Hold your fire," Will orders, but a second bolt wings out and punches a neat hole through a steel breastplate. The man is knocked back into the second rank, quite dead. His bowmen are expert shots, and they know that they have the ability, even at a hundred paces. "Oh, be damned to it then. Fire as you see fit, lads."

Another fifty quarrels speed out, and the centre of the enemies front line dissolves in a welter of death. One man, foolish enough to be decked out in the finest clothes, and sporting great ostrich plumes in his velvet cap, is struck a half dozen times, and another takes a bolt in the mouth and out the back. It carries on and hits a man in the second line in the neck.

The disciplined second line step over the dead and dying and quickly fills the many gaps. Pikes are lowered, the line bunches up into a solid phalanx, and then hurls itself against the outer gate. It is sturdy enough, but Surrey's men are well prepared, and soon heavy axes are brought to the fore.

John Beckshaw shouts commands, and directs his pikemen to thrust outwards at the axe men, but they are protected by their own long spears. When one man is killed, another takes up his axe and continues the determined assault.

The gate is almost two hundred years old, and made of wooden cross pieces, bound with rusting iron. It is only an inner barrier, and not meant to stand up to a direct battering such as this. The wood is rotting in places, and the great axes soon begin to gouge out large chunks of the gate. Beckshaw's men fight valiantly, even recklessly, and they begin to take casualties.

The company sergeant sees that John Beckshaw is pushing himself forward, thrusting with his sword, and he grabs at him and pulls him back from the fray. "Desist, sir," he cries. "You can do little with that against a pike. Here, take this." He bends and picks up a pike, dropped by one of his own wounded fellows. As he straightens up an enemy shaft spears through the gate and rips into his chest.

John Beckshaw grabs at the pike and rushes to fill the gap. He pushes the long handled weapon outwards, and the point encounters flesh. He twists, and is rewarded with a scream from the enemy side. Men fall, wounded and dying on either side, and Henry Black's men, goaded on with the promise of great wealth, step over their slaughtered friends, and continue an unabating attack on the gate. Then, without warning, the cross ties give way, and the gate disintegrates.

"Form up, boys," Henry Black says from his relative place of safety. "Six abreast, and go for the next gate. It is no more than a thing you might hang on a garden fence. Once through it, and we are inside. Then we will have the run of the Tower."

Behind the battle, Tom Wyatt is moving through those who usually hang back in any battle; the surgeons, the bearers, and the camp followers. He asks, now and then, if any know where Colonel Henry Black is. He offers them sight of a poem he has written about an old lecher, and claims it is an urgent despatch from Norfolk.

Some simply shrug, and others swear they do not know the fellow. Then one young lad comes to him from the crowd of Londoners who have come to see the king saved.

"He gave me a penny," the boy says. "Just for a moment's word. I took it in good part, but he had the look of the very devil about him, sir. You're that Tom Wyatt, aren't you?"

"You know my poems, child?"

"Nah... I saw you getting thrown out of Nell Thumper's knocking shop, last week… and she did say 'piss off Tom Wyatt, and no more credit'."

"I see, famous for my debts," Wyatt says. "I have a meeting with the Pope, lad, and am in a hurry to be gone. Can you show me to this fellow?"

"It will mean your death, sir," the boy tells him. "For I see you would do him harm, and you are just not good enough."

"I care not for your opinion," the poet snaps. "You know him by sight?"

"No, good sir… listen to me, and it might save your life. This Colonel Black has the smell of a born killer on him… not unlike Will Draper. Such men are able to kill without a care, and they know their job. Black will kill you in a moment, if you fight fairly."

"I am listening." Tom Wyatt sees that this boy is no mere urchin. "You work for Draper?"

"His special agent for the Aldgate, your honour. My name is Joe Rodney. Now, will you heed my advice?"

"I will, Master Rodney," Wyatt tells the small child. If Will trusts the boy, then he must too. "Speak on."

"Call him out, and he will skewer you with one thrust. The man wears his sword low, for ease of draw, and he has knives at his waist, in the back of his belt, and hidden away in each boot."

"You are thorough, good sir," the poet observes. "You observed so much?"

"It is my task in life. I watch, and I make notes to send on, if need be." Joe Rodney hawks his throat, and spits out onto the packed earth. "Are you armed?"

"My sword, and a dagger," Tom Wyatt confirms, "and a small duelling pistol in my doublet."

"Let me see it." The pistol is shown, and hidden back away again. "That is a piece of shit, sir. I wager it fires a quarter inch ball, and is useless over ten paces."

"Perhaps." In truth Wyatt does not know. He won the gun in a card game, and has never even fired it.

"If you are intent on this thing, you must be bold; bluster your way right up to the man. Then you place the muzzle to his head, and pull the trigger. At that range, he will be killed, or sorely wounded. If he is not killed at once, draw your knife, and drive it firmly into his ear ... like so. This kills the brain in a moment, Then turn about, and walk away, quickly. His men will be shocked at first, but then they will wish to rip you limb from limb."

"That sounds fair enough," the poet replies. "If I can stop this fellow, and save my friends, death will not be unwelcome."

"Ah, I see. You are one of those fellows who see death as some great conclusion to a lost love, or some such. I do not think any one woman is worth dying for… only living for."

"You did not know her," Tom Wyatt says. "She was the stars in heaven, and the beating life of my heart."

"You make her sound like a queen," Joe Rodney tells the poet. "Now, let us find this harbinger of your death."

"You think I will fail then?"

"Yes, I think he is too much for you, sir. That is a compliment, for you are a man of gentle soul… who can love to the point of death. Come, and keep close to me, these bastards would rob you for a groat coin."

"We must hurry, for the soldiery are starting to move forward. Once the fight is on, my task will become all the harder."

The boy leads him past mercenary Flemish crossbow men, busy winding back their strings, squires and pages, sharpening daggers on whetstones, and others putting pike heads to the grindstone for a final edge.

There is also a tent, wherein four girls

are busy easing the younger soldiers 'nerves', for twopence a tup. They will make a tidy fortune this day, and some of their customers will never return for a second helping.

"Is he on the foremost rank?" the poet asks, and he receives a cackle of laughter in return.

"I told you, he is far too wily a soldier. He will let his men batter their way in, then come after, and do his slaughter. The battle is won, without him taking a risk. We are near. Just remember to get as close as you can, and do not hesitate. If the shot does not kill him…"

"Yes, I know. Stick him in the ear, and make myself scarce."

"Good luck… and there he is, I see, loitering in the rear ranks. See how they are all looking away from you? I would help, but I am only a child, and not yet ready for my own grave."

Tom Wyatt looks across to where his enemy stands, and he understands what the child means. Colonel Henry Black is as tall as Richard Cromwell, and almost as huge. He is ten years younger than Cromwell though, and his bulk is all heavy muscle. Here is a man who can kill bare handed, Wyatt thinks, and his heart skips a beat at what he intends to do.

"What is your business here?" a short, officious fellow demands, as he approaches his quarry.

"I have an important message for Colonel Black… from Norfolk."

"Lord Norfolk," the man snarls, and Henry Black turns around to see what is afoot.

"Who are you, man?" the colonel asks, coldly. "Not one of mine, I think?"

"Sir Thomas Wyatt," Wyatt says to Black. "I have a…"

"The poet?"

"Yes, for my sins."

"I know your bawdier work," Black tells him. "Though all of the love a dove bits make me puke up my blasted guts. Well?"

"A message," the poet says, limply, "from the Duke of Norfolk."

"Really?" Henry Black nods, and turns to look out, over the ranks that are forming. "Come closer, Master Poet, and speak with me. Is old Norfolk here then?"

Tom Wyatt steps much closer, until he is but inches from the back of his quarry. His fingers close about the butt of his small pistol, and he eases back the firing wheel. It is a modern design, and the iron wheel must only strike the flint to ignite the powder charge.

He slips his free hand to the knife in

his sash, and draws the pistol. The colonel is oblivious of the action, and does not move, even as the poet pushes the muzzle right into the back of his head, and squeezes the trigger.

*

"Father... Jesus!" The Earl of Surrey jumps to his feet, and the whore in his lap tumbles to the ground. "I was just... just..."

"Hiding away from danger, you spavined lump of donkey excrement," the Duke says, and punches him in the gut. The terrified earl doubles over, and takes a second fist on his chin. He, quite sensibly, falls down, and waits for the anger to subside. "Why did you not tell me that the king is inside the Tower of London?"

"I did not think it mattered, sir," Surrey wheezes. "Colonel Black assures me that he can take the place, and put the king in our power."

"You frigging great ass. It only works if Henry believes us to be his saviours. That chance is now gone. He will send secret messages to Cumberland, Warwick, and his Border Lords. Inside the month, thirty thousand men will arrive, and release the king from our bondage. Then Henry, in his infinite wisdom will have us all beheaded. Is that clear, you cur?"

"Yes." Surrey is crying now, for he suspects he is about to be chosen to carry the blame. "You will claim I acted alone, and support the king."

"Something like that. Where is that cocky bastard Henry Black?"

"At the front line, sir."

"Better still." Norfolk gives orders, and his steward, anxious to secure his golden thanks, sees to things. The duke has a thousand heavy cavalry with him, and they are to be arrayed, and sent charging into the 'rebel' troops.

"Malcontents, sire," Norfolk will explain. A few hundred men, who have misled others into rebellion. "They are dispersed now, and their leader killed. A fellow called Black… a mercenary, out for a profit."

Surrey sees that he might yet survive, and congratulates his father on his brilliance.

"Yes, we can blame Colonel Black, but only if he is killed. otherwise, he will hang us all with his wild stories."

"Then let us charge. Come boy, you have a sword, and will ride with me in the first rush."

Surrey is dragged outside, and pushed up onto a heavy charger. His father tells him to hang on, and not halt until he reaches the

Tower's courtyard. He grips the reins with one hand, and hangs on to his sword with the other. He cannot escape the thought that his moment had come, and he was about to die.

The heavy cavalry forms up in four lines abreast - each two hundred and fifty strong - and advances. At first the foot soldiers think that reinforcements are here, but then they perceive that they are being charged at, and they begin panic.

The big horses gather speed, and long lances are dropped into the couch position. Those in the rear ranks of infantry start to run as the cavalry bears down on them.

"What is this?" Colonel Black roars, and Tom Wyatt fires. The powder is old, and produces little more than a spark. It is enough to push the lead shot from the barrel, but only an inch. the slug pops out of the muzzle, and bounces off Black's thick skull. "Murder, sir?"

The poet draws his knife, and strikes, but Henry Black moves fast, and grips his wrist. He twists, and the blade tumbles free. Then the enraged mercenary forces Wyatt to his knees, and takes his head in his two big hands, and starts to squeeze.

It is his party piece back in Ireland, where he would entertain his men by executing prisoners in such a way. It is slower than a knife, but much more painful for the victim. The poet feels the grip tighten, and fears his eyes are about to burst from his face. He is not wrong. After the eyes are gone, the skull starts to crack and splinter, until you can see the brain beneath. Finally, after the intense agony, comes death... welcome death.

So be it, Tom Wyatt thinks. Let me die for my unrequited love. His mind is closing down, and he has a pain behind his eyes. There is a loud popping noise, which he fancies is one of his eyes going.

"Bugger me," the Duke of Norfolk curses as his pistol shot seems to have no effect. "This one is not for dying." So he fires his second pistol. The lead ball hits Henry Black in the chest, as did the first, and he grunts as if stung by a bee. He sees that he is under attack from his own side so releases his hold on the poet, and draws his sword.

"Norfolk! You treacherous old bastard," Black says, and staggers at the duke as blood pours from his two wounds. A dozen cavalry troopers, now dismounted, bustle in between the two men, and shield their master from Black's rage. Tom Wyatt fumbles for his dropped knife, then staggers to his feet.

"You satan's spawn," he says, and

stabs at the man's back. the blade hits leather, and skids away. Then another hand is on his, guiding the point to the throat. Wyatt thrusts, and the point opens an artery. A fountain of blood sprays out, soaking everyone within a dozen yards, and the huge mercenary collapses to the ground.

"See father… I can do it," Surrey says, and takes the knife from Tom Wyatt's shaking hand. "Thank you for the help, Tom."

"The usurper is dead. Long live the king. Long live Henry." This from the steward, starts Norfolk's cavalry cheering, and the foot soldiers, so recently cut down in their hundreds join in. They want only to be on the winning side now.

The fighting between the two gates suddenly ceases, and Will Draper wonders what has come about. It is then that the Duke of Norfolk appears, and hails up to the General of the Examiners.

"Good day, Draper… a fine day for a fight, what?"

"My dear Lord Norfolk," Will Draper says. "You are under arrest, by order of the Attorney General's Office. John, chain the fellow, and then find his son… they are both in this, and must face the court together."

"Will, don't do this," Norfolk calls up

to Draper. "Are we no longer friends?"

"God damn you, sir. I have lost more than thirty good men today, and slain over five hundred of yours."

"Oh, do not worry about that. I can replace them within the week. There are plenty of starving peasant lads ready to join my army."

"Take him away," Will says, and the once great Duke of Norfolk is taken into the Tower of London, and lodged in a damp cell, close by Traitor's Gate.

*

"Norfolk is in chains?" Tom Wyatt cannot believe it. "What does the king say?"

"That he is a traitor, and must pay the penalty for his wrong doing." Will pours out more wine for them. I am to ready both of the Howards for trial tomorrow morning, and see that the execution yard is fit to use."

"My God, then he is serious."

"Our friend in Antwerp predicted as much," Mush says. "He thinks the man must over reach himself, and end on the block. Now it has come to pass."

"Not before time," Richard Cromwell says. "I was before a firing squad, a moment from death, when the fighting ceased. Now I am to go drinking with their sergeant, who is an old acquaintance. God's tender mercy, or some strange happenstance?"

"Some cavalry arrived, unexpectedly," Will says, "and I think it caused the ordinary soldiers to panic, and then break. Once it starts, an army can vanish in minutes. You must recall how the Baglione army in France broke once their own cavalry were cut down."

"We were in a strong position today," Mush replies. "I cannot understand why Norfolk allowed the attack. He must have known the king would never forgive him."

"True enough," the younger Cromwell says. "Now he and his son must pay the inevitable price for treason."

"Then here is to the trial." Tom Wyatt raises a glass. "Will the king be there?"

"I hope not," Mush says, ardently. "It will go far quicker without him."

"If he does appear, do not call me to testify," Tom Wyatt says. "I came late, and my words would only muddy the waters a little."

"Why would we call on you, Tom?" Richard asks. "It is not as if you actually did any fighting, is it?"

"Just so," the poet says, and drains his glass. "Late, as usual, old friend."

"Here is to a speedy trial, and a swift

execution of the sentence." Will Draper raises his glass, sure that he has, at long last, brought his man to justice.

*

Thomas Howard, the infamous Duke of Norfolk, is astounded to find himself in a ten foot square stone cell, with a leg iron linking him to the wall with a yard long length of heavy chain.

"Fucking morons!" he yells at the heavy iron bound door. "Do you know who I am?"

"Shut up in cell number five," a voice replies, "or I'll heat up my branding irons, and tend to your foul mouth."

'But I am Norfolk."

"And I am the Queen of Sheba," the voice replies. "Now, give us a kiss and shut your mouth."

"Insolent dog," Norfolk mutters, then thinks of something to try. "I have gold, fellow.

"How much?"

"Thousands."

"With you?"

"No, not actually on me."

"Then shut up."

"My strongroom at Arundel is heaving with gold and …"

"I should let you out, so that you can nip off there, and fetch me a huge bag of golden Angels?"

"That's it."

"That sounds fine, Your Lordship, but I should go there alone, and have your men hand the treasure over first."

"I could write a note," Norfolk concedes. "Then you would return, and let me out?"

"Of course."

"You are lying, aren't you?"

"I am." The voice breaks into laughter. "Sleep well, sir… for on the morrow, you are for trial, and I have never yet seen a 'not guilty' verdict handed down by your peers."

"Then let me send a message to my son." Norfolk sees that the boy might be able to go to Henry, and explain it all.

"For a price, sir." The gaoler says, and a hand appears at the grill.

"I have a few coins," Norfolk says, and searches his purse. He finds an Angel, and a handful of copper coins to throw to any lepers, to keep them distant from his noble self. "Eleven shillings, and four pennies." He reaches as far as he can, and just manages to drop them into the waiting hand. The man pulls his closed fist back, and counts.

"Ten shillings and fourpence," he says. "For one of the shillings is a foreign one, struck in the Brabant mint, and not worth a fig here."

"Good fellow, I beg of you…"

"Very well, what do you wish to say to My Lord Surrey? When you know, just shout aloud, for he is but two cells down from you, and he will be at your side tomorrow."

"Oh, such a cruel fate," the Duke of Norfolk curses. "We must pray that Henry gives us a fair hearing."

"Father, is that you?"

"It is, son. We are for trial this next morning, and must play to our strengths."

"Have I any, sir?"

"Yes… your clever way of keeping your mouth shut, unless I address you. It may save our lives if you say nothing. Let me speak for us."

"That suits me, sir," Surrey replies, but cautiously. "Though I hope you do your best for me."

"I will, my son," the maudlin duke replies. "For you are my own blood, and I freely acknowledge it."

"Thank you, father," says Surrey, "for I never thought myself to be another man's bastard. Mother did not stray until some years later. I was ten when I first caught her making the beast with Master Weams."

"The dance master?" Norfolk is surprised, as he always thought the fellow was a raging sodomite. "The insolent swine. I shall personally flog him to death, when we are finally released."

"He is already dead, sir," Surrey says, repeating some gossip he has stored away for some time. "It seems that Sir Egbert Dalton came home from a hunt early, and Weams was busy swiving his wife upstairs. The wicked fellow heard his doom approaching, and leapt out of the window. As he dropped, his hose caught on the spiked lintel, and he was left, swinging in mid air."

"Oh, to have seen that sight," the duke chuckled.

"Dalton came into the room, saw his wife, still panting and naked, and rushed at Weams. In his fright, the man slipped out of his hose, and tumbled to the ground. They say his head cracked open like a walnut."

"A fine end to a fine bastard," the duke pronounces. "I am much cheered, boy. Are you chained?"

"No."

"Those dirty bastards," Norfolk

growls. "They seek to humiliate me. Why, even the gaoler will not take an honest bribe!"

*

"How much did he offer you?" Will Draper asks, and John Beckshaw, who has just pretended to being the gaoler, holds out his hand.

"Ten shillings, and untold wealth to come. He has a strongroom at Arundel, with thousands in it."

"I shall move to have it confiscated, as soon as the duke is condemned."

"Is our evidence sound?" Tom Wyatt asks. "I saw Norfolk arrive, and his cavalry rode into his own men."

"Bad management," Will Draper replies. "I have seen eager horsemen break their own lines, just to get at the enemy."

"Then Norfolk killed Henry Black," the poet says. "At least, he shot him twice, but the man would not lie down."

"Did he know Black?" Mush asks the pertinent question. "By reputation, yes of course… but by sight?"

"I don't know," says Wyatt.

"Norfolk likes you, Tom," Mush says, as he tries to puzzle out the meaning of the day's events. "He knows you are the kings favourite versifier, and he sees you being murdered. So, he fires at your attacker. It is what any of us might do."

"Yes, that makes good sense," the poet concedes, "but I am not a versifier, you cheeky little bastard. I am the King's Poet, as from this last week. It brings me in a hundred a year, for which I must make up the odd rather rude rhyme."

"Then you are a bloody lucky versifier," Mush says, and grins at his friend. "I am glad that the ogre Black did not squeeze out your eyes, though your brain would be no great loss to humanity."

"Then we have our proof." Will Draper is nervous, at this, his moment to finally destroy his enemy. "We have Norfolk's own troops entering London, uninvited, and then them laying siege to the Tower. Surrey is with them, and Norfolk arrives at the moment of our threatened defeat."

"We also have the evidence of Colonel Black roving the shires, murdering anyone who might be hiding close friends of the king,"

"We have depositions?" Will asks, and Richard Cromwell laughs at his disquiet.

"Rafe Sadler's lawyers have sought out every survivor they can, and taken down their evidence. It is clear that this Black fellow was their leader, and that he was the Duke of Norfolk's man."

"Rafe knew to do this?" Will asks, because the plot had come just recently. "How so, Richard?"

"That was my doing," Tom Wyatt tells him. "I am the court poet… little more than a fool in men's eyes. So, I hear things, and Surrey has a mouth on him that would condemn him ten times over, but for his nobility of birth. He boasted of how 'his man' was busy 'putting down' a few peasants in the shires. I passed this on to Rafe, who thought it wise to investigate."

"A stroke of good fortune," Will replies, "aided by your astute thinking, my friend."

"I merely passed on the news," the poet tells him. "It was Rafe who acted. I am a follower, Will, not a leader."

"You do yourself a disservice, my friend," Will says. "You led the cannon against the Malatesta bastard, and took command in many skirmishes. You are a clever man, and that is your main attribute."

"Then use my cleverness," the poet urges. "Do not call me as a witness on the morrow… or let Norfolk do the same. It is not wise."

"But you saw the attack from their side," Mush tells him. Your words would sway the king, and no mistake."

"Then Henry will be there?"

"He insists upon it. He is here, within the Tower still, boasting to everyone as to how he halted the charge, and directed the battle to its end. I fear he will want to be both judge, and jury."

"Norfolk's lawyers will not have any of that," Wyatt says.

"He has not asked for a lawyer," Will replies. "I think he must be hoping to throw himself on the king's mercy, and hope to weasel out of the whole mess. I can see the king relenting, because of their noble blood, and settling for a heavy fine. Arundel will soon be Henry's new estate, and Norfolk's men, the king's own."

"Then he will not lose his head?" the poet asks. "It seems odd that a man can be boiled alive for a chicken, yet go almost scot free for treason."

"I think it depends on Henry's mood," Richard Cromwell offers. "I shall keep close to him this night, and dun the duke in a subtle way."

"Subtle, Richard?" Mush asks, and raises an eyebrow. "How will that be… such words coming from a raging bullock?"

"I shall ignore the implied insult, little monkey, and tell you."

"Pray do." The room is rapt at Richard's ideas on subtlety.

"I shall remind him of how Norfolk did help bring down poor Queen Katherine, and then marry him off to *La Boleyn,* his own niece... and a proven whore. Then I shall mention Wolsey. That is always good for a maudlin tale about forgiveness. At the right moment, I will reveal how Lord Percy came to get the task of making the arrest. I have it in writing... an order, with Norfolk's seal upon it!"

"Christ, Richard, we have a genuine Norfolk seal of our own. We could fake anything, if we wished."

"The king is happily ignorant of that fact, Will," Richard says, "and I lack your morality to that degree."

"What next?"

"If more is required, I can point to several plots of late, where Norfolk's hand was suspected. The king has been too lenient, and will see that the only way forward is a swift blow of the axe. The duke will be in the next world by the day after tomorrow."

"Let us hope so," Will concludes, "for

a freed duke would be the most dangerous enemy a man could hope for, and we will all be on his *Vindicatio*, and no mistake!"

*

"Breakfast, My Lord!" A slot opens, and a beaten metal tray starts to appear. Norfolk leaps up from the narrow wooden cot he has spent a sleepless night in, and crosses the tiny cell.

"Some eggs, made into an omelette, I think… with rashers of bacon, and a few pork sausages."

"Daft bugger," the voice says. "Here, and don't slop it on the floor."

The tray contains a slice of hard bread, a mug of murky, well watered ale, and a scoop of thick porridge. There is a wooden spoon, and nothing else.

"What is this?" Norfolk demands. "I paid you a goodly bribe this last evening, and expect a better repast before my trial.'

"Bribe, you say?" the voice drops to a growl. "Not to me, you didn't. Has some fool been in here, and stolen my gelt?"

"It sounded like you," Norfolk replies. "Common, and nasty."

"This is my kind voice, sir," the gaoler says, somewhat hurt by the remarks. "Your money never reached me, and I am sorry for it, as the wife has a fine cut of ham roasted, and some fresh eggs. How much did they trick from you, My Lord?"

"All I had on me… ten pounds in gold, and another five in silver coin. There were some pennies, but I save them for the poor benighted lepers. Let us say a round fifteen pounds, in all." There, Norfolk thinks, that will redound on the thief, if he is ever found out.

"I thank you for your candour, My Lord, and will ask the missus to slice you enough ham to keep body and soul together. What about your son?"

"Let the fat little bastard go hungry," Norfolk says. "I have been up half the night trying to get him to understand what '*keep your mouth shut*' means. I fear his great gob will be my undoing at trial."

"I could slip in and strangle him for you, sir, if that would help, but a favour like that would cost," Abraham Wake says. He jests, of course, for he has his orders from Will Draper, and has been a Cromwell man for years. They wished to retire him on a pension after the 'execution' of his old master, but he is not for going. So, he remains in place, with his secrets untold. Loyal to the *Mijnheer* in Antwerp.

"How much?"

"Five hundred, and some land?"

"Too much. I'll have to take my chances." Though I thank you for the offer, and might look to employ you at some future date, Master Wake."

"I admire your optimism, Lord Norfolk, but the odds are three to one on you getting it in the neck. I think your last day is upon you. I shall make sure the axe is well honed."

The gaoler is a simple man, but a clever one, and he has his own ideas as to whom to address his complaint to. He makes his way up from the dungeons, and slogs across the courtyard towards the White Tower.

As he arrives, Will Draper is coming out, and the two men, old friends of yore, exchange greetings.

"Good day, Abe," Will says, and sees that the man is not happy. "Is there some problem with your prisoners?"

"I've come to complain, Sir Will," the gaoler starts. "My prisoner was duped last evening, by someone claiming to be me."

"Ah, yes, my dear Master Wake. Most unfortunate, but it was a jest in poor taste."

"The jest included My Lord being robbed of all his worldly wealth," Wake continues.

"That is so," Will confesses. "He wished to bribe someone, and our man obliged by taking what was on offer. I am sorry if this upset you."

"Only the taking of a bribe, as was by rights mine to take, sir. His Lordship was most aggrieved, just now, and claimed the coins to be all he had in his purse."

"A trifling amount," Will explains, and reaches for his bulging purse. "Shall I round it up, for your inconvenience?"

"No need. Just give me the full amount His Lordship spoke of, and honour is satisfied, Master Will. Fifteen, he claims."

"Shillings?"

"Pounds."

"The lying bastard!" Will says, but sees that the duke has had one last victory over him. "Pounds it is then. Will golden angels do?"

"You are a true gentleman, sir, and have been all these years I have broken bones for you."

"Not so many, I hope?" Will Draper is not a cruel man, and he has kept his recourse to torture down to the barest minimum.

"Barely a dozen in the last ten years," the official Tower torturer agrees. "Now that brother in law of yours is a regular; at least one a month, and as for the Attorney General... why he has them delivered by the cart load, every Tuesday and Thursday. The poor buggers scream, of course, and say what they must, and that be that. Though I had one in here the other week who insisted on swearing to a plot against the king. I did for him, as I was told, but now, I see he was speaking the truth. Some tale about a rogue going about, as if under the Duke of Norfolk's command."

"When was this?"

"Two weeks ago. I took down his words, and sent them off to Sir Richard Rich's offices."

Then Rich knew about the uprising two weeks ago, Will ponders, yet did not speak until just the day before it was to happen. Once more the rogue has used the weapon of information to gain his own ends. But what were those ends? How did it benefit him?

Had Will understood the world of high politics better, he would have understood how Rich benefits. By revealing the plot, he is made to be an honest and loyal fellow. Further, there is the chance of bringing down Norfolk, a powerful enemy. The confession, obtained under duress, but offered freely, and repeatedly, would seem to indicate that Norfolk was actually provably innocent. This last point would show Will Draper that his case was not as sound as it might be. All that remains for Richard Rich to do, is decide on when, how and if, he might use it.

For the right price, the duke might yet show himself to be guilt free, and escape the block. Such intangibles are, however, beyond Will Draper's ken, and he must go into a trial that he thinks already won, with enough against him that might yet let Norfolk go free.

6   Trial and Punishment

The Tower of London is vast, yet is so much built up over the centuries, that a decent venue for such a huge show trial is hard to find, at first. It is Richard Cromwell who comes up with the idea, but only through a coarse jest he makes over dinner.

"Where will we try Uncle Norfolk then?" the king asks, seriously, and Richard sees a chance to poke fun at the old man again.

"Why, the Wakefield Tower, Your Majesty. Then the King of the Beasts shall be above the King of Men."

"How mean you, Dick?" the king asks, much puzzled by the comment.

"Why there is a great long room on the ground, and it is exactly below your fine zoo, sire. As Norfolk pleads for mercy, the lion shall roar. That lion is you, sire, and Norfolk is your meat."

"Ah, well spoken, Dick… and quite apt, I think. Have them clear the room, and set it ready for a trial."

"But sir, think of the stink," Cromwell says. "It will be enough to make a man gag."

"Oh, do not worry about the stench,

my boy, for I am determined to be done with this business, and the scoundrel Norfolk, before luncheon is upon us. His head will adorn this tower before nightfall."

"Then your mind is set, sire?"

"Like a rock, firm against all battering. Did Norfolk spare my beloved Cardinal Wolsey, whom I loved like a father, or his own niece, whom he tried and had killed?"

"The woman deserved it though, sire," Richard says, judiciously. It does not pay to think well of Henry's second wife. "Then there was so much other he did, but that he was forgiven for."

"Yes, he has gone too far now," the king concludes. "A toast, gentlemen… to the Wakefield Tower, and its roaring lion!"

"We might feed Norfolk's carcass to your lions, sire, but I fear they would spit it out, for fear of being poisoned by the bilious old bastard!"

The chamber erupts into laughter, because every man has heard the king's boast, and they know that the great Norfolk is finally to fall from grace.

Tom Wyatt, the poetic knight, stands then, and begins to contrive an ode to suit the happy occasion. The court falls silent, as the master of ribaldry clears his throat, and begins to speak. His voice is melodious, and many a woman has fallen under his spell, because of the elegant beauty of his words.

> *"Though Norfolk's guilt is clear to see,*
> *and wise men must use the law*
> *the wicked rogue may yet go free*
> *and escape the lion's maw."*

"Not in my den," Henry calls out, and he gets the laugh. Tom Wyatt bows, and continues.

> *"The king is wise beyond compare,*
> *and well understands this season,*
> *His judgement will be true and fair,*
> *as he listens to the Howard Treason."*

> *"The swine has moved to take a crown,*
> *from the head of our dearest lord,*
> *Norfolk sought to do Hal down,*
> *and now must face his reward"*

> *"For trying hard to lay Henry low,*
> *Norfolk's reward should be,*
> *a death both lingering and slow,*
> *beneath the gallows tree."*

"By the great fucking horns of the

devil," Henry curses. "You have it there, my boy, and in only four verses. My Lord Norfolk is a low scoundrel, and he must be smitten, hip and thigh. The bastard shall pay for his damned infamy."

"After a fair trial?" the poet suggests.

"Oh, yes, of course. there must be a fair trial," Henry replies. "Then he shall go to Master Wake."

*

"Do we have enough men to form a jury?" the king asks, even as he enters the great hall of the Wakefield Tower. It is typical of his lack of forward planning, and shows how much he needs good men about him. It is Rafe Sadler who steps forward, and whispers into the receptive royal ear.

"We are rather lucky that Ned Seymour is in the city, sire. Your brother-in-law expected to pay a curtesy visit on you, his most noble relative, and finds himself as the senior jurist. Then I have invited Sir John Russell, your own personal herald. He knows your own mind in this matter, and he can be trusted to reach the correct conclusions."

"Both sound fellows,"Henry replies, "but I must have at least six… for it is the law that dear Tom Cromwell did put in place, to ensure a fair trial for all. Never less than six, or more than fifteen is the rule."

"Your ever reliable Dick Cromwell makes three, Sir Moses Draper shall be our fourth, and I thought myself a suitable fifth. The sixth man is Heneage, who did volunteer himself without being asked. A noble spirit, if a little dim. He will understand where his duty lies, Your Majesty."

"A fine panel," Henry decides, for it is weighted with two men who hate Norfolk, and four who simply dislike the man. "They will be fair as is needed, I warrant."

"Undoubtably, Your Royal Highness. Now, to the matter of the after trial proceedings… I thought the next day, in the small forecourt just outside the White Tower. Your Majesty could watch from a high window, if he wishes?"

"If they are found guilty," Henry says, quite properly, but he nods his agreement to the arrangement anyway. "I doubt we have ever had a genuine father and son double execution before. At least not in my lifetime. I shall commute the sentence, of course. All this quartering, and dragging of entrails is really quite barbaric, and the swift blow of an axe will suffice."

Henry walks into the hall, and the babble of chatter dies away. He crosses to where they have set up a throne on a dais, as befits his station in the realm, and he sits down.

"Give order, for His Sovereign Majesty King Henry, the eighth of that number, King of England, Wales, Ireland, the Calaisis, and France. Head of the Church of England." Sir Peregrine Pond declares, and then stands behind his master, in place of Sir John Russell, who is on jury service for the next hour or two. The king gestures with his hand, and nothing happens. There is an uncomfortable wait, until Rafe Sadler hisses from the jury box.

"Bring up the prisoners!" and a guard leaps to obey. Norfolk and Surrey have spent a bad night in the dungeons, and both look unkempt, and faintly disreputable to the court. Apart from the jury, there are about fifty other gentlemen crammed onto long benches found in the other towers, and they set up a low, almost inaudible hissing at sight of the two accused. Henry smiles. The dice are loaded, and ready to roll.

"Charges, fellow," Rafe Sadler whispers to the Clerk of the Court, a fresh faced young man from Barnaby Fowler's practice. Iain Bantry clears his throat, and starts to speak.

"Your Majesty, Lords, Right Honourable Gentlemen… it is charged that on the fourteenth day of this month…"

"Not Guilty." The sudden pronouncement from Norfolk throws Bantry for a second, but he is well trained, and soldiers on.

"And that you did conspire to make war against the king, by means of…"

"Not Guilty."

"…your son… who did join you in this treasonable…"

"Not Guilty," Norfolk snaps. "Not guilty of anything Will Draper can invent to throw at me. Not guilty to the lies, not guilty to the calumnies laid unjustly at my door, not guilty of it all, sire."

"Then we must hear the evidence," Henry says, gruffly. He was hoping for a quick plea for mercy, and the offer of a huge payment to save his neck. "Who prosecutes here?"

"General Sir Will Draper, sire," Will says, and stands up. "I will show that the duke inaugurated a reign of terror against your own subjects, for his own purposes, and that he then headed a conspiracy to take the city of London unto himself, using his own household troops, and yeomen archers.

Further, I shall show how his plan went askew, and the attack was thwarted by the king's own presence of mind in fortifying the Tower of London. Said Norfolk then suffered the desertion of his foot soldiers, and the defeat of his entire army, by the king, and a few hundred of his most loyal Examiners."

"Bollocks to that, Draper," the duke responds with a great roar. "You have some proof? Then let us test it."

"My Lord, do you intend defending yourself?" the king asks.

"I do, Hal… and my idiot son too, whom is not fit to speak to his elders or betters alone. If you so please?"

"It is your choice to make, My Lord," Henry replies. Will notes that the king has accepted the use of his 'Hal' persona without rebuke.

"Colonel Henry Black was employed by the duke, on a mercenary basis, in the June of last year."

"Not so," Norfolk replies. "The idiot son hired the fellow, not me. The boy also paid him a ridiculous salary."

"Nevertheless, the man took your orders, sir." Will insists. "Some of your men have sworn to this, and claim he often rode in your company."

"Then that proves I knew the man, if only in passing. A duke does not befriend a mercenary, sir... as a king should not trust one either." The imputation is clear, that Henry converses with a man who once earned his pay by chasing Welsh bandits over mountains, and butchering Irish rebels. The audience titter at the unexpected acerbity of the remark, and the king gives them a sharp, disapproving look.

"Then you deny that this man was ever in your employ?"

"I deny nothing, Draper... so bring the rogue in, and let him speak."

"Colonel Black is dead," Will confesses. "Killed at the height of the battle's fervour."

"By me," Norfolk says, and the audience gasp at the revelation.

"An unlucky mishap," Will says to the duke. "Or a careful plan to cover up your plotting?"

"A stroke of good fortune," Norfolk replies. "I came to save a king, but found myself saving a dear friend of this court... Sir Thomas Wyatt. Black, for evidently it was he, was murdering the young man, when I shot him... twice. Both rounds hit him in the chest, but he seemed impervious to the wounds. He drew his sword, and would have split me asunder, save for my son, who drew his dagger, and plunged it into the foul creature's neck. Hardly the actions of two men in cahoots with the actual villain of this entire fiasco."

"You killed him to keep him silent," Will Draper says.

"In front off around six thousand witnesses, sir?" Norfolk sniggers, and waves to someone in the audience. "What say you to that Sir Rizz?" 'Rizz' Wriothesley, who has slipped into the back row is mortified. He has recently broken with the duke, on bad terms, and now, the crafty old swine is dragging him into things. "Well, did you ever see me with this fellow, sir?"

"No, Your Lordship, but…"

"Of course not," Norfolk says, smoothly. "It is a fiction, made up to dun me, by a jealous person, in this chamber."

"Then you deny sending him into the shires on a mission to discover the whereabouts of people you wanted dead?" Will demands.

"Not Guilty," Norfolk says, "to everything. Who are these folk I wish dead so earnestly?" The prosecution cannot name names, or the king will want to know why

Thomas Culpeper and Lady Jane were in hiding.

"Honest folk, sir," Will snaps at the duke. "People of impeccable character."

"Who cannot even show themselves in this court?" Norfolk grins, and makes a rude gesture at Will. "*That* to your invisible witnesses, Draper. Show me some real evidence, or be damned to you. If this is but a travesty, to have me killed, then let us be done with it… but the king is here, and I expect real justice from so important a quarter. Hal is a dear friend, and will see that true justice is done… unto the letter of the law, as dear old Tom Cromwell was wont to say. What say you to that, Hal?"

"This court must be a model of probity," Henry says, but curses his decision to sit as judge. A lesser man could not be so easily manipulated into being strict with the law. "When Will Draper is done, your own evidence will be heard, and put in the balance. Then we shall see about these heinous charges of treason."

"Not Guilty, sire."

"Your men captured my city, and meant to take me prisoner."

"Yes, Hal, they did," Norfolk says, and there is another gasp from the onlookers.

"For they thought it a command from their Lord… that is, myself."

"And it was not?"

"Your Majesty," Will Draper insists, "are these not questions for the prosecution to investigate?"

"Of course," Henry replies, somewhat flustered at the implied rebuke for his interference. "Though I am keen to hear an answer to my question. Did Norfolk's men storm my city?"

"As you wish, sire. The prisoner is directed to answer… simply. A 'yes' or 'no' will suffice."

"I am sure it would, but I must reply with a 'possibly'."

"Possibly?" Will says, and it opens the floodgate for Norfolk. He has been, erroneously, given leave to expand on his word. In the jurist's box, Rafe Sadler groans at the mis-hit.

"The order was given by Black, when he saw the walls undefended. Once inside, it was an easy matter for him to pretend I was in command. Men thought him to be my go-between, and did as he said. He invaded London, of his own accord, just as he raided in the southern shires. Without either my knowledge, or my permission."

"Why would he?" Will brings the exchange back onto familiar ground. "How could he hope to hold the city, with six thousand men?"

"I think he meant to secure His Majesty, and use him as a bargaining tool," Norfolk offers, ingenuously.

"Against whom?"

"Any who oppose him," Norfolk replies. "I think he was hungry for gold, and might want to ransom Hal for a huge amount. Then he would return to his Irish lands, and live the life of a great robber Lord. Such men are revered in that Godless country."

"This is all nonsense," Will Draper declares. "You employed him, through your son, and you sent him to invest the city. Imagine his surprise at finding the walls abandoned, and the king safe in the Tower of London."

"A bad day for him," Norfolk says. "That must be when he decided to attack the Tower. The men trusted him, and thought the order came from me. So, they prepared for battle. I was some way from the city, when the news came to me, and I dressed in my best armour, and took horse at once with every man I could muster… a thousand of the very best heavy cavalry, I think."

"Your intention was to support your main force, with cavalry, and take the king hostage."

"My intention was to stop Black from destroying the Tower, and endangering dear Hal's own life," Norfolk tells him. "I am sworn to the king, in both body and soul, and could never betray him. Now, what of these murders I am accused of in Suffolk and Kent?"

"You know the counties, sir?"

"Know them, I own half of them," Norfolk replies, and this raises an encouraging laugh from the audience.

"I have here," and Will holds up a sheaf of sworn affidavits, "proof positive of your guilt. Each one speaks of Colonel Black at the head of about fifty riders, burning, raping and plundering a series of villages. Individually, they mention that Norfolk is their master. Must I read them all out, My Lord Norfolk?"

"No, let me see them." Norfolk takes the papers, and reads, his lips moving over the words. " Hmm… 'Thy came at dawn, and did terrible murder to six of our men, and did take two of the women for their pleasuring. They boasted of being in 'Norfolk's pay'. Poor misused creatures, I say… and here is another... and I quote 'They came early, and did do murder on us. Three men and a boy killed, and the cattle stolen. They did boast at being Norfolk's men, and '*in his pay*'. How cruel, and how close to one another. Now, what is this... a different tune? No, again they say Black is '*in Norfolk's army*' and the poor surviving peasant notes that the men all swear to be '*in the duke's pay*'. Sire, these are not affidavits, but confessions of an unimaginative clerk, who thought they would not be compared by this court. I move to strike them from evidence, and hope they have not blackened the probity of the prosecuting officer."

"As you say, My Lord," Henry says to the smiling duke. "Such a closeness of the words lead me to agree with you. Remove the offending papers, General Draper. Now, how does that leave us?" The king has allowed the duke a hit, for old time's sake, but he still wishes the trial to be done, and sentence passed in time for his next meal.

"It leaves us with the distinct possibility that Colonel Black was, even then, working to his own ends, and not under my son's direction," Norfolk explains. Will sees he must fight back hard against Henry's monstrous ruling.

"It means nothing of the sort, sire," he declares. "These folk are honest, and truthful. That they each heard the claims against Norfolk is clear, but some idle clerk has recognised a pattern, and used it by rote. Black was under orders to Surrey, who is a weasel liar, and a damned rogue... and Surrey is under his father... Norfolk."

Then Black *was* Norfolk's man?" the king asks, somewhat confused, but willing to be told.

"Yes, sire... he was, until his death. Every action was at Norfolk's behest, and it is he who is standing here today, on trial for his life."

"Then it is proven," Henry decides, "for no common officer would ever formulate so clever an idea. Why, to steal a king, and hold him hostage for gold is... quite the most wicked thing, and only likely to be done at a great man's hand. I think you should consider yourself as being proven against in this one instance, Norfolk."

"That I was in official command of Black at that time?" Norfolk asks, and the king walks right into the trap.

"Yes, that is precisely it. You were in official command, sir."

"Do you perhaps recall the *Battle of*

the Spurs, Hal?"

"Of course I do... like yesterday," the king says, wistfully. "I drove their army from the field, and won the day almost single handed."

"And do you recall the truth of the matter, my friend? Do you recall how your council did say you were far too young to lead? They allowed you to fight, but put a wiser head in charge of things. They chose a man who had beaten the Scots, outfought the French, and put down two uprisings in Yorkshire, and Kent. That man was I, my dear friend."

"It was," Henry concedes, and he goes red faced at the memory of what is to now come out.

"You accepted my command over you, most graciously, and swore to serve me in battle, *exactly* as I directed you. Then I ordered you to take the middle ground, and stand firm. I recall the very words, Hal. 'Do not advance, no matter what the provocation' I said to you... and then I even put it in writing."

"I confess that you did," Henry mutters. "Stand firm, and do not move. The very words, as I recall."

"And as soon as I rode off, to launch

a right wing attack on their weaker flank, what did you do, Hal?"

"I charged them."

"Louder please, for the benefit of the jury, sire."

"I charged home, and won the day," Henry tells them.

"Thus breaking the chain of command. I was not there, and could not enforce my orders. You ignored me… oh, to be sure, you won the day, but against my explicit orders. Is that not what Black did? He had a warrant, sealed by my idiot son, and he misused it to show he was indeed, '*a Norfolk man*'. Does that not make sense, Hal? Might not the men he commanded believe him too? If so, then I am innocent of the charges concerning the shires."

"It would seem…"

"Sire, the summation and verdict must wait until the end," Will puts in. The duke has driven a hayrack through the prosecution, by alluding to some fanciful battle from another life. Henry is in danger of being overcome with sentiment. "I have stated the facts against His Lordship, and believe them to be both true, and accurate. The affidavits may have been dismissed, but the survivors words are there still, on their lips. I can call each man up as a witness, if you but give me the consent, sire."

Henry's love of his people does not extend to listening to some overfed yeomen farmers complaining about murder and taxes for hours on end. Besides, he grows hungry, and wants to be done with this thing, at at his lunch.

"That these folk exist is proof enough, Will," the king coaxes. "I shall take their word for it that Black's men spoke of being in Norfolk's pay. However, I can see a valid argument that says Black had deceived his men, for some further purpose. Have we any real witnesses to hear?"

"I have several aldermen, who witnessed the incursion into the city. It was a market day, and many hundreds saw what came about."

"What will these aldermen say to us, Will?"

"That Black declared himself to be from the duke, and under orders to secure the city, and take Henry into protective custody."

"Protected... from whom, sir?" the king snapped at Norfolk, who shrugs his shoulders. "Who are my enemies, that I must be so protected?"

"Do not look to me, Hal, for he was

not really under my orders. I knew nothing, until my idiot son sent me a messenger, to warn me of what was going on. Like you at the eternally famous 'Spurs', I donned my armour… new from Lombardy… you must visit, and see it for yourself… and rushed into battle, without a thought about orders, or chains of command. I had a king, and a kingdom, to save."

"Quite so, old fellow." Henry ponders for a few moments, then makes his decision. "I will accept the statements made by our illustrious aldermen at face value, and not trouble them to appear in this court. Again, they believed their ears, when Colonel Black spoke of being Norfolk's man. That might well be true, but it remains that Black might have lied, and misused Norfolk's name to his own ends. It is unclear, and you must make it clear, my boy. Fish…"

"Pardon, sire?" Will asks, and hopes it is not the poppy juice talking.

"Fish, damn it… can you not smell it, sir?"

"There is a certain smell, sire," Will replies, his nose twitching at the unpleasant aroma.

"Fish for lunch, Your Majesty?" Rafe Sadler ventures from the jury box. This is unlikely, as the king has an aversion to fish, other than at dinner.

"It is for the new animals, sire," Sir William Laxton, a junior warden of the Tower of London offers from the benches. "They are found on the far off shores of Ireland, and about Cornwall. They are a cross between a lion, and a fish… sea-lions, we call them, and they live on fish alone."

"Fascinating, young man. Who are you?"

"Sir William Laxton, sire."

"Excellent… now, sit down, and shut your blasted mouth," Henry tells the startled fellow. "I am for my luncheon, and we are not getting on."

"Sire… might we move on to the investing of the city now?"

"With all speed, Will," the king urges, for his stomach is rumbling. "I am much bothered with hunger, for breakfast was sparse this morning."

"Camp rations, sire," Will says. "I think the men appreciated how you did take rough with smooth, during the battle. They noted well how you inspected the ordnance, and kept the men at the embrasures, with crossbows at the ready. It is a pity that you were not able to take your sword up, and dash them into pieces." This is a mishmash of half truths, but the king will swallow it readily enough. Camp rations consisted of a six egg omelette, a bowl of porridge, and thick slices of boiled ham hocks. All washed down with a bottle of good Portuguese red, and a quart of weak beer. As for his noted bravery, the king was noted as standing behind every cannon in turn, as if to shield himself from any stray crossbow bolts.

Had the tower been breached, and men flooded in, Henry would, no doubt, have soiled his own hose, and dropped his sword. Still, the king has a version he can live with, and he is grateful for Will Draper's kinder interpretation of his actions.

"Yes, we missed a damned good fight there, my boy," the king muses.

"One that should never have happened, sire," Will tells him. "Colonel Black is… was… a very fine soldier: a tactician, and a ruthless commander, but he could never aspire to become king. His actions were the actions of a man being directed… a man obeying his orders. Those orders told him to take London, and make the king safe from other attacks on his person. No such 'other' attacks were likely, but he obeyed, either the duke, or his so called 'idiot son'. And I agree with the duke on that point. the son *is* an idiot without equal, so it *must* have been done at the direction of the father."

"Got you there, Tom," Henry says, with a sly chuckle. The duke notes that he is now 'Tom', and that the king's attitude is still there to be swayed. "This Colonel Black was your pawn, was he not? Did you order him to steal my city from me?"

"Not I, Hal," Norfolk swears. "Nor would my stupid son. It was all the doing of this rogue, Henry Black. He won over my men by claiming I was in charge, then led them against you. I can only suspect he was after a massive bribe to leave … or in the pay of some other conniving lord. There are a few I could name."

"Name them, sir!" Henry demands. "For I would know who loves me not."

"The Pole family, or those still alive, and hiding in France. Kill, or capture you, and England returns to the Roman church."

"They are a broken reed, and lack the ability to fund so elaborate a ruse," Will Draper says with a mocking smile. He cannot allow credible alternatives to be set up, and must focus the king on Norfolk alone.

"Then we have the Percy clan, brooding away up in Northumberland. They have never forgiven you for persecuting the family over Harry Percy's connection to my niece, *la Boleyn*."

"*La Putain*, more like," Henry curses, and bangs his fist down with force. "Must you mention that vile woman's name in front of me, Tom?"

"Only that I might then prove my own innocence, Hal," Norfolk replies. "I have saved the best for last… the Scottish king."

"Most unlikely," Will says, but the audience have started muttering amongst themselves. There have been wild rumours about a possible Scottish invasion for some weeks now, and this statement only puts some flesh on the bones.

"Really?" Norfolk grins at this, for he can see that the king is stricken with the very idea. "Let us suppose that Colonel Black was under the orders of King James. He suborns Norfolk troops into believing they march for England's salvation, and marches on London. As soon as news of his success reaches Perth, the King of Scotland will march south with twenty thousand Highlanders at his back. They would be in Berwick within two days, and at the walls of York at the end of the week."

"But why?" Henry asks, with a quake

in his voice.

"Why, to have your throne, sir," the duke chimes in. "With you either dead, or captured, he could roam the countryside, at will. He would find Princess Mary, and Elizabeth... even Edward, and so end the Tudor line for ever. Then who would the crown fit, Hal?"

"Why, him, of course," Henry says, with real horror in his voice. "A damned Stuart on my throne."

"Yes, imagine that, Hal... a foreign king sitting on England's throne."

"The dirty bastard!"

"Sire, this is but a story, made up to fit the facts." Will Draper wishes to God Above that the king had stayed at home this day, and let them get on with the business of killing one troublesome duke, and his asinine son. "The Scots are *not* invading."

"Only because I stopped them," Norfolk puts in. "They know Black has failed, and will not now gamble on an unsupported invasion."

"That makes sense,' Henry says, and Will sighs at his gullibility.

"Sire, it is a story," the Examiner states. "Had the Scots meant to move, they would have to be a gathering of the clans, much discussion, and then a final consensus. This all takes about two months, and I have six agents in Scotland, pretending to be either Scots, or foreign traders. One of them, at least would have seen the signs. Nothing has come to my ears, and James is *not* on the move. Besides, the French would want to be involved too. Or we might blame the Bulgars, or the far off Turcomen for the deed… or, and let us think on this… we might just go for the obvious answer… which is so often the truth of things. Lord Norfolk is under a heavy cloud, and out of favour with you, sire. So he decides on a great plot to restore his fortunes again. All he needs is the right sort of a man, and that is when Henry Black turns up. The damned man is a consummate soldier, without a conscience, and he wants gold. They meet one another, as attested to by one of his own stewards … Master Albert Perry …"

"That lying bastard, I sacked him for stealing from me."

"Last week," Will reveals, "after he caught you fornicating with his youngest daughter, a girl of thirteen, against her will. You dismissed him, and threatened to have him killed … by Colonel Henry Black, who was then by his side."

"That is a damned lie!" Norfolk rues

letting the man live, and curses his own lust for the girl. Though 'unwilling' he had offered her money enough, and only took her by force when she refused him. A girl like that does not have the right to refuse her lord, and the father should have minded his own business.

"Master Perry, distraught at his cruel treatment, sought employment with a certain Sir Gregory Cromwell."

"A fine young man," Henry says, helpfully, for once. "He is married to one of my dearest Jane Seymour's sisters, and so is my brother-in-law. His word is his bond and I shall hear nothing against him."

"Thank you for that, sire. A most honest assessment of an astute and decent young man. Gregory saw the misery the man was in, and took him on as an overseer of his flocks."

"Then he has sheep?"

"About eleven or twelve thousand, Your Majesty," Will replies. "It seems the animals have an affinity with him. Then the man told his tale, and Tom Crowell's son saw the import of it. He wrote to me, and I took a deposition. The man is without, should you wish to meet the poor wronged fellow."

"I doubt it, Will" Henry says, conscious of his need for food. 'Give me the gist of it, if you can."

"In short, he describes how he found his daughter being ravished, and of how the duke did mock him, and then dismiss him without a penny in wages. Then he goes into detail, and reveals that the bully boy is none other than Colonel Henry Black, a man of great stature, and brutality. The man was 'under the command of Norfolk alone, and 'jumped to obey his every word'. No Percy's, and no Scots, sire... just the good old Duke of Norfolk, who calls you 'Hal' most shamelessly, as if he loves you well, but who but a day ago was coming here to see you put in chains."

"Chains?" Henry gulps, and beckons for a drink. It is the weakest beer possible, and he spits it from his mouth in a great spray, "Surely not that?"

"Sire, Norfolk was chained during the night, to stop him from fleeing. It is the common practice."

"Not for a king," Henry blusters.

"But Your Majesty, was not one of your predecessors killed with a red hot poker rammed up his arse? Then there was the one who was starved to death, and another strangled... but that was in France, I think."

Will plays on Henry's terror of

overthrow, and the death that would follow. It is his fear of this that makes him a bad king, as he persecutes the catholics, those with any contrary opinions, and even those he simply suspects. it has the desired effect.

"Norfolk, you wicked swine," Henry says. "You would chain me up like a dog? Why I shall pay you out for this, fellow."

"But, Hal …"

"Do not 'Hal' me, you cunning old rogue," the king replies, heatedly. "I am hungry, and will finish now for my repast. Afterwards, I shall finish up your sorry tale, and pass down my verdict on you both. It seems that your claim to having an idiot son is true, so I am of a mind to spare him, and have him locked up in a House of Lunatics. You will not meet that fate, sir."

"Sire, am I to be condemned without a defence?" Norfolk asks. "Are we then in Spain, and under Inquisition rules?"

"You may have a half hour, after my meal has settled. Let us say at the third hour?" Henry stands, and Sir John Russell rushes forward with a walking cane, and to take some of his great weight on one arm.

"Lean on me, sire, lest that damned leg fails you," he says.

"Oh, loyal Russell, what better

servant could I have than you? This leg irks me so, for I am the same weight now, as when I was a lad of twenty five."

"Your Majesty is a tower of strength to us," Russell replies, using the usual rote of wildly inaccurate praises that seem to fit the bill. "Even the mighty Dick Cromwell cannot best you in arm wrestling. He is a sore loser, often enough, always claiming as to how his elbow slipped, or he was distracted."

"Such mendacity ill suits my gentlemen," Henry mutters. "Norfolk has shown himself to be a man of straw. See that he gets only prison rations for his luncheon."

"Yes, Your Majesty."

There is no luncheon service in the Tower's dungeons, and Lord Norfolk must face the rest of his trial with hunger pains, gnawing at his vitals.

*

Rafe Sadler has arranged a fine meal for his friends, and they gather in the White Tower. The king, as befits a judge, must eat alone, to avoid him being compromised. There are cold chickens, diced into quarters, a side of roast beef to be sliced at will, and some very fine French and Flemish cheeses. The bread is still warm, and there are strawberry preserves to smother on it.

"How was that?" Will asks, and it is Rafe Sadler, the brilliant lawyer, who gives his expert verdict.

"To be honest, you started badly, and then let it all go to shit," he says, and his friend is crestfallen. "Then, you regained your breath, and came back strongly. The business about the girl being raped was a clever ploy."

"I regret to say that it was all true," Will replies. "The girl caught Norfolk's eye, and he simply dragged her into a barn. The father arrived, and took a sharp beating from Henry Black."

"Which proves that Norfolk commanded him, and that the duke then lied *under oath* to the king. Henry saw this, at once, and has decided the duke's fate. All the evidence in the world will not sway Henry now, for he feels to have been personally slighted. I doubt anything can save the duke from death."

"What about this claim to have not known, and thus turning up late?" Mush asks of the lawyer.

"He did not notice six thousand of his men marching to London?" Rafe snorts with laughter. "Then to claim he was coming here to stop Colonel Henry Black from his base actions… fanciful, at least. No, Norfolk was on his way to reap the harvest of victory, without risking his neck in battle. Henry will note this, and think him a coward. As the king has his own fears in that direction, I think it will seal Norfolk's fate. Death for them both, I think. The king will not want to pay the support of the lad in a madhouse."

"Then it is done?" Richard asks the lawyer. "I can look forward to an execution, followed by a quieter life?"

"Yes, unless.." Rafe Sadler leaves the sentence hanging in the air, for Norfolk is a wily old bird, and he might yet talk Henry into a lesser punishment.

"Dear God," Will prays, "may we have the bastard, at last… amen."

"Amen," they all reply, but how often does God listen to such selfish prayers?

7 The Defence

The jury come back into the hall, after a good luncheon, and they have all taken a little too much of the free wine provided. It can loosen the tongue, and encourage them into asking all the wrong questions. To this end, Rafe Sadler has warned each of them to keep silent, no matter what.

"Just nod your heads, when I say so, and utter but one single word when it be asked of you… 'guilty'. Understand?"

They do. Each of them has cause to hate the duke, and they all wish him either dead or disgraced. They sit, then have to jump up, as Henry enters the room. He appears to be pain free, and ready to proceed. Will understands what has happened at once. The king has resorted to his poppy juice earlier than usual, and has taken too much. They are all in for a rare old time of it now, he thinks.

"Be seated, gentlemen. We have a half hour to spare, and I intend listening to Lord Norfolk's pleading. There is to be a dance at Whitehall tonight, and I must have the matter done with in time for me to change. Fancy dress, you see. I wonder who shall be the horse's arse this year… for I recall that it was poor Surrey last time, and soon enough, he will not be available."

"Sire, I think there are enough in court to find a decent horse's arse amongst," Will says. "For my part, I hope to go as the avenging angel, and Miriam shall be Mother Earth. She tells me the dress is quite risqué."

"Marvellous tits... your wife, Will," Henry observes. "Oh, the pleasure you must take in rubbing your face into..."

"Sire!" Rafe Sadler, who does not understand about the freeing effects of the magnificent poppy juice tries to bring the talk back to legal matters. "Might we get on?"

"I'd like to get on Lady Miriam," the king says, and nudges Will in the ribs. "Though there are some fine fillies in our stables this year, are there not, my dear Examiner in Chief?"

"Undoubtably, sire," Will replies.

"Lady Janice, for one." Henry half closes his eyes, and smiles at some recent thing that has pleased him. "She has lips of gold, and can nibble a man's fruit like a five bob tart. Now, where were we, lads?"

"Sire…"

"Call me Hal." The order is issued, and all who are in earshot are stunned into silence. The idea of calling the King of England Hal, is quite beyond them all.

"Then... Hal...sire..." Sir Rafe Sadler stutters, self consciously. "We are to hear Norfolk's evidence."

"Righto! Let us get on with it, Rafe," Henry says. "I am the judge, you know, and must soon make up my mind. Though I must warn you, I am ready enough to see some heads falling on the morrow."

"My Lord Norfolk?" Rafe prompts, and the duke stands up, so as to be seen by all. He strikes a pose he imagines is noble, but it only makes him look as if he has a problem with his tights.

"Shit yourself, Tom?" Henry asks. "Or do you save that for sentencing? By God, but I shall watch them cleave off your proud head, and stick it onto a spike, with pleasure. Who is our executioner these days... not that fellow..."

"Abraham Wake," the Duke of Norfolk says.

"That's the man."

"No, sire... I am calling Abraham Wake as a witness for the defence," Norfolk tells the king, and there is a surprised gasp from the audience.

"Silence, you arse kissing load of sodomites," Henry snaps. "This is not some bawdy playhouse, but a solemn court of law.

Now, Norfolk, you want to call the very man who will execute you on the morrow?"

"I do, sire," Norfolk says. "He is a prime witness to my innocence."

"Bollocks," the king groans. "This will all end badly."

"As in a bawdy playhouse's finest tale, Your Majesty. Now, pray bring in the official executioner, and torturer of the Tower of London."

The great doors swing open, and Abraham Wake is ushered in to meet his betters in a chamber he has never been allowed in before now.

"Master Wake?"

"Your Lordship."

"Is this then really you, and not some cock-a-dandy misusing your name?"

"It is I, sir… in person, and at the court's service. though I cannot think how I might be of service… other than in the cutting off of Your Lordship's head soon enough."

"Tell me about one of your prisoners… Walt Horeshem."

"He came, he talked, he died," Wake says. "That is the whole story, sir."

"Sure enough, but what did you talk about?"

"I simply listened, sir. It was some

nonsense about an uprising against the king. I get about one a week of those, so did not really pay it any heed."

"Really?" Norfolk smiles, like a hungry cat. "Were any names mentioned in this plot?"

"I recall one that came up a few times," Abe Wake says. He is aware that he is being pushed into saying something that might hurt Will Draper's case, and he does not like it. "Poor Horsehem spoke it several times, which led me to apply my methods more severely. I had to either break him down, or confirm what he said."

"And did he break?" Norfolk asks.

"Yes, of course, but not before he convinced me that there was some truth in what he said."

"What name did he give you?"

"Colonel Henry Black, sir," Abe Wake admits. "He swore the man was a part of a plot against the king."

"When?"

"Oh, about three weeks ago."

"Did you have him sign a confession?" Norfolk asks.

"His hands would not cope with it by then," Wake says. "I wrote it down in a report, and passed it along to the right people."

"Bugger me, an executioner who can write," the king expostulates. "How can this be, fellow?"

"I was taught by Master Thomas Cromwell, Your Majesty. As fine a man as ever walked this earth. He used to pay for lessons so that poor fellows such as I might get on in this hard world."

"Dear Tom… how I do miss him," Henry moans. "Done to death by you, Norfolk… you scheming two faced bastard son of a whore. I should pass sentence now, and be damned to you and your ilk."

"Sire, you are married to my own sweet niece… and she is a Howard."

"For all the use she is… with her bloody damned headaches all the time. I want a woman, sir… not an invalid." Henry pauses and looks at a spot on the far wall, where he fancies he sees a writhing snake-like thing.

"I shall speak with her, as soon as I am judged innocent, sire," Norfolk replies. "Now, Master Wake… this report you wrote… where did it go?"

"To the new Attorney General's Office's at Austin Friars, Your Lordship."

"Ah, now we are getting somewhere," Norfolk says, with the air of a man who already knows the end of the tale. "Then you may step down, sir, and I thank you for your memory."

"Is it done?" Henry asks.

"One more witness, sire," Norfolk says.

"Great festering warts, you impudent fellow. I have to get into costume, and the damned thing is a bastard to get just right. The girls love it. I shall have my pintle in something sweet this night, or wish to know the reason why not. Get on, man!"

"Call Sir Richard Rich, Attorney General of England." Will Draper's heart goes into his mouth, as he realises that Norfolk knows about the fatal report. The Attorney General is already in court, sitting quietly at the back. Now he stands, and makes his orderly, and sedate approach to the witness stand.

"Pick your blasted feet up, Rich," the king roars. "What ever possessed me to raise you up so high? Why, you are little more than a carrier of piss pots. Hurry along."

"As Your Majesty commands," Rich says, and almost runs to the stand. He almost trips, and makes himself look like a capering fool, with arms and legs going like a windmill. Then he hurries through the swearing in on the great bible, with the king frowning at his tardiness.

"Sir Richard," Norfolk says, "do you recall receiving this report?"

"It came into my office, about two or three weeks ago," Rich says. "Though I was not shown it until yesterday. I contacted General Draper at once, and advised him of the threat to the city. He called up his men, and rushed to foil the plot."

"Then it was a plot?"

"In so far as a wicked deed had been plotted, but instigated by a single man."

"Name him, sir."

"Colonel Henry Black," Rich says, and he turns to face the king. "Under questioning, my prisoner swore that Black had stolen an impress from Norfolk's office, and was using it to forge official documents. These documents were to prove that he acted at your behest. The colonel's plan was simple, and quite ingenious. He started out by suborning a troop of men, about fifty, into believing him the duke's man in every way. Then he simply moved on to make it so everyone in Norfolk's foot companies thought him to be Norfolk's own man. That is how he came to have six thousand men at his beck and call."

"Do you believe this to be the truth?"

Norfolk asks, and Rich responds with a warm smile.

"Your Lordship is a good and faithful servant of the king," he says. "It is only that this Black fellow was so cunning that you are here today. It was Black who stole your army, and Black who brought them to London. He used your son to add veracity to the plot. Why, if Surrey was here, then Norfolk must approve. So, your own men went to war against their king."

"Outrageous," Henry mutters, but he sees that something huge has just occurred. "Explain more fully, Rich, and stop that disgusting smirking at me."

"As you wish, sire. The duke has been an unknowing dupe in all of this. A stupid, almost jester-like figure, unworthy of his title."

"Steady on!" Norfolk complains.

"He was used, until the truth came to him, via his son, a renowned idiot, and then, he acted like Zeus coming from the heavens. He called his cavalry to order, and charged home. The foot men were broken, and dispersed, and the duke was confronted by Colonel Henry Black, a giant without equal, who was slaying our court poet."

"That was a damned shame," Henry

says to no one in particular. "For he is a fine poet, though with as dirty a mind as a Roman Catholic priest."

"Quite, sire." Sir Richard Rich continues to hammer his nails into Will Draper's case. "Lord Norfolk discharged two pistols into the man, and was about to be run through, when the son struck with a dagger. This blow proved to be the fatal one, and the battle was won… not by an Examiner army, but by an ageing duke, and his idiot son. Sire, the Duke of Norfolk has saved your crown for you, and should be soundly applauded for the deed, not tried for his life. The man is as innocent as a lamb. Far too stupid to be the leader of so heinous a deed. I believe that… that… sire?"

The court is silent, save for a low snoring noise from the throne. Henry has begun to doze, and the sudden cessation of all talk makes him start awake. He looks around, and sees a sea of expectant faces looking back at him.

"Right, all done? It saddens me, Norfolk… for we are old friends… but you will be taken out from this place and put to death. I think we might even leave in the 'hung, drawn and quartered' bit, because you have been so long winded about it all."

"But sire," Richard Rich says, quite aghast at the verdict, "the Duke of Norfolk is proven to be innocent. I have a sworn report, that exonerates him."

"You have?" Henry frowns. "I must have missed that part. Exonerate, you say?"

"Beyond all doubt," Rich confirms.

"Is this so, Draper?" The king looks to his Examiner General for his verdict, and Will can do no other than agree.

"It seems so, Your Majesty," he replies. "As this evidence is embedded in the past, it has a veracity that I cannot question. The duke is exonerated, and I can offer nothing further against him."

"Right then, this trial is over." Henry belches loudly, and waves a hand at the duke. "Off you go, Norfolk, and try not to get into any more muddles."

"Yes, sire, as you so wish." The duke of Norfolk bows, and steps down from the dock. Surrey follows, unable to believe his good luck. He is confused as to where this 'evidence' has come from, but he thanks God for it. "Then I shall see you at the fancy dress ball tonight then, Hal?"

"Oh, you're still going then, Tom?" the king asks, almost conversationally. The trial is done, and he can forget that but a moment before he was going to send the man to the axe.

"It would seem so, my dearest Hal… and besides, they need my boy to be the horse's arse again."

*

The audience are shocked into dumbness at the sudden ending of the trial, and the verdict, which has cost most of them money. Only Tom Wyatt has bet on Norfolk, and he has made a tidy sum of twenty pounds on the wager.

"You wagered on Norfolk being found innocent?" Mush asks.

"I had a feeling," the poet replies.

"A feeling?"

"Yes, that he would come up with something. Though the series of events does seem to show him to have been an innocent fool in the matter."

"How can it be so?" Will Draper demands, angrily as they gather outside the courtroom. "The man is as guilty as sin itself."

"Then how comes this report to be written?" Tom Wyatt asks. "It cannot be a clever forgery, for you know the very man who wrote it.'

"Yes, I believe Abe Wake," Will

admits. "If he questioned the fellow, he would have the truth from him. The man was broken on everything from the rack to the ball crusher, and he never wavered from his tale. He *knew* a seal had been stolen, and he *knew* that Black was suborning Norfolk's troops. That tale points to it being Black alone who was after the king... for whatever evil purpose. Perhaps the Scots had made promises to him, after all?"

"I do not believe it," Richard Cromwell says. "The man is as guilty as can be, and he has escaped from us again."

"The king will have to reward him now," Will concludes. "He will give him more land, and let him come back into the inner circle. This has been a bad day's work for us all, my friends. We have been duped, and may never know how. I blame myself for our failure. There were signs, and I ignored them, so intent was I on ruining the man. In truth, he has almost ruined me with the king. Henry will think twice now about everything that I tell him."

"The blame belongs to all of us," says Mush. "Perhaps we should have simply killed the damned fellow, and risked the consequences."

"Henry's wrath?" Richard shakes his

head. "By God, lad, but you would not want to feel that. It would be more than a few heads lost. It would be the ruin of us all … our businesses… or families. No, better this way by far. We lose, yet keep our lives, and our dignity."

*

"Free," Norfolk says into the fresh air of the courtyard, and his son capers about like a fool, and slaps his thighs with mirth.

'We have outdone them again, father," he boasts, "though, for the life of me, I cannot see how we did so."

"We… little fellow?" The duke cannot help but sneer at his son's lack of intelligence. "You think your old man such a fool that he would go directly against the king, without the most careful planning?"

"God's own good luck, I would say," Surrey replies, and he receives a sharp cuff across his head. He moves away, out of range of any further assaults, and rubs his stinging ear. The duke's men, still encamped about the Tower send up a ragged cheer as he comes into sight, and start up with a ribald song about him, with much allusion to his bad temper, and renowned sexual precocity.

"Sing away, you damned bastards," he says. "Norfolk is free. Now, we can start to make England great again."

"Father, should we not just keep our heads down?" says Surrey. "Our enemies are all around us still."

"They are all confounded," Norfolk declares. "Henry will see how they tried to bring me down, with false charges, and contrived evidence. I shall be his first minister again… not that great blustering fool, Dick Cromwell… and the power of the King's Examiners shall be curtailed."

"Draper will not tolerate that." Surrey cowers away from the raised fist, but the blow is not landed.

"Draper has taken his best chance, and he has lost," Norfolk tells his son. "I have seven thousand men in the city, and it is only natural that I use them to guard the king. The Examiners will be ordered back into barracks, and my men will assume bodyguard duties over the king."

"Henry will not allow it," Surrey says with a rare insight into court politics. "It is as good as surrendering himself to us."

"How can he deny me?" the duke asks. "I am proven innocent, and the saviour of his kingdom. By the time I am done, Will Draper and his brood will be finished."

"We have just been delivered from

the jaws of death, by a stroke of good fortune," Surrey replies. "Can you not see how we should draw in our horns?"

"You really are an utter fool, boy." The duke sees that he must explain all to his son, if he is to keep him from losing his nerve. "It is proven... beyond any shadow of a doubt... that Black worked alone, is it not?"

"Yes. The confession, taken down weeks ago, proves that, father. We are, despite me knowing otherwise, quite innocent."

"Just so. For we both know that Black was really our creature... do we not?"

"Yes. I was wondering about that part of it," Surrey says. "Why would this Walt Horseham fellow be so insistent on naming Colonel Black as he did?"

"Because he was being tortured, of course," Norfolk replies, with a broad grin on his face. "The pain was such that he did as all men do. He broke down, and confessed what he thought was the truth."

"I do not understand."

"Ninny, how could I sire you? When this plot was first mooted, I foresaw the dangers that lay before us. So much might go awry. So, I had our agents find Horseham, and put him in league with Henry Black. I told Black to employ him; to take him into his confidence, but claim that he was the ringleader of the plot. To this end, I gave Black my official seal, and various other documents, so that he might appear to be acting independently."

"And Black accepted this?" Surrey asks. "Did he not flinch at making himself look the master of the plot?"

"Not at all. He knew that he would be rewarded beyond avarice, if he succeeded, and hanged if he did not. I told him that if I was protected, and it went awry, I would see his family in Ireland were looked after. He thought this a fair offer, and so convinced Horseham to join him in his plotting. The man was a devout Roman Catholic, and thought he was doing God's work in pulling Henry from his throne."

"Then he was really Black's man?"

"He was. He believed the colonel was the sole villain of the piece, and he was quite willing to help him against the king. He was told to get in touch with others like him, who want the old church restored, and prepare them for rebellion. Black hinted at a return to the old church, once the king had been taken hostage, and the fool believed him."

"He really believed it?" Surrey shakes his head at how easily a man can be swayed, if he is promised the right thing.

"He did. That was the important thing, you see. Then it was arranged for him to be informed on, and arrested by Richard Rich's agents, who sent him to the Tower of London. Once there, my little plan unfolded perfectly. Horseham was put to the question extraordinary… and he was found to be wanting. Old Abraham Wake is an expert, and he soon had the fellow talking. Only, instead of informing on a few dissident catholics, he blurted out everything he '*knew*' about Colonel Black."

"Then it was all in place, before we moved against the king?"

"It was. Had you done the job properly, and taken Henry, I would have had no need for Rich's help. As it was, you messed up again, and I was forced to intervene. I had to defeat my own army, and make sure Black died… then bargain with Rich to come forward and show the letter."

"Rich knew?" Surrey worries at this, for the Attorney General is a dangerous snake of a man.

"As soon as he saw the report from Abe Wake," Norfolk explains. "I had to promise him certain things. In return, he was to produce the document, if we were ever tried."

"But he warned Will Draper against us," Surrey complains.

"Only at the last moment," Norfolk says. "He sought to have a foot in each camp, as I would do."

"Then we have won?" Surrey likes the idea that, after years of being thwarted, his father has finally won out against the Austin Friars cabal. "Draper's power is finally broken?"

"Oh, he will still have his usual duties," Norfolk says. "He can see to the king's messes for him, and waste his time hunting down murderers and thieves, but he will never hold sway over the king again. Not in my lifetime."

"Then what of all of the others?" Surrey asks. "Dick Cromwell, Rafe Sadler, and Mush Draper?"

"Richard Crowell has been protecting Lady Jane Boleyn," Norfolk replies, with a smirk. "Henry has a certain dislike for the woman, and will frown on his Privy Councillor helping her. I think we might find something to charge her with, and that will force Cromwell to act. If he helps her, the king will drop him."

"And Sadler?"

"A small man. He will want to stay in office, and I shall let him… in return for his support."

"Yes, that might work," Surrey enthuses, "but Mush Draper is a different sort of a fellow."

"Yes, he is fiercely loyal to his brother in law," Norfolk agrees. "Perhaps we might simply have him killed. A robbery gone wrong, or an accident on the river?"

"It has been tried before." Surrey is well aware of how the Austin Friars gang seem to lead charmed lives.

"By bloody amateurs, my boy," Norfolk says. "His Austin Friars bully boys have all melted away, and he is alone now. I think we can arrange an accident for him, without too much trouble. He is prone to drinking in the most dangerous places, and a fight starts so easily. He might just find a blade in his ribs."

The Duke of Norfolk is one of those men who are clever enough to survive, but vain enough to endanger their gains. Because he has managed to evade the axe, the duke thinks himself to be, once more, in the king's great favour.

It is true that his men hold London, for now, but the other great lords will not let him keep the city. Suffolk and Cumberland hate him, and will push to have him withdraw his troops. As they can vastly outnumber him in the field, he will eventually have to comply, or risk open warfare.

His failure to see how much the king loves Will Draper is also to be his downfall, as Henry will not suffer his favourite Examiner to be brought low. Nor will the king allow any interference with his other ministers, whom he fears to lose.

Norfolk has survived the axe, but it is to be his last triumph, and his greatest trial is yet to come. Henry is beginning to turn against his new queen and, like Anne Boleyn, she is a niece of the duke. It must reflect badly on his taste in women for his king.

*

"Rich played us false," Mush Draper says, over his mug of ale. "We should have slit the bastard's throat, years ago."

"He warned us," Will replies. "If not, the plot would have worked."

"But he knew... weeks ago."

"He says not," Will argues, "and I cannot prove otherwise. I suspect he knew, and lost his nerve at the last. He told us, so that he might show himself to be innocent."

"Then he acted against Norfolk too,"

Tom Wyatt says. "It is as if he means to be well balanced... and thus betray us all in equal measure."

"Rich has his own game to play," Rafe Sadler says. "It will suit him to have saved Norfolk, in some way. I dare say it will become clearer with time."

"For now, I am made to look like an utter fool," Will complains. "The king will wonder how he came to be locked in a tower, fighting off loyal Englishmen, and it will reflect badly on me."

"Not so, my friend," Tom Wyatt puts in. "Rafe and Richard will whisper in the king's ear, and see that he remains against Norfolk. We missed our chance today, of course, but another will present itself... for the poor old duke cannot live without intrigue, and he will slip up."

"Then we must try to return to normal," Will says. "I want a dozen of our best men to guard Henry, and I want to replace Norfolk's men at the city gates."

"He will not like that at all," Richard Cromwell says, flatly. "He holds London by the throat and will be most loath to relinquish his grip."

"Then we will not inform him of our actions," Will says. "Mush, can you gather together a decent sized mob… of say, a hundred people?"

'An angry mob… or an organised one?" Mush asks.

"Not too well behaved, and with a leader who knows how to handle himself," Will explains. "Let them start a disturbance near one of the city gates, and draw the guards to them. Then they must melt away, without hurt to anyone."

"And our men slip in, and take possession of the gate?" Mush guesses.

"Yes, I think so." Will drains his tankard. "If we can place our Examiners at a couple of the gates, in good numbers, Norfolk dare not use force to dislodge them. Then, when Charles Brandon finally arrives with his Yeomen, we can allow him free entry."

"A good idea," Rafe Sadler says. "Norfolk will have to watch as the city fills up with Suffolk soldiers. The king will side with Suffolk, of course, and complain at having to feed too many troops. I will agitate for Norfolk's men to be stood down, then sent back to their own shires."

"A bloodless victory," Will says to them. "Norfolk will be back where he started from, and the crown will be safer than ever."

"Thank God, and our devious ways,"

Tom Wyatt tells them. "Now, I must be off, for I am to escort the Archbishop of Canterbury to Rome."

"Yes, that will be another thorn pulled from our flesh," says Will. "With Tom Cranmer gone, we can get rid of Culpeper and Dereham, and warn the queen to behave herself."

"Consider it done, my friend," the poet says. "He is waiting for me, even now, at Eustace Chapuys' house, and we will be at sea before the next dawn."

"Is it true, that Chapuys is going with you?" Rafe asks.

"Only as far as Bordeaux," Tom Wyatt replies. "It is to encourage Cranmer, and ensure he does not get cold feet."

"The little fellow has been a good servant to Henry, whether he likes it or not," Richard Cromwell says. "Let us toast him, gentlemen."

"To the little frog," the poet says affectionately, and they raise a glass. Everything, it seems, is going well.

*

"Gone?" Eustace Chapuys is poised in front of his mirror, as he tries to place his new cap, just so. He pauses, and frowns at his servant. "What do you mean... gone?"

"Gone, as in 'not here', master," Alonso Gomez says. "His room is empty, and he left a note."

"A note?" Alonso Gomez is a loyal servant to Chapuys, but he cannot help but be annoyed by his habit of asking questions that do not need to be asked.

"Yes, a note. Sealed with his ring, and addressed to you."

"To me?" Gomez grinds his teeth, for now he must confirm it and receive another inane response.

"To you, sir… and before you say 'to me' again, might I suggest you read it? I fear it contains very bad news."

"Bad news?" Chapuys asks, and Gomez groans, and rips the document open. The wax is still soft, and that means that Cranmer has only just departed.

"Give me that!" Chapuys says, sharply, and reads the contents. "It is from the archbishop."

"Really?" Gomez says. "Shall I follow him?"

Chapuys digests the short message, which begs his forgiveness for his actions, but he cannot leave without a final word with the king, and his heart sinks.

"Can you find him, and bring him

back without harm?" he asks, and Gomez shakes his head.

"I can ask him to come, but I cannot compel him… unless at knife point, and someone would be bound to see, and call for help. The archbishop is well known, and I, as you often say, look like a real cutthroat."

"Perhaps I could…"

"Keep out of it, master," Gomez concludes the sentence. "You do not have the power to stop him from seeing the king. We would have to kill him, and you do not approve of that."

"No, I do not," Chapuys says. "Then I must warn Will Draper. If things go badly, he must know what to do."

"He should kill Thomas Culpeper, at once," Gomez says.

"There will be enough blood shed, if the archbishop says the wrong thing," Chapuys says. "Let us hope he is circumspect with his words."

"Master, if we believe that, we would not be sending him to Rome."

*

"I am here to see the king," Cranmer tells the guard on the gate at Whitehall.

"Aren't they all," the young guard says. "So, what have you come as then, sir?"

"I am the Archbishop of Canterbury," Thomas Cranmer says, a little taken aback by this odd reply.

"Yes, I can see that now," the man says. "I suppose it is better than being the Queen of the May, or the Horse's Arse."

"I beg your pardon?" Cranmer is quite bewildered by this odd turn of conversation. "Let me pass, fellow."

"Just as soon as I see your invitation, sir," the guard tells him.

"Invitation?" Cranmer is confused even more. "I am the…"

"Bishop of Cloud Cuckoo Land," the man says. "Yes, and I'm Hereward the Wake… only without my arse painted blue. Now, invite… or bugger off."

"But I *really* am the Archbishop of Canterbury."

"Just passing, are we, Your Lordship?" the guard says. He knows that any great visitors are accompanied by flunkies, and sealed papers. They do not just turn up, unannounced, and claim to be the buggering Archbishop of Canterbury. "Now, get lost, before I stick my spear up your arse!"

The archbishop cowers away from the threat, and scurries off towards Westminster, where he hopes for a kinder welcome. The guard grins at the old fellow as he leaves, and then waves over to the man guarding the next entrance.

"See that, Charlie?" he asks. "The old bugger only wanted to get in to the fancy dress ball, without an invitation. I chased him off, good and proper."

"Funny business that," Charlie Fox replies. "You'd have thought that the Archbishop of Canterbury would have an invite, wouldn't you?"

"The… oh, Christ on His Bloody Cross… Sir! Wait…come back… I was but jesting!"

*

Will Draper is at home, preparing for the king's ball, when Alonso Gomez comes calling. He explains the purpose of his visit, and concludes with an apology.

"I offered to chase the man, and kill him, but the master does not condone such things, and he stopped me."

"Thank you for the kind thought, Alonso," says Will, "but I fear the cat is out of the bag."

"The cat?" Now Gomez is confused. Even after all his years spent in England, he still cannot understand some of the language. "What bag, señor?"

"I mean that the secret is out," Will tells him. "Cranmer will insist on seeing the king, and then... who knows?"

"You have Culpeper?"

"Yes."

"Kill him."

"I dare not. The king would ask why, and I have no ready answer."

"Say he was a traitor."

"I have just accused Norfolk of treason, and been made to look a fool," Will tells the Spaniard. "The king would not believe me. He would want proof, and I have none. All I can say is that he is suspected of swiving his wife. You see my problem?"

"I do, sir." Gomez puzzles for a moment. "Perhaps the bishop... he does not tell Henry. What if he keeps silent?"

"How could that be?"

"It is a hard thing to tell a king that which he does not wish to hear," Gomez says. "He may lose his nerve."

"Or God might strike him dumb," Will says. "No, I must go to the ball, and see what happens. What say you to my costume?"

"Wonderful, sir... what are you?"

"A Barbary pirate captain," Will tells him, and Alonso Gomez smiles and nods. He has sailed with the Barbary pirates in his younger days, and the costume is wildly inaccurate. He doubts that any of his former shipmates would wear a silk shirt when calico was so easily available.

"Shall I come with you, sir?"

"No." Will Draper is resigned to his fate, and will see what the evening brings. "Stay with your master."

"Now Cranmer is gone, Master Chapuys is free to attend the ball," Gomez replies. "He is coming as an ostrich bird."

"He is?" Will smiles for the first time that day. "Where will he find enough feathers?"

"Oh, he'll find them," Gomez avows. "Even if he has to strip every hat in his wardrobe."

*

Lady Jane Boleyn is back at court, and she wonders at the vagaries of royal life. But a few days before, she was an outcast, forced to scrape a living from a few acres of land, and now, she is back in favour, as Queen Catherine's most senior lady in waiting.

Her lover, Richard Cromwell is instrumental in this, and he assures her that he is faithful to her, and will marry her as soon as possible. Her star is in the ascendancy once more.

Her reprieve from a life of penury comes at a price though. She must insinuate herself back into Catherine's good offices, and make sure the girl does nothing more to arouse suspicion about her past.

"I want to be 'Mother Earth'," the queen pouts, and stamps her foot.

"Well, you cannot be, madam," Lady Jane tells her. "Lady Miriam Draper is *always* Mother Earth. She has the figure for it, and the king approves of her costume. You must be a nymph, or some other sort of a creature."

"I could go naked, and say I am Venus, risen from the waves."

"You will dress modestly, Your Highness." Lady Jane is tired of trying to placate the stupid child, and speaks her mind. "The king must think you to be a modest maid, in all things. So, you shall wear a long dress, and a headdress to cover your face."

"I will not."

"Oh, but you will, Catherine," Lady Jane tells her. "Your precious Cully has vanished, and might reveal his treasonable ways at any time. He will say you are his lover, and Henry will demand to know the truth. You must say that Culpeper lies, and that you are faithful. It is the only way to save yourself."

"You mean Henry might put me aside?" Catherine asks.

"Madam, if you are suspected, he will have you executed. As he did with Anne Boleyn."

"Nonsense. Besides Cully will never betray me. He says the court are behind him, and will rise up against the king. Then we shall see about things."

"Are you quite mad?" Lady Jane snaps. "Cully is a squire... no more. He is either in hiding, or taken. He has no power over anyone, and the court will go to his execution without a murmur."

"But, he said..."

"Madam, you are in a world of dreams... Culpeper's dreams. The boy is living out a fantasy, and I fear he will die for it. Do not join him in his delusion."

"Will the king be angry at me?"

"Henry is angry at the world, my girl. We must turn his wrath aside, and blame Cully. You must swear your innocence, if asked, and let him go."

"Henry will kill him."

"Madam, he is already a dead man," Lady Jane says. "Remain calm, and deny it all. The king may believe you, and so punish others in your stead."

"What about Cranmer?" Catherine asks. "I told him… things."

"Do not fear about that one, Your Majesty," Lady Jane tells the queen. "He must be upon the Channel by now, and half way to France."

*

'Forgive me, sir," the guard says, "but I did not recognise you. I was only following orders, you see?"

"You are forgiven, my son," Cranmer says, and places a finger on the man's head, in blessing. "Now, please let me pass. I must speak with the king."

"That I shall, Your Worship, but I fear you will struggle to see His Majesty this night. The place is full of revellers, and most of them are in costume."

"The king is an imposing size," the archbishop replies. "I shall find him."

"Then pass on in, sir, and good luck," the man tells him.

"Here, fellow… take this… to keep you honest." Cranmer presses a shilling into the man's hand and the fellow grins and pushes the coin into his own purse.

"Bless you, sir, and did not dear old Tom Cromwell use to say the very same thing to me? Often he would drop me a bob, and say it was for honesty's sake."

"Yes, the poor fellow," Cranmer says. "I miss him… as does the king."

"They say the good die young." The guard opens the door, and bows the archbishop through, content that this means he will live a long life, if nothing else. "Good hunting, sir."

Archbishop Thomas Cranmer is fifty two years old, and of a sickly disposition. He dreads facing up to the king, and speaking to him about the matter that has come to haunt his every hour. Queen Catherine has spoken plainly to him, but under the seal of confession, about her intimacies with at least two men.

The one, an affair before marriage, she might well be forgiven for, but the second indiscretion has taken place after the wedding, and that is what may well doom the girl. Cranmer foresees a terrible end to it all, and racks his brain for a way to keep faith with the king, yet spare Catherine the block.

"Tom… I was not expecting you here tonight.' A sleek looking fox, complete with glass eyes in its head, and a mane of red fur down the back, trots across to him, and holds out a hand to clasp. "Are you on the king's business?"

Cranmer is just about to explain to the fox that it is none of his business, when the mask is pushed back to reveal Bishop Stephen Gardiner beneath.

"Oh, Gardiner… it is you," the archbishop says. He is shaking, and unsure of how to proceed. "I come to see the king, though I doubt he will wish to see me, old friend."

"Then you must be the bearer of bad news," Bishop Gardiner guesses. "I doubt Henry will thank you for it… not on the night of his great masked ball."

"Just so. I should be on my way to France, but my duty conflicts with my conscience."

"A worrisome thing… a conscience," Gardiner replies. "I try not to let mine get in the way of things. What is the problem?"

"I cannot say," Tom Cranmer tells the bishop. "I am sworn to the secrecy of the confessional."

"Oh, one of those, is it?" Gardiner shakes his head. "Some scoundrel seeks to hide their misdeed by confessing to his priest, and thinks himself safe. Tell all, and be damned to the rogue, Thomas."

"It is not so easy," Cranmer says.

"Then keep faith, and anger the

king," the bishop tells the old archbishop.

"You now begin to see my quandary," Cranmer replies. "I cannot repeat what I have been told. It risks my immortal soul, and the life of someone who does not deserve to be betrayed by me. Yet, my duty is to the king. What can I do, Gardiner?"

"Hello there, Archbishop Cranmer." The most extraordinary creature, a small, beady eyed animal, covered in feathers of all descriptions bows. "You fled from me, quite without warning."

"Chapuys?" Cranmer must muster all of his willpower not to laugh at the sight. "What, in God's name, are you?"

"The Ostrich bird of far off Araby," Chapuys replies. "I have flown here to save you from yourself, sir."

"The soul and the body are two different things, Eustace," Cranmer tells the strange bird. "Henry sustains the one, but I must cherish the other. I shall go to Rome, if it is willed by the king, but I must also look to my spirit. I am caught between two roaring fires, Señor."

"I know what ails you, my friend," Eustace Chapuys says. "I have tried to keep you from this deed, in the hope that a happier solution may be found. You *must* keep silent."

"Speak to Henry," the fox says, "and keep your honour, Thomas."

"Sir… this is none of your business," Chapuys tells the bishop. He crooks a finger, and a man, dressed up, for all the world, like a murdering cutthroat steps from the shadows, and takes the bishop by the elbow. "Let my man, Gomez escort you into the ball."

Stephen Gardiner needs only one glance into the eyes of the Spaniard to know that he should comply. He bows to both men, and allows himself to be urged towards the next set of doors.

"Now, promise me, Archbishop Cranmer… you will not speak to Henry about the queen."

"I am torn, Eustace… torn betwixt honour and duty." The archbishop sees that he is damned either way, and wrings his hands in dismay.

"As God is my witness, you must not speak to Henry about the queen,' the little Savoyard says. "It would mean her immediate death… and the death of others. You must see that?"

"Yes, I understand."

"Then promise?"

"You ask too much of me, Eustace. I am a poor creature,' Cranmer tells him. He is not a brave man, and he does not know which action will cause him the most harm. Tell, or remain silent.

"I ask for you to keep the sanctity of the confessional," Chapuys presses. A man's religion is all he really has in the world to hang on to, and he fears Cranmer will risk his soul, rather than keep Henry in the dark. "You must not speak of it."

"Very well." Cranmer comes to a decision, and raises a hand to his heart. "I swear I shall not speak to the king… nor to any other living soul… about the queen's matter. So help me God."

"You are a good man, Thomas," Chapuys says. "Shall we leave now?"

"And miss the ball?" Cranmer smiles at the ambassador. "Henry expects you now, and he will be amused by your outfit."

"Amused?" It has not occurred to Chapuys that his feathered display is anything other than an accurate portrayal of the fabulous Ostrich bird from the land of the Mussulman. "How so, sir?"

"Oh, never mind," Cranmer says. "I, for my part am going as a Man of God, and that too is a charade."

"The king will ask why you are not at sea," Chapuys muses.

"I shall tell him that I need his permission to leave England… which is the truth. No great lord, either secular or clergy, may leave the country without the king's say so. I must have his word, if not his written permission."

"I see." Chapuys would rather put the man aboard Miriam's cog, and be done with it. "Then that is what you must do, my friend."

Of course, Archbishop Cranmer thinks, if he keeps the secret of the confessional, what need is there to go to Rome at all?

"This Roman business," he asks. "It is all a flummery, is it not… designed to get me out of England?"

"I know not, sir," Chapuys lies. "I think that is a matter for your Foreign Office, and whomsoever is in charge of it these days."

"Richard Cromwell, which tells me everything," Cranmer says. "Now, let us dance a little jig, Eustace, for old time's sake. I think my trip to Rome may yet be postponed!"

8 Masquerade

"Bring Rafe Sadler to me," the king asks, and Sir John Russell goes out into the outer court. Rafe is leaning against a window sill, and flirting with one of the many ladies in waiting. He is a married man, with seven children, but still enjoys the chase, without the capture.

"Sir Rafe," Russell says, "he is asking for you."

"How is his temper?"

"Better. The poppy juice Will gives him is wearing off, but slowly. Until just now, he thought himself dancing with the fairies."

"God save us." Rafe almost crosses himself, but does not. "He is either addled with drugs, or mad with pain. What does he want of me now?"

"He seems to be still confused about the trial." Russell pulls open the inner court door, and announces Rafe's presence.

"Is that you, boy?" Henry asks. "I am in need of your advice."

"At your service, sire."

"How came Norfolk to live this day?" the king asks.

"Sire, he gave proof of his innocence, and you released him."

"Was I duped then?"

"No, sire. You sat in judgement and made a fair decision, based on the evidence offered. That evidence was strongly in his favour."

"What about Weston?" The question comes from nowhere, and Rafe Sadler is caught unawares. "There was no evidence against him, yet I sent him to his death. I am of a like mind about poor Norris too. Found guilty, without real proof. You see what I mean?"

"Sire, they spoke treason against you," Rafe says. "They were both as guilty of it as could be."

"Norfolk is as guilty as sin too, but the *evidence* says otherwise." The king is clearly coming to terms with reality, as the huge doses of poppy juice he has been imbibing start to wear off. He sees, as if from afar, that his actions, of late, have been drastic, and he is temporarily dismayed.

"Your Majesty has acted with the best of intentions at all times," Rafe says to the king. "Weston and the rest are in the past, and they met their end because they had to."

"Were they guilty?"

"The court adjudged them to be, Your Majesty," Rafe explains. "The king can advise, but it is for the courts to decide. You are blameless."

"Yes... I am." Henry rubs his eyes, and calls for wine. "Damn me, but my leg hurts. I need some of Lady Miriam's magical potion. Find Will Draper for me, and bid him bring me a dose at once."

Rafe bows, and makes his way to the outer court, where he searches out his old friend.

"We have a problem with the king," he says, as he comes upon Will and Tom Wyatt.

"Yes, I know, Rafe," Will says. "Cranmer is on the loose."

"He is?" Rafe wonders if this day can get any worse. "Then we are in for a wild time of it, my friends. Henry's mind is clearing from all the potions you have been feeding him. He begins to doubt his actions, and seeks to blame others for his failings. He speaks of Norris and Weston, as if he just now thought them to be wronged."

"It is the poppy, no doubt," Will says. "It eases the pain well enough, but can make a man feel... odd."

"Odd?" Rafe asks. "You must keep him addled, or 'odd' will become something altogether more sinister. The king cannot be at fault. If he starts to question past trials, he will look to blame anyone but himself. Every lord in England will be blamed, and the entire government will grind to a halt."

"It cannot be so bad," Tom Wyatt says. "Look, here comes dear old Chapuys. Let us hope for some better news from his quarter. Master Eustace… how goes it?"

"Success," the Ostrich bird crows to his friends. "I caught Cranmer as he came into the palace, and played upon his morality. The man is torn between two stools, but he has sworn, in the name of God, and with hand on heart, not to speak to Henry about this dangerous matter of the queen."

"Thank God for that," Will Draper says. "On the morrow, we must dispose of Culpeper and Dereham. I shall say we found Cully's grave, and that he died during the plague. As for Francis Dereham… who will even miss him?"

"Not a single soul," the poet tells his friend. "The man is a weasel of a fellow, who looks to live off soft hearted women. I could find you ten who would drive a knife into his black heart, if given the chance."

"Then he must have a fatal fall," Mush Draper says. He is standing in the shadows of a deep alcove, and watching the revellers as they arrive. So few of them are left who ever opposed Tom Cromwell, and the young Jew is pleased at how the years have treated the Austin Friars crowd. "Perhaps we might also arrange for some other accidents?"

Tom Wyatt taps out a beat on the window sill with his fingers:
> *"The great lord trips, and breaks his bones,*
> *and the son goes tumbling after,*
> *one duke slips on some wetted stones,*
> *and the earl hangs from a rafter."*

"Hush, Master Poet," Will Draper cautions. "It is not only Norfolk and Surrey we must tend to, one day. Richard Rich has also played us false. Did he not back both sides, so that he might appear to be the hero of the piece?"

"Then my *Vindicatio* has three more names to scratch out," Mush says.

"Perhaps we should take instructions from our important friend in Antwerp," Will replies. "His is a far wiser head."

"He will advise us to caution," Mush complains. "I could send for Ibrahim, and some of the lads. A couple of accidents, and a robbery gone wrong is all that is needed. Then we have done for them all, and can get on with the running of England once more. The Mijnheer sees greater land reforms, and an adjustment to taxes, so that the rich might pay more to the crown revenues."

"Henry will never let Austin Friars rule him alone," TomWyatt guesses, quite correctly. "He will form a council, and bring in enough conservative sorts to balance us out. Richard, Rafe and you, Will, against Tom Audley, Stephen Gardiner, and the archbishop. We will be mired down again, and unable to reach a sensible decision about anything."

"True. We need one man to come to the fore. As did Cardinal Wolsey in his day, and Lord Mortimer in days gone by." Will Draper sighs. "Even another Tom Cromwell would do us nicely. I wish we could somehow resurrect him."

"You forget something, my friend," the poet reminds him. "Each of those men fell from grace. Wolsey was disgraced, and died of a broken heart, whilst the other two went to the block."

"Yes, the king can be a harsh master," Rafe says. "He awaits you now, Will, and begs for a drop of the magical juice. He is suffering."

"We must be careful. Miriam tells me that it can drive a man quite mad, if he imbibes too much."

"Tell Henry that," Rafe replies. Will

searches in the pouch at his waist, and brings forth a small phial made of horn, and with a cork stopper keeping in the precious liquid. He holds it up between finger and thumb. It is all that keeps the king from going into his terrible rages, and Miriam pays almost fifty pounds in gold for so small an amount.

"Then let me dose him, and ensure we all have a good evening," the Examiner declares. "Mush, stay close to Henry, if the archbishop should approach him, and make sure that he keeps his word."

"Do I kill him if he speaks out of place?" Mush asks.

"It will be too late then" Tom Wyatt explains. "For that which is, must then be was, and once it is was, it may never be is again."

"I wish you were 'was', you annoying fellow," says Mush and he gives his friend a playful shove. "You mean that the horse would have already bolted?"

"Just so. If Tom Cranmer speaks, we can do nothing about it… but in speaking, he will have condemned his immortal soul to Hell. I doubt the archbishop will risk hellfire, even for his king."

"Thank God it is not down to Stephen Gardiner, Mush says, "for the Bishop of

Winchester would sell his own mother to the devil, if it would advance him."

"Stephen is keen to keep in with Henry," the poet replies, "but he would not go so far. He knows it would earn our enmity, and he fears Austin Friars anger more than the kings, I think."

"Let us hope so," says Mush. "He has a quick wit and a smooth tongue for a priest. I think he might well end up better advanced than any of us!"

*

The king has changed his mind about being the Sun God, and his four dressers are busy arraying him in his new choice of costume. He is clothed in six yards of fine white linen, draped about him in a most regal fashion.

About his ample waist is a golden girdle, inset with dozens of precious rubies and sapphires, which is laced up as tightly as they dare. A chaplet of golden laurel leaves sits upon his head, and in his right hand, he carries a golden lightening bolt.

"Who am I?" he asks as Will Draper comes into the throne room. Will thinks the poppy potion is still confusing him, so answers in kind.

"You are Henry, King of England,

sire," he replies. "Are you quite well?"

"No, Will… *who…am… I?*" He does a clumsy pirouette, and holds out his dangerous looking thunderbolt.

"Oh, yes I see." Will considers the ridiculous figure the king cuts, and tries to imagine what heroic personage he is meant to be. "Thor?"

"Who?"

"The old Norse God of thunder, sire," he says. "Or even Woden himself… the king of all the gods."

"No, do not think Norse," Henry replies. "Think on a grander scale."

"Roman?" Will guesses.

"Oh, piss on the bastard Romans, my friend. Greater still."

"Then you are one of the gods of the Greeks?" Will chances, and Henry is pleased at being recognised as such with so little prompting.

"Make sure they all know that I am Jove," he tells one of his dressers. "Then, if any other has dared come as me, they can bugger off and change into a costume more meet to their station in this court."

"Yes sire." The young man disappears to warn the court, and save the blushes of anyone who might have chosen badly.

"You have it?" Henry asks, once they are alone, and Will produces the poppy concoction.

"Let me mix some into your wine, sire," he says. "Then you might jig the night away.'

"There is a new French dance," the king says. "One must hop upon every fourth step, and kiss the lady's hand. I shall use it to test out which of the queen's girls look kindly upon me."

"Will not the queen be present, Your Majesty?" asks Will.

"I doubt she will last an hour," Henry says. "Though her headaches have subsided somewhat, since Lady Jane came back to court. I hope I have not made a mistake in forgiving that damned woman, Will. I only did it for Dick Cromwell's sake, you know."

"An act of true friendship, Hal," Will says. He chances using the king's first name, so as to test the waters.

"Yes, you and he are my best friends, save for Charles, of course. I am thinking about a new Privy Council, and would have Dick and my dear Lord Suffolk on it. I even thought about choosing you, Will, but there would be dangerous whisperings."

"Whisperings, Hal?"

"Yes, damn it. About your past life," Henry says. "The rumours are hurtful, old friend. They speak of a dubious parentage... a Roman priest involved... and a murder."

"Oh, those silly tales," Will replies, with a smile. "My father died when I was but a year old, and the old village priest took me under his wing, and taught me to read and write. That is why I have good Latin and French, sire."

"Hal... we are alone, and so I am your Hal, as I am your Will... no, that is not so. You are my Will and you are to call me Hal, or Harry. This poppy drink is powerful stuff, my friend. Tell me about the priest you killed. No, do not deny it. I see it in your eyes. Did he deserve it?"

"He was selling himself, Hal," Will says. "He would refuse to say mass, or even bury a poor soul, without taking all the coins poor people had. He thought to rob me, and refused to shrive my dead family... so I cut his throat for him."

"Good fellow." Henry waves his lightning bolt, menacingly. "Now we have rid England of his sort for good. I am the church, and I will not tolerate... I will not... er... what was I saying?"

"How much you want to dance with

all the pretty girls," Will says. "You feel happy, and your leg is less painful, is it not?"

"Why yes, that is so." Henry even does a heavy jig. "Let us get to it, my boy, and be damned to them all. On the morrow, I will elevate you to a baronetcy, and place you on the Privy Council."

"Your Majesty does me a great honour," Will Draper says. It is what he has hoped for, and now, he has it within his grasp. His palatial Draper House is on the river, close to the Templar's Church, and he has a mind to become the Baron of the Inner Temple, or simply... Lord Templar. Lady Templar, he thinks, will be very pleased at the further increase in their stature. "Shall we dance?"

*

"You look pathetic," the Duke of Norfolk tells his son. The Earl of Surrey is encased in the back half of a cow, complete with udders. "It was bad enough you being a horse's arse, but this is ridiculous."

"Rizz is the front half," Surrey explains. "I know you dislike him, but he is in favour with the king, and that is good enough for me. Now we are found innocent, we can start to gain our revenge over those swine who dared charge us."

"You blithering idiot," the Duke of Norfolk says. "We were as guilty as sin. It is only my forward planning that has saved our necks for us. Now you want to go off, seeking revenge. I forbid it, do you hear me? You will not make a move against our enemies, unless I approve it. Do you understand, child?"

"Yes, sir."

"Good. Then be a cow's back end, if you must, whilst I am an altogether superior creature. What say you, my poor idiot boy?"

"Perfect, as usual, sir," Surrey tells his father. "I doubt anyone else will think to dress up as Jove. I like the thunderbolt."

Surrey is being mendacious, for he has already taken action against those he believes have tried to do him down. A good time shall be had by all, but after the ball is over, and Will Draper leaves the palace, a dozen men are in waiting for him at the riverfront, and they have explicit instructions.

*

The evening meal is started early, and restricted to just a dozen courses, so that the dancing might start all the sooner. The main courses, a roast boar, spit roasted geese, and a side of beef, are set amid a range of game pies, custard tarts and fancy marzipan figurines, and the whole is washed down with good Italian wine, and excellent Kentish ale.

Candles, expensive wax ones, rather than the cheaper and smellier tallow sort, are lit in embrasures all around the walls, and two huge chandeliers are lowered, and lit. Each great circlet of iron holds a hundred and fifty candles, and the combined light thrown off is enough to illuminate the dance floor.

The courtiers are not ones for showing much imagination, so the great hall is occupied by no less than twelve 'fiersome bandit chiefs', three 'fairy princes', four 'Turcoman Lords', one man dressed up as a bush, and many more with nothing to conceal their identities, other than a small mask, or a few pieces of lace hanging from their caps. There is also the obligatory horse, and a rather ridiculous looking cow with huge udders and a mouth that opens and closes on a string.

Tom Wyatt is clothed in a wide doublet, with long pieces of velvet hanging down to the ground. He delights in telling the ladies that they are bedroom drapes, and he is the bed. It is but a short step to invite them to lie down on his well plumped mattress.

His wit, and his reputation work well for him, and he slips away twice for a quick tryst in a side room. It is during one of these little escapades that he sees Archbishop

Cranmer pacing up and down, outside the great hall.

"Have courage, sir," the poet says to him, in passing. "Henry is in a good mood. Just go up to him, and beg his leave to travel to Rome. Nothing more."

"Yes, you are right. Faint hearts never win anything, young man. Thomas, is that you?"

The poet removes his head from Lady Dorothy's ample bosom, and smiles, beatifically at his godfather.

"The same, sir. A simple sinner, about his simple sins," he confesses. "Shall I escort you in?"

"If the lady will excuse you," the archbishop says, stiffly. "Be sure that the sins of the flesh will find you out, Lady Dorothy."

"Love is patient, love is kind. It does not envy, it does not boast, it is not proud." The poet sees that the archbishop does not quite place the words. "One Corinthians, verse thirteen, sir. Love is not something to be punished for. You might bear that in mind, when thinking about the queen, and her silly, misunderstood words to you."

"I have given my word, young Thomas, and more... I swore it, hand on heart," Cranmer snaps. "Not one utterance shall pass my lips." He touches the cross hanging at his neck, and repeats himself. "Not a single word, you knave."

"Then let us make our way through this press of humanity, Uncle Cranmer, and beard the king upon his great throne."

*

The evening's dancing has begun with a stately Pavane, which is little more than a slow walk back and forth, with the odd bow and curtsey thrown in. It is suitable for the older gentlemen of the court, for they need not do anything more than stroll, and show off their finery to the ladies. At one point, a capering cow tries to join the dance, but it is despatched by Mush Draper, who kicks it brutally up the arse.

Surrey gives a yelp of pain, whilst Rizz laughs. He is the front of the animal, and out of harms way. He guides his rear end past several more gentlemen, who are all aware of whom it is in the back end, and each one lands a kick of varying degrees on Surrey's inviting posterior.

"Damn me, are they doing that on purpose, Rizz?" the earl asks, despite his face being muffled in his comrade's rear.

"Not at all, old fellow," Rizz replies. "It is just the custom. Why, I dare say that the horse is getting a similar treatment."

"Oh, very well then," Surrey decides. "If it is the way of things… but did you see father's face when he saw how the king was dressed?"

"By Gad, yes!" Rizz is enjoying himself enormously. "Two Jove's in the same ballroom, and one of them a king. Poor Norfolk went under the table, and came out as a Roman senator. Quick thinking, what?"

"One side, you silly creature!" The Archbishop of Canterbury wishes to get to the king, and no farmyard animal can stay his progress. He is unable to resist the urge, and boots the unfortunate cow up the arse to make it move along.

"Oh, you bastard," Surrey squeaks, and the clergyman is surprised at where the blasphemy issues from.

"Watch out behind," Rizz warns, and he emits a most noxious fart. Surrey holds his breath and curses his luck. No matter how hard he tries to work things in his favour, he always seems to end up as the hind end of one creature or another.

The elegantly danced Pavane gives way to a '*Cinque Pas*' which is another slow parade, involving a little five step shuffle of the feet. Henry enjoys both slow dances, and uses them to view those ladies who are likely to be available. It is the custom for those who are spoken for to cast down their eyes, whilst the gamer ones smile back, quite brazenly.

Unfortunately, Queen Catherine is feeling quite well, and wants to dance the night away. She makes a great show of staying close to her husband, and takes his hand for the energetic Galliard. She hops around him, and admires his own little leaps with renewed love in her eyes.

"Sire, you dance most beautifully," she says. "I hope to see such gallant moves again later, in the comfort of my own chamber."

"What's that, madam?" Henry strains to hear over the music. Catherine, who has been cold towards him for weeks, and usually has a sickly headache, is now being most forward. "What of your throbbing head?"

"Lady Miriam has given me a powder that eases all ills, sire," Catherine says. "Now I look forward to some other thing throbbing. Let us not tarry overlong at the dancing. I have a longing that will only be satisfied by the touch of a real man. Oh, the thought of what I want to do to you is… almost sinful."

"Almost, madam?" Henry asks with a sly wink.

"Almost, sire. For is not such a thing expected between man and wife?"

"It is. Oh, Catherine, you make an old man very happy."

"There is no old man here, sire," Catherine says to him, looking about her. "I see nothing, but great experience, and wonderful skill. Tonight I shall lie with Jove, and like Europa, beneath her bull, I shall prove fertile."

"By God, yes!" Henry is delighted. the poppy juice makes him feel invincible, and his young wife is simpering for his love. He cares not that she has muddled her myths, and cultures, for she is the most beautiful girl in the hall, and he is her lucky husband.

"Come, sire... the Volta," a voluptuous Mother Earth says, and pulls him back onto the floor. Henry smiles like a child, as Miriam whirls him around, in a frenetic spin that borders on the lascivious. Hands touch, and the gentlemen are permitted liberties that would usually earn them a sharp slap. Miriam's magnificent bosoms almost leap of their own accord, and keep the king distracted for the full duration of the dance.

At last Henry is allowed to stop dancing, and he staggers over to his throne, and sits down. He is the happiest man in

Christendom, and his world is complete. His wife adores him, his enemies have been given a scare, and Will Draper is set to bring the Privy Council under his thumb for his king.

"Will shall rule the council, and I shall rule him," he says aloud. Then he realises that he is talking to himself, and looks about to see if anyone has noticed. There is no-one near, save a rather tatty looking cow. The king grins, and in time honoured tradition, he kicks it up the arse. Surrey lets out a string of curses, the gist of which is that he 'will gut the pox ridden bastard who did that'. The curse, coming from the cow's rear as it does, makes for a surreal effect.

Henry finds this hilarious. In fact everything is suddenly hilarious, and he cannot help but laugh. For good measure, he lands a second kick, and finds the Earl of Surrey struggling to escape through the ragged udders.

"You bastard arsehole!" he cries, and is about to fumble out the dagger he has secreted in his doublet, when he recognises the king. "Pardon me, sire, I was addressing the fellow that was behind you. Good dance?"

"Excellent, young Surrey," the king tells him. "To think, but this morning, I was going to have your head on a spike. How I did smile at such a thing."

"Yes, so amusing, sire," Surrey replies. He steps clear of the wreckage of the cow, and bows. "Both father and I were so pleased. Innocence is always a good reason not to cut a fellow's head off, don't you think?"

"Ha!" Henry finds this remark to be funny too, and he slaps Surrey on the back, so hard, that he actually staggers forward, and falls onto his knees. "Up, lad. No formality here, what? Tell that father of yours that I am still wondering how he escaped the block. Tell him that the next time he irritates me, I shall have him fed to my lions... alive... like the Romans. Tell him I shall enjoy the spectacle."

"I shall, sire," Surrey says. "Though then, who will you have to vent your rage on?"

"Oh, I'll find someone," Henry says. "I am on a promise this night, young Harry. What say you to that?"

"Does the queen know?" Surrey says, and the king stops laughing.

"What say you?"

"Sire?"

"You imply sir... you actually dare to *imply*?"

"Only that your way with the ladies is

world famed, sire," Surrey tells him. "I can scarce keep up with your conquests."

"You little creep," says Henry. "I suggest you bugger off, before I change my mind, and have your gizzards drawn out of your backside."

"At your command, Your Majesty," Surrey replies, and slides away. As he is still attached to the front half of the cow, Rizz is dragged backwards, complaining that he cannot either see or hear a thing.

"Loathsome little turd," the king pronounces.

"I beg your pardon, sire?" The archbishop, accompanied by Tom Wyatt, and with Mush Draper lingering nearby, is shocked at being addressed thus.

"Not you, Cranmer," Henry tells the cleric. "By God, but I would not think to address my most senior churchman in so mean a manner. You are my man, sir. Are you enjoying the ball, my old friend?"

'My old friend' is a good start, Cranmer thinks. He bows serenely, then offers his hand to be kissed, as is the usual custom. Henry takes it, and examines the great ruby ring that is the archbishop's insignia of high office.

"Nice ring, Tom." Better still, the

archbishop thinks. I am Tom now, and the time is upon him. All he need do is ask for official permission to travel. "How can I help you?"

"Sire. I require your permission to travel abroad."

"Oh, where to?"

"Why, to Rome, Your Majesty."

"Rome... why would you want to go to that piss stained dump of a place?" Henry asks.

"To negotiate with the Po... that is, I mean... the Bishop of Rome."

"Negotiate?" Henry frowns at this. He recalls something about a Papal request, but it has gone from his mind now. "Out of the question. That corrupt fellow excommunicated me. The slack dog must realise that I have done the same to him by now."

"Quite so, sire," Thomas Cranmer says. "You excommunicated the whole Roman Catholic world last year... citing their heresy. Then you *do not* wish me to go to Rome?"

"No, it's a bloody stupid idea," Henry decides. "Write to Rome instead. Tell them that *I* run the church in England, and that *I* intend supporting every protestant prince in

Europe against them. Tell them, Tom, and be damned to them, and to their Latin bound ideology."

"Your Highness, that might cause another rift," Cranmer says. "Might I not suggest you let Richard Cromwell write the letter... or Sir Rafe Sadler?"

"Good idea. That is what I pay them for, I suppose. Yes, let them take the blame if it comes to war, or some other such mischief. Anything else?"

"No, sire. Nothing at all." The archbishop sees the relief on Tom Wyatt's face, and Mush Draper moving away with a satisfied smile on his face. He bows to Henry, and holds out his hand again. This time, Henry leans forward to kiss the ring, and Thomas Cranmer clasps the king's hands in both of his.

"May the Good Lord bless you, and guide you in the difficult times to come, sire. May your goodness and mercy cast a light over us all. Amen."

"Yes...quite... amen, old fellow," the king says. "No need to take on so. It's only a letter... and it will save you from weeks of sea sickness, what?"

Archbishop Cranmer backs away, bows again, then disappears into the crowd.

Mush, Will and Tom Wyatt all breath a sigh of relief. The danger has passed, and they can get on with tidying up the loose ends.

On the morrow, Barnaby Fowler will receive a message concerning Thomas Culpeper, and Queen Catherine's life will be safe. Tonight, the queen will do her duty, with enthusiasm, and make the king content.

"Come, Will… dance with me." Miriam Draper, looking wonderful in her revealing 'Mother Earth' costume wants her husband to spend time with her, and now, he can. The danger is averted, and all is well with the world.

"Yes, let us all make merry," Will declares. "Mush, Rafe, Tom, find partners. Let us dance the night away. We have come through the shadow of the valley of death this night, and we are unscathed."

"Amen," Rafe Sadler replies. "May we now all be in for a quieter life."

*

"Bloody odd fellow," Henry mutters to himself. He has never liked having priests about him, because they remind him of all his sins… confessed to, or not. "How can you enjoy yourself, with a damned archbishop in the room?"

"Bloody bishops." This is from a

Roman Senator, who is losing his wrapping, piece by piece.

"Norfolk, is that you, old fellow?" Henry frowns at the half naked man beside him. "I thought you were dead."

"Not I, sire," Norfolk replies. "I wager it was some other fellow who merely looks like me."

"What?" Henry thinks on this, then grins. "Ha! A jest, old friend. Why, I am glad I did not kill you this morning. I am running short of friends these days."

"Yes, only your enemies multiply, sire." Norfolk chances, but Henry is not having any of it.

"If you now mean to dun Will Draper… then have a care Norfolk, for I am minded to make him into nobility on the morrow."

"A good idea, sire, for I have always resented having to cross swords with a man of such low birth. Son of a Catholic priest… and murderer of his own father."

"What's that?" Henry is aghast at this. "His own father? How mean you, Norfolk?"

"His father was a priest, and he murdered a priest," Norfolk says. "It seems odd that he should know two such men. Is it not more likely that he simply murdered his own father to conceal his almost satanic birthright?"

"By God, but I shall change my mind in a moment, Your Lordship, and have your head cut off right here, whilst the Volta still goes on. Out of my sight, and do not return until you can come up with a less lame story than that. Be off, you insolent issue of a Turk's arse!"

Norfolk, who is as thick skinned as any man in England, retreats, and wonders how next to undermine his enemies. He is running low on ideas, and cannot see that he is a spent force.

The king sits down on his throne, and considers the last few minutes, and their import. Norfolk is a shadow of his former self, and can be pushed to one side. Henry will have those troops of Norfolk's still in London placed under the command of Charles Brandon. In this way, his greatest friend will command more than half the soldiers in England.

Then there was the disquieting business with the Archbishop of Canterbury. Why would the fellow insist on speaking with him about so trivial a matter as a mission to Rome, and why in the midst of a revel that was not to his taste?

Curious, if nothing else, Henry muses. It was as if Cranmer wished to impart something of importance to him, but was restrained in some way. The man has no love for Rome, Henry muses, so why even entertain the idea of going there? The king has forgotten, because of his poppy induced state, that it is Richard Cromwell who has set this ball rolling, and that it was he who manoeuvred him into sending Thomas Cranmer abroad.

"Bloody strange," Henry says, again, and the queen goes flying by, in the arms of one of his young squires. He smiles, because it is he who will be holding her come bedtime. Not some lame excuse of a young pup. This makes him think of Thomas Culpeper then, and he resolves to demand his reappearance, the next time he sees Will Draper. Dear Cully is missed, and Heneage is a poor substitute as his 'privy man'.

"Rough hands" The words come out so loudly that a passing horse stops in its tracks. Henry hands out the customary kick to the rear end, and Sir Thomas Heneage grunts in pain as his own head is rammed into the rear of the horse's front.

The rapid change in the king's wife has been effected by Miriam Draper and her magic potions, and by Lady Jane Boleyn, who seems to have a soothing effect on Catherine. Whatever the cause, he is grateful for the change in his wife's behaviour, and shall take full advantage of it this very night… if he remains sober enough.

Henry is aware that he still has only one son to come after him, and that a sudden fever, or an unexpected accident in the joust, will leave him with nothing but daughters. If he can give another boy to Catherine, things will be more stable, and the Tudor line shall be assured for another hundred years.

Tom Wyatt is standing on one of the tables, and proclaiming a rude ditty about a proud sailor's daughter from Tangier, who enjoyed drinking a beer, whilst Will Draper is tiring his wife out on the dance floor. The dancers have dwindled now to a handful, and the obliging squire bows to Catherine, and slips away to meet his own lover. The queen sees Henry looking, and gives him a saucy curtsey. It is a promise for things to come, he thinks.

"Damn me," Henry says, and he strikes his favourite pose… hands clenched into big, meaty fists, and placed on his broad hips, "but it is a fine life, and no mistake!"

"Life is for living, and is so sweet,

but treat it badly and she is fleet,
each moment we pass, if ill spent,
will send us down to a hot descent."

Sir Thomas Wyatt is down from his table top for a moment, and whispers his silly little couplet into Henry's ear. The king ponders on the meaning of it, and thinks it to be some kind of a warning to him.

"You seek to warn me against good living, Master poet?" he asks.

"I seek only to entertain you, Your Majestickness."

"That is not a word, is it?"

"It is now, sire," Wyatt replies, rather drunkenly. "For we poets are the blacksmiths of the spoken word. We heat the letters in our fires, and hammer them out on the anvil of truth. Let me invent such words as might adorn a king."

"You are a dunderhead, Tom," the king replies, affectionately. He is in the best mood he has ever experienced, and prepared to love his fellow man with arms held wide. "Has a king ever had such loving friends?"

"Your Majestickosity does you credit, sire," Wyatt continues. "You are, without a doubt … a man of rare abilities… a man of his age. Has ever a kingdom been ruled by so benign a ruler? Why, save for a few minor upsets, we have all lived happily under your benign thrall."

"Minor upsets?" Henry is about to realise that the poet is luring him into something, when a rather scruffy looking creature, not unlike a half plucked goose springs forward, and grasps Wyatt by the arm. The extraordinary bird then attempts to pull the poet away from the king.

"Come away from the king, sir," the bird chirps. "You are drunk, and not fit to stand."

""I know that voice," Henry says, and he snatches at the p*apier-mâché* beak that covers the lower face. "You are no ostrich, sir… but a frog. Little Chapuys, as I live and breathe, and ready for the oven, I see."

"Your Majesty's sense of humour does you credit, sire," Chapuys says.

"Your *Majesticknouses* sense of anything," Wyatt mutters, and gets a sharp dig into his ribs from the little Savoyard.

Henry has a heady mix of poppy juice and wine inside him, and the world seems to be an unreal place to him now. It seems quite in order for him to be surrounded by a talking horse, giant ostriches, and surly poets, who think it is perfectly alright to dun their king.

"You are drunk, sir," he tells the poet.

"Tomorrow you will be sober."

"And tomorrow, you will still be king," Tom Wyatt replies. "Why do we not exchange our rolls? You can write my poetry... for you have a good eye for a rhyme, and I shall rule England... for I have a good eye for justice."

"Why ever not, my dear friend?" Henry thinks now that some clever jest is afoot, and he is intoxicated enough to play along with it. "I imagine that a poet's life is a pleasurable one."

"Why yes, sire, it is. You but whisper 'dove' and 'love' into a soft white ear, and ladies fall into your arms, like apples from the tree. As king, I would just *demand* their favours. Then there is the joy of being paid an Angel or two for the labour of a week. Again, as king I would simply take what I wanted. Am I qualified, Hal?"

"Come away, sir," Chapuys insists, and at that moment a gentleman who is dressed up as a cutthroat of the worst kind appears, and escorts the poet back to his table.

"My sincere apologies, sire," the ostrich says to the king. "Our poetical friend cannot take his wine. He meant nothing by his jesting... nothing against you, that is."

"He hints that I am not a good king,

Master Chapuys."

"Good kings seldom live long, Your Majesty," Chapuys replies, diplomatically. "Is it not the clever ones... the pragmatic ones, who rule the longest?"

"Then I am an unkind monarch?"

"No, sire. You love your people well, but that does not mean you cannot be a stern father to them. Tom Wyatt merely points out that you have to be different from other men. You cannot live by their rules."

"Ah, dear Erasmus..."

"Eustace, sire... like the saint."

"Yes, of course. Eustace. It is plain that you understand me well. The emperor made a good choice when he sent you to me. Do we pay you?"

"Pay me, sire?" Chapuys is quite shocked at the suggestion. "I am the emperor's man, and it would not be meet that I took money from the English purse."

"Nonsense. I shall speak to Rafe Sadler, and have you placed on one of our pension funds. A couple of thousand marks a year will not go amiss."

"Thank you, sire." Chapuys sees that the king's eyes are glazing over, and that he has little sense of anything that is being said.

"Think nothing of it, Master Ostrich,"

Henry tells him. "Anything else?"

"I could do with my own palace to live in," Chapuys says. "Perhaps Hampton Court?"

"See Dick Cromwell, and he will see to the lease."

"And perhaps you might give me an island or two?" The little diplomat is having a fine time of it. "Cyprus would be nice. Oh, and a thousand pounds in gold... each month?"

"Of course. Consider it... con...oh, I feel odd. Am I right in thinking that there is a lobster making love to a mermaid yonder sir?"

"They are just kissing, sire," Chapuys says. "Might I call your attendants, and they can help you to your ease?"

"When I was a boy, they called me the 'spare prince' behind my back," the king says. "Well, I've shown them, haven't I, my dearest little froggy?"

"Yes, sire. You have shown the world. Now, pray sit, before you fall down."

*

"Lady Miriam ben Mordecai Draper, Baroness of the Templars," Mush says into his sister's ear, and she sees the mischief in his eyes.

"Then how long before Sir Moses Draper becomes Earl Moses of the Bulrushes?" she replies. "We have not fared badly, have we brother?"

"Not at all, sister." Mush looks about him, at the last few dancers, whose legs are finally giving out under them. "I see some thirsty courtiers, and they will be searching for wine."

"Let them search as much as they wish," Miriam says. "I am engaged to supply the viands and the drink, at a cost not to exceed seven hundred pounds. They must move on to beer, if I am to clear my usual profit."

"Four hundred on the seven?" Mush asks, and Miriam nods.

"The king spends enough on one dance to support ten gentlemen in luxury, for a year. If I can pare down the costs, the margin is mine to keep. Sometimes, as with Master Cromwell's wake, I lose money. Seeing our illustrious *Mijnheer Cornelis* to his grave cost me over two hundred and fifty pounds. Not counting the bribes that Will handed out to all and sundry."

"How is the Draper Company faring, sister?" Mush has no real interest in business, but he feels as though he should show willing, for Miriam's sweet sake. She has spent over twelve years toiling away at her financial empire, and her menfolk take it for granted. "Are my shares prospering?"

"Why this sudden interest, Mush?" Miriam asks. "You hold a thousand shares in out venture, out of a hundred thousand. Pru Beckshaw tells me that she can sell them tomorrow for twenty five pounds a piece."

"Then I am worth twenty five thousand in shares alone?"

"In a way," Miriam replies, and takes a deep breath. Such niceties about commerce are beyond most Englishmen, who prefer to hunt foxes and deer, or go to the better whore houses. "Your one hundredth part brings you in eighteen thousand a year, mostly from trade. We also own tanners yards, ale houses, houses to lease, and two ship's chandlers in Yarmouth and Bristol. These produce a steady income, which we use to oil the wheels of government."

"Bribes?"

"No, not bribes. Gifts to men who can help us. Now Wriothesley is the coming man with Henry, he must have a thousand a year, and Rafe's corps of clerks are kept honest with an extra hundred a year on their salaries."

"What about the Portuguese vineyards?" The question is insinuated into the conversation almost as a by your leave, but Lady Miriam smiles, and shakes her head at her brother's lack of cunning.

"You want to leave England again?" she asks. Mush has ever wanted to travel to the Holy Land, and he is not getting any younger.

"I could visit the Portuguese interests, and then go on to see how our agents in Puglia and Cyprus are faring."

"Then go on to Jerusalem?" Miriam asks.

"Why not?"

"Because you may never come back," she says, honestly. "I could not bear to lose you, Mush. Besides, my husband needs you. He cannot handle England by himself. The king is going to raise him up to the peerage, and place him at the head of his new Privy Council."

"I overheard about the baronetcy, but as for Will leading the council …you are sure of this?" Mush sees that all the world will be there for the taking. "Does our friend in Antwerp know?"

"Not yet," Miriam tells him. "It has only just been spoken of, by Henry. I shall see

Kel, or tell the master on my next visit to the *Palais de Juis*. I am there twice a month, these days."

"Norfolk will not like it, of course," Mush says.

"The duke is not to be on the council," Mush's sister says. "Will is to be the king's voice, with Richard, Rafe Sadler and the Attorney General taking pride of place. Then Archbishop Cranmer and Bishop Gardiner will make up the religious wing, with Tom Audley owning his place as Lord Chancellor. Beyond these seven men, there will be a secondary group who must take on the burden of office. Barnaby Fowler is to command these fellows, and he will have the best legal minds in England at his finger tips."

"What about Charles Brandon?" Mush asks. "He will feel slighted, considering that he is the king's childhood friend."

"My Lord Suffolk is to have a special rank at court," Miriam says. "He is to be the king's private gentleman, as is Rizz Wriothesley, and other nobles. It gives them high rank, but no actual power. Will shall tell him that he is to be commander in chief of the army of all England, and he will not have time for council duties too. The duke will accept this, for it is true. He will have a dozen garrisons to keep up to the mark, and all of the Tower's ordnance."

"And you have worked all this out in the last hour?" Mush asks his sister, and she giggles.

"Of course not. I and our Dutch friend have been considering it for months. It was plain to see that Norfolk was about to lose his place, and that the Privy Council must crumble away. We reason thus: who can keep Henry's enemies in check? My husband. Henry has no choice in the matter. He cannot leave Norfolk in place, and the Earl of Surrey is a fuddle brained prat-a-dandy. Nor can he let the politicians take control. They would run away if the French but farted at them. No, it has to be my Will. He will do a good job, and we will all prosper."

*

"*Listen well to my sorry tale,*
of how I took to good strong ale,
and tarried long o'er maiden's virtue,
wallowing in their wicked stew."

Tom Wyatt declaims from his table top perch, but few are listening now. Only one man is attentive, and he fancies himself to be a critic of the first order.

"Bollocks," Rizz says, from the wreckage of his cow costume. "You use 'stew' in the vernacular, Master Poet… to mean 'bawdy house' do you not?"

"I do, Sir Rizz, you benighted little turd… which I can rhyme with 'bird' or 'word'." Wyatt bows to his tiny audience.

"Then you seek to couple it to 'virtue'," Rizz says. "Might not it be better to use 'head' as in maidenhead, and put it with 'bed'?"

"Are you trying to thoroughly annoy me, Rizz?" the poet asks.

"Of course," Rizz replies. "Speak with Will Draper for me, Tom. Ask him to offer me an honourable place on the new council, rather than some post that involves cleaning out the jakes."

"He does not trust you, Rizz," the poet says, "and with very good reason."

"I can keep a secret."

"Really?" TomWyatt is tired. He has courted danger by annoying the king, and now he is ready for some lady's bed. "Prove it. Tell me what you keep so secret… and I shall be the judge."

"Thomas Culpeper," Rizz says.

"What of him?" Wyatt says, his voice dropping to a menacing whisper. "He has gone missing, these last few weeks."

"He is living at old Weston's place,"

Rizz says, just as softly. "Can it be that Will Draper wants him out of the way? The king would be angry, if he knew. Cully kept from the king… and his new queen."

"What do you want to keep your mouth shut, Rizz?" the poet asks.

"Just Will Draper's trust, Rizz says to the poet. "I have known for some time, yet stayed silent. Speak up for me, Tom."

"You will remain silent?"

"I swear, upon my honour." Rizz does not see any benefit in telling Henry about Culpeper's strange hiding away, and thinks he will do better under the Austin Friars wing. "Though Henry is going mad with worry about the little bastard. It seems he cannot do without the fellow. You know he is mad, don't you?"

The king is mad?" The poet thinks now about Henry's strange behaviour this very evening. "Are you sure?"

"No, Tom Culpeper is mad," Rizz says to the poet. "He talks to himself, and utters the most ridiculous rubbish one could imagine. He sends gifts to all the great men at court, and thinks them to be his friends. I think he has some plot in mind, but he is the only plotter. It is in his mind alone."

"Then he is quite harmless," Wyatt

says.

"Just so, Master Poet… but then I ask myself… why does Will Draper have him locked out of sight? What can it be that makes the general so nervous of the man?"

"You had best leave it there, Rizz," the poet says. "I shall speak to Will for you."

"Good man," Rizz says, with a cheeky grin. "You are rather drunk, sir… so will you remember to keep your promise?"

"I am never as drunk as I look, my friend," Tom Wyatt replies. "My word is my bond."

"That is enough for me then, my friend. May Master Cully's silly little secret remain so."

"Amen," the poet says, and falls off the table with a great crash. He bounces up, as if it is a usual occurrence, and puts it down to him taking God's name in vain.

"Are you hurt?" Rizz asks.

"Of course I am," Wyatt replies with a wicked grin. "No one applauded!"

9 Two Notes

"Will shall make a fine king's counsellor," Mush says, loyally.

"The only bar is his low birth, and the stupid rumours about his fathering," Miriam tells her brother.

"You know he is the son of a priest, do you not?" Mush says. "He also killed another priest."

"Two priests," Miriam replies. "A rogue who tried to shame his dead family, when he was seventeen, and another fellow… Father Dominic, an Irishman… in the north, who was preaching sedition."

"Ah, yes, I forgot that one," Mush says. "It was when he met John Beckshaw, I think. He cut the man's head off, with a single blow, and sent the rioters packing."

"That is so," Miriam explains, "and his birthright is no secret. My agents inform me that Will is the son of a Scottish farm worker, who came south from Stirling, with his master. The master, a minor laird of the MacLeish clan, died of the plague a year later, and left Angus Draper stranded. He indented himself to a yeoman farmer near Chester, for six years, and took a wife. They had two children, before Angus died in an accident.

The widow only survived because the village priest took her in, as his housekeeper."

"The fellow who taught Will to write, and chatter away in Latin?"

"Yes… Father Gwyllam. He was like a father to Will, until he was moved to Wales, and a new man put in his place." Miriam sighs. "It was an ill starred action. The new man was a rogue, and he dishonoured Will's dead mother and sister. So, Will killed him, and ran away to join the army in Ireland."

"Is there a point to this happy tale, sister?"Mush asks.

"Yes, there is," his sister tells him. "Those great men … great through an accident of birth… will resent Will's history, and seek to bring him down. I cannot let that happen. Will Draper, Lord Templar of England, must be guarded by my best people, and that means you, my dear brother. You must be ever at his side, and ready to defend him against those who would see him low."

"I cannot do it alone," Mush says, as his thoughts of a sacred trip to Jerusalem fade once again.

"I have already engaged Ibrahim to act as your man," Miriam says, "along with a dozen other cutthroats. All goes to plan, brother, and we are soon to enter into a time of prosperity and peace, not seen in England during our lifetime."

Mush Draper sees that his future is not his own; has *never* been his own, and that Tom Cromwell and his sister are pulling all of the strings, like a pair of benign puppet masters. He must dance to their tune, as usual.

All of Thomas Cromwell's enemies are either dead, or ruined, and Will's old master shall rule from afar, without either let, or hinderance. Miriam is his good right arm, and heir to his legacy of making England into the greatest power on land and sea.

"Then the Holy places must wait," Mush says. "How can I leave, when England is soon to be managed by a Jewish housewife, and a man who has been dead this long time past? I shall tell Isabella to unpack her clothes again."

"She is not here tonight?"

"No, we thought it best not."

"She is ill, brother?"

"No, Miriam… she is with child."

"You meant not to tell me?"

"It is our third time at the well," Mush says. "The other two did not take hold, and she was greatly upset by their loss… as was I."

"How far along is she?"

"Four months," Mush confesses. "I meant to leave her with her family in Venice, and travel on alone."

"She must take to her bed, and rest," Miriam says. "Get her through the next month, and the child will be safe."

"I wish to be a father," the young Jew says. It is something he thinks will make him whole, like declaring his faith, or going to the holy shrines. "If God grants me a child, I will become a better man, sister."

"You are good enough for me now," Miriam tells him. "Let it be a daughter, to balance my own boys, and so that our blood might be passed down, as prescribed in our Holy Books. Life is getting better with each passing day, Mush… and I believe our futures are to be both profitable, and secure."

"Lady Miriam… thank God you are still here." Sir John Russell is breathless, having run about the court, trying to find a lady of good character. "I am instructed to find a lady of true honour, and honesty, then bring her before the king, at once."

"Does the lecherous pig have no scruples," Mush snaps at Sir John. "My sister might look like Mother Earth in her clever gown, but her fallow field is not meant for Henry's plough."

"Take care, my friend," Sir John says, and looks about to make sure they are not overheard. "To curse *this* farmer might bring a charge of treason upon your head."

"The king has always desired my sister," Mush complains.

"Mush, you know I would not dishonour Lady Miriam in so crude a way. I am not the king's pimp, and he does not have designs on your sister."

"Is it the poppy juice he seeks?" Miriam asks, and Russell shakes his head, confounded as to a reason for the sudden upset.

"No, it is not that, though his behaviour is mighty odd this evening. He is expected to visit the queen tonight, and he withdrew to his private chambers, so as to prepare himself. The next I knew, he was cursing and swearing like an old soldier, and there were tears welling in his eyes. He is distraught at something sent to irk him, and evidently cannot speak of it, save to a matron of good repute. He commands me find one, but it is not that easy. Thanks, in the most part, to Tom Wyatt, there are few 'honest' ladies at court. Then I thought of you, my dear lady, and my task is done. Come with me at once, Miriam, else the king will have a great seizure, and do himself some serious hurt."

"You begin to intrigue me, Sir John," Miriam Draper says. "What can it be that the king may not confide even in his best men?"

"I know not, My Lady, but Henry is rending apart his Jove costume, and lamenting his good nature. He rants about making Tom Wyatt into a king."

"It sounds as if he has imbibed too much of my elixir," Miriam says. "It will not harm him, but he might well have a few odd dreams."

"Well, just now, he sees himself persecuted," Sir John tells her. "He mutters that the whole world is against him."

"Dear God," Mush snaps, "that means he is getting ready to ruin some poor bastard. I pray that it is not anyone of my knowing."

*

"You will never get a boat down river at this time of night, Thomas," the ambassador says to the archbishop. "Pray come home with me, and spend the night in comfort. We can drink some of the excellent Moroccan wine that Lady Miriam sends to me. The Mussulmen are forbidden strong drink, of course, but they still grow the grapes, and sell their produce to we wicked

Christians."

"Thank you, Eustace. I was worried about finding a bed for the night," Thomas Cranmer tells the little Savoyard diplomat. "Might I trouble you for a candle too, so that I might read my scriptures before I go to try and sleep? I seldom close my eyes for more than three hours in a night."

"My manservant, Gomez will help you," Chapuys says, and does not mention that that same fellow has offered to cut his throat twice now. "I shall have wine brought to us, and we can talk, or play chess… as you so wish. I too can seldom sleep much. I often wonder if it is my bad conscience pricking away at me."

"Not I, sir," the archbishop says, as they walk the few hundred yards to Chapuys' house, next to what was once Austin Friars. "My conscience is clear, and I am at one with my God."

"You have shown yourself to be an honest man, sir," Chapuys replies. "I asked only that you did not speak to the king about Catherine, and you held your tongue. Now, you do not even have to go to Rome, but may return to Canterbury Cathedral, with your good name unsullied."

"That is so," Archbishop Cranmer

tells the Savoyard diplomat. "I contrived a way to satisfy both sides of my conscience, without actually breaking my word. I swore not to speak of Catherine's wickedness, and I have not. Not one word has passed my lips, yet my duty to the king is fulfilled."

"What is that?" An alarm bell rings in Chapuys' head, and he glares at the archbishop, who is sweating, and who looks a strange shade of purple. "You have satisfied *both* of us, My Lord... how can this be so?"

"I have done what I have," Cranmer says, defiantly.

'Oh, dear Christ hanging from His Cross, Tom, what have you done?" Eustace Chapuys can feel the ground opening beneath his feet.

"My duty."

"Then we are ruined," Chapuys tells the archbishop, "and we must see bloody murder done again!"

*

The king is perched on the window seat in his bed chamber, and he almost jumps to his feet when Miriam is shown in. He curses his servant, and orders the room to be cleared. As usual, at bedtime, Henry is accompanied by several gentlemen of the household, and they are put out into the corridor.

"Lady Miriam, thank you for coming to me so promptly. I asked for any virtuous lady, but I hoped in my heart that it would be you."

"It seems Sir John Russell was at a loss to find anyone else suitable, sire."

"Yes, a sad reflection upon my wicked court," Henry says. "I am in need of your matronly advice, madam, for I am beset by the most evil doubts."

"At your service, as ever, Your Majesty." Miriam sees that it is her advice that is needed, rather than that she has committed some unknown offence against the crown. "How may I help?"

"Look at this." Henry holds out a tiny, folded piece of parchment. "I found it when I started to undress. It was tucked into the cuff of my blouse. I can only think some clever hand has been at work, and slipped it there. When, I cannot say, but it must have been whilst I greeted someone."

"Who, sire?"

"I cannot think." The king is quite distraught. "Apart from my servants, and one of the squires… oh, and Archbishop Cranmer, of course… none have come close enough. Pray, read it, and give me your opinion." Lady

Miriam Draper has a sudden, sick feeling in her stomach. She knows that Cranmer has kept his word, by keeping his silence, but has he used some sophistry to ease his conscience?

She takes the note, and reads.

Sire,

The queen is young, and prone to youthful indiscretions. Look upon her favourably.

The words are conciliatory in nature, but liable to fan the smoke of mistrust into a roaring fire. Miriam reads it again, and tries to find the best way to interpret it for Henry.

"It tells you nothing, sire," she says, but the king shakes his head.

"No, it tells me everything, Lady Miriam," he says. "It explains the sickly headaches, and Catherine's behaviour. I think she does not love me."

"Or it might allude to some girlish silliness," Miriam persists. "She might have held an unfulfilled passion for some innocent squire, or been loved from afar by another. It is how children are."

"You must advise me honestly, Lady Miriam," says the king. "I cannot allow anyone else to suspect the queen, lest it redounds on my own good character. What am I to do?"

"You wish to keep this a secret, sire?" Miriam asks. "Or do you wish me to speak with Catherine?"

"I want to know if she is faithful, or not," Henry says, but he does not mean it. He wants someone to tell him that the queen is blameless, and he has not been cuckolded. His pride will not stand another blow. "*La Boleyn* was a whore."

"Catherine is a child, sire... not another Anne Boleyn," Miriam tells him.

"Does that mean she is innocent, or not?" Henry asks. "This note writer is sure that something is amiss."

"Your informant hides his face, sire. How can he be believed?" Miriam sees that she might use this anonymity to soothe Henry's suspicions, if only Henry continues to claim he does not know who it is.

"It was Cranmer," Henry admits, and her hopes are dashed. "He placed it in my sleeve, as he took his leave. I am sure of it. The queen must have confessed all to him."

"I doubt it, sire," Miriam replies. "The archbishop is not worldly wise, and might easily mistake a casual remark for something quite different. For instance, I might say how I do love my king. You, as a man of great understanding will know that I mean a love other than the carnal, but our poor Cranmer might think I suggest something quite different."

"You think so?" Henry asks, and his agitation lessens. he is more than willing to be convinced, and he suspects that Miriam will guide him through the difficulty. "The queen has become most loving to me in these last few days."

"That is because her sick heads are abating, sire," Miriam explains. "My apothecary gives her powders to take, and the pain is much lessened. As soon as she feels better, what does she do, but invite her loving husband to her chambers. It is her duty to give you children. The girl loves you, sire."

"That is not the question, Miriam," Henry says. "Of course she loves me. The note, damn it, hints at some *previous* sin. I must know that she is like 'caesar's wife' in this, and above suspicion."

"If Cranmer knew anything, he would tell you," Miriam insists. "He has possibly heard some salacious gossip… quite untrue, I think… and does not know what to do about it. So, he hints, and hopes you are wise enough to exonerate the queen. Does he not urge you to look upon her favourably? Why would he do that, if he thinks her to be guilty in the eyes of God?"

"Yes, you speak good sense, my dear." The king is becoming convinced. "Cranmer is an old woman in these matters, and I must not listen to him."

"A wise decision, Your Majesty," Miriam says. "Let me take this note, and 'hint' to the archbishop that he should keep his nose out of royal affairs."

"Yes, he should keep to church matters," says Henry. "His own domain is the Holy Scriptures and the secrets of ... *the confessional*. My God, Miriam, what if the queen has confessed to the man?"

"Would he not say?" Miriam's heart sinks. The king has hit upon the truth, and the idea is lodged in his mind, like a monolith.

"No, I doubt he would... but he *would* hint to me." The king looks at the deadly note again. "I must know the truth of it, Miriam. I am minded to ask your husband to investigate the matter for me. For I can trust his word, can I not?"

"Sire, if you do ask Will, he may give you an answer that does not sit well with you. What if he finds some minor thing that can be blown out of proportion?"

"Not by me, madam," Henry says, unctuously. "If it be nothing, I will not make it more than it is. Though I *must* have the truth of it."

"Then give him the order, sire," Miriam says, "and may God guide his hand. For my part, I would let sleeping dogs lie."

"Would that I could," the king says, "but there is the royal dignity to consider."

Of course, the royal dignity must be considered, Miriam thinks. Henry cannot allow his own character to be impugned, and any hint of him being a cuckold must be stamped upon. The die is cast, and the muse of fate will have its say, as it always must.

*

Thomas Cranmer has slept on his actions, and realises that he has done the worst possible thing in slipping a note to the king. Henry is not one for half measures, and the archbishop sees that he will not give anyone the benefit of the doubt, if it makes him look less of a man.

"What have I done, Eustace?" he moans at breakfast. "I have used sophistry to trick you, and have tricked myself. The king will know it was me, and make his assumptions."

"Yes, he will," Chapuys tells the

cleric. "He will think how the queen has spurned him, and put the worst construction on things. He shall think she has a young lover."

"She has though."

"Yes, and the fellow has been removed," the ambassador explains. "We have him safe, and Catherine needs only to claim herself virtuous. So simple…yet she listens to your ill advised advice, and actually confesses. Whatever made you suggest it to her, Thomas?"

"It is a mere formality. I suggest they confess, and they lie to me. God still sees what is in their hearts, but I am not party to it. I never thought she would be so damned truthful. I have listened to Henry's confession for the past ten years, and it never varies; nor does it contain any actual sins that can be punished."

"You should wait until he takes his poppy potion," Chapuys says. "Then he will tell you anything. Last night, he promised me a thousand silver marks a month, and a royal palace to live in."

"Then he may think my note to be a part of his overheated imagination?" the archbishop asks.

"Only if it has now vanished," the

little diplomat replies. "No, once out of the bag, this cat will have sharp claws," Chapuys says. He sees now that Henry must have Catherine investigated, and wonders if Will Draper can still save her from the block. "Catherine may get a second chance to swear her innocence, and she must take it."

"I cannot possibly take a second confession."

"God forbid!" Chapuys throws up his hands in horror. The archbishop has done quite enough damage with the first effort. "I am sure that General Draper can find a more pliable priest. You protestant clerics are very easy to bribe."

"You are unkind, Eustace."

"And you are a fool, Thomas," the little man snaps. "One simple thing, and you fail."

"She confessed."

"Only because you assured her that it was in confidence. Then you break your vow to her. I hope God can forgive your pragmatism, sir."

"I thought…"

"No, you did not… other than to see how you might save your own face."

"Perhaps I should leave."

"Yes, I think so." Chapuys is not in a

forgiving mood. Queen Catherine is a Howard, and the Howards are a Roman Catholic family. This suits the Emperor Charles well enough, and he will not want another upset. "Good day, Your Eminence."

"Must we part on such bad terms, Señor Chapuys?" Cranmer is close to tears. "I have come to love you as a friend over these last weeks."

"We still have an unfinished game of chess, sir," Eustace Chapuys concedes. "Perhaps you might call back this evening, and I will close out my victory."

"I have just taken receipt of the new book by Erasmus," Tom Cranmer says, his spirits lifting a little. "It is his *Ciceronianus*, but in English for the first time. I think it a rather jolly read."

"Come to supper, and we shall investigate the shortcomings of Cicero together," Chapuys says. The man, after all, is a useful ally for a foreign ambassador, and he cannot be spurned so readily.

*

"The king instructs me to look into the queen's history," Will tells his wife, and she informs him about her late night liaison with Henry.

"Cranmer has set the cat amongst the

pigeons," she says. "The note damns her without saying anything, and now Henry wants to know the truth."

"Could he not have asked me, before they married?"

"He was eager to bed her then," Miriam sneers. "Now, with his precious 'honour' at stake, his mind changes."

"I am caught in a bad place," Will complains. "If I look, I will find. We all know that, do we not?"

"Then suggest to Henry that the queen goes to confession again."

"How will that help?" Will asks.

"Buy the priest," Miriam tells him. "Tell the king that you will arrange for the confession to be overheard. Then school your man well, and have him ask the right questions. Do you love the king? Have you a lover at court? Will you ever betray your king?"

"Yes, I see. She must say she loves the king, for we all must. She does not have a lover at court… for I have him in custody, and she will never seek to betray the king. These are clever questions, my dear."

"Then you can report to the king, and let him draw his own inferences," Miriam explains. "He is as vain as any man alive, and will believe what he wants. Catherine will be exonerated, by the king, and all you need do is make Culpeper and Dereham vanish."

"You are clever… for a woman," Will says, and she grins at his nerve.

"Thank God I am, Will Draper, for you keep your brains in your sword arm, more often than not."

"Enough, I bow to your superiority, my love," he says, "though I cannot admit as much to Mush and the others. I must seem to be master of the house."

"Then it is a good job we own twelve. I shall rule in the other eleven."

"We own twelve houses?" Will asks, somewhat taken aback at the news. He is constantly surprised at his wife's head for business, and can seldom think in sums over the odd few hundred, which would keep a gentleman for a couple of years. Miriam deals in thousands of pounds, Ducati, and Brabant coin each day.

"In England," she replies. "Three more in Antwerp, and another half dozen in Venice and Genoa."

"Then we are not short of a place to hide?" he says.

"We are Drapers, sir… and we do not hide," Miriam tells her man. "Find us a willing priest, and let us try to salvage what we can from Cranmer's mess."

"I shall make it my priority, my love," Will says, and he buckles on his sword. "Just how much are we worth?"

"You will forget again," Miriam says. "You always do."

"Then there is no harm in telling me, my sweet. I will not bandy it around. It just fascinates me at how clever a wife I possess."

"About two million pounds in shipping and land," she tells him, "and another two in ready cash. Then there are the loans we own, and the security attached, which comes to about three million."

"I cannot conceive of such vast sums," Will confesses. The yearly income of both France and England is hardly a match for so great a fortune.

"Yes, that is why you forget, husband. It is easier for you to let me handle it. Perhaps it is my Jewish heritage?"

"Do not mock me, my love. You know I bear no ill will towards any creed. My own boys are of your blood, as much as mine. Besides, you are a Coventry wench... the king says it is so."

"Then may God save the king, and let him turn from this destructive course he is setting himself upon." Miriam cannot insist enough on what her husband must do. "Search hard, husband. Find a pliable pastor for us to employ, and be quick about it. The king will want an answer, and he will want it soon."

*

"You wish to put aside the queen's confession?" Archbishop Thomas Cranmer is dumfounded at so devious a suggestion. "For what purpose?"

"To save the queen from embarrassment, My Lord Archbishop," Will Draper says. "It is perfectly clear that you misunderstood her childish passions… no more than the holding of a hand, or a peck on the cheek, I assure you. Now, because of your sophistry, Henry thinks his wife has betrayed him, and seeks answers where there are none to find. The queen is innocent."

"That is not the sense of it that I took. I am not that simple, Sir Will. I am a married man."

"To a sensible widow, I hear?"

"Yes, that is so."

"Then she is excused her past?"

"There is nothing to excuse."

"Because it was before your time?" Will asks, and the cleric smiles and relents.

"If the king asks, I will say I am unable to name anyone who has asked for confession. If pressed by him, I shall ask him if I might reveal some of the many sins he has told me about over these past few years in his service."

"A clever solution, sir." Will stands up to go. "Would that you had thought of it before you hid a note in the king's sleeve."

"I panicked." Cranmer is honest about it, and thinks it will exonerate him from further castigation, but there is a price to pay, of course.

"Very well. I can see that. One last thing… can you recommend a thoroughly bribable priest?"

"Of the new church?"

"Yes."

"Then you do mean to have Catherine confess again?"

"Yes, under strict supervision."

"The Reverend Jeremiah Cropper of the Church of St Agnes in Harlow. I am about to de-frock him for usury, and indiscriminate fornication within his flock. Use him quickly, before his powers are gone, and the bawdy house claims him."

"He sounds perfect. How much need I offer the fellow?"

"Enough to keep him drunk for a week. More and he will grow suspicious."

"He will keep silent afterwards?"

"God above, no. He will boast to everyone about how the queen chose him to confess her sins to. The king will hear about it in days…and Catherine will be exonerated."

"That will do nicely, sir. I have left a donation for the church poor with you clerk. A draft on a Brabant bank for one thousand pounds. Pray forget this conversation ever took place."

"I do not need your bribe," Cranmer says, somewhat shocked at the offer.

"No, but the poor do. It will feed them bread and soup for five years, if spent wisely. Good day to you, sir."

Will Draper is relieved to leave the archbishop's palace, and return to Draper House. He will make the short ride over to Harlow on Moll, his aged Welsh Cob. She is almost fifteen years old, and only up to short exercise these days, but the odd ride out is good for her, and it reminds Will of his early days, when they were both young.

"Is it done?" Miriam asks, as soon as he arrives home.

"It is. I have only to go to Harlow, and bribe the new priest. He will come back with me, and I shall present him to Catherine this afternoon."

"Thank God, then we are back on course. England cannot stand another scandal."

"I shall take Moll."

"Are you sure? The stable lad says she is grown old, and easily tires."

"One last ride," Will says.

"And then?"

"She must grow old gracefully, and spend her days in a meadow. As must I, one day."

"Husband, you are not yet thirty three years old," Miriam says. "The prime of life for any man."

"Perhaps," Will replies, "but I am not the man I once was."

"You do not need to be," Miriam replies. "You have me and the children, and enough to retire on."

"The king will never let me. He must keep us all until we are beyond our time. Then he culls us, like those old rams... when our tupping days are done."

"God forbid, husband," Miriam mutters. She is all for a good tupping with her own old ram. "Serve him well, and slip in another, when the time is right. The master in

Antwerp will have someone in mind. He always does."

"Yes, I dare say Rafe will want to die in harness, and Barnaby Fowler is a most capable fellow."

"Then there is Kel Kelton," Miriam says. "He is a most pragmatic fellow, and eager to satisfy."

"He is too quick with the knife for my liking," Will replies. "A cooler head is needed. Some clerk that shows promise."

"Henry will want another Will Draper," his wife says. "A strong man who can use a sword as easily as a ledger. Have you no up and coming young fellow to bring on?"

"One or two, perhaps," Will replies. "but none of them blooded yet."

"The age of reason is coming, husband," says Miriam. "Diplomacy will rule the world, and sharp tongues will do better than sharp daggers, I suppose."

"I have never yet talked a villain out of trying to skewer me, my love,' Will offers. "Diplomacy is all well enough, but we must still remember that most things are achieved by threat, rather than sweet words."

"That is man business, and I shall leave it to my man." Miriam knows when to let things be, and her husband will digest what she says, and come to a mutually acceptable answer. An answer that she will accept, with some modification, if needed.

"How shall we tell the queen?"

"About what?"

"Her confession, you ninny," Lady Miriam says. "She is the queen, and we cannot simply turn up and say 'madam, here is a priest, come to take your confession. She must be notified of our intentions, and warned to be ready. It is only a curtesy, I know, but one expected by our betters."

"Will a note do… hand delivered on a velvet cushion, stuffed with strands of gold… or one of my men on his knees, with the parchment in his mouth, like a puppy dog bringing a bone?"

"A simple note, by messenger will do, I think," Miriam replies. "Though a nice seal, bearing our new coat of arms will suffice."

"We do not possess such a thing." Will knows, even as he speaks that his wife has, by some miracle of foresight, taken care of the matter. She opens her purse, and pulls out a wooden stamp with an embossed head. It shows a Templar's broadsword, with a chaplet of thorns entwined about it.

"Master Tom suggested it, three

months ago," she explains. "The design was his own idea. I suppose he saw how the wind was blowing, and guessed at your elevation."

"Like hell he did," Will marvels. "My bet is that he has had Rafe and Richard whispering in the king's ear. 'Oh, if only you could bring Draper into your council, sire, but for his low station' and 'nothing too grand, sire... perhaps a baronetcy where his house is?'. The king ponders this, and lo and behold...Baron Draper of the Templars. The old fox must be catching some of Pru Beckshaw's second sight."

"Accept it, my love." Miriam kisses him, lightly on his cheek. "In the meantime, send the queen her note, and let her have the day's warning. Impress on her the importance of the thing."

"Of course."

Will goes off in search of a decent scribe. His own hand is neat enough, but not as stylish as some of his boys, trained by Rafe and Barnaby at their lawyer's dens. He finds Anthony Porterfield in the kitchen, begging food from Maisie, who has come back to London to see her kitchen is still being well run in her absence. She is heavily pregnant, but as robust as ever.

"You boys will ruin the master, with

your eating." she curses, but hands over some onion soup and bread. Will takes a bowl for himself, and sits with the lad, who looks half starved.

"Hungry, Anthony?"

"Always, master."

"Then eat up, for I have a task for you. There is a note to go to the queen at Whitehall Palace. It must go into her hands alone, and none other."

"Not even the king's, sir?"

"No, not the king's. If he thinks to stop you, conceal the note, or destroy it. The contents are for Catherine alone."

"Am I to write the note too?" the young man asks. It is not unusual to take a verbal message and transcribe it later.

"Yes. I must be off soon, so leave it to you, lad. Here is my seal. When you are done with it, return it to Lady Miriam."

"Of course, master. Might I know the content of this note… the better to write it down."

"Of course. Start with the usual flourishing…Your Most Regal Majesty, etcetera. Then say something like;

Catherine,

General Draper shall call on you in the afternoon of tomorrow, with a pastor of good repute. He will take your confession, and absolve you. The answers to his questions will be repeated to the king, so I must warn you as to how you make answer. Sign it for me."

"Right, master." The lad slurps down his soup and goes off to the small clerks office that Marion maintains at the front of the house. On the way he is stopped by two other clerks, begging advice, and he is delayed a half hour.

"Damn me, Tommy," he curses, as a third one comes to him. "I must get a note written, and delivered to the palace before dinner. Let me be, for the sake of Christ." They let him be, and he finally picks up his quill and writes down the necessary flourishing introduction.

It is then he concentrates on Will Drapers words, which must be conveyed to Her Majesty. He recalls that they seemed somewhat verbose for a short note, and so settles on the *gist* of them.

It will save time, and effort to condense it, he thinks, and the meaning was clear enough… was it not?

He writes:
Madam,
You are to confess. To this end

General Draper will call tomorrow, with another. Be truthful, for the king will hear your answers.

He signs it, and folds it for sealing. The new seal is impressive, and the effect of the whole says 'this is an important document'. Then he writes out a pass, allowing him free access to the palace for the day, and appends the new seal. It looks most official, and the guards, most of whom do not read at all well, will accept it, and let him pass without hinderance.

*

Will Draper is content that his instructions will be carried out, and he sets himself the task of ordering up his horse, and enough provisions to last him through the length of his coming journey.

Moll senses that she is needed, and her ears prick up as her master comes into the stables. They have shared many adventures together, and the old Welsh Cob is ready to carry Will wherever he may wish.

"Good girl," Will says, as he pats her neck. "A gentle ride, and then a well earned rest, I think."

10 Apocalypsis

Anthony Porterfield borrows a friends black doublet, which is newer than his own, and has the famous embroidered 'C' on the sleeve. The insignia still carries weight with those who have ever dealt with Thomas Cromwell and the Austin Friars' gang.

He arrives at the south facing entrance of Whitehall Palace, where the usual supplicants are gathered, hoping to get inside and lobby some great lord or, at least, his secretary. He pushes his way through the merchants and bankers who besiege the palace, and holds out his cleverly forged entry pass for the guards to study.

"Come now, good sirs, and behave yourselves," he says to the men he jostles aside. "One must have a valid pass to get past these good fellows." He gestures towards the two armed guards, who have orders to turn away any without the right sort of papers. "See here, a genuine pass… like this one."

"Bastard little jack a nape," a rotund wine seller snaps. "I've been waiting here for three bloody days. How do you ever manage to get a pass?"

"Why, you must speak with the clerk to Sir John Russell," Anthony replies.

"And where do I find him?" the man asks. Anthony smiles, and turns up his open palm. The man growls his displeasure at the implied request for a bribe, and drops a silver coin into the open hand. "Well, where do I find this fellow, you damned robbing rogue?"

"His name is Oswald Green, sir, and he has an office in the west wing of the palace."

"How do I get to see him?"

"Just show your pass, and they will let you in."

"But… why you cheating little…" Anthony Porterfield slips the shilling into his purse, and is through the door in a moment.

"There is always a fool waiting to be parted from his money," he tells the grinning guard. "Where do I find Her Majesty, good fellow?"

The sergeant at arms is no fool, and he knows when there is business to be done. He holds out his own hand in turn, and receives a sixpence for his advice.

"Main corridor, until you come to a narrow staircase, guarded by an Examiner, young sir. Go up a flight, to the long gallery, and the lady is holding court there. Some foolish game that has come over here from the French is taking place."

Will Draper's man thanks the fellow, and follows his instructions. His pass takes him to the long gallery, where he finds the queen and her inner circle of ladies and gentlemen playing at a frolicsome game of boules.

"My turn, I think," Catherine says, and takes up the polished wooden 'jack'. She tosses it, too daintily, and it falls short of the mark. One of the gentlemen makes a conciliatory clucking noise, and begs her to take the go again.

"For a sudden gust of wind must have spoiled your aim, my dearest queen." It is Tom Wyatt, who has called 'by chance' and stayed for the sport. In truth, he has a message from Miriam, warning him to keep close to Queen Catherine, until Will comes back with his tame pastor.

"You would have me cheat, kind sir?" Catherine asks, and giggles. She is the queen, and they will let her win anyway.

"A fair chance for a fair lady," the poet replies. He is quite the most handsome man in the gallery, and all of the ladies want to catch his eye. Next to him is John Lascelles, the ardent protestant reformer. He is there with his sister, who he hopes to find a place for within the queen's household.

"What have we here, Master Wyatt?" Lascelles asks, as Anthony Porterfield bows to them all. "Another fellow to help the queen to victory?"

"Just a simple messenger, sir," the young courier says. "I have a note for Her Majesty."

"Then hand it over, boy," Lascelles says, and holds out his hand.

"For the queen's hand alone, sir."

"Impudent young pup," the older man says, and goes to snatch the paper away from the messenger. Anthony sways backwards, and takes a firm grip of Lascelles' outstretched wrist. He gives it a gentle tweak, and the courtier yelps in pain.

"For the queen, sir," Porterfield repeats, and Tom Wyatt laughs at the byplay.

"Catherine... see here is a bantam cock, come to deliver you a *billet deux* from your loving husband."

Catherine smiles at the mocking tone, and curtseys to the poet. She must keep up the fiction of her husband's great prowess in the bed chamber, but only the night before, after the ball, he was quite unable to perform his manly duties.

"His Majesty is as loving as I could ever want him to be," she says. "I wonder what he wants of me now?" She takes the note, breaks the seal, and begins to read. She is not an educated girl, and must move her lips as she digests the contents.

She sees that Will Draper is going to call, and is intent on drawing the truth from her. This truth will then be passed on to Henry. It is a disaster. The King's Examiner insists on the truth, and she is caught in a trap.

"I am undone," she says, and begins to cry. Tom Wyatt is confused, because he understands the note to be her escape from danger. "The king will know all, and I shall be shamed in front of the whole court."

"Know what, madam?" John Lascelles asks, before the poet can stop him, and Catherine bursts into great flows of tears.

"About Cully, and my other lovers," she tells the astonished gathering. "How I did let them take liberties with my person, and even did promise myself in marriage to that amiable rogue, Francis Dereham."

The gallery empties in moments, as all those present realise that a disaster of the worst kind is bearing down upon the young queen. Tom Wyatt takes the note from her, and reads it. The 'gist' of it has changed the meaning, and terrified the queen into her rash statement. He sees that he must act at once, before the damage becomes too great for him to repair.

"Master Lascelles, close the doors, and fetch back those ladies who have fled from here. I must speak with them about this silly misunderstanding. Can I rely on your good will, sir?"

"I know my duty, Wyatt," the man says. "Calm the queen down, and I will do what must be done."

"Good fellow," Tom Wyatt says to the mean minded reformer. "You will earn my favour, and that of greater men than I. You, boy, attend on me. Where did this damned note come from?"

"From my master, sir," Anthony Porterfield replies, as he senses that something is going dreadfully amiss. "General Draper spoke to me… and I copied it down… somewhat later."

"And changed the very meaning of it, you damned idiot," the poet guesses. He turns to the queen, and begs her to cease her crying. "Madam, there is no harm done here. General Draper means only to have you confess again, but to a more genially minded priest. The man will attest to your honesty, and love for the king."

"He will?" Catherine dabs at her eyes,

and snuffles herself into silence.

"Yes, Your Majesty," the poet insists. "Master Lascelles will stop your ladies from gossiping, and see that no word of your outburst gets abroad. He wants a place for his sister, so he is easily bought. Pray, do calm yourself down."

"Sir, I have made a grave mistake," Anthony Porterfield says to the poet. "I have no excuses... and should have paid better attention to my errand."

"There is no real damage done, lad," Tom Wyatt replies. "The thing is contained, I believe."

Outside the long gallery, John Lascelles struggles with his conscience, and decides that he cannot let his own good name be smeared by involvement in such a sordid mess. He goes straight along to the offices kept for the use of the archbishop, and demands entry.

"I must speak with Archbishop Cranmer," he demands of a grey haired old fellow who looks like the emptier of chamber pots.

"I am Cranmer, young man," the old man replies. "And you are...?"

"John Lascelles, My Lord Archbishop," Lascelles tells the odd old fellow. "I am new to the court, from Cambridge, and ..."

"I do not need a life story, sir," the archbishop snaps. He has had a long night, and a morning full of upset, because the queen must be saved. Will Draper is bringing in a second priest, and all is to be smoothed over. "What do you want of me?"

"Sir... the queen has been unfaithful to the marriage bed."

"Not so, sir," Cranmer says, though he is somewhat taken aback by this bald statement of the facts. He looks about himself, to see if any prying eyes are watching this dangerous exchange. "It is just common hearsay, wickedly put about by idlers, and hysterical women. Who told you this perfidious pack of lies, my son?"

"Why, the queen herself, sir," John Lascelles replies. "She has just informed the entire court of it. She lies with Thomas Culpeper, and also Francis Dereham. Now she fears the king will exact his vengeance upon her, and her defilers."

"You have misunderstood, sir."

"Not I, My Lord Archbishop," John Lascelles replies, smugly. He thinks Martin Luther's rigorous doctrines are what the country needs, and is all for banning everything that makes life a pleasure. "She is immoral, and not fit to reign in a decent protestant country."

"The poor lady suffers from rather bad headaches," Thomas Cranmer tells John Lascelles, as if this explains everything. "She really is being misunderstood. You misheard, sir… and I strongly advise you to accept that."

"Misheard? Then I and a dozen others must have misheard her declarations," Lascelles insists. "You must tell the king about this, at once. If not, someone else will whisper in his ear, and you will look most untrustworthy."

The entire point of the whole affair is that no one tells the king anything, Cranmer thinks, and this is not how it is meant to be. He is not a man who can think on his feet, as Tom Cromwell could, and he scrabbles about for some breathing space.

"We must not be hasty," says the archbishop, but John Lascelles has an answer ready. "I should speak with the queen first, and then with my fellow bishops. You, and those with you, must hold your tongues until we can arrange for a proper investigation."

"The secret is out, sir. if you do not get to Henry first, he will only doubt your loyalty. Let us go to him, at once, and show him how he is protected by our zeal. Let him see how the new English church ... the *true* church... looks after his immortal soul for him."

"But if we are mistaken, Master Lascelles..." Cranmer finds himself wishing that Alonso Gomez was nearby, so that he might silence this fool for him, then recants the wicked thought.

"The queen did confess to adultery, Archbishop Cranmer, in front of me, all her ladies in waiting, Lady Jane Boleyn, and that dreadful poet fellow."

"Tom Wyatt?" Cranmer sees that the queen has been watched carefully, by two reliable people, and the archbishop cannot understand how things have gone so badly wrong. "The poet was there, and he still let this happen?"

"Yes, I suspect he will be amongst her lovers too," Lascelles says, with the self righteousness of the truly dull man. He is in a loveless marriage, and suspects that Tom Wyatt is a little too friendly with his wife. He is not mistaken in this belief, but he lacks the proof to confront the amorous poet and accept a cuckold's horns for his trouble.

"The queen's lover? No, he most

certainly is not," Cranmer snaps. "Can I not dissuade you from your dangerous course, sir?"

"Not for a thousand pounds, My Lord," Lascelles says. "If you do not take action, and at once, I shall make known my knowledge to every gentleman in the court. Further, I shall see that the pastor of my church preaches against her immorality this very Sunday."

"I see you are not for turning."

"I am a rock," Lascelles tells the archbishop. For one giddy moment, Tom Cranmer thinks to send for Mush Draper, and have him threaten the fellow into silence. Then he realises that it is too late, and a dozen tongues are already wagging. Henry will hear of it, no matter what, and then wish to know why his archbishop has remained silent. The time for secrecy is passed, and Cranmer must look to saving his own hide.

"I shall put on my garb, and walk with you to the rose garden," he tells the insistent puritan. "It is where Henry will be at this hour. The king so loves his *Rosa gallica versicolor*. The Tudor rose is a powerful emblem."

"He will be angry." John Lascelles sees now that he is not to get away with simply informing on the queen, and that he must repeat his sordid tale directly to the king.

"Angry? You greatly understate the case, sir," Thomas Cranmer says to the stubborn fellow. "Which is why I intend letting *you* tell him that his wife is a whore."

"Strong words, sir," Lascelles says. He is a prudish fellow, and does not like to hear such language. "The common whore takes money."

"And Queen Catherine does it for nothing?" Cranmer almost slaps the man in the face. He is the sort of puritanical idiot who is beginning to spoil the new church, and he wants nothing to do with their pinch faced lack of humanity.

"The queen does it, sir... and that is the point." Lascelles watches as the archbishop puts on his outer robes, and hangs a fine jewelled crucifix about his neck. To the puritan, this adornment is close to idolatry, and he reviles it.

"Then what will you say to the king, if you cannot bring yourself to use profanities?" Tom Cranmer asks. "That his wife is *untrue* to his bed... or that she is *wayward*? However you word it, my boy, he will want to kill someone with his bare hands, and you are to be the messenger."

"He must be told." Lascelles holds such puritanical views, and adultery is high on his list of personal dislikes, that he will risk the danger.

"Yes, he must," Thomas Cranmer says. "By you, young man… a fool who cannot see what he is doing to England, and who will end his days as a martyr for a cause that does not want him. May God save us all!"

*

Will Draper finds his wayward priest in a low drinking tavern on the Harlow road. He is directed there by a pleasant young girl, who works the taverns for her daily bread.

"Bless him, but Pastor Cropper is a real gentleman, sir," the girl says. "He always gives me a shilling, and never asks for change. He does the fastest confession I have ever known, and a girl is absolved in the twinkle of an eye."

"Then he is a happy drunk?" Will asks the girl, and she nods, enthusiastically. "I've never seen another who could out drink him, sir, and he does his holy duty, drunk or sober."

"Then point me at him, wench, and take this for your trouble." The girl looks at the golden Angel in her palm, and sees that it is enough to last her a week or more. It makes her frown.

"Here, you ain't going to hurt him are you?" she asks.

"No, I just want to use him for a while," Will tells the girl. Do I really look like such a dangerous fellow, he thinks. "The Angel is to buy your silence, my girl. You have not seen me, and you know nothing about Pastor Cropper's business with me."

"For an Angel I would lie to the devil, master." The girl slips the coin in to her purse, and looks about her. A rough looking fellow is lounging close by, and he sees the transaction.

"Bugger, that's torn it," the girl says. "Black Billy has his eye on me."

"Your pimp?"

"Not mine, sir. He watches all of the girls, and takes his cut. If not, he can get nasty with us."

"What is your name?"

"Sal Ginley, sir."

"Wait here, and I will speak with this rogue," Will says. "Hold Moll's head for me. She is not likely to bite… though I am." He crosses the road, and Black Billy stands up to meet him.

"You watch me, fellow?" Will asks, and the man gives him a long look.

"I simply watch, good sir," Billy replies. "Can I help it if you cross my sight?"

"Your glance irks me, you lazy dog. I suggest you take your roving eyes somewhere else… where they may not ever be turned on me again."

"This is my corner," the man tells Will, "and I stand here, doing my business."

"Watching?"

"I keep an eye on the girls, and see they are not made light of."

"You pimp off them, you saucy fellow?" Will smiles, and drops his hand to the hilt of his sword. Black Billy sees a man in his middle years, wearing the expensive clothing of a courtly gentleman, and he knows the sort. They think that their place in life allows them to push common folk around.

"My business is my own," Black Billy says. He thinks he has the measure of this dandy, and will not back down from any confrontation.

"*Sir*," Will Draper snaps. "It is not fit that a common rogue forgets his manners. You will address me as 'sir', or 'My Lord'." Billy looks about him, pointedly, and grins.

"You seem to have left your army at home, My Lord," he says. "Have a care at how you treat me, lest I think to chastise you for your uppity ways."

"Mistress Sal… in fact, all of the working girls in Harlow… are now under my direct protection,' Will tells the ruffian. "To this end, I think it best that you move to another place… some miles hence."

"Will you make me, Lord Fop?"

"Of course." Will steps back, and puts a yard between them. "How shall it be? Leave or fight. It all the one to me, fellow, and I will let you choose your fancy."

"My fancy?"

"You do not have a sword," Will points out. "So, shall it be fists, or knives?"

"After I beat you senseless, you will come back with the magistrate, and have me taken up," Black Billy sneers.

"Then kill me," Will replies. "It is a small matter. Kill me, and drop my body into the river. Who then can point the guilty finger at you?"

"Put aside your sword then, My Lord," the man says, and starts to take off his jacket. Will Draper catches him, as his arms are still entangled in the sleeves, with a swift right and left to the chin. Black Billy staggers backwards, and Will comes on, without remorse, and hammers home another half dozen heavy blows.

Black Billy finally disentangles himself from his coat, but all the fight has left him. Will sees that his cheap victory has done the job, and he gives Billy a shove that sends him to his knees.

"Enough?"

"Foul!" Billy says, and spits out fragments of broken teeth. Will steps forward, and places the blade of his knife against the man's throat.

"No, sir… this is the foul. You will leave Harlow, now. If you return, I will send a couple of my men here, and they will finish the job. Do you understand?"

"My family are…"

"Take them with you," Will Draper says. "I dislike pimps, and these girls are under my protection now. Be on your way, at once."

"He'll not settle with that," Sal Ginley says, when Will returns to her side. "He will give it a few days, then come back."

"Then tell the other girls to join together, and refuse him. Better still, give him a few coins, and send word to my office here. You know the Examiner garrison, out on the Cambridge road?"

"Good customers, sir," Sal says.

"Then send to them, and bid them

help you. I will leave orders for them to help you out in this matter. One of my sergeants will come along, and thrash the rogue again. The third time, and he shall end up feeding the rats by the river."

"Sir, we are just whores."

"Honest ones, who do not deserve to be robbed," Will says. He feels good at the deed he has done, but wonders how he will explain to Miriam that he has taken a town full of prostitutes under his wing. She will surely understand, he decides. "Now, I must see my inebriated priest."

"Bless us, but no… do not call him 'priest' sir, for he is firm in his beliefs, and tells us all as how the Roman Church is a heresy against the king's church."

"Apart from the fornicating, and the drinking, he sounds like an ideal sort for the new church," Will muses.

Pastor Jeremiah Cropper is sitting in the *Raven's Wing* with a huge earthenware tankard in his hand. He is down to his last few coppers, and is reduced to drinking cut beer, at a half penny a flagon. It is like drinking water, and the man of God is not happy.

"Pastor Cropper?" Will asks, and the man struggles to his feet. "I am Sir Will Draper, General in Chief of the King's

Examiners, and I would speak with you."

"Over a drink?" the pastor asks. "A *decent* drink."

"Wine?"

"Or black rum," Cropper replies.

"Then I shall have some brought, at once. Will you eat with me?"

"I never eat, sir," Jeremiah Cropper says. "It tends to get in the way of my drinking."

"Some soup and bread," Will tells the tavern girl. "A bottle of your best rum, and a red wine, if you possess such a thing."

"We have a nice Portuguese, My Lord," the girl replies. "The owner has it brought in from foreign parts."

"The owner?"

"The Draper Company, sir," the girl tells him. "They own most of the better taverns between here and London."

"Really?" Will sees that he is remiss in not knowing the depth of his wife's business doings. "Does a pretty dark haired woman visit?"

"From Drapers, sir?" The girl looks confused. "This ain't the place as a lady would come to. No, there is a travelling fellow, who counts the profits, and sees we are all paid."

"His name?"

"Why, Rob Buffery, sir. As honest a fellow as I have ever come across."

Rob Buffery is the retired soldier who stood by Will's side once, when they fought off a score of Inquisitors, and then settled down to run a busy tavern in Cambridge. It seems that Miriam knows a useful man when she meets one, and has brought him into her service.

"Then you are well served." The drink comes, and the soup is plentiful and hot. Will eats, and the pastor drinks.

"Might I ask what you want with me, sir?" Jeremiah Cropper asks.

"Your cleric's head, my friend," Will replies. "I have a young girl, in need of an understanding confessor. I am willing to enlist you to my cause with the promise of ten pounds."

"You could get a man killed for so much," the pastor replies. "Do I know this girl?"

"Her name does not signify. It is a simple matter," Will tells the man, who is half drunk again. "I will give you the questions to ask, and you will see the lady answers in the right way."

"I know how to take confession, my

good sir," Jeremiah Cropper says. "I have given absolution to half the damned cutthroats in the home shires. As long as they admit to something, I can clear their way into heaven."

"For a fee?"

"Of course. Usually I only ask for a couple of shillings. I suppose great people have greater sins to hide?"

"None of your business," Will Draper tells him. He despises men who use the cloth to hide behind, and his toll of corrupt priests is one he is proud of, but this one seems to be cut from better cloth. "I want the lady absolved, and you on your way before nightfall. If you speak of this to anyone, I will have to have you killed."

"Dear Christ, sir… I am not a violent man," Cropper replies. "I care not what the girl is about. Blindfold me, if you wish, and I will absolve whosoever you place in front of me. It is not for man to dish out God's punishments for him."

"Then drink up, and we will be on our way, Pastor Cropper. You shall know the lady's name when we get nearer to our destination."

Will mounts Moll, and watches as Jeremiah Cropper struggles to climb up onto the sway backed nag the Examiner has hired for him. It is an easy ride back to London, and neither man needs to be a great horseman. On the way, they talk, and Will finds himself actually liking the fellow, and his views.

God is to be loved, and will love in return, Jeremiah thinks. It is not for man to decide what is in God's mind, and that makes both Catholicism and Protestantism redundant.

"We must love one another," he declares, "without verminous bishops making up rules. I dare say I will end up on the pyre for my thoughts."

"You say God sees us, with or without the church," Will asks.

"That is so. You cannot hide from Him, sir. Now, who am I to absolve?"

"Queen Catherine."

"Oh, bugger it," Jeremiah Cropper swears, "I knew I should have asked for more."

They are within sight of the city walls, when Moll comes to a halt, and refuses to carry on. Will Draper slides down from her back, and rubs he ears.

"Tired, old girl?" he whispers, and strokes her neck. "It's time we found you a green field to live out your days."

"She is old," the pastor says, and he climbs down from his own mount. He pats Moll on the flank, and runs a hand over her withers. "Twelve?"

"Fourteen, more like," Will replies, and Jeremiah Cropper nods his head. He is the second son of a farmer, and knows his animals, if nothing else.

"She is blown, sir," he says. "See how her girth shivers?"

"She must rest."

"No, sir," Jeremiah Cropper says to him, softly. "It is not a short rest she needs. See now how she is starting to lather? Your mare has had enough. She will go no further"

"Nonsense." Will Draper cannot accept so bald a statement, especially from a drunken priest. "She will be fine, after a rub down and…" At that moment, Moll goes down onto her knees, then subsides, very gently, onto her side. The King's Examiner steps back, and chokes back a cry of dismay.

"Her heart is failing," Cropper says. "I have seen it before with other animals. It is as if they know when it is time. You must end it, now, before she suffers too badly."

"End it?"

"Think of the pain, sir," the priest tells him. "If you love the creature, then you must help her on her way."

Some gentlemen are on the Harlow road, with their hawks, and the highly strung birds are startled when a single pistol shot rings out.

*

Henry is sitting within one of the rose arbors that dot the long circumference of his private garden. At this time of year, the bushes are bare, but in the summer months they would be heaving with luscious Tudor roses, a sturdy blend of white and red.

The king's courtiers watch his every move, so that they might take their cue from him. They laugh when he laughs, clap when he claps, and even dress as he dresses. If Henry decides that yellow tights are in fashion, everyone follows suit.

Today, because he is dosed with Miriam Draper's poppy potion, Henry's body is fooled into thinking it is warm, and he is dressed in the lightest doublet and hose his dressers can find. In the spirit of true obsequiousness, his courtiers are decked out in a similar way, and their teeth are chattering in the early December air.

"Blast me, but here is that damned priest again," the king growls, as Archbishop Thomas Cranmer makes his appearance.

"The fellow will be sitting in the privy with me next… see if he doesn't." Sir John Russell laughs, politely at the jest, but wonders why the man is here. He is detailed to see that Henry is not disturbed with any more nonsense about the queen, and the archbishop is becoming a nuisance.

"Shall I send him on his way, sire?" Russell says, moving forward to cut off the cleric. It is then that he sees the fellow following Cranmer, and thinks otherwise. It is John Lascelles, a whey faced puritan, who can bore the pennies from a dead man's eyes. It seems that Cranmer has a new acolyte, and a harmless one at that.

"No, let him come," Henry says to his personal messenger. "Who is that coming with him… a black crow?"

"Better a crow than a raven, sire," Russell jests. "It is Master Lascelles, out of Nottinghamshire. He advocates the abolition of dancing, laughter, and the tupping of willing wenches."

"A cheery fellow indeed," the king replies, and laughs at his own remark. "Perhaps Cranmer wants him to save my immortal soul."

"Sire, without dance, jesting or swiving, who wants an immortal soul?"

"Ho! Well said, Sir John." Henry is in an excellent mood now, and he waves the archbishop forward in the spirit of a benign master ready to give a hearing to a loyal subject. "Now then, Tom... that is, my dear archbishop... what is it I can do for you?"

"Sire, might I name..."

"Master Lascelles," Henry says. "I am aware of the gentleman, and of his rather puritanical views. Is he here to pray for my immortal soul... or just to stop me doing a robust jig?"

"Sire, I am here to bring you sad news," Lascelles says, his voice betraying his upset at being so mocked.

"Oh?" Henry thinks for a moment, then shakes his head. "Is someone dead then?"

"No, sire."

"Have the Scots invaded, or the Welsh rebelled against me... no? Then I am at a loss, sir. Spit it out, man."

"Your Royal Highness, the queen is distraught, and almost in a state of collapse."

"What... my Catherine?" Henry looks about him for one of the many doctors he employs at such great expense. "How come you to know this?"

"I was with her, sire... when the news

came." Lascelles is drawing the thing out, but he is beginning to regret being the chosen messenger. Sir John Russell sees that he has been circumvented, and thinks hard as to how he might shut the fool up, and get him from the king's presence.

"Thank you for the warning, sir," Russell says. "Now leave us, so that the king might repair to the queen's side, and tend to her… lovingly."

"No, sir." Lascelles steels himself to speak on. "Word came that Queen Catherine is to be questioned, sire."

"Damn me, fellow… I know. I ordered it. Will Draper is to investigate, and put my mind at rest."

"The terrible news quite unhinged the queen, sire, and she did make a most fulsome statement… concerning her past indiscretions." A dread silence falls over the court, and Henry is struck quite dumb. Cranmer stands back, and leaves Lascelles to make his own way forward.

"You speak thus of the queen, sir?" John Russell snaps. "Let me run this dog through, sire!"

"I knew it." Henry whispers the words, and John Lascelles gives a sigh of relief. "The note, and then the headaches, should have told me. Is it Wyatt?"

"Your Majesty!" Cranmer cannot stand by and watch an innocent man blackguarded. "Tom Wyatt is not the viper here, but someone closer to your heart."

"A name, sir," Henry snaps.

"Francis Dereham," Lascelles says, because it is the first one he heard.

"Who?" Henry cannot recall anyone of that name. "The gentleman is unknown to me."

"He was the queen's favourite, some years ago," Lascelles tells the king.

"But… she is only seventeen now, you damned idiot."

"Yes, sire," Lascelles says. "She was but fourteen at the time. Since then, she has formed a lustful attachment to a page called Thomas Culpeper." This strikes home like a dagger, and Henry is almost physically sick.

"Cully?" he gasps. "Cranmer, is this true?"

"It is what Master Lascelles tells me, sire," Cranmer says, diplomatically. In this way, he can absolve himself of most of the blame, and claim that the revelation was all Lascelles doing. "For my part, I was simply waiting for General Draper to complete his investigation."

"That is the right and proper course," Henry says. "This fellow's method has caused me much upset, and if it be untrue, I will seek his swift punishment."

"Then General Draper is to continue with his …"

"Oh, Tom… she is guilty. I can see that now, and so is Culpeper. The dog has deceived his king, and fled the consequences. I want him found, and I want the queen taken into custody. As for this Dereham fellow… if he actually exists… arrest him too. Good day, Master Lascelles, and thank you for your unwavering candour."

'Your Majesty… it was but my duty. To keep silent would lay me open to charges of misprision of treason." John Lascelles bows low, and retires from the garden. As he leaves, he sees the king looking after him, then whispering to Sir John Russell. He smiles, because there will be some small reward coming his way. Perhaps even a chance to further his religious views with the king's council.

"Misprision?" Henry asks.

'The deliberate concealment of a treasonable act, sire.'

"Bloody lawyer talk."

"He is certainly a man with two faces,

Your Majesty," the king's messenger says, in the hope of dunning the obnoxious fellow down.

"Russell, mark me well," Henry whispers. "When this business is done, I want that fellow dead. No trial, or investigation is required."

"I understand, sire."

"You will do this for me?"

"With great pleasure, Your Highness. I know a man who can make such things come to be."

"Good fellow, John," Henry says. "Make it as unpleasant as possible."

"As Your Majesty commands me, sire," Sir John Russell replies. "He shall pay for his puritanical impertinence." Sir John is a man of his word, and he will not rest until Lascelles is ruined.

*

The overnight cog from Gravesend to Antwerp ties up at the Draper Company dock, and Kel Kelton leaps ashore. He runs the few hundred paces up the hill to the *Palais de Juis* and hammers on the front door. The old Flemish woman answers with her usual surly manner.

"Wotcher, mate," she asks in her fractured English, picked up from the house's

English servants. "It's too early for this. The *Mijnheer* is only just out of bed, *ja*?"

"Who is it, woman?" Cromwell has an intense dislike for the old woman, but she came with the house, and neither he, nor Miriam has the heart to throw her into the street. "Never turn away a visitor."

"Blimey cock," the woman grumbles, and moves off to fetch some breakfast for them both. "Is only the little bastard…that Kel. You eat?"

"Yes, I eat," Kel tells her, and pushes into the house. Cromwell opens his study door wide, and beckons him in.

"Keep quiet, lad, for the children still sleep, and I would keep them in that state for another hour." Cromwell pours out two mugs of watered beer, and offers one to his messenger. "Well?"

"Bad news, sir," Kel Kelton tells him. "An arrest warrant has been issued for the queen."

Henry must be seen to be investigating thoroughly," Cromwell assures Kel. "It is a formality."

"She has confessed to having carnal knowledge of Francis Dereham, and ThomasCulpeper."

"Dear Christ… why?"

"God knows. It seems some stupid clerk in Will Draper's employ decided to re-word a message to her, and she thought herself undone."

"Witnesses?"

"At least fifteen," Kel says. "It looks as if John Lascelles is the main accuser."

"The man used to work for me." Cromwell recalls a thin, untrustworthy looking fellow, with strange views on Christianity. Because of his wildly puritanical ideas, Cromwell had been forced to let him go. "I dismissed him, for his foolishness."

"Now he has his revenge," Kel ventures. "He went to the king, with Archbishop Cranmer. I knew we should have slit his throat, when we had the chance."

"It is not Cranmer's fault," Cromwell says. "He is trapped. If he does not support the allegations, he will be suspect himself."

"Henry has gone very quiet," says Kel Kelton. "Whitehall Palace is as if in mourning, and the court speaks in hushed voices. The queen is in the Tower of London... the same apartments as Anne Boleyn once occupied."

"Who arrested her?"

"Sir John Russell, and Charles Brandon. It seems that the Duke of Suffolk is still in favour."

"Of course he is." Cromwell knows that, for the last month, Suffolk has been recruiting Norfolk men to his own banner, and has the largest number of men in London. "He is Henry's faithful shield. What about the Duke of Norfolk?"

"At Arundel, and swearing his innocence of the whole thing. He says he had no idea about his niece's wickedness."

"Then she is quite alone."

"Will the king kill her?"

"Of course he will. The royal dignity has been offended," Cromwell replies. "What about the two men involved?"

"Dereham is lodged in a cellar at your nephew's house in Cambridgeshire, and Culpeper is under Barnaby Fowler's protection."

"They must both go to the Tower of London," Cromwell advises. "See that the king knows they are taken prisoner by Will Draper. It will do him no harm."

"Draper has failed you, master."

"Enough of that talk," says Tom Cromwell. "Will is my good right arm, and he has never let me down… even when I wronged him. His fault seems to be in trusting the matter to a clerk. Who is it who let him down?"

"Anthony Porterfield, sir," Kel replies. "Shall I kill him for you?"

"For a stupid mistake?" Cromwell shakes his head in horror. "I placed the boy with Will. His father once did me a very good turn, and I sought to repay him by employing the son."

"He failed you, Master Tom," Kel persists. "At least have him beaten."

"And if I listened to you, every person who ever crossed me would have his throat cut... including several archbishops. No, that is enough. Anthony has made a mistake. See he is sent to Rafe Sadler's law offices, where he can spend his days copying out writs in a musty office."

"As you wish, sir."

"Oh, now you are peeved at me, my boy." Cromwell sighs, and drinks down his beer. "I miss English ale. One day, I shall be dead for real, and our work must go on. I need steady men about me, Kel. Are you steady?"

"I am loyal, master."

"Yes, but are you steady?" Thomas Cromwell repeats. "Mush has become steady. He listens, and thinks, before he acts. Will Draper and Rafe Sadler are steady, and they have the king's ear. Then there is my own nephew... a rock of steadiness... who considers everything twice before he speaks. If you wish to get on in the world, you must forget your overtly violent ways, and become ...well... steady"

"Oh, yes, I knew there was something else," Kel says. "Richard is unwell, and has taken to his bed."

"What is this?" Tom Cromwell is taken aback, because his nephew never takes to his bed, save once, when he had been poisoned by a rogue priest. "Is it the sweating sickness, or worse?"

"It is a sickness of the heart, master," Kel explains. "When they took Queen Catherine prisoner, Lady Jane was with her, and they added her to the warrant. It seems Richard has made certain promises to the lady, and cannot see how to save her from Henry's wrath."

"Is there evidence against her?"

"I fear so," says Kel Kelton. "The rumours are that she did help Catherine meet with Culpeper."

"Rumours are not proof, Kel."

"The king has an unnatural dislike for her, as if she has crossed him in some way."

"Then she is a dead woman," Tom Cromwell says. "If Henry dislikes her anyway, this will give him his chance to rid the court of her, once and for all."

"Richard will get over it," Kel says. "He will see that he must cut all ties with her, and condemn her actions."

"When he thought me dead, at Henry's command, Richard went about the court wearing mourning whites, and lamented my passing to any who would listen. He is the loyalist of men, and I love him for it. See that he does not suffer for his devotion to Lady Jane, Kel."

"Yes, master."

"Is that all of your bad news, Kel, or do you save the best for the last?"

"No, sir, that is all," Kel says, "save for Will Draper losing a horse from under him. He was uncommon upset about it."

"A horse?" Tom Cromwell guesses what is coming, and feels sadness for his old friend. "Was it Moll?"

"Yes, his old cob," Kel says. "I did not think him to be so sentimental about such things."

"He was ever one for taking in strays, Kel," Cromwell replies. "You do well to thank God he did, else you would not hold your current position. It was Will who found you a place at Austin Friars, and it was he who let you ride with him that first time. You owe the man so much."

"I have saved his life before now, Master Tom," Kel objects. "Are not honours even?"

"Comradeship cannot be measured in favours given and received, Kel. That is nothing but common bartering." Cromwell thinks that his young man has risen as far as he might, and any further advancement would only ruin his already fragile sense of right and wrong. "I want you to travel to the north for me. My agent in York has retired, and I need a trustworthy man to take his place for the nonce."

"York?" Kel sees this as a huge step down, and he is not happy. "That is a job for a clerk, sir. I will be wasted there."

"You will watch the Scots for us," Cromwell says. "Things will be dull in London, after this business with the queen is done, and you will find more adventures in York than the capital."

"Maisie will not want to leave you, sir. Nor will Lucy." Kel's two wives rule him, and they enjoy living and working in Antwerp. This news will not sit well with them at all.

"Then you may think to leave them

both behind," Cromwell tells him. "You will only be gone for six months… perhaps less… then I shall find you something nearer home."

"Why?"

"You question me?"

"No… I am sorry. I shall go to York, as you wish." Kel knows that the alternative will be harsher, so keeps his mouth closed. Cromwell is satisfied. He sees, clearly, that there are bad times coming. Times that may bring down destruction on friend and foe alike. If the king is intent on vengeance, there is no telling where is suspicious mind will take him.

Richard is a Cromwell, Rafe Sadler is an old Cromwell man, and Will Draper holds a lot of military power. If the king thinks to protect himself, innocent heads may be at risk. For the past month, the old Privy Councillor has been posting his best men to far flung corners of England, in the hope of preserving Austin Friars' fragile power base.

"You send away our most loyal men, sir," Kel tells him. "I hope you know what you are doing."

"Yes, I hope so too," Cromwell says. "Now, let us take breakfast, and speak of pleasanter things."

"Ibrahim is back from Genoa." Kel

tells his master.

"Ah, my untrustworthy Moor," Tom Cromwell says, with a sparkle in his voice. The man is a favourite of his, and he rejoices at his safe return.

"Yet you send him to deal with your enemies abroad."

"He speaks five languages," the old Privy Councillor says. "Whereas you find English hard. I needed a man who could talk to the Genoese."

"About flowers?" Kel sneers.

"About poppies," Tom Cromwell replies. "The juice is a wonderful boon for mankind, and I would increase the supply, so that common men might afford it."

"The Chinamen say it is hard to grow," Kel says.

"They lie as a matter of course. The plant grows quite wild, on any old piece of ground," Tom Cromwell says. "They tell us these lies to keep the price up. Ibrahim has procured some seeds. I intend growing our own. This will force down the price, and stop the foreign swines from cheating us."

"Then I am pleased for his success, Kel replies, "for Miriam's potion will be the saviour of mankind."

"Amen to that," says Thomas

Cromwell. If nothing else, he thinks, I will give mankind a gift that all can benefit from.

*

Ibrahim ben Raschid, son of a peasant farmer from Andalucia considers himself to have come far over the years. Having once been in the employ of the Spanish Inquisition, he has moved on to better things, and now serves the prestigious Draper Company.

Since conniving over the 'death' of Thomas Cromwell, he has become a trusted envoy for the late Privy Counsellor. Now he finds himself returning from Genoa with a rare and valuable package. The few seeds he has procured from an Indian merchant will help break the monopoly enjoyed by the great Cathay mercantile houses.

He escapes from Genoa ahead of a small army of easterners, intent on his murder, and the return of the poppy seeds, only to find himself dogged by them once back on dry land.

His ship, owned by the Draper Company line is safe enough, but once it docks in Gravesend he is in mortal danger again. He arms himself with a cutlass, and a pair of pistols, and sets off to find a cog to take him across the Channel.

He is walking down the quayside when a dozen armed men, Indians, Lascars and Chinamen come from nowhere and surround him.

"Good day to you, sirs," Ibrahim says to them. "A fine day to die, I think?"

"The seeds," a tall Indian demands, and holds out his hand.

"Take them," Ibrahim says, and draws his pistols. The Indian gestures for his men to rush the Moor, but they do not move. He orders them again, but still they stand their ground.

The quay is stacked with crates and bales of wool, ready for shipping, and along the top of these men are crouching, each with a musket trained down onto the Indian and his men.

"Trouble, Ibrahim?" Mush asks.

"You are late, my friend," Ibrahim says. "I feared I would have to slay them all myself."

"There will be no killing today," Mush tells his friend. "You, sir... surrender, and we will put you back on a ship this very day. Or fight, and die where you stand."

The Indian sees that he is outnumbered, and that his men's knives are bested by muskets and long swords. He bows, politely, and signals for his men to put away their daggers.

"My masters will be displeased," he says. "We will have to return our fees."

"Better out of pocket than dead and buried," Mush tells the man. "Now, follow my men, and they will see you safe back aboard the next ship to Genoa."

"I have the seeds," Ibrahim boasts, once his would be assassins leave.

"We never doubted you," Mush says.

"Really?" the Moor replies. "Then why have your agent follow me?"

"Ah, you saw him?"

"As did our enemies," Ibrahim explains. "His body was found in the harbour just before I sailed. I fear he was not s good as you thought."

"Poor fellow," Mush says. "I will see his family are looked after. He was there to protect you, not because we doubted your loyalty, my friend."

"Of course not," Ibrahim says. "I never doubted it. Now, is the cog waiting?"

11   A Bad Business

"His Majesty instructs me to inform you of his displeasure, General Draper." Sir John Russell has no choice but to deliver these stinging words, as the king is sitting right behind him.

'If I have offended His Majesty, in any way, he shall have my immediate resignation," Will replies, and the king gives a polite cough, so as to indicate that he will speak now.

"I do not seek your resignation, sir," Henry says, "but you compliance. I instruct you to do a thing, and it is still undone. What am I to make of that?"

'Does His Majesty speak of his orders to find Thomas Culpeper?" Will addresses Russell, who has to suppress a grin. The king mutters an oath under his breath, and pushes his messenger aside.

"I speak of that very thing, sir," he snaps. "Why do you disobey me?"

"Thomas Culpeper is in custody, sire... as is Francis Dereham. They can be conveyed to the Tower, whenever you so wish."

"I so wished three weeks ago, My Lord Templar. Yes... I have confirmed your elevation, sir, thinking you were my sworn man."

"I am no one else's, Hal," Will Draper replies, and the use of his given name makes Henry gape in astonishment.

"You dare 'Hal' me, sir?"

"At your own command," Will persists. "I am to call you 'Hal' when we are alone, as you must call me 'Will'. It is a mark of our friendship, as were my actions in keeping Culpeper and Dereham out of the official record."

"What is this nonsense?" Henry stirs in his seat, and begins to think he has missed something. The idea that he might not be fully aware of all that has passed makes him uneasy.

"Not *none sense*, my dear Hal, but good sense," Will replies. "Had I taken them up, and put them in the Tower, we would never have the truth of things. The queen would simply say they lied, and that would be the end of it. By keeping them apart, I have made the queen think herself abandoned, and forced her into a rash act. It is the right thing to have done. She has confessed, and that is that. Besides, you only wanted Cully back at court, and knew nothing of this Dereham rogue."

"Oh." The king sees that Will speaks good sense, and his anger evaporates. "I thought it must be something like that, but Sir John does go on so. See Russell, you were wrong to doubt Lord Templar, my own Examiner General."

"A thousand pardons, Will," Sir John Russell says. "Whatever was I thinking of?"

"What are your orders, Hal?" the new Baronet Draper of the Inner Temple asks. "A trial, and then a swift execution for them all?"

"No, I think not. Catherine can wait upon my pleasure, and Cully and his friend can feel my wrath. Have them both put to the question by the Tower torturer."

"Hal… they have both confessed their guilt." Will sees no point in torture for the sake of it.

"Then we certainly have the right men," the king says. "I want them broken, almost to the point of death, and then, I want to watch Cully die."

"As you command," the new Lord Templar says. His elevation is a proud moment for him, but he sees that he still must bow the head to Henry, and do his dirtiest work. "Do you have any preferences? The wheel, or hot irons are both tried and tested. Then again, you might want them tied hand

and foot to four horses, and torn apart." His sarcastic remarks are quite lost on the king, who favours the more exotic forms of torture.

"I am sure Master Wake will know what to do," John Russell says, hurriedly. He takes Will by the elbow, and moves him away from the king.

"Do not bait him, I beg of you, Will," he says. "I have spent all day dissuading him from 'making an example' of Thomas Culpeper's entire family. He was for hanging the father, the mother, and his brothers, and then burning down the damned house."

"He is raving mad."

"Your wife's poppy juice does not help," Russell replies. "It makes him feel like a god. If he thinks it… then it can be done. Perhaps you should give him less."

"It is too late. He craves it, like a child after honey." Will sees now that the potion is a two edged sword, and not safe to hand out without care.

"Then do as he wants, and keep away from court as much as you can," Sir John tells him. "For, one fine day, he will recall that your wife is as rich as anyone in Europe, and that she is a Jewess. Oh, yes, he will remember, as it suits him. On that day, he shall think up some slight you have given him, and blow it out of all proportion. You might find yourself arrested by your own Examiners, and charged."

"I will have Miriam move back to Antwerp," Will tells his friend.

"Discreetly, my friend," John Russell advises. "The least thing starts him off these days."

"We have nurtured a monster in our bosoms," Will muses. "Can we then complain when he bares his fangs at us?"

"This blood letting might satisfy him for now," Russell replies. "He sees you as his friend… along with the Duke of Suffolk, and that is in your favour."

"Suffolk is hardly ever in court these days," the new Lord Templar says. Does he avoid the king on purpose?"

"He has a new woman. She prefers the country life." Russell grins at the idea of Charles Brandon being kept from court by a wench. "She abhors gambling, and will not have strong drink in the house."

"You jest."

"I do not. Brandon abstains these days, and goes to church every other day."

"Then miracles do happen." Will cannot help but smile. "What does Henry think of all this?"

"He knows nothing. Brandon begs leave from court, because he is busy seeing to the defence of the realm. With your men holding the city, he must see to the ports, and the shires. He has a brisk way about him that gets the task done."

"Then I wish him luck," Will Draper says. "May he have a long life, and a happy one… without wine!"

*

The queen's apartments have been thoroughly searched, but without any success. If any incriminating documents exist, then they are well hidden. Will leaves men looking, and goes to the Tower. He speaks with Lady Jane Boleyn, and promises to help her in any way he can.

"You must deny any involvement in the queen's business," he says, but she is not for listening to good advice.

"I think it better if I throw myself on Henry's mercy, and confess what I know. He will see I am but a minor piece on the board, and forgive me."

"No, he will kill you, madam," Will tells her. "Keep silent."

"I dare not. What if Catherine denounces me?"

"For what?" Will sees that there are

still secrets that may never be fully uncovered. "Did you conspire to help the queen in her recent adultery?"

"Not as such."

"That will not do, madam," Will says, sharply. "What did you do?"

"Nothing, save deliver the odd letter or two, but I do not know the contents... I swear."

"You gave Culpeper letters from Catherine?" Will sees now where he might find the absolute proof he wants.

"Yes... two."

"Then I must leave you, Lady Jane, but I pray for you to heed my words... deny everything. Claim Culpeper is a mad fool, and the queen an empty headed girl. I will tell the king that this is so, and he might relent, and spare you, if only because Richard Cromwell loves you."

"Yes, my dear Richard," Lady Jane says. "We are to be wed, you know."

"My congratulations, madam," Will tells her, but he can see a look in her eyes that tells him she is beginning to give up. It is the look a stag has when it is finally brought to bay, and has nowhere else to turn.

*

The Lord Templar sees now that it is

Catherine who has been the rasher of the two, and that it is she alone who dares send letters to her lover. He hopes, against hope, that Culpeper has been unwise, and kept them somewhere safe. He gives orders for the man's quarters to be thoroughly searched, and even insists that the floorboards are to be prised up.

Barnaby Fowler leads the search of Thomas Culpeper's quarters, and after an hour, he is ready to admit utter defeat. There is nothing of any interest in the sparsely furnished rooms, save a nice brace of pistols, tooled with silver, and a magnificent Spanish saddle. Both were destined as bribes; one for the Duke of Worcester, and the other for Will Draper.

"The fool thought he might buy such men with these gifts?" Fowler muses, and one of his men, a bright young fellow from the Austin Friars' camp picks up one of the pistols, and aims it at the wall.

"A fine piece of…" The gun explodes, and hurls a heavy lead ball into the plaster, inches away from Fowler's head. "Jesus!" Paul Werry cries, "I did not think it loaded, master."

"You blithering great oaf," Barnaby Fowler swears. You might have killed someone… damn it, you might have killed *me*. I think you should make sure the other one is safe too." Paul Werry puts down the discharged gun, and picks up the second weapon. He opens the pan, and blows out the pinch of powder within. Then he eases the trigger down, and taps the gun against the wall. It is hard enough to dislodge any ball, but nothing comes forth.

"Empty?" Barnaby Fowler asks.

"Probably," the younger man says, and he looks down the barrel. He gives a satisfied chuckle, and slips a finger into the muzzle. A tightly rolled parchment is within. "Look, sir, a letter."

Barnaby Fowler takes the document, and unrolls it. It is a letter from Catherine, Queen of England. The hand is childlike, and the language is disjointed, as if composed by two different hands. The lawyer suspects that Lady Jane Boleyn has been party to the composition.

Master Culpeper,

I heartily recommend me unto you, praying you to send me word of how that you do. It was showed me that you was sick, the which thing troubled me very much, and will, till such time that I hear from you.

Praying you to send me word how that you do, for I never longed so much for a thing as I do to see you, and to speak with you, the which I trust shall be shortly now.

That which doth comfort me very much when I think of it, and when I think again that you shall depart from me again it makes my heart die. To think what fortune I have that I cannot be always in your company.

My trust is always in you, that you will be as you have promised me, and in that hope I trust upon it still, praying you that you will come when my Lady Jane Rochford is here. For then I shall be best at leisure to be at your commandment, thanking you for that you have promised me.

I send you my man whom I dare trust, and I pray you take him to be with you, so that I may sometime hear from you one thing. I am as I said afore, and thus I take my leave of you, trusting to see you shortly again, and I would you was with me now, that you might see what pain I take in writing to you.

Yours as long as life endures,
C

It is Catherine's downfall, and the words condemn her lover too. Barnaby

Fowler rolls up the parchment, and tucks it into his doublet.

"Well done, Master Werry," he says to the pleased young man. Had you not shot that wall, we would never have found it. Here, take this." The lawyer hands a coin over to the lad.

"A golden pound, sir?" he says, wide eyed with surprise.

"Yes," Barnaby Fowler replies, in time honoured tradition. "It will keep you honest."

*

"Good day, sir, I am Abraham Wake, the senior torturer of the Tower of London. It is my born duty to exact confessions from you both."

"We have already confessed," Francis Dereham says, from where he hangs in chains. "For the love of God, man."

"God does not get down her too often, for it is nearer Hell than Heaven," Wake replies. "I have my orders. You are both to be tortured… with Master Culpeper receiving special attention.'

"Then get on with it," Dereham says to the torturer. "How shall it be?"

"Quick, for you, sir," Wake explains. "I am not a cruel man. You must be seen to be ill done to, so I shall break one of your arms, and one of your legs, and beat you about the face. It will look worse than it is. The court will approve, and then... off to the gibbet."

"And me?" Tom Culpeper is bemused by the turn of events. He has gone from living the life of a gentleman, in a fine house, to being stretched out on a bare wooden table in the blink of an eye. "The Earl Warwick and My Lord Suffolk will hear of this. You dare to threaten me, fellow?"

"I dare sir, for it is my vocation." Wake knows of the wild stories, and that no great lords will come to save the poor wretch.

"You fool," Cully tells him. "Even as I speak, great men are rousing their forces to come to my aid. The Examiners will storm this tower, and set me free, whilst Norfolk and Suffolk shall pull Henry from his throne, and hand me his crown."

"Fair enough, sir" Abraham Wake tells him, but sees that he is quite deranged. It is never good to torture the mad, he thinks, as the condition is catching, and might infect him as he works. "I shall deal with poor Master Dereham first, then see to you. If your rescuers have not arrived by then, I fear I must start on your fingers."

Francis Dereham is a scoundrel, but

he prides himself on his courage, and he does not scream until the blocks are placed on each side of his thigh. The steady pressure, as the mallet does its work and tightens the solid oak blocks is too much to bear, and when the thigh bone splits, he cries for his mother.

"Nearly done now, sir," Wake tells him, soothingly. "You have stood it far better than most." One last tap, and Dereham passes out. "There, now he can rest. Come now, Master Culpeper, we must get on about our own business. Where is your army... not here yet, I see?"

"They are delayed," Cully says, and tries to pull himself free. "Perhaps if we give them another hour?"

Abraham Wake knows that any delay is only cruel to the victim, so he starts. The pincers are red hot for a reason; so that as the fingers are snipped off, the searing heat cauterises the raw wounds. Cully passes out as the torturer reaches the middle finger of the right hand. He remains unconscious as Wake removes two fingers from each hand, and breaks the thumbs, but he wakes up in time to feel something cold and hard being placed about his genitals.

"Oh, dear Christ!" The imprecation is cut off by a long, wailing scream. The huge pliers crush down, and end Cully's adulteress days for ever. After a rest, Abraham Wake will return to his task, and break most of the bones in Thomas Culpeper's body, save the legs, which he will need to walk into court.

"I did it. I did lay with the queen," he mutters through swollen lips. "I swived her, time and again."

"Yes, I know, sir," Abraham Wake replies. "It makes no never mind. Soon done now." The hot irons are an afterthought, and they score wicked welts across his flesh, but he is beyond feeling now.

"Done?" Sir John Russell asks from his dark corner. "The king wishes it to be painful, Master Wake."

"Then he has his wish," the torturer tells the gentleman. "Any more, and he will die. Let me have his wounds tended, lest they fester."

"Yes, of course. I take no pleasure in this, Master Wake." Sir John Russell wrinkles his nose up at the stench of burnt flesh. "It is just that the king insists."

"Bless, sir, but I understand." The Tower's long serving torturer replies. "We all want a bit of revenge, now and then. It is only that the king can demand it on a greater scale. Perhaps, if he came down here, and did it himself, he might find a spark of humanity in his soul."

"That is dangerous talk, sir," Russell says, but he cannot disagree. "Can you arrange the executions?"

"How many?"

"Three, at least."

"Then the queen is guilty too?"

"Can you doubt it?"

"Twenty pounds for the three, and I get to keep the clothes."

"Fifteen, you rogue."

"Twenty, or find another," Wake tells him. "I care not for killing women. They wave their arms about, and want to pray to distraction."

"Very well, twenty it is."

"Payable up front, and not refundable," the old torturer says. Later, he will write out a report of the day, and hand it over to Kel Kelton, who will take it to Antwerp on his next visit.

*

"The queen says you encouraged her to pay immoral attention to Culpeper, madam." Mush Draper is put to interviewing Lady Jane Boleyn, and he sees that it is a test of his loyalty to the king. "Forgive me for asking, Jane. I would rather not have this terrible task."

"Then listen well. I counselled them both against it," Lady Jane replies, "but they would have none of it from me. I could not dissuade them."

"But you still allowed it to continue?" Mush asks. "You could have reported your suspicions to me, or Will."

"It was known by many at court," Lady Jane tells Mush. "Why am I singled out? Her own uncle knew."

"Norfolk knew?" Mush sees that this, if put into evidence, will be another nail in Norfolk's coffin lid. "You are absolutely sure?"

"Of course he knew. He was hoping that Cully made her pregnant, so it could be foisted off onto the king."

"You have proof?"

"Do you have proof of my guilt, my dear Mush?"

"Only Catherine's admission. She swears she was led astray by an older woman, and that this makes her somehow 'less' guilty."

"She thinks this will save her?" Lady Jane laughs at the absurdity of the thing.

"I imagine so. Once she confessed in front of a dozen witnesses, she was forced to find a scapegoat. The king, however, will not believe a word of it."

"Then I shall go free?" Lady Jane thinks she might yet escape.

"Not yet," Mush tells her. "Rafe and Richard whisper to the king, daily, and it is likely he will have you confined in the Tower of London for some time. Then he might well forget you, and let the charges slip."

"Really?"

"It is what we hope for," Mush tells her. "Once he has done for Culpeper and Dereham, he will attend to Catherine. She cannot hope to live. After that, his lust for revenge might waver."

"Then I must pray my luck holds," she says. She stands, and paces the small chamber. "Might I have a larger room, sir?"

"I shall see what can be done," Mush replies. "Abraham Wake is an accommodating fellow, for a price."

"I have no gold."

"Richard will pay. He is intent on your release, and can afford it."

"We are promised."

"I know, but it is best the king does not find that out, else he will suspect you *both* of treason."

"Is it treason now to love, Mush?"

"Everything is treason, if the king wills it," the young Jew tells her. "All the poppy juice in the world cannot stop the king's leg festering, and the poison eats him up inside. It gnaws at his soul, and lets him think the most preposterous things."

"Then he might not live?" Lady Jane asks, and Mush shrugs his shoulders.

"It is treason to even think such a thing, Jane," he replies. "Though his passing would save many lives. He has decided that the northern counties must be subdued, and has the Lord Warwick hanging innocent aldermen and farm boys from the oak trees by the score."

"Then I must hope and pray."

"Yes, but do it silently," Mush advises her. "There are ears everywhere, and they would like to report you to Henry for a golden crown or two."

"Is life so cheap then?"

"Thomas Cromwell hoped to make England a better place, but things are no different than they were. Innocent men hang, and others are condemned on the word of scoundrels. Professional spies, who work for themselves have become a thing of today."

"You have my statement now, Mush. How will it go?"

"I shall tell Henry that you deny helping his queen, and that I believe you. If that helps, then so be it. Until then, you shall have better quarters, My Lady."

Mush stands, and bows to Lady Jane, then slips out of the chamber. Abe Wake is outside, waiting. Mush takes a purse of silver from his belt and hands it over.

"A better room, Abe, and see that her food is plentiful, and her bed is well made."

"As you wish, Master Mush," Abe Wake says. "How is the *Mijnheer* taking things?"

"Badly," Mush says. "He longs to be able to return to England." The torturer puts a finger to his lips, and nods to the nearest corner. He has good ears, and thinks someone is listening. "Still that is not likely, is it?" As he speaks, Mush moves towards the place, like a cat, and reaches around into the darkness. He comes back with a thin little fellow, whom he has caught by the ear.

"Ho!" Wake grins. "If it ain't Master Grimm, the Duke of Norfolk's new executioner. What ho, Artie… lost your way to the White Tower?"

"Just passin', Master Wake," the man squeals. "I was curious as to who was loitering in the corridors."

"Why, it is Sir Mush Draper, my friend," Wake says, "and he is not partial to being spied upon."

"Spied? Not me, old friend. I heard nothing anyway. Nothing, save about some foreign gent, and I did not understand the meaning," Grimm says.

It seals his fate. If he reports how a Flemish gentleman wishes to return to England, it will set cleverer minds in motion, and place Tom Cromwell in a place of danger. Mush draws his knife, and thrusts it up, under the man's ribs, and into his heart. The little man looks at him as if in reproach, then slides down to his knees. Mush eases him down to the cold stone floor, and pulls his blade free.

"Can you dispose of the body for me, Abe?" Mush asks. "I regret causing you the trouble, but he could not live."

"I'll drop him into the moat, for the rats to devour," Wake confirms. He is easy with the casual murder, for he understands its necessity, and he is still a Cromwell man. "I never did like the scummy little bastard. He would hurt for hurt's sake."

"Then I have done us both a favour," Mush tells him. "What if the Duke of Norfolk misses him?"

"What if he does?" Abe Wake says.

"The duke is hardly in a position to start fussing, is he? Henry thinks him involved in this latest scandal. No, he will hold his tongue and wonder at his toady's disappearance."

"Then I must be off and make my report," Mush replies. "Henry is impatient these days, and will want to know how my interviews went. He pores over every word, looking for any sign of treason against himself."

"Good luck, my dear sir," Master Wake says, and he means it, most sincerely. If the king is set on finding treason amongst his closest courtiers, then he will find it, even if it does not exist. There are very hard times coming for some.

*

Sir John Russell returns to Henry, and describes the torture of Culpeper in the most graphic detail. The king nods his satisfaction at how expertly the fingers have been cut off, and pops a sweetmeat into his mouth.

"What day are we, Sir John?" he asks.

"It is the last day of November, sire," John Russell replies.

"Then the two men must go to the Guildhall on the morrow, and stand trial. I am assured of their guilt, and the jury is to be notified of my unwavering belief. They are to be found guilty, and sentenced to a traitor's death."

"Sire… I can see how this common fellow, Dereham, deserves that fate, but Cully was your favourite. In his way, he loves you well. Almost like a son unto a father."

"Yes, you speak well for him, Russell, and I am minded to forgive him for the treason. Let it be adultery then, and only the axe is to be his punishment."

"You are a wise ruler, sir." Sir John bows. "His family will appreciate the kindness of their king." The family will heave a sigh of relief, for traitors forfeit all they own, and the land and house is in Cully's name. His death will not inconvenience them now, and the family wealth, for what it is, will be safeguarded against confiscation.

"As for the women…" Henry stops, as if something sticks in his throat. "Catherine Howard is guilty of the most wicked sin against me. She must also face her own trial, but not just yet. She and the damned Boleyn woman are to be kept locked up. The Howard woman shall be held at Syon House, and Lady Boleyn can reside within the Tower, but in decent chambers. We will ruminate on their fates, and see what the new year brings."

"Yes, sire." Russell knows that there

is a move to have Lady Jane exonerated, or at least, forgiven, but now is not the moment to try and further her cause. "I shall see to it at once."

"Where is Rizz?" Henry asks. He is to lose one favourite, so must bring on another to take his place.

"In the outer court, sire."

"Send him in to me."

Sir Thomas Wriothesley bows as he enters, and sees that the king is in a much mellower mood. It is a relief and he ventures a genial smile.

"Your Majesty is looking so much better today," he says. "You are feeling so too, I hope."

"I am, my boy," the king admits. "For the pricking thorn in my side will soon be pulled, and my honour left untarnished."

"Excellent news. How may I serve you, sire?" Rizz knows the king wants something, else why summon him? Henry likes those he trusts close by, so that he might demand a favour whenever the mood takes him.

"I want you to attend tomorrow's trials, my dearest boy. You are to carry this with you." Henry hands over a royal scroll, bedecked with seals. "It will mark you out as my own trusted man. Stand by the jury, as if to guide them, and make sure they reach the correct conclusion. Then you must attend the executions, and tell me how they went."

"An honour, sire." Rizz is overjoyed at the thought. Men will see how high he stands in the king's favour now, and it will do his worth no harm at all. To be in the king's favour means that the Lombard bankers will reassess his standing at court and give him greater credit. With access to money, he can dress better, buy a new horse and a pair of decent falcons.

With good birds of prey on his arm, and a fine hunter beneath him, he will be an ever present when the king rides out. This will rank him alongside the Lord Suffolk and keep him ever in the kings vision.

"I value your loyalty, Rizz," Henry tells him, "and I look forward to your report."

"I am Your Majesty's most loyal servant," Rizz says, and he bows himself out of the throne room backwards.

"Damned fine lad," Henry says to Russell. "We must do something for him. Is not there a High Sheriff's post going in Shropshire?"

"He would have to live there, sire," Russell replies. "You might consider making him Warden of the Ports. Then he can remain at court."

"Does it pay enough?"

"Three hundred a year, sire."

"That will do for now," Henry says. "Have it arranged, John."

*

"Lord Templar, Your Majesty," the court chamberlain announces, and Will Draper strides into the throne room with a confidence he does not fully feel. The king holds out his big hands, and clasps both of Will's in his.

"My good and faithful servant," Henry says. "I knew you would not fail me in my hour of need."

"Of course not, sire."

"Tell me, how long did you have Culpeper in custody for?" Henry asks. He is not stupid, and he sees now that Cully's disappearance was nothing to do with the plague. For his part, Will is taken aback, for this is a conversation he has already had with Henry, and he fears that the poppy juice is affecting the king's mind.

"About a month, sire," Will admits again. "I knew he was guilty, but I dared not charge him without proof. Once the proof came to light, I was able to reveal his whereabouts."

"You lied to me?" Henry asks, and then frowns. The words are familiar, as if he has asked this question before.

"I did, Your Majesty," Will says. "It was for your own good. Had I told you, your honour would have forced you to act at once, and some of the guilty might have escaped your wrath. You would not have lied, even to right a wrong, sire."

"True, It is ever my downfall. I am far too honest a fellow, and cannot abide deception." Henry says it, and in a short while, he will believe it. "I forgive you for your mendacity, old friend. It was a wrong, but done for the right reasons."

"Thank you, Hal." Will bows, and sees that the king is flustered now, as he recalls some earlier conversation.

"Have we spoken of this matter before?" he asks, and Will has his answer ready to use.

"I do not recall it, sire," he says. "Perhaps you have thought about the thing so hard, that it was imprinted on your mind?"

"Of course. I have been thinking on things, and saw that Cully must be being held somewhere. The mind does... some odd things to you, old friend."

Too much poppy juice does much the same, Will thinks, and resolves to try and wean the king off the potent medicine.

"No matter, sire," Will says. "The felons are caged, and but await your royal decisions."

"The dates are set for the trials."

"Then that is that, sire," Will says.

"There is but one more thing that you can do for me," the king says. "If ever I speak of marrying again, knock me on the head, and throw me into the Tower."

"I will need that in writing, sire," Will says, and they both laugh. The Draper family are in the clear once more, and it will be business as usual, come the morrow. Two men, and a queen must die, but that is nothing to the wider world. The English are an odd race, and the foreigners expect the occasional bloodletting over common adultery.

"What will the French say?" Henry muses.

"Bugger the French," Will responds as expected. "The Holy Roman Empire will not be bothered. Eustace Chapuys assures me that the emperor has enough on his plate with the Nurnberg riots at the moment."

"Then all is well," Henry says."How sits the new title, my friend?"

"It sits better on my lovely wife, sire, who loves being Lady Templar," Will says. "My men still call me General Will, and that is as it should be, of course. It keeps my feet firmly on the ground."

"Dear Will, now you are ennobled, it must be ever Hal and Will between us."

"As you wish, Hal," Will Draper says. "I am honoured by your friendship." Ten years ago he was fighting for his very life in a stinking Irish bog, and now, he is made to be a fine lord. Funny how things work out, he thinks. He is finally dismissed, and there is time enough for him to visit home and see the children for a while.

He cuts through the rose garden, now covered in a fine frost, and emerges from the east gate. It is little used, and the guard has slipped away to find himself a hot brazier to warm his hands against. The usual beggars are loitering, and they set up a cry for alms when he appears amongst them.

"Alms, master?" one of them begs, and holds out a hand. Others cluster in, and beg for a coin or two. Will cannot refuse them, and always has a bag of pennies to hand out, he bends his head to find his purse, and it is at that moment one of them hits him from behind. The blow is savage, and it makes him fall down onto one knee.

A second beggar kicks him in the side, and Will catches his foot, and twists it hard. The man yelps in pain, and a third man swings his club against Will's head. The blow knocks him senseless, and the last thing he recalls is being kicked repeatedly in the ribs and the back. He blacks out, and the beggars lift him, and carry him down to the water's edge. A sleek boat is waiting, manned by men with concealed faces.

"Hurry now," the Earl of Surrey commands from the boat. "Bind him, and get him on board, you scum."

"Cut his throat, sir?" one of the men asks. "It will only take a moment."

"Later, Naughton," Surrey says, "after I have taught him a lesson or two in manners. My Lord Templar shall disappear this day, and never be seen again."

"Better to cut his damned throat, sir," the man says. "Let him live, and he will have you, as sure as can be."

"Not again," Surrey says, as he recalls how he has been constantly humiliated by the man over the years. "Now he is in my power, and he must play out this little game by my rules."

"This is Will Draper, sir," Naughton

persists. "He does not think of this as a clever little game. He is a born killer of men. He has never been bested, and few of his opponents have ever lived to boast of it. If it is a game, then the general plays by his own rules, and no mistake. Kill him now, I implore you, or risk his anger later. The man is the devil himself, and will destroy us all if he gets a chance."

"Enough!" Surrey must have his hour of pleasure and he is in no mood for a servant's advice... no matter how good it is. "Take him to my house in Peterborough, and shackle him, hand and foot, in the cellar."

"The old root cellar, sir, or the one your grandfather used to use for his... his little pleasures."

"Oh, there are two are there?" Surrey is suddenly interested. He has never been below stairs, and news of a further secret cellar intrigues him.

"The old duke was keen on using a riding whip when he was in the saddle, sir," the man explains. "My father tells me that he used the cellar for his swiving, so as not to disturb her ladyship with all the screaming. I believe their are manacles fitted to the walls."

"The saucy old bastard," Surrey says, with true admiration. "Yes, that sounds quite the place for my friend. Lock him up soundly... you hear?"

"Yes, Your Lordship. Are we to feed him?" Naughton asks. He has no qualms about starving their captive to death, but he must have orders.

"Every other day," Surrey says, with a childish smirk on his face. "And then only a little bread, and some water."

"It will make him weak," Naughton says, "His muscles will waste away, and he will become maddened with thirst... but I would still rather we just cut his throat, My Lord Surrey."

"Would you rather take his place, Master Naughton?" Surrey means it, and Naughton falls silent. "That is much better. I think you must get on, before we have some nosey courtier poking themselves into my business."

"Yes, sir." Naughton signals to the men, and the boat is quickly boarded. It is not possible to reach Peterborough via the river, but the Thames will allow them an easy egress from the city. Then they must put their captive in a cart and deliver him into his final captivity.

Naughton, who is somewhat cleverer than his master, has Will Draper's weapons taken from him, and also his new doublet. It is a present from his wife, and is adorned with rhinestones at the collar and the cuffs.

"Make sure it is stained with his blood," the man instructs one of his men. "I will see to the placing of it." Naughton waits until they are through a couple of bends in the river before he splashes ashore, and lays the doublet on the water line. It is far enough in to get a soaking, but not to be pulled away by the tide. He walks down the shore for a few yards, and drops the ivory handled dagger in the mud. He treads it into the wet ground, yet makes sure enough is showing for it to be easily discovered. It is not much of a deception, but enough to fool many folk.

Harry Howard, the Earl of Surrey sees none of this, for he is not for the discomforts of a rowing boat on a darkening night. He has a hired palanquin waiting at the south exit of the palace, which will take him to Bishopsgate, where he will be outside the city walls. From there, he has a comfortable carriage waiting for him.

By the next morning, he will be at his manse ... a huge, grey thing, purloined from an out of favour Bishop of Ely, during the bloody Wars of the Roses. Surrey thinks himself to be quite the man, having bested the infamous Will Draper, and gives no consideration to the dozen men he has had to employ in gaining his own ends. His enemy is in his power now, and he cannot wait to start exacting his revenge.

"On with you, lads," he cries to the palanquin bearers. "An extra sixpence to share, if you do not jog me over much!"

12 The Searchers

Sir Thomas Wriothesley is the coming man at court, and he is treated as such by all those wise enough to see it. The king favours him, even in front of Rafe Sadler, because he is of more noble birth, and he uses him to carry out those tasks he thinks Sadler is too ethically minded to complete.

Since his knighthood, Rizz has been granted vast tracts of church land in the southern counties, and done things for Henry that would make most men blanch. He has rooted out the king's enemies in Yorkshire, and condemned them, without trial. It is even rumoured that he 'turned off' several malcontents himself, happily kicking away the ladder, and watching them jerk and twist their lives away.

Now he is to carry out one more task for his sovereign lord. Henry wants to know how Thomas Culpeper and Francis Dereham go to their deaths. The king has boasted at how he will watch the men die, but he is not able to travel, because of his throbbing leg, and he is averse to standing in a cold courtyard for so fleeting a pleasure.

Each man is guilty of the same sin, but Cully is to be honoured. Henry does not wish him to suffer the agony of a traitor's death... but just to die.

"Nice and quickly does it with Cully, Master Wake," Rizz tells the ageing Tower torturer. "Culpeper is to go with great dignity."

"Dignity?" Abraham Wake grins at this. "They all piss themselves at the end, sir. They cannot help it."

"Just as long as it is fast," Rizz replies. "The king wants to be merciful."

"Then let him go," Wake mutters, and goes off to see to the length of the rope, and the sharpness of the axe.

"Damned surely fellow," Rizz says, and turns to Mush Draper and Barnaby Fowler. "You will bear witness, gentlemen, that I have instructed the fellow to make Cully's end swift?"

"We shall," Barnaby Fowler confirms. He has no business there, but during his weeks as Culpeper's gaoler, he has come to like the poor fool. "Though the lad is quite mad, you know. He is not really fit to hang and the king must know it. Lord Templar thinks he should be placed in a mad house."

"Tell the king of your concerns, Master Fowler," Rizz replies coldly. "The verdict and the sentence was written out a day before the trial."

"Then the king openly flouts the laws of England," Mush says.

"The king *is* the law," Rizz tells him. "Now, who is this coming along here?"

"Master Kelton," Mush says. "He works for the Draper Company, I believe, and he wishes to witness the final act."

"Why, what business is it of his as to how these men meet their ends?" Rizz asks, and Mush cannot tell him the truth. Kel is there as Tom Cromwell's eye witness, and is to report back on the morrow.

"Good day, Sir Thomas," Kel bows to Rizz, who preens at the recognition. "I am here, acting for Lady Miriam Draper. Both of these rogues have loans with our company, to the tune of over a hundred pounds each. I am to see what they leave behind, in the hope of recouping our outlay."

"You seek to dun the condemned out of money, even as they go to meet their maker?" Rizz grins at the thought. The bankers must lose out in the end, and it amuses him to think of how they will mourn the loss of income.

"I am to retrieve what I can and reduce our losses," Kel lies.

"The clothes, and anything in their

purses, go to Abraham Ware," Rizz explains the niceties of a judicial execution. "I fear you will come away empty handed, fellow."

"Then I will go to their families for our money," Kel says, with a careless shrug of his shoulders. "Someone will have to pay for their profligacy. When do we start?"

"Soon enough," Rizz says. "You gentlemen may watch, of course, but I cannot spare troops to keep you safe. The mob can get a little boisterous at these affairs, and my pikemen must guard the prisoners, and then ring the gibbet."

"We can easily make shift for ourselves, Rizz," Mush Draper says, and taps the hilt of his sword. "Though I doubt many would wish to riot on poor Cully's behalf."

"Perhaps not," Rizz replies. In truth, he has brought along fifty pikemen to keep himself safe. Since he began acting against the king's enemies for him, the mob have taken a dislike to his face. He is often pelted with stinking fruit, or shouted at and abused in the streets. "These scum will fight over anything."

"Scum, sir?" Barnaby Fowler is ready to pick a quarrel with the man, whom he finds to be the worst kind of courtier. "You arrested a Calvinist last week, and broke him on the rack, without resorting to a trial. These 'scum' resent such high handed actions by the king's *guffer*." The insult in the word is clear, for Rizz is only there to '*guffer this*' or '*guffer that,*' not act as Henry's private henchman in chief. The mob hate such men, and will do him harm if given the chance.

"I sought information from the man, not a confession," Rizz says, in his own defence. "If he had committed a crime, I would have had him tried, of course."

"You racked an innocent man… for information?" Mush finds this to be quite repugnant. It is not how Tom Cromwell sees the way forward for England.

"Not innocent. I needed to find a confederate of his, and he told me where to look. Then he confessed to having illegal books in his possession."

"After you stretched his bones some more," Barnaby Fowler says, with mounting disgust. "It is against the law, sir. You should have a legal warrant, and witnesses to the deed."

"Speak to the king," Rizz says, and he sees that he will easily win this particular argument. "Henry commands, and I obey. The man was asked, and refused to answer. That alone was bordering on treason. He had to speak up, and I fear that the rack was an obvious choice."

"You actually turned the wheel yourself," Barnaby says. "Did it give you pleasure, sir?"

"I resent that," Rizz says, rather haughtily. "You imply that I take pleasure in inflicting pain."

"Then call me out," Fowler tells him. "Strike me with your glove, and demand some satisfaction."

"I do not brawl with ... commoners."

"Is that out of good taste, or cowardice?" Barnaby Fowler is quite prepared to push Rizz into a fight, and kill him. "Call me out, sir, and be damned to you."

"The king will forbid it," Rizz says, but the barb has struck home. He knows he is a coward, and he hides behind his new office like a shield. "The Attorney General says duelling is illegal."

"Richard Rich is a worthless, perjured little shit," Mush puts in, and Kel Kelton sniggers. Though Cromwell is abroad, and 'dead', his work goes on, and part of that work is to foil the advancement of Rich, Norfolk, and men like them. Will Draper is now the head of the Austin Friars faction, and he will lead the struggle.

"We should have cut his throat, all those years ago," Kel Kelton says. "Now, are we getting to it, gentlemen? I have a cog to catch, and the tide waits for no man."

Sir Thomas Wriothesley - Rizz to his diminishing circle of friends - signals to one of the guards, and the sorry spectacle begins to unfold.

"I thought Will might attend," Mush says. "He is with the king though, and I doubt he can escape."

"His Majesty is most verbose these days," says Barnaby Fowler. "Will says that Lady Miriam's marvellous new potion can heal a dead man, but it can also loosen his tongue, and give him visions."

"Visions?" Mush thinks such things are for hysterical nuns, or charlatans looking for a way to steal your purse. "The holy kind, you mean?"

"No, far from it. Last week, Henry was convinced that this small dog was talking to him. The poor little creature is called '*Crommie*', for it has a most unfortunate resemblance to the master. Henry found himself in conversation with the poor mutt."

"What did it say?" Mush asks, and Barnaby chuckles at the question.

"Nothing, of course," he replies. "For it is but a dog. The king told Will that the poor thing was uttering the most dire threats against the crown... in a Scottish accent."

"*Mashugana*," Mush curses. "The dog was Scottish?"

"No... the dog was..." Barnaby stops, as he sees that he is being jested against. "The upshot was that Henry wanted the animal tried, and executed. Will took the traitorous talking dog back to Draper House, where it now lives happily with Gwyllam and his siblings."

"Ah, yes, I know the beast," Mush says. "Though it has barely spoken a word since joining the family."

"Your jests are almost funny... now hush, here come our culprits, and.... sweet Jesus, but what have they done to them?"

It is a piteous sight. Thomas Culpeper, once the most beautiful boy in the court, looks like an aged beggar. His hands are swathed in bandages, his body is scarred with welts and burn marks, and one of his arms hangs useless at his side.

"Master Wake is an expert at his job," Mush says. "Though Francis Dereham seems to have been better used. At least, he can walk without support."

"It was Henry's idea," Rizz says, for he fears another verbal attack from men he hoped were his friends. "I counselled against such wicked treatment, but he overruled me."

"Yes, I can just see you standing up to the king," Barnaby Fowler snaps. "I wager you gave him a real tongue lashing."

"Let it be," Mush tells his comrade. "The damage is done, and that is that. Now we must do our duty, and watch this wicked thing progress."

"They swived the queen, Mush," Rizz objects. "That is an offence that cannot be forgiven."

"Dereham lay with her three years ago, before the king knew her, and the evidence against Cully is not conclusive. I wager that a good lawyer, or even an ordinary one, like my friend Barnaby here, could put up a stout defence."

"Yes. The boy is disturbed, as if by demons," Barnaby says, ignoring the sly dig at him. "Then there is the letter. It speaks of talking to one another, with no mention of a carnal act. Then again, it is sent from the queen... and there is no reply. Culpeper did not encourage her in the least. The boy is not competent to act against the king."

"Nevertheless, the damned fellow is

guilty," Rizz insists, "for the king says so, and the king cannot be wrong. To suggest as much is treason, as is even thinking he might ever err. You will find these laws are binding, as written by poor Thomas Cromwell."

"Yes, they are sound enough," Barnaby Fowler admits. He can do no other, for he has helped write many of them. "They are good laws, if not abused."

"By the king, sir?"

The lawyer sees the clumsy trap that Wriothesley sets for him, and avoids it skilfully.

"By those who might badly advise him, sir," Barnaby Fowler replies. "Is it the king's fault if he listens to bad advice? What if things unravel, and someone mentions the cardinal to him? Or Tom Cromwell? See how well *their* detractors have faired."

"Cardinal Wolsey is history," Rizz declares, and Cromwell is a proven traitor."

The blow comes in low, and hard. Rizz can do nothing but expel the air from his lungs, and try gasp in more. He almost doubles over, and Barnaby takes his elbow, and keeps him upright.

"It is only that we are in front of witnesses that you still live, Master Rizz. One more slight against my old master, and I will see you are found in the Thames, with eels eating out your eye sockets. Do you understand me, sir?"

"I am the king's chosen man," Rizz wheezes as he tries to remain upright.

"As was Tom Cromwell, Thomas More, Wolsey, Norris, and Culpeper. Do you see a pattern, sir?"

"I can scarce walk," Rizz complains.

"Nonsense. The thing was but a love tap, Rizz," Mush Draper tells him. "My friend here can punch you so hard, your teeth would come out of your arse!"

*

"How went it, my dear boy?" The king has his conciliatory face on. He wishes to show that he is full of remorse over an act he could not avoid. "I so dislike having to condemn someone I once thought of almost as a son."

"Sire, he was a loathsome traitor," Rizz says, consolingly. "You loved him, as the man you are, but you condemned him as a king. It could not be avoided."

"Yes, you speak only the truth, my friend. Did he make a good end of it?"

"Enough of one, sire. He made great play of his injuries, which I found to be somewhat pathetic. Then I gave the order to have them brought forth. Both Tom Culpeper, and Francis Dereham were tied onto hurdles, and drawn from the Tower of London to Tyburn. As they were not of noble birth, they could not be executed within the Tower precincts."

"Quite right. We must observe the etiquette of the occasion. The crowd behaved itself, I hope?" Henry always fears the mob, for if they ever found a good leader, he would need a hundred thousand men just to hold London and his palaces.

"I had a troop of pikemen, sire, and several armed gentlemen with us. There were some crude remarks shouted out, concerning Culpeper's immoral behaviour with the queen, but I sent my stoutest men into the mob, and had some of their thick heads broken."

"I should think so too," Henry agrees. "The rabble cannot be allowed too many liberties." The king does not know that a roughhouse developed, and several innocent onlookers were clubbed senseless.

"We reached Tyburn at the appointed hour, and set about the task. As you expressed a wish for him not to suffer, I so ordered it that Culpeper went first. The lad made a rambling exhortation...to me, about how his people would soon come and rescue him. He seemed to be confused. Then he begged the common people to pray for his soul, and this was met with the usual coarse jests. With much play on the *soles* of his feet soon dangling high, and even cruder things about the queen's carnal desires, I thought it only meet to hurry on."

"I commuted the hanging and drawing, did I not?" Henry is in the thrall of his poppy juice potion, and is finding it hard to separate the reality from the make believe.

"You did sire, and when the crowd saw that he was not to hang, they grew quite restless. Culpeper was standing on the ground by the gallows, I gestured to him, he kneeled down, and his head was stricken off with one clean blow."

"Then it was as it should be," Henry says. "A humane end for a once loyal servant. May God forgive him that which I could not."

"Then Francis Dereham, a man of poor breeding and low morals, was brought up, and he made as if to make a long speech, but the mob were having none of his sudden show of unctuous piety. They pelted him with rotting fruit and small stones, until he stopped. Abraham Wake pushed him up the turning off ladder, and they put the noose about his neck. He was slow hanged, and he kicked for a few minutes, until the executioner bid him to be lowered, whilst he still drew breath. Then the fellow took up a cleaver and dismembered Dereham. He drew out his bowels, and held them up for all to see. Then he beheaded him, and quartered the body. Most neatly done. Both their heads are now set on London Bridge."

"You have served me well, Rizz," the king says. "I have a mind to find you a another new post. What say you?"

"I might serve you best as a secretary to the new council, sire."

"Splendid idea," Henry says. "I shall have Will Draper confirm the post, as soon as possible. Is he in court?"

"No, sire. He is absent. Perhaps he is travelling abroad again?"

"Yes, I suppose so. Still… as soon as he turns up… what?"

*

Miriam Draper has preparations for Christmas well underway. The *Palais de Juis* is to be full of guests again, and the feasts will be spectacular. Maisie and Lucy are in charge of the food, and they have excelled themselves, drawing ingredients from the four corners of the known world.

"What about the wines, My Lady?" Maisie asks. "With so many guests, we might run low."

"Send word to Mijnheer Karel at the Bruges warehouse," Miriam decides. "Have him send over another three barrels of the cheap French, and two more of the sweet Portuguese."

"As you wish, madam," Maisie says to her mistress. "They will drive you to penury. Never have I seen such gluttons."

"It is Christmas," Miriam scolds her chief cook and house keeper. "I must see that Will's largess is enjoyed by all."

"Then we are to feed the poor too?"

"Them first," Lady Miriam tells her. "Both here, and at the London houses. Good soup… with meat in it, and a ha'penny loaf of bread each."

"That will be a thousand loaves, and a hundred gallons of soup," Maisie says. "Do you know what that will cost?"

"Sixty pounds, a feed," Miriam says. "The twelve days of Christmas, by three meals a day. How are your sums, Maisie?"

"A hundred and eighty pounds a day for seven houses," Maisie says. She knows how to do her accounts right enough. "That is twelve hundred and sixty pounds, by the twelve days."

"A little over fifteen thousand pounds," Miriam tells the girl. "A small price to pay for keeping the poor people fed."

"You're soft in the head," Maisie says. "You can't feed the world."

"Then I must feed those that I can."

Maisie shrugs, and goes off to see how the game pies are coming along. It is still a fortnight off the festivities, but the meat and game must be hung for as long as possible.

"You are a good woman, Miriam," Tom Cromwell says. He is loitering in a corner of the great hall, with Gwyllam, her eldest son. "You never turn away anyone."

"What is this?" Miriam Draper feigns annoyance. "Are you children playing nicely?"

"Uncle *Tomas* is showing me how to creep up on the enemy." Gwyllam, despite his mother's attempts to turn him into a little gentleman, has his father's martial outlook.

"Really?" Miriam sees the sword at her son's waist, and frowns at Tom Cromwell. "A real sword, Master Tom?"

"The boy won the weapon in battle," Cromwell says, defensively. "You should let him learn how to use it. A man must know how to defend himself in this wicked world."

"I understand, but not today. I have too much to do, and your help would be appreciated. I need a guest list, and an idea of where I am to board them."

"Oh, the usual will come," Thomas Cromwell tells her. "Eustace Chapuys has written, and will be here on the Eve of Christmas. Then there will be Kel, Richard, Mush…"

"Write it down," Miriam says to her permanent houseguest. "I cannot possibly remember it all."

"Of course," Thomas Cromwell says, as he realises Miriam is more fraught than is usual. "Are you unwell, my dear?"

"No, I am not."

"Perhaps a chill?"

"No."

"Then a…"

"I am pregnant," Miriam snaps.

"Oh, my dear girl!" Cromwell comes to her, and gives her a hug. "No wonder you are so out of sorts. How far along are you?"

"Not far," Miriam tells him. "I thought it all behind me, and now… a fourth child."

"Mother," Gwyllam asks, "what does pregnant mean?"

"It means my work will be made

harder from now on, my little man, and I will have to have Pru and the rest of my girls do more for the business."

"I will help," Gwyllam tells her, solemnly. "I will guard your boats."

"Keep away from the harbour," Tom Cromwell tells the child. "Do your guarding at home."

"Yes, Uncle *Tomas*." Gwyllam says, then grins at a happy occurrence. "See now, Uncle *Tomas*… here is Master Kel. He will help me."

"I was not expecting you just yet, Kel," Cromwell says. He senses from the young man's face that something is wrong.

"I caught an earlier cog, Master Tom," Kel says. "I have urgent reports for you. Might we go into your study?"

"What is it?" Miriam is no fool, and she knows when trouble calls. "Tell us, Kel."

"It is business, Lady Miriam," Kel replies, "but his demeanour gives the lie to what he says.

"Damn it, Kel," says Tom Cromwell to his messenger. "She will have it from you, one way or another. The woman is worse than the Spanish Inquisition. Speak out and let us all know what is amiss."

"As you wish, sir." Kel takes a deep

breath. "Master Will saw the king three days ago, and left the palace at Whitehall. Since then, he has not been seen. Our people are searching everywhere, but he is not to be found."

"I don't understand." Miriam is shocked, and sits down by the fire. "Missing, you say?"

"He did not attend the council, yesterday," Kel explains. "I sent to Draper House, for fear that he was ill, but his servants thought him to be off about his business."

"You thought to see if he was with Mush or Richard?" Cromwell asks.

"Mush is leading the search, master," Kel replies. "I am afraid the general has fallen into some bad company."

"See that every man is employed at finding him," Cromwell tells him. "Spare no expense."

"Have someone speak with the river men," Miriam says. "If there is a body, I must have him back."

"There is no thought of that," Cromwell says. "I dare say he is on the trail of some malcontent, and hiding away."

"May God hear your words," Kel says, but he has his doubts. For Will Draper to vanish so completely speaks of evil, unknown things afoot, and of some bad times to come.

*

The king reads the death warrants again, and picks up his quill. It is a simple matter to scrawl his name across them, but he vacillates.

"Sir John, how goes the arrangements for Christmas?" Russell is caught off guard, and struggles for an answer.

"The feast is planned, sire," he replies. "Draper House will cater, as usual. They have given us a very good price."

"How much?" the king asks. He cannot be seen as a stingy monarch.

"Twenty five thousand pounds, sire, and I believe there are to be jugglers included in the price."

"Do you not think executing the queen will dampen the occasion?"

"Not if it is kept private, sire," Sir John tells the king. He sees the king still hesitates, and makes a guess at what Henry is thinking. "Then again, you could always postpone the event, until you are better disposed to make your decision."

"That is exactly my thinking, my dear Russell." Henry is delighted that his right hand man agrees with him. "I could let them wait, and sign these warrants at a later date.

You follow?"

"Perfectly, sire," Russell says. "Why, you might even see fit to relent your righteous anger and consider leniency at some future date. Your clever wit wins out again."

"Yes, it does, does it not," Henry says. The thought of clemency has not crossed his mind, but he now sees that it might make him look rather good in some eyes. "Now, my dear fellow… you must call me Hal in private."

Bollocks, Sir John thinks. I am now the king's close friend. He is moving onto dangerous ground, for those who the king destroys, he first makes into comrades.

*

The troop of mounted men moves across the flat Cambridgeshire countryside apace, and heads for the squat grey manse in the distance. Their leader is Tom Howard, the irascible Duke of Norfolk, and he is on a mission even he cannot believe he is undertaking. He is on an urgent quest to find Will Draper, the Lord Templar, and save him from whatever has befallen the damned fellow.

He is the first to be suspected by the Austin Friars gang, and he has enough trouble on his plate just now to become involved in a war with them. His revenues are being eroded, and most of his yeomen have been given to Suffolk. He is out of favour again, despite all his recent fawning, and even Henry thinks he has done some harm to his favourite soldier of fortune.

"Bog crawling Irish scum bag," he snarls, for the tenth time that day. "As if I would soil my noble hands with that priest killing turd." It is clear that he is under suspicion, so the duke decides to exonerate himself by offering his services in the wide ranging search.

Mush Draper and Richard Cromwell are convinced that their beloved King's Examiner is either dead in a ditch, or being held captive for ransom, within the city of London. In four days, however, no ransom demand has been received.

Then Henry puts the cat amongst the pigeons by declaring his belief that his best man has been kidnaped, and taken either abroad, or to some gloomy castle in the shires. The Austin Friars crowd think that this is a rather stupid idea, because of the difficulty of getting so well known a figure out of a city that is being double guarded at every hour of the day and night. Gates are manned, walls are patrolled, and boats are searched.

The king, however, has spoken, and Mush curses at having to pull precious agents from the search for so wasteful a task. It is then that Norfolk plays his master stroke. He goes directly to Henry, risking his wrath, and offers his services in the faltering search.

"Let my lads scour the shires, Hal," he begs. "We have had our differences in the past, but Will Draper is the backbone of our administration, and he must be found."

Henry, who can be a sentimental fool at times, finds this offer touching, and accepts. Norfolk has formed three flying columns of armed men, and proposes to send them out to search the further shires.

"God's speed," the king says. "Would that my damned leg was mended, and I would ride with you."

"I could choose no better man, Hal," Norfolk replies. "Why, damn it, but was it not I who had to chase your dust at the Battle of the Spurs? Am I the only one left who was there on that glorious day?"

"By God, yes… you were there, Tom, as was old Cumberland. I fear the rest are dead," Henry recalls. "You bade me wait, but my blood was up."

"By the time I managed to catch up,

you had cleared the field of the French. I was second behind you, but did not even have to draw my sword. Such a victory, eh, Hal?"

"You served me well, Tom," Henry says, in his maudlin voice. Norfolk is touching a nerve, and the king recalls the battle that he remembers, and his great victory. In truth, he was a young monarch with a strong head, who needed protecting from his own stupidity. Norfolk and Cumberland, both seasoned soldiers, had surrounded him with six thousand heavy cavalry; an impervious wall of armour against twenty thousand French peasants with pitch forks or scythes. They ran, as soon as the English juggernaut rolled towards them.

Most, mainly at the rear, escaped, and only the front ranks had to be broken. The English vanguard smashed home, and slaughtered a few hundred unlucky French peasants. Now, the king recalls how he charged alone, and swept the heavily armed French aside. It is a strange world when the truth is nothing more than what a king thinks.

Norfolk sees he has moved Henry, and he strikes.

"I have always tried to serve you well, my dearest Hal... as I will serve you again in your new Privy Council."

"Ah, yes... well, you see Tom, the thing is..."

"Mind you, at my damned age, you must not expect me to turn up for every meeting, or even kick a few fat arses in Parliament," Norfolk says, rather cleverly. "Your Majesty must use me sparingly, and look to the new blood coming through. Perhaps I might sit back, and merely advise you on the more important issues?"

"Damn me, why not?" Henry thinks this a good way to keep everybody at their ease. Norfolk will not interfere with the day to day running of things. "You must have a suitable title."

"How about 'King's Special Advisor?'" Norfolk suggests, and the label is applied. By the next day, the king will be convinced that he thought up the idea all by himself, and that the newly created post was all his own doing. The Duke of Norfolk has, in one brief meeting with the king, secured his position on the Privy Council, and taken a post that suggests he is placed above the ordinary councillors.

In return, all he has to do is make a good job of looking for Will Draper. He does not have to be found. In fact, Norfolk thinks it likely that an enemy, like the Fuggers, or the

Bagliones have had him murdered, and his body will be floating down to Gravesend on the ebb tide. Still, the search must continue.

"Sergeant Lewis... five men to secure the gate,' he commands. "Fanshaw, be so kind as to post your fellows around the perimeter. This fellow is like an eel, and can slip out of our hands with ease."

"Do we fire on them, if they try to run, sir?" Lieutenant Fanshaw asks.

"Best not," Norfolk replies. "His mother would not approve."

The house is not fortified, but the walls are sturdy, and the small windows are barred. It would take some time to batter their way in, but the door opens, and a young footman comes scurrying out.

"Your Lordship, we were not warned of your coming. There are no preparations in hand. Let me call the stableboy, and have your mounts tended to."

"Stop your damnable grovelling Snade," Norfolk snaps. The lad is known to him because, in earlier times, he has swived the mother, who was then a buxom dairy maid on his estate. "We are not stopping, but I must speak with my son at once."

"I shall fetch Lord Harry at once, Your Lordship." Moments later, and the lord of the manor, Harry Howard, the Lord Surrey, comes to the door.

"God in a cheap whorehouse," he swears, but good-naturedly. "Whatever has made you bestir yourself, and ride so far from Arundel, father?"

"Don't give me that load of bulls bollocks," Norfolk growls. He is on horseback, else he would slap the little monster around his grinning face. "My men and I seek Will Draper."

"And you think I would entertain that turd?" Surrey replies. "I would sooner swive a poxed jade than sit at the same table as he. I said we should have killed him, many years ago. Why would he be in Cambridgeshire anyway? I doubt Peterborough is his sort of a town. Save for the bones of Katherine of Aragon, a decent market, and two knocking shops, the place is as lively as dinner at Tom Cranmer's palace."

"You dolt… how long have you been here?" Norfolk is in no mood to hang about, but he has sworn to search the county from end to end, and his son has a house, gifted to him by his mother.

"Oh, about a week, I think?"

"Six days, sir," Snade, the footman adds, helpfully. "I recall it well, for Tuesday is the servants meat day."

"What, I feed you bastards meat?"

"Just the one day a week, Your Lordship," the lad explains. "The expense is docked from our wages."

"I should think so," Surrey says, quite outraged at the thought of his servants guzzling ham and beef. "There, father… six days we are told. Why is it important?"

"The stinking Irish bastard has gone missing." Norfolk is losing interest. His son was not in London when Draper went missing. "The king demands we search for him."

"Then drag the rivers," Surrey says with calculated contempt in his voice. "Such fellows always end up with a knife in their ribs, or their throat slit from ear to ear."

"Have you…?" Norfolk feels foolish at asking, and Surrey pre-empts him by answering the unasked question.

"I swear, on all I hold precious, that I have not cut Will Draper's throat, or stabbed him in the dark. Nor has any of my men killed him. There. Satisfied?"

"I had to ask about it, lad. You must see that?"

"Father, I know you have never been able to love me, but I am your son, and that means a lot to me. Was it not I who warned you about Culpeper's mad dreams? Did I not warn you about the Austin Friars dogs, when I was yet a youngster?"

"Then we may search the house?" the duke asks, and his son does not flinch at the perceived insult.

"Do as you frigging well wish, sir," Surrey says, coldly. "Let your men search each floor, carefully. I have tapestries that cost more than they will earn in five lifetimes, and vases of such exquisite craftsmanship that they cannot be replaced."

"I'll have Fanshaw and Lewis search, and warn them I shall skin the flesh off their arses if they damage anything." Norfolk is abashed at his actions and feels as if he has slighted his son's nobility.

"Thank you, father. Might I interest you in a rather fine Venetian vintage I recently laid down?"

"A free drink is a good drink, my boy," Norfolk says, mellowing towards his son. A good wine will cure most ills, and his arse is sore from all the riding he has done this day. "Gad, sir, but my arse hurts."

"I have a salve, father," Surrey tells the old duke. "It is made in Egypt, by descendants of the last Pharaoh."

"Really, what was the old fellow's name?" Norfolk asks. "For I hear they ruled all the savage world."

"Christ knows... Rum-titty-bum, or some such nonsense," Surrey says. "Shall I have one of the servant women apply this unguent for you, sir?"

"Is Nelly Bull still with you?" the old man asks.

"She is, and the minx is as skilled as ever, sir."

"Then I shall submit my arse to her tender ministrations. Might I have a bed chamber, my boy?"

"My very own, father," Surrey says, and the old duke is touched by the gesture. He takes the willing Nelly Bull into the room, and in between some rough love play, she anoints the duke's posterior with the thick, greasy concoction.

It is not until two days later, marked by a lessening of pain in his rear, that the Duke of Norfolk decides to swive the girl who is charged with warming the beds at Arundel. As soon as he throws aside his clothes, she begins to laugh.

"Damn you, wench... what is it?"

The ointment, bought by a gullible Surrey, at great expense, from a travelling mendicant, has an unwelcome side effect, and Surrey has used it to play a prank on his obnoxious father. The Duke of Norfolk's arse is dyed blue, and it will take at least a month to wear off.

"I shall kill the stinking little bugger," Norfolk curses. "I so swear!"

*

The Earl of Surrey is proud of how he has hoodwinked his own father, and made him think his word is good. Yes, he has not *killed* Draper, and nor have any of his men.

The old duke's men have searched each floor of the huge house, including the cellar, without success. They do not know that there is another, deeper dug cellar, and its door is masked by a dusty old tapestry depicting the Rape of Lucretia.

Inside, hanging by his wrists, but with his feet just touching the compacted earth floor, is Will Draper, Baronet of the Inns of the Temple. This Lord Templar thinks his shoulders will soon give way, but he cannot complain, for there is a cloth stopping up his mouth.

Surrey is in no hurry. He will wait until his blue arsed father and his men have gone, then return to his little games. He taunts Will Draper, about how easily he was taken, and hints at what he might do when Miriam Draper lowers her defences.

"I might just let you rot here," Surrey tells the suspended lord, later. "Or beat out your teeth. Do you recall how you humiliated me, in front of the court?"

"No," Will says, through cracked lips. "I humiliate so many, that your own personal grief means nothing to me."

"Insolent bastard!" Surrey slaps Will Draper's face, but the blow is feeble and the Examiner smiles at his persecutor.

"Like a girl," Will mumbles, and this time, Surrey uses his balled fist. It is enough to draw blood, and make his prisoner wince. "Perhaps you might have one of your men do it for you, Surrey. There is a certain way to do these things. Were it I doing the punching, your face would already be a bloodied pulp."

The next few slaps increase in intensity, as Surrey works himself up into a fine rage. He has longed for this moment for years, but now, he finds it a hollow victory. If he had bested the man with the sword, or wrestled him to the ground, it would mean something, but thrashing a helpless enemy is no fun, after the first few punches. Still, he muses, it is better than nothing.

"Then I must devise a more

interesting way for you to leave this world," the young lord tells Will Draper. "In the meantime, you may think on this my dear Lord Templar. Your family have had no word of you for the past five days. My house has been searched, and my father's stupid men found nothing."

"Then you have caged a lion," Will says through bruised lips. "Think on about Caesar, in the king's zoo. His mane is threadbare, and he is slower now than he once was, but yet a month ago, he caught a fellow at feeding time, who did not take enough precautions. Caesar ripped off his arm, and then devoured it. Think of me as Caesar, you little arsehole."

"Very well then, and I shall think of your buxom Miriam as Caesar's wife," Surrey replies.

"She is not part of this."

"One day, she will accept that you are dead, and seek solace. I shall try my hand at luring her to my bed, but I wager the likes of Tom Wyatt, or that devilish blackamoor rogue you have about the place, will breach her crumbling defences. When it happens, I shall let you know how she did wail under their lusty thrusting. In the meantime… I shall let you hang, like an unripe carcass. " Surrey grins, and leaves the small cell.

"Finished, My Lord? the gaoler asks of his master.

"For now," Surrey tells him. Lock up tight, and conceal the door again. I would not put another visit past my father, or even a call from Mush Draper."

"Am I to get a good fire going, My Lord?" the man asks. "It takes a couple of hours to get the charcoal glowing white hot."

"A fire?"

"A brazier, sir," the man says. "So that we might prod the fellow with heated irons, and pinch his flesh with pincers."

"No torture."

"Pardon, sir... but is that not why you took this fellow?" the gaoler asks.

"You do not need hot irons," Surrey tells the fellow. He has just, most laboriously, finished reading Niccolò Machiavelli's works, and thinks he has a notion on how to cleverly manipulate an enemy. "You just need the right idea planted in a man's head. I have set him thinking now as to how his wife's fertile acre might soon be ploughed by another farmer."

"Wickedly done, My Lord," Pol Humphrey agrees. "Though I would pay someone to swive my wife for me."

"Yes, she is an ugly old sow," Surrey

says. "Whereas Lady Miriam Draper is thought to be one of the greatest beauties in the court. Any man would be jealous of so great a beauty, and fear for her chastity"

"Then we let him ponder," Pol Humphrey says. "In the dark?"

"No food either," the Earl of Surrey concludes. "A pint of water, or weak ale each day, to stop him dying on me."

"Yes, sir," Pol smiles, and double locks the cell door, before lowering a crosspiece into place. The room, no more than two strides long, and one wide is plunged into total blackness, and Will Draper closes his eyes, and spits out the blood that flecks his lips. The pain, at least, tells him that he is still alive, and that is the important thing.

"I've been through worse," he mutters to himself, "though I'll be damned if I can recall when."

*

The shoreline scavenger is a child of no more than six or seven, and he works the edge of the river as the tide ebbs. Some days, he is lucky enough to find something of small worth: small coins, the odd shoe or boot, or some discarded wood, ripe to be made into kindling.

"Anyfin' Joe?" his comrade asks, and

the lad shrugs his little shoulders.

"Nah, this stretch is no good, Gums," Joe replies. The lad is quite toothless, at seven tears old, hence the comic name. Then Joe stops in his tracks, and lets out a cry of joy. In the mud, he see the glint of golden brocade and runs over to find an almost new doublet of exquisite manufacture.

The garment is covered in Thames river mud, but instantly recognisable for what it is worth. The brocade alone would fetch two shillings of anybodies money, but intact, Joe knows it will fetch five pounds from some poor courtier who wants to impress his fellow squires, or pages.

Of course, the two boys will not see anything like five pounds. There is a strict hierarchy amongst the fences of London, and the rules must be obeyed. By the time everyone has his cut the lads might be lucky to see a few shillings from the deal.

"We could try to flog it to some gent, and cut out …"

"Not likely, Gums," Joe cuts him short. "Big Archie will cut us bad if we cheat him. Let's get over to his place right now."

"What's it worth to us, Joe?" Gums asks, excitedly. "It must be some lord's best tucker, surely."

"Ten bob?"

"We could live for a year on that," the boy says, and if they stick to their usual diet of old bread and watered down ale, they can. Then again, they could live like lords for a fortnight, and have something to remember. "Lor' pal, we've cracked it."

They are so busy planning their new life, that Joe walks over the exposed hilt of the dagger, and only notices it because he is barefoot, and he steps onto the exquisite ruby in the butt.

"What the f.. dear Christ on His Cross, it's a knife." Joe digs it free, and sees that the handle is encrusted with fine stones. It is ornamental, rather than a weapon to kill with. Something to impress, when it is left on the table outside the king's court. Tiny Scottish pearls pick out the letter 'D' on the handle.

Joe cannot read, but he recognises the symbol, which flutters from a hundred or more pennants on water craft up and down the river. Everyone working the Thames has been told to watch out for any clue to the whereabouts of Will Draper, late of the King's Royal Examiners.

"Change of plan, my dear mate," Joe says, "for we are off now to see Mistress

Maisie Kelton, over at Draper House."

"Why, it ain't the meaty soup day, is it?" Gums asks. "All we will get is a bowl of warm onion soup, or a tongue lashing."

"Maisie will see us," Joe replies. "She will know the true value of our wares, and see as how we get our fair reward for this morning's work."

"And some bread with the onion soup, maybe?" Gums hopes.

13   For theDead

"Here, let me see what you have," Maisie Kelton says, in her very best 'bad tempered' voice, but the older of the boys shakes his head, stubbornly .

"Deal first, missus," he insists, and Maisie has to suppress a smile. Many waifs call for soup, or to earn a copper splitting logs, but this one was different. For all the world, he reminds her of her own Kel.

"Free soup for a year."

"You dole it out free every mornin' anyway. A lady as pretty as you shouldn't lie to a little lad, as it gives you wrinkles." Joe, however, can smell the broth bubbling on the huge kitchen fire, and little Gums is already sitting at the table, with a wooden spoon in his hand.

"Oh, I am pretty now, am I?" Maisie says. She is heavy with child again, and her rough edge is worn smooth by the compliment. "What is it anyway... some rubbish off the river bank?"

"A dagger."

"We already have too many about the place," Maisie says. "More than in Antwerp." She prefers life in Antwerp, but she is near her due time, and she trusts the English midwives more than some foreign woman who cannot speak her tongue. "If it is a decent one, I will give you lads a shilling apiece." It is Kel's birthday sometime this month, though they could never say exactly when.

"Oh, you'll like this knife, Mistress Maisie,' young Joe says, casually. "For it already has a famous insignia upon the hilt."

"It bears the 'D'?" The boy nods, and unfolds the ruined doublet. Even as he does, the girl recognises the best doublet, bought for audiences with the king. It is festooned with semi precious stones, and cost Miriam almost sixty pounds.

"Master Richard will wish to question you," she says, and Gums is up, and out of the door in a moment. Maisie stares after him in mute surprise.

"He don't like questioning," Joe explains. "One of the Attorney General's men questioned him so hard, he ended up wi' no bleedin' teeth left!"

*

Damn this English water, Cromwell thinks to himself. It is almost two days since some boy found Will Draper's dagger, and only now is he getting news of it. He cannot blame Kel Kelton, whose move to York has been suspended for now, but the curse of being a dead man with no voice. If only he could speak to the king, and steer him into the right channel.

"How sure are we that…"

"We are sure, master," Kel says, with a lump in his throat. He realises, only now, just quite how much he owes to the Examiner General. "I have seen the dagger many times, and he once even let me wear it at one of the Royal Examiners parades. Lady Miriam recognised it too, as did my Maisie. Then there was the doublet to consider. I have brought both items with me, sir."

"Were they much soiled?"

"They had been at the water's edge for a few days, master," Kel says. "The Thames is full of all kinds of shit, and the tides have been unkind."

"The knife did not sink then?" the inquisitive part of Thomas Cromwell asks.

"No, it was embedded up to the hilt in the sludge, else it might have been drawn out by the ebbing tide, and carried into deeper water."

"Then we must be grateful for that, at least," Cromwell tells him. "How is poor Miriam taking it? Does she still think he might walk back in through the door?"

"When I left, she was lighting candles

throughout Draper House," Kel confesses, "and gathering those few who know, to help her sing the *Kaddish*."

"The Jewish lament. Then she has given up all hope," Thomas Cromwell says. "The *Kaddish* is a song praising the God that they cannot name, and entrusting the lost soul to him."

"Why do they not know their God's name, master?" Kel Kelton asks, and Thomas Cromwell smiles at the young man's glaring gaps in his learning. He hoped to make him into a decent lawyer, but the lad is too willing to cut corners, and prefers settling disputes with a blade across the throat, or a sword into the ribs.

"But they do know their God's name, Kel," he tells him. "It is only that their faith forbids them from uttering it out loud."

"Then do you know it?"

"There a few names… some say thousands, and others insist on there being only eleven, but I know most of the more famous ones."

"Then tell me."

"So that you might taunt Mush Draper with the knowledge?"

"Sir, surely he is from Coventry, not the lands of the Hebrew."

"Very well, you rogue. How might you use it?" Cromwell asks.

"I can use it to warn him. I can use it towards him secretly. He might think to be wary of attack, if I say the word."

"I shall give you this knowledge, and watch how mature you have become." the 'deceased' Privy Councillor says. "I shall note it in my diary, and…" Thomas Cromwell is suddenly struck speechless, and he puts a hand over his eyes, as if he was Saint Paul, and he has just been converted on the road to Damascus. "That is it!" he cries. "A way to speak directly with the king, yet remain in the world of the dead. I must get to work at once. You are to find me some old paper, or parchment will do."

"Sir, I am for York, am I not?"

"Bugger York," Thomas Cromwell says. "You and I, my boy, are about to perpetrate the greatest fraud ever."

"And what of Will Draper?" Kel asks, rather surprised by Cromwell's sudden enthusiasm. "Do we mourn him, or let poor Miriam do that alone?"

"We all grieve in different ways, Kel," the old lawyer says. "Miriam will rend her clothes, put ashes on her head, and wail out her *Kaddish* for the lost soul. Those of

Austin Friars who recall how he was always ready with help, or loan a few shillings until payday, will retire to a tavern of good standing, and drink to his memory. Mush will miss him most, of all the men, for they were like brothers to one another. My way of trying to come to terms with this wicked deed is to throw myself into some magnificent scheme. Now, are you for helping me, or watching the Scots scratch their arses up on the borders?"

*

In truth, everyone mourns the passing of so fine a fellow as Will Draper, save for the man who knows the truth. The Earl of Surrey hopes for many happy hours, watching his arch enemy starve, and rot away, until that happy moment when he can start the tortures in earnest.

"You pace like a cat, Draper," he says through the cell's iron grill.

'Like a lion," Will mutters, and turns to pace the three steps from end to end. Then he will pace the two short strides across.

"A mangy old beast, who will be put down at the first hint of an escape attempt," the earl tells his prisoner. "I hear that your wife has accepted your sad demise."

"Miriam would not give up hope."

"It seems your doublet and knife were

found on the Thames bank. As they were recognised by the newly made widow, she was clear about her belief. You are now quite dead, sir... to everybody. Why, my agents even tell me that she sent the doublet and knife abroad, for some uncle to look at. Once it is verified, this fellow, a banker I believe, can have all the money unlocked and placed at her disposal. Damn it, stop pacing, or..."

"Or what?" Will Draper sneers. "If you come into this cell alone, I will wrap my chain about your scrawny neck, and choke the life from your body. No, if you wish to enter my domain, bring two big strong men with you, and hide behind them."

"You impudent bastard!" Surrey is tempted to open the cell door, and go in with the riding crop he always carries with him, but he has not the courage. "If you do not cease all this walking to and fro, I will have you shackled to the wall by *both* wrists."

"Very well, if it annoys you so much, Your Lordship," Will replies. "How come you to hate me so much?"

"Because I am descended from English kings, on both sides, and because of this I would stand third in line behind Henry Tudor, and my father. Then you come from some Irish bog, and the king calls you brother.

That is my place, you worthless peasant's boy."

"But the king loathes you, and did, long before he ever met me," Will says. "You are a person who easily attracts such noble sentiments."

"Yes, but he would have mellowed as he aged, and I would take up my father's mantle. You see? Surrey would become Norfolk, and he would rule, with Henry, and then, with young Edward."

"As the law dictates," Will Draper says. It is your birthright… right or wrong."

"But you would always be damned well there, uncovering plots, fighting against corruption, and killing for the king. You have, just now, tried to have my father and I ruined with your intrusive investigations."

"It is my job, I seek the truth," Will replies, and starts to pace the cell again. It is little more than a large rectangle of soil, scooped from the earth, and lined on all sides with foot square slabs of granite. A man might chisel away for ten years, just to loosen one stone. "I am the tool that keeps you and your ilk safe. Lose me, and the dangers of the world come ever closer. To my knowledge, I have saved the king from assassination on at least two occasions, and helped to bring down your dangerously vain cousin, Anne Boleyn."

"That slut brought it down on her own head," Henry Howard, Earl of Surrey, sneered. "Besides she was guilty."

"Of adultery?" Will asks. The longer he keeps the fool talking, the further away is the next beating, he reasons.

"Oh, I doubt that," Surrey chuckles. "Unless Tom Wyatt was dipping his pen into her pot. No, I mean of the business with her brother, of course."

"That is all a complete nonsense," Will tells the earl. "A concoction to make the other charges stick."

"When I was twelve years old, the Boleyns were on hard times, and came to live off us at Arundel. I fancied Anne, and thought she might take my virginity from me, so I waited until night fall, and slipped into her room. Anne was astride George, and riding him like a prize stallion. Now, stop your pacing, fellow!"

Will digests this news, and also the more important information that his doublet and knife are in the hands of Thomas Cromwell in Antwerp. He wonders if Miriam has sent it to him as a courtesy, or because she has understood the clues held within the two things. He thinks the former, but hopes for the latter. It will ease her sense of loss. He ignores Surrey, and continues to stride back and forth, as his shackle allows. Just knowing that the action infuriates the pompous earl gives him a small sense of pleasure.

"Right, that's it... I warned you." the earl snaps. "Men, come hither, and give this saucy fellow a sound beating!"

"Come on in yourself, little Harry," the King's Examiner snarls. "Let me test you against my withered muscles."

Naughton has three more men with him, for he has learned his lesson. Two men are not enough, and his previous partner is nursing a broken nose, and a jaw that will not mend before Easter time.

"Right lads," he tells his rough helpers. "One to each arm, and keep clear of his head, for it is like a battering ram. Once pinned, I will move in with Bad Ted, and lay into his ribs. We shall soon have him crying for his blessed mother."

Big Jimmy, a renegade Scot, wanted for murder in Perth, and Don the Dung Shifter, a brawny man of no intelligence, lunge in and pin Will's arms to the wall. Then Ned Naughton and Bad Ted, a pimp and misuser of small children, move in to exact their pound of flesh.

It is as Will Draper hopes. With his arms held firmly back against the wall, he can then use the leverage to bring up his lower torso, with both heavy riding boots to the fore. Naughton manages to twist away, and takes a glancing, but painful blow to the hip, but Bad Ted finds a heavy leather boot embedded deep into his groin.

The impact is enough to dislodge something down below, and the man gasps in pain, and horror. He makes a terrible gurgling sound, and grabs at the offended portion.

"Me fuckin' crown jewels," he snorts, and topples over to the ground. The restrainers are surprised, and loosen their grip, enough so that Will Draper can throw himself into the attack. He gets his yard long chain around Naughton's neck, and starts to squeeze, whilst a second savage kick crushes another man's knee cap.

"Dear Christ!" Surrey, terrified by this reversal manages to get out of the cell door, and thus out of range. The key is safely in his purse, and Draper cannot escape, thank God. Bad Ted is on the floor, and pulls himself towards the door, whilst the other two seek to get far away from this dark avenging angel. If his arm was unfettered, he would kill them all, without remorse. To emphasise this point, he chokes Naughton until his face goes blue, and then thrusts him, gasping and coughing, out of the cell's heavy wooden door.

"Lock the bloody damned thing, Naughton," Surrey screams in a mad panic, "and hire another ten men. I want hard men, men who can fight, and know how to beat a man who is already chained up. Do you understand me, you blasted dolt?"

"Yes, Your Lordship," Naughton says, through cheeks blushing with broken veins, and lack of air. "I'll see the stinking bastard is done for, once and for all. I said, right from the start, that we should just cut his bastard throat and be done with it. The man is born out of Satan's own womb."

"No, I want him to feel some real pain." Surrey crosses to the cell door, and peers through the tiny aperture. "For now, he must simply starve. I am riding to London, where I must call on poor Lady Miriam, and express my deepest sympathy for her loss. Why I might even give her the benefit of my manly lance."

Will lunges, and throws out his foot like an arrow. The distance is too great, of course, but the sudden attack makes Harry Howard jump back in fright and lose his footing. He tumbles into the compacted earth and sends a cloud of dust into the air.

From inside the cramped space of the tiny cell there comes the eerie sound of confident laughter.

*

"Master, I am exhausted," Kel Kelton complains. "Might I not have a few hours sleep?"

"You can sleep on the boat," Tom Cromwell says, and Kel sees the truth of this, but he must sleep alone, and not have the company of either Maisie or Lucy, who have just returned from London. "This is of the greatest importance. Do you seek to refuse me?"

"Never, master." The accusation stings Kel, and Tom Cromwell sees the look on the young man's face. He has gone too far and hurt a loyal servant. "I have shed my own blood for you, have I not?"

"You have." Tom Cromwell puts a hand on Kel's shoulder. "I should not have said so ridiculous a thing to you. Of all my young men, you are the one amongst many who will do for me unto death, without question. Am I forgiven for my stupid remark?"

"Is that not what good families do,

sir… forgive one another?" Kel is Austin Friars, through and through, and has a personal high regard for Cromwell, who raised him from petty thieving on London Bridge, to being a successful 'man of business' worth two thousand a year, and who has something the master calls 'gilt edged' investments with the Italian banks, worth over thirty five thousand in Brabant Ducats. "Enough of this though. Your orders, master."

"You are to deliver this message to Miriam, by word of mouth. Nothing on paper, and so nothing to betray our thoughts. Listen well my boy, and be on the next cog to leave Antwerp."

*

"Pardon me, missus, but there is some fine lord at the door, saying he is here to see you." Winnie has been with the Draper's for three years, and has just been promoted to the post of senior front door opener. It is to be the height of her attainment, but she is content not to be back on the streets begging for food. "I bade him wait, whilst I fetched you from your important business. He had a name as near made me laugh."

"Really, Winnie… that is not how we treat guests, even uninvited ones," Miriam starts, but Pru Beckshaw is with her, and places a hand on her arm.

"No, Winnie did well enough," Pru says, with a far off look in her eyes. "How did he upset you, girl?"

"Sorry M'am, but he poked me with his riding stick, an' was rude. Called me a slut, and bade me fetch you, as if you could not refuse him anything."

"Such hubris. Old, or young?" Miriam asks, annoyed at the unkind thought that has sprung to her mind, unbidden.

"Young fellow, mistress," Winnie replies, and Lady Miriam sees that she is right in her suspicion.

"Then it is not Norfolk," Miriam decides. "It must surely be the son, to be so arrogant. The Earl of Surrey thinks himself above even God."

"Yes, thart's it, the Earl of Slurry," Winnie says. "Right fitting name, if you arsks me, Lady Miriam."

"I saw this, as I slept last night," Pru says. "We must meet him in the great hall, and be very wary. He is no friend of the Draper Company, and seeks some advantage from you. I 'saw' him eating at your table, and he was sitting in Will's chair."

"You are sure?"

"It was as if in a dream, but the

meaning was clear enough," Pru says. "This sly weasel means to take advantage of you, my dear, and thinks to do so whilst poor Will is still away." Pru insists that Miriam's husband is simply 'travelling', and shall turn up in the fulness of time with a merry tale to tell. "Your husband is in a ... a small place... I think, but need only step through the door and come back to you."

"You know this?"

"I see shapes... nothing more."

"Then this small space you speak of might well be a coffin?" Miriam asks.

"I do not see the dead," Pru replies. "I see only a hint of what is either now, or to come. Will is alive... or was when last I 'saw' him."

"Then let us go to this intruder and see what he has to say for himself," Miriam decides. "Let the weasel show his teeth."

They compose themselves in the great hall, and have Winnie show the gentleman in.

"About bloody time too, you dimwitted trollop," Surrey growls, even as he enters the fabulously spacious chamber, and raises his riding crop above his head.

"That is not a good idea, sir" Lady Miriam says, but she is too late with her warning. Winnie, who is almost fifteen stones of muscular London peasant, catches Surrey's wrist in mid air and disarms him. Then she flexes the crop a couple of times, until it gives, and snaps with an audible cracking noise. She takes the two pieces, and stuffs them down the earl's fancy doublet. Surrey is too stunned, and frightened by the raw savagery, to speak, and simply watches, as she turns back to her mistress.

"Th'earl of Slurry, madam," Winnie announces, and curtseys. She withdraws, and Miriam Draper gestures to the seats at the long table, as if nothing out of the ordinary had just passed.

Harry Howard decides to go along with this, rather than get off on the wrong foot with the soon to be widow. Like his father before him, Surrey is absolutely convinced of the order of things: God, Henry, Norfolk, Surrey, and that makes him a cousin to the Almighty. It is only since the Draper Company made an appearance that the Norfolk dominance of both king and court has been questioned.

He strolls over to where a flagon of wine, and some bread and cheese stands out for any weary traveller, chooses some cheese, and sits down in the biggest chair available.

It is Will's chair.

"Good day to you, madam," Surrey says, as his opening gambit. "I hear that your husband's doublet and dagger have been found in the Thames, and that you must now entertain the prospect of a long widowhood."

"Thank you for your gallant words of consolation, My Lord Surrey," Lady Miriam replies, astonished at the thickness of the young lord's skin.

"I aim to please, My Lady," Surrey tells her. "It is difficult for a woman, even a well set up one like you, to face being in widow's weeds for the rest of her life."

"That is most presumptive of you, sir," Pru Beckshaw says, shocked at his casually cruel manner. "The Lord Templar is not yet declared dead by any legal authority."

"The king is dressed in his finest mourning white this morning," says Surrey.

'Then he is presumptive too, My Lord." Pru half closes her eyes, and forces herself to concentrate on the aura that surrounds this wicked man.

"Your lady in waiting appears to have gone to sleep, madam," Surrey says as Pru subsides into silence. This interview is becoming stranger by the minute. "Might she not retire, and rest herself, or should I simply poke her into wakefulness?"

"That would be most unseemly, sir, for me to see a young gentleman whilst alone," Miriam replies. "I do believe you seek to compromise me with your attentions."

"Good God, no," Surrey says. "I have nothing but the highest regard for you Lady Miriam. My one concern is that you will be left alone now, in a dangerous world."

"Why do you think I must remain a widow for evermore, Lord Surrey?" It is not a conversation to Miriam's taste, but she is keen to see where it will lead her.

"Why?" Surrey looks amazed that she has not yet thought about it "You are the widow of one of the richest, and most powerful men in England. The king will not allow you to choose a new husband for yourself. Henry will turn to his advisors, Audley, Cranmer, my father, Dick Cromwell, and Sir Rafe Sadler. It is for them to decide on where you marry. You are a powerful political pawn, and must be used to the best of ways."

"Mostly fair and honest men, My Lord," Miriam prods. "And what will these esteemed gentlemen advise?"

"That your vast fortune; a fortune that powers England's economy, must be secured for the state. To do this, you must marry an equal… or a better… within the English court. Lady Templar cannot possibly marry a low born commoner."

"I think that is completely out of the question," Miriam tells the earl. "Then where must I turn, Harry?" The earl thinks that her using his given name is a good sign, rather than like the cat smiling at the canary.

"Well, we must cast around and find others to put on the eligible list."

"Others, Harry?"

"Others than myself, my dear Lady Templar," Surrey tells her, without a blink of a suggestion that he does not understand his crassness.

"Oh, I see," Miriam says, and wonders where this ridiculous conversation will go next, when Pru suddenly opens her eyes, and starts to speak in a low, melodious tone of voice.

"The father wishes to best the son, and his wishes are fulfilled. For the one will steal his coat of arms, and the other will watch him perish."

"What rubbish is this?" Surrey asks, and perceives that it is a sort of threat to him. The old duke will outlive him, the woman says, and be at his death? "Make it clear, woman, else I have you taken up for black hearted witchery."

"She does not know what she says, My Lord," Miriam says, soothingly. "It is a medical condition."

"Then she should take care as to whom she decides to insult, madam."

"My Lord, it could be anyone she talks about, and her silly prophesies seldom come true."

"I see an earl who is held back by a duke, and he frets over his future. Do not, good sir, for I tell you this, you will see your father in the Tower, under sentence of death, and finish with your head held high above him," Pru says.

"Now, that's more like it," Surrey tells Lady Miriam. "Old Norfolk's head ends on the block, and mine shall be above his. I think she has something there. Yes, the old bastard should end his days like that."

"You have given me much to think on, My Lord," Miriam says. "Might I beg a few days to decide what I want to do?"

"Oh, no rush, my dearest woman," Surrey replies. "I have got to get rid of my first wife yet!"

*

"Bird up!" The cry, from one of the game keepers, alerts the gentlemen to the hunt. Some pigeons and a few water fowl are scared out of hiding by the dogs, and the gathered hawkers raise their arms, and poise their own falcons for the kill.

"Wait for it!" the Duke of Norfolk growls at Sir John Russell. "Loose to early and the prey is missed."

"Just so, Tom," the Duke of Suffolk calls. "Watch to your right!" Norfolk sees a pigeon cutting away, and unhoods his bird. The magnificent creature cocks its head to one side, then launches itself into the sky. Both Suffolk and Russell follow suit, and all three falcons are climbing into the sky, trying to get above their prey.

"Now we wait," Norfolk says.

"Like for news of Will Draper?" the Duke of Suffolk says.

"Draper is certainly dead," Norfolk says. "See how my bird glides? Dead and dropped in the river."

"I cannot believe it." Suffolk is genuine in his belief. He has watched Will Draper for years, and knows he is not one to be caught out in so easy a manner. "We have not searched hard enough."

"We have searched… oh, good kill, Lord Norfolk… everywhere," Russell tells the others. "And yours too, My Lord Suffolk. Damn but my thing has missed his way… and

I paid twenty pounds for him."

"A good bird will set you back at least a hundred, Russell," Norfolk tells him. "Besides, I know we have looked everywhere, down to the last stinking hovel. I even rode up into Cambridgeshire, and caught my lump of a son unawares. We searched the little bastard's home from top to bottom. My men found nothing, but laughed at his pretensions."

"How so," Suffolk asks.

"The silly bugger collects old tapestries, and hangs the damned things from the walls on every floor, Why, he even has one in the cellar. A mucky one about some tart called Lucretia… with her tits out, and everything."

"Your lad was ever a saucy young fellow," the Duke of Suffolk says. "Why, I wager that every one of us has roistered with him, at one time or another. What say you, Sir John?" Russell has just managed to retrieve his falcon, who having missed his prey, decides to savage the feathered hat of another guest.

"My pardon, Señor Chapuys," the king's minder says, as he wrenches the bedraggled cap from the bird's talons. "I will buy you another."

"No matter, Sir John. Attend to your friends, who seem intent on discussing the fate of poor Lucretia."

"Never heard of the girl," Sir John protests. "What is she claiming?"

"She was a Roman lady," Eustace Chapuys says. "Dishonoured by the king's son, she killed herself."

"Oh, her," Sir John says. "Then I shall, at least know what these fellows are going on about."

"And I must ride for London, my friend. I have enjoyed watching your hawking. Your bird killed my ostrich feather cap with great style."

Eustace Chapuys makes his excuses, and sends for his horse. The others spend their time failing to bring down another bird, and when the horse finally comes, it is the Duke of Suffolk who comes over to bid the ambassador farewell. The duke holds out a hand to the little Savoyard, and as they shake he leans forward, and speaks in a husky whisper.

"Your hand, Master Chapuys," he says. "I perceive that you do leave us early, sir?"

"I do," Chapuys replies. "I have urgent business to attend to."

"Then you understood?" Suffolk says, still with his voice muted.

"Yes, as you do, My Lord," the old ambassador tells him.

"Then ride, sir, and I pray we are right, and that you will be in time. God's speed, my dear Eustace."

"*Adieu* Charles," Chapuys replies, and puts spur to horse. At the last, these two men, from different worlds, are joined in a mutual friendship, forged out of their love for Will Draper. As he rides off, a second horse, ridden by Alonso Gomez falls into Chapuys' wake. The Spaniard is sworn to keep his master safe, and he thinks that now that oath might be tested once more.

*

Mush Draper is visibly shocked when Richard Cromwell enters the great hall at Draper House. The once gargantuan man is but a shade of his former self. His hair is beginning to grey at the temples, his skin is a of a chalk like pallor, and he is leaning on a thick bamboo cane.

"Richard, come here and sit by the fire," Mush says. "You look worn out, and ready for some hot ale. See, I have a poker already heated."

"It has been a tiring journey, old

friend," Richard replies. He begins to cough, and puts a handkerchief to his mouth. "The coach must have hit every pothole on the way. The hot ale will most certainly revive me though. Good day to all here, and may this meeting prove to be a success."

"It most certainly will, Master Richard," Kel Kelton says. "I have news from a certain friend over the water, and I have given it to Lady Miriam."

"It must be good news to bring together such a collection of rogues under one roof." This is from the handsome black man leaning at the mantlepiece. Once a make believe prince of Abyssinia, then a failed explorer, Ibrahim, a Spanish Moor, is now attached to the house of Draper. "Rob Buffery is no angel, and old Edwin Tunnock is a born murderer. As for you others…"

"I am a loyal lieutenant in General Will's Examiners," Jeremiah Cord says. He has no wish to have his past as a coiner and cutpurse brought up, "and this rum looking fellow is Sergeant Tam Jones. Now *he* is a bad lot."

"You are all dangerous men." The eight men all turn and bow towards the door. Lady Miriam is standing there, with her husband's doublet and dagger in her hands.

She crosses to the huge table, and places the articles down on it. "Now let us see if you are clever ones. Pray examine this doublet, and the dagger, then tell me what you think."

The motley gang cluster around the two items, which they have hitherto only seen at a distance. It is the Moor who breaks the heavy silence.

"You say that Will Draper was killed on the river bank, whilst wearing this?" The 'Abyssinian' grins, and shakes his head. "Then his assassins must have used a garrotte, or slowly poisoned him to death."

"Perhaps it was Archbishop Cranmer, and he simply bored poor Will to death," Miriam says. "You see what I mean though, Ibrahim?"

"He does, and so do we all now," Mush says. "Several men must have been involved. If they struck him down with knives…"

"No holes," Richard Cromwell says, catching up with what they could all now understand. "The doublet would be rent open with slashes, or punctures from a thrust. Will was not killed in this, my dear Miriam."

"And the dagger?" Miriam asks.

"Just so, my lads," Ibrahim enthuses. "Who here has not robbed a foeman after the battle is done? The spoils of war go to the victor, do they not?"

"Yes, this dagger is worth a hundred pounds in jewels alone," Mush confirms. "What self respecting villain would leave it behind?"

"True enough," Miriam says. "I think the doublet was left to identify Will, and the dagger was put there to make sure the finder went for his reward. A young river waif called Joe brought it to me. He is now one of our pages, and will be given a good education."

"Then the chances are, Will still lives?" Richard asks.

"Why else fake his death?" Mush conjectures. "If he is dead… leave his body to be found, not his doublet."

"I agree," Ibrahim says. "Your husband is taken captive, My Lady, and is being held somewhere."

"That is why I have summoned you men here today." Miriam must be wary of her words, for only half the room know the Antwerp secret. "I knew Will was alive… I could feel it, but I also know we have searched everywhere for him. Then, a friend of mine, travelling in Flanders suggested where we might look for Will."

"An astute chap, to know what is

afoot from that distance," Edwin Tunnock says, with a sly smile at the Moor. It was they who smuggled Cromwell from his cell in the Tower.

"I met him, by chance, during my travels," Kel Kelton says, and reported his views to Lady Miriam."

"What was his thinking?" Rob Buffery, an ex soldier who had once fought alongside Will Draper in Ireland and then Flanders asks.

"That so clever a ruse would take several hard men, who all must be paid, and then the cost of locking Will away, and seeing him to be well guarded."

"There we have it," says Ibrahim. "If we agree that Will lives, then we must agree that someone with wealth and power is behind the plot. Now, all we need do, is discover who it is, and where he has Will."

"My money is on that Norfolk bastard," Edwin Tunnock says. "He would cheat himself, for the fun of it."

"Or his son," Tunnock says.

"Or both?" Mush asks.

"Then again, the Fugger Bank would be able to fund this," Miriam says.

"Then that is why you want us, all loyal men, here today?" Richard says.

"I can think of three names rich enough, malicious enough, and we need to watch each of those factions like a hawk."

"Whomever it is, Norfolk, Fugger or Surrey, they might not go near Will's prison for days... or weeks."

"I know, but it is the best we can do, short of someone else knowing that which none of us know."

There is some commotion, and the great hall's doors are flung back. The dramatic impact is somewhat lessened by the appearance of two mud spattered men of middle height, and middle years. Alonso Gomez falls into step behind his master, and they advance on the gathering.

"Lady Miriam, it is I, Eustace Chapuys. Forgive this intrusion, but I come to tell you that I know where your husband is. It is all to do with a tapestry!"

*

The chances of rescue appear slim to Will Draper, and a lesser man might well despair. He survives on a cup full of brackish water each day, and a crust of bread every other day. He gnaws his fourth crust, so guesses he has been chained to the wall for eight days. In the darkness it is impossible to tell the passing of time.

His main guard, and tormentor is Pol Humphries, a big brute of a fellow, who likes to goad him through the small window behind the tapestry. Will accepts the man's loathsome behaviour because, to do it, he must open the small window in the cell door, and so let in a little welcome light. It is on his third visit that he finds Will Draper cowering in the corner nearest the door.

"What is it, you stupid bastard?" Pol asks, and Will turns frightened eyes on him.

"There's something… alive in the dark. Can you not hear it?"

"Pol laughs, and goes on his way, but the idea sticks in his mind. Dark things live in the darkness, he muses, and it may not always be a rat. His superstitious nature comes to the fore, and makes him wonder.

"It slithers, keeping to the darkest places," Will says on the next visit, as if talking to himself. "I dare not sleep, for fear it comes for me."

"I hope it does," Pol chuckles and closes the tapestry again. There is little fun to be had taunting a man who is going mad. He reports this to Ned Naughton, who is in charge of the castle, whilst Surrey is away in London.

"Twelve men to guard a bloody

nutter," Naughton moans. "Let him turn insane then, and the earl might finally let us cut his bloody throat."

"Do I treat him any differently?" Pol asks, and Naughton laughs, nastily.

"Why should you?" he asks, then he understands and wants to kick the gaoler up the backside for his stupidity. "Ah, I see. You think that madness is catching, like the plague, don't you?"

"Is it not?" Pol asks. He believes that the touch of a lunatic is likely to pass on his madness, and he fears for his own health.

"Old wives tales," Naughton tells him. "Or else every mad house would be run by madmen, would it not?"

"Oh, yes… that's right," Pol says. "I never thought of that."

"Which is why I'm in charge around here, you moron, now get back to your duties."

Pol returns to his guard duty. He sits outside the hidden cell, and fancies he hears odd, wet, dragging noises, as if some 'thing' was dragging itself towards the cell door. He wonders, irrationally, if a satanic creature has tunnelled in, but the cell is always empty of monsters when he brings the prisoner's water in each morning.

Then, on the ninth night, Will Draper tries the chain, and finds that he has lost enough weight to pull his wrist free. It is not easy, and he loses the skin from his wrist and knuckles, and cuts his right thumb almost to the bone. He is free of his shackles, but still locked within the confines of a sealed chamber.

Pol is dozing when the noise starts, and he jumps up, as if ready for a fight. It is only the poor mad fool he has locked up. There are some low grunting noises to be heard, and the sound of a heavy body being dragged across a floor.

"Sweet Christ!" The voice is shrill, and terrified. "Keep it away from me. Oh, please… help me…. aghhh."

The scream tapers off, as if the victim is being pulled away, down a long, dark tunnel. For the first time, Pol suspects his own fancy is true. Some beast that digs its way in, and devours all he finds. He fetches a torch, and pulls aside the tapestry of Lucretia.

He holds up the blazing torch, opens the small window, and looks inside. For a moment, he cannot believe his eyes. The chain hangs on the wall, quite empty, and there is a lot of blood on it and spattered over the compacted earth floor. Worse of all, the cell is completely empty. The creature, it seems, has come in the darkness, and taken its terrified prey.

Pol draws his dagger, and unlocks the cell door. It opens outwards, so he is able to survey every inch of the floor. In one corner, the compacted earth has been scuffed and clawed at, as if by some reptile. He shudders, and steps inside. Pol glances to right and left, and at the low bunk. It is too low to hide under. Will Draper is, quite worryingly, gone.

"Jesus," the gaoler mutters. "Eaten by a monster." It is his last thought, as Will Draper, who has wedged himself across the ceiling, at full stretch, lets himself fall. Every muscle aches, but he knows he has but one chance. He falls right on top of a terrified Pol, and grapples for his throat.

The big gaoler is sure the beast has come back and he tries to scream. In that moment Will manages to grapple his hands about the thug's head. He grips hard, and twists, sharply. There is a loud snapping noise, and the big fellow crashes down to the floor, his neck snapped like a twig.

The feeble light stings Will Draper's eyes, but he must not stop. Next are the stone stairs, which he must mount, until he comes to a way out. On the way, he must kill any who oppose him. It is a weak plan, but one that is his only hope of salvation. If he cannot overcome them all, then he will die fighting. He lurches to his feet, and takes Pol Humphries knife from his lifeless body. There are torches every few yards, and he is fast getting used to the illumination.

"Stairs," he mutters, as if encouraging his own actions. No one else is coming, he tells himself. I must shift for myself. He starts up, and is half way up the stone flight, when a shape appears above him.

"What's all this then?" It is Ned Naughton. Surrey's wicked henchman sees the feet of Pol Humphries sticking out from the cell, and realises that Draper is out, and still a dangerous man. "I told His Lordship, right from the start to let me cut your throat, you bastard. Now I'll have to kill you anyway."

"You talk a lot," Will replies, and lowers himself into a defensive stance. It is because Naughton has the advantage; a sword, which he draws with a flourish. "Let us get to it, you worthless pig. I want to finish the job I started. Do you still ache from where I struck you?"

"I may be a pig, but it is you who is to be spitted," Will replies, menacingly.

Behind, faintly, there is the sound of shouting, and the heavy clash of steel on steel. Ned Naughton looks uneasy at the sounds, and moves down a step.

"Careful now," Will says, and begins to circle the knife, as if to draw his attention to the blade. Whilst on the stairs, he is at a disadvantage, and needs to turn the tables on his adversary. He fakes a sudden step up, and Ned Naughton puts in a thrust. The blade misses its mark, and Will can put his shoulder into the man's chest, and barge him off the steps. The ruse works, and his enemy is sent toppling out into the air.

Naughton cries out in anger, as he falls the six feet to the ground. On impact, he lands on hands and knees, with his sword a yard distant. Will sees his chance and jumps after his enemy. He feels the dagger go through fabric and flesh, but it is not a killing blow.

"You murdering bastard!" Naughton screams, and shrugs the weakened Examiner off him. He sees where his sword has fallen, and staggers over to retrieve it. Will is on his own knees now, with his blooded dagger in his hand. He drives it into the hard soil floor, by his boot, so that it is hidden from sight.

"You are done for," Will Draper says

to Naughton. "You must lie down now, and go to your maker."

"Not with a nick such as this, My Lord," Naughton replies as he touches the wound in his left side. He picks up the sword and turns to display his torn tunic, and the smear of blood staining it. "I seem to have you at a disadvantage, sir. You are disarmed."

"Then I must yield to you," Will says, and lowers his head in submission.

"Oh, gentlemen's rules is it now, My Lord?" Naughton sneers. "I play by a different set of laws." He advances, raises his sword and aims for the throat.

"As do I, sir," Will says. He pushes himself up and forward, inside the thrust, and brings his right hand up, with the retrieved blade in it. The aim is still not good, but it is enough to make Naughton cry out and drop his weapon. "The law of the wild country."

Will Draper's eyes are red rimmed, and his lips are drawn back in an almost feral sneer. He stands, still holding the knife, and walks his enemy backwards, not allowing him to fall. He comes to a halt as Naughton's back touches against a cold stone wall, and leans into the task.

By the time Chapuys and Mush come rushing down to the cellar, where Lucretia has given up her secrets, Will has gutted his man, with the efficiency of a butcher about his job.

"Dear God, my friend... enough," the little Savoyard says. He takes Will by the elbow and leads him away.

*

"The moment I heard that Surrey was in the habit of hanging expensive tapestries on cellar walls, I knew it," Eustace Chapuys says. "Why hang the Rape of Lucretia over a bare wall, unless there was yet another door behind it? I saw how the old duke had been fooled into thinking he had searched everywhere, and that a further chamber must be hidden within Surrey's house. Why hide the existence of this cell, unless it was occupied by a special felon? The Duke of *Norfook* gave the game away, quite by chance, and I and my faithful servant raced to get help. Thank God you gentlemen were gathered together at Draper House."

"We knew you were alive, Will," Mush says, as they ply him with another glass of wine, and choice cuts of the best meat in the house. "Only that we did not know where, until Eustace came along with his clever deduction. I and the others took horse, and came here at once. We little expected there to be an army waiting on our arrival."

"Yes a dozen surely rogues put up a grand fight," Rob Buffery explained, "and we were forced to slaughter them, to a man."

"They fought like veritable demons, sir," Jeremiah Cord tells his redeemed commander. Why, Tam Jones took a nasty stab in the shoulder that will take some time to mend, and the Spanisher servant was cut about a little too. Though I have never seen anyone kill like Master Gomez. It was as if the very devil was guiding his hands, and every blow went home."

"Then there are no fatalities on my account?" Will says."I am, at least, glad for that, lads."

"I fear Edwin and Richard are not as fearsome as I once thought them to be," Mush mutters to Will. "I suppose old age reaches us all in the end."

"Taking my name in vain again, Mush?" Richard Cromwell says, reaching for a lump of cheese. "I killed my man, did I not?"

"You are unwell, my friend," Mush replies. "Once, you would have been first into battle, and swinging a woodsman's axe like a mere child's plaything."

"We all remember things as better than they were," Richard Cromwell replies.

"For instance, I remember when you were thought to be such a pretty boy. Now poor Isabella has a chattering monkey for a mate."

"Eat and drink, lads," Will says. "I for one do not care who made the most kills. After finishing off Naughton, I had not the strength to take on another dozen men. It is a pity they all died though."

"Yes, a few witnesses would have helped us prove the Lord Surrey's guilt," Mush says. "I wager he has his alibi concocted again, even before we found you, Will."

"Of course. He might claim that Naughton acted on his own behalf, and intended asking a ransom. Henry will fall for it, yet again."

"Then you say the word, sir, and I will see the fellow does not see another dawn," Alonso Gomez says from his seat by the fire. He has a cut over one eyebrow, which makes him look more devilish than ever before. "I can make it look as if he died in his sleep, if that is your wish. A most tragic accident, no?"

"Yes, even bishops can succumb to such a death," Eustace Chapuys says, rather shame-faced. The murderous Spanish servant, Gomez, has done as much for him, albeit

albeit without permission.

"We must use the law," Will Draper says. "I would like to think Thomas Cromwell would approve. What say you, Kel?"

"I would say that our old master would insist on it, sir, though I would also like to slit the dirty bastard's throat open for him."

"Perhaps, if he is listening to me, in heaven, he might send me word on how to act?" Will sees Kel's smile, and knows he will have his 'heavenly' answer within a few days.

"And what now?" Richard Cromwell asks. "Are we to let the little rat go unpunished?"

"Do we have any lamp oil in the place?" Jeremiah Cord asks. He is a huge man, almost as big as Richard Cromwell, and his voice is deep and commanding.

"I am sure there must be some, seeing all these lights about the house," Mush says.

"Then let us all take a treasure each, for our troubles," Cord says, "and pile the rest up against the walls and windows. We soak them in the oil, and put a torch to the lot. Each floor is timbered with well seasoned oak, and the whole place will go up like a bonfire. It will seem like a simple accident, and the earl will never be able to tell if anything is missing."

"A cunning idea," Chapuys says, "but I must refuse my share of the spoils. I was at the rear, and my own sword remained unbloodied."

"You have done more than any of us, sir," Jeremiah Cord replies, firmly. "Shall we vote on it?"

"All those in favour?" Will says, and there is a resounding 'aye' from them all. Will knows exactly what he will loot from the doomed castle, and the thought of it makes him smile for the first time in days.

Later as they make their way back towards London, Will Draper turns in his saddle, and watches the sky grow a deep, blood red. It is a good blaze, and the locals rush to fight the flames. The conflagration is too much though, and few of the peasants care to risk their lives for the Earl of Surrey, whom they all detest with equal vigour. Afterwards, they are all quite astonished to find a dozen dead bodies in the burnt out husk of the castle.

*

Harry Howard, Earl of Surrey, is a mere shadow of a man. In the two months since his castle near Peterborough burnt down, he has heard nothing from either Ned

Ned Naughton, or any of the other twelve men he hired. Apart from that, he is aware that wherever he goes, there is a Cromwell man there... drinking where he drinks, and whoring where he whores.

"It is too much, sire," he complains, rather ill advisedly, to the king. "I must feel safe in my own shires."

"Too much, sir?" Henry glowers at the spoiled young earl. "I shall tell you what is too much, sir. It is too much that I must suffer daily pain from my damned leg... that is too much. Now you snivel about the place, like some damned snivelling... thing... about a man I thought lost to me. Then he is returned to me, with some tale of derring do, Barbary pirates, and an adventure with Prince Ibrahim. Now you want to dun him down, yet again? What has he to do with your house burning down? How could he put it to the torch whilst escaping from a gang of Moroccan pirates off the coast of Tangier? You must learn a lesson from your father, who has been very quiet, these past two months."

> "*One man's place is hard earned*
> *and another he must inherit*
> *one mans home was all burned*
> *and he can scarcely bear it.*"

Tom Wyatt, who is close to Henry

these days, trying to distract him, chants the little ditty, which he swears is going the rounds of the common people.

"There, you see," Surrey complains to Henry. "Now even Wyatt does it."

"Does what, sir?" the poet says. "I merely repeat a witty ditty. Has it some meaning to you?"

"You know how much Will Draper hates me," the earl moans.

"Not so, My Lord," Tom Wyatt tells the ashen faced earl. "Why, I shall prove it. I am invited to dinner tonight, at the Draper House. You must come with me, and meet this ogre you so fear."

"Never." Surrey is not to be swayed.

"Well, I think it a fine idea," Henry says. "What time, Tom?"

"About seven, sire?"

"We shall be ready," Henry says, thus inviting himself too. "Right, Surrey?"

"Er… why, of course, sire… I mean…"

"Shut up." Henry grins. "I shall not miss a chance to gaze on Lady Miriam's magnificent… gardens again."

"As you command, sire," the poet replies, with a mischievous smirk. "I shall see that Sir John Russell has your royal barge ready for six."

"Yes, we shall progress by water, and appear like wraiths from the mist."

"Cloaked in the mists of night,
Hal does sally to the fore,
and beholds himself such a sight,
as makes his belly roar.
Great pies of crusty hue
and fish upon his plate
Henry's palate is err true
as each full dish he ate.
Come now, one and all, I say,
and let us all indulge,
in Miriam's finest food, this day,
and watch our stomachs bulge."

The court poet utters the little rhyme off the top of his head, and several courtiers clap their appreciation.

"You ad lib, sir?" Henry says, with awe in his voice. It is a gift he would love to have, but he is aware that he must labour long and hard on his own poetry. "It is a gift."

"A gift to utter such poor rubbish, sire," Tom Wyatt says, judiciously. "How can one ever forget your magnificent '*Green Groweth the Holly*'? Such power in the words… '*As the holly groweth green,*
And never changeth hue,
So I am, and ever hath been,

Unto my lady true.' Such fine words, Your Majesty. Perhaps you might recite the whole poem to young Surrey this very evening, so that he might understand the true meaning of beauty?"

Surrey is trapped. He cannot disobey the king, and Tom Wyatt stays sat by his side for the rest of the day. He is escorted to the barge, and placed second in the huge entourage that the king must have, even for so casual a flying visit.

The long barge eases away from the shore, and begins to make its way down river towards the now famous Draper House, whilst Henry discourses on the merits of his own poetry when compared with the Italian school, or even poor Tom Wyatt. Everyone is pleased when the craft finally moors at the Draper quayside, and they can debark.

The king waits until they can tie up fast, and so avoids getting wet feet. A watching lad from the house runs off and alerts Will to the arrival of his 'unexpected' guest at the landing stage.

"Your Majesty, this is a most pleasant surprise," General Will Draper, the new Lord Templar, gushes as the party reaches the great house's main entrance. "I trust we have enough food ready to stretch around your people."

"Oh, just a bowl of soup and some stale bread for them, Will. They will eat in the kitchen, with the other servants, what?"

"As you command, sire," Will says, and gestures for one of his lads to come over. "Joe, have them set out the long table... the one we brought from Austin Friars great kitchen... and see our guests are well fed, as is fitting."

"Yes, master," young Joe says, with a sharp bow.

"Smart lad... one of your lawyer students, Will?" Henry asks.

"Yes, sir. He is a veritable jewel. Now let me... I say, Wyatt, you old rogue, is that Surrey with you?" There is a sudden silence in the huge hall. "Why Harry, my old friend, where on earth have you been keeping yourself these past few months?"

"Oh... here and there," Surrey replies in a small voice.

"Then we must make new arrangements over the seating. I thought myself at the place of honour until the king came, and now, I must shuffle down another place. For Norfolk is before Surrey, and Surrey before Suffolk, then comes poor Templar. How is your dear old father keeping these days? His health is good, I hope?"

"Er... yes," the Earl of Surrey says. "I believe so."

"Never mind, old boy, he can't live forever... and you will advance one day... all in good time, what?"

"Er... yes, quite."

"By God, but this is a fine thing, sire. Dining with my king, and all my dearest friends. We must roister the night away. Damn, but it is really good to see you again, Surrey. let me get you seated."

The king is amazed, yet pleased at this apparent rapprochement, and allows himself to be steered to the seat of honour. Will sits two places to his right, and Miriam to his immediate left. It is for Surrey to take the remaining place, and he sees that, despite his show of loving friendship, Will Draper will have his day, and his say.

"Sit Harry," Henry commands. "I see you have put up some new tapestries since last I called, Lady Miriam. I rather like the one hanging over Surrey's chair. Rather saucy depiction, what?"

"Yes, Your Royal Highness, I think it a little too explicit for public viewing, but it draws a great deal of attention. My husband tells me that it is called 'the Rape of

Lucretia'."

"Really?" Henry says, with an odd look on his face. "I recall she killed herself afterwards. Is it not a hard world for women, my dear?"

"Yes, sire… a hard world, but we keep going. We must. Wine my Lord Surrey?"

The earl holds out his goblet, and Miriam fills it for him. He wonders just how the Drapers will enact their revenge on him, and he shudders at how Lucretia must have ended up at his back.

Culpeper is dead, and rumour has it that Catherine will soon follow him to the block. That means that the Howards have furnished two queens for Henry, and each has been found to be guilty of adultery and treason. If his dynasty is to survive, he must stir his father into action.

The food, as usual, is exceptional, but it is all just ashes in Surrey's mouth. Across from him, the ambassador, Chapuys sits, with a large, ornate garnet ring on his finger which was once a Howard heirloom, and Mush Draper is sporting a fabulous gold and amethyst brooch given to the Norfolk family by the King of France.

They mock me, he thinks, and his heart grows cold at the thought. If they can be so bold, it is because they understand that he is a beaten man. Never, he tells himself. If it takes a decade, I will have my revenge.

"Hal," Will Draper calls, across Surrey, "we have a new fool with us tonight."

"Oh, leave poor Surrey alone," Henry says, and laughs at his own jest. The table follows suit, and Surrey must smile at his own ridicule.

"A real fool, sire," Miriam says, and claps her hands. At once, a green clad man, with bells on his cap and at his ankles comes tumbling into the great hall. He is thin, hunch backed, and as agile as a cat.

"Has any one ever told you that you look like the king, sir?" he says to a startled Henry. "Only you are better looking!"

"I am not!" Henry snaps back, before he realises the jest. Then he laughs, and tosses a coin at the fellow.

"I only accept gold coins," the jester says. "It saves me from having too heavy a purse." As he says about his heavy purse, he cups a hand over his codpiece and makes a lewd lunging gesture at the assembled guests.

"Ho! The fellow is a bawdy one," the king says, in delight. "Tell me another, you dirty fool."

"What is the difference between the

King of France and a turd, sire?"

"I know not."

"No, nor do I."

"By God, Will," Henry gasps between laughter, "I swear that you give the finest dinners in all England!"

*

"Norfolk is a broken man, sir," Kel Kelton reports back to Thomas Cromwell. "He walks like an old man, and stands only with the help of a stick. I doubt he, or his bastard son, will ever be a threat again."

"Good, but we must remain vigilant, my boy," Tom Cromwell says. "It when the dog is wounded that it is at its most dangerous."

"They are watched around the clock, master," Kel assures the old man. "One false move, and we can have them silenced."

"Of course, but as a final resort only. How is the king keeping?" Thomas Cromwell asks. "I miss him so very much."

"Mad with pain, or stupefied with drugs, these days," Kel replies. "Lady Miriam's confinement is but another month away, and Draper House is prepared for the great event. My sharp tongued Maisie has dropped again… a blue eyed daughter with my good looks and her sharp brains. Richard is … Richard, sir. At least he is out of his bed, and trying to save his lady love. How goes it here?"

"Such news, my lad. Isabella is in her bed, and due any time now. Is Mush crossing to be here with her at the right moment?"

"This week," Kel Kelton tells his master. "I think he hopes the child will arrive before he does. He fears for the girl, and seems to love her to distraction."

"As I fear for England," Cromwell says, a faraway look in his eyes. "Though our latest plot will help, if only we can find enough unsullied pages, my boy."

"I paid a visit to a company in the Strand, who used the new fangled Caxton Press for a while, then got themselves arrested by Sir Thomas More. I bought the building and the press for three hundred pounds, and acquired its stock of un-cut parchment. Over two thousand quarto sized pieces of good quality cotton and flax mix."

"You used a fake name, I hope?" Tom Cromwell asks, his voice excited at this excellent news.

"I bought it through a Dutch company, owned by two German fellows who do not exist," Kel says. "The entire contents, and the press, are to be shipped over to Ghent, and then on to Antwerp, next week. You might start at any moment, sir."

"The uncut parchment must be authentic," Thomas Cromwell says. "The king is no fool, and he will see through any ruse that is not up to the mark."

"My people use the best inks, and know how to age a document," Kel tells him.

"We cannot use your forgers," Cromwell says. "The writing must be mine, and mine alone. It will take time, but I find I have a lot of that these days."

"As you wish, sir. In that case, I shall have the ink and paper brought here by secret means, and that will be that."

"Then we are ready to proceed?"

"We are, sir," Kel replies. "Have you told Will Draper yet?"

"And have him interfere?" Cromwell chuckles. "No, let him find out for himself, and then we will see how clever he really is."

"A pound says that he spots the ruse at once." Kel Kelton will do all in his power to deceive everyone, but he has a high opinion of Will Draper's keen mind.

"Your wager is taken," Thomas Cromwell says. For the first time since his 'death' he feels firmly in control of everything once again. "For I am '*dead*' certain of my ground!"

"If your plan works…"

"It will work," Cromwell insists. "We have the materials to hand, and the contents of my memory to harvest. If we play our cards right, Henry will dance to our tune once more, and I will be able to keep my beloved England on the right course."

"The Thomas Cromwell way," Kel Kelton says. "May God look favourably on our machinations, and keep them safe from discovery."

"Amen to that," Thomas Cromwell replies. He knows that his secret is safe with Kel, and can only hope that no one else suspects what he is about to do.

*

Isabella Draper, far from her home in Venice, and taken in hand by the efficent ladies of Draper House goes into labour but a few days later, and spends many hours in bringing forth a child for her husband. There are complications with the birth, and the doctor hints that there will be no more children. Mush does not care. He is a father, and his beloved wife will recover her health, slowly but surely.

Three weeks later, Miriam Draper is overseeing the loading of a boat with goods for one of her many market stalls when she feels the sudden pain of contractions. It is her fourth child, and it does not wish to wait. Pru and Marion Giles scarce have time to get her to bed before her waters break, and the child, a robust girl, comes screaming into the world.

"Yes, scream away," Miriam says, "for this is a bad world, little one. Would that we could all cry just like you."

When word reaches Thomas Cromwell, he has a golden bracelet made to fit the girl when she is of marriageable age. It weighs in at four ounces, has small rubies set in its girth, and is worth the price of a small riverside house.

"Our friend abroad is far too generous," Will Draper says when he sees the fabulous gift.

"He seeks to give all our children their independence," Miriam tells him. "It is the way of my people to help their children on their way in life. He has paid for Gwyllam's education, and sent precious gold and jewels for the others. It is his way of saying thank you to us."

"For what?" Will asks. "I serve him well enough, but I still put the king first."

"Perhaps you do," Miriam says, "but it is odd how Master Tom still seems to come off best each time."

"There is always a first failure," Will says. "He will overreach himself, and find that he cannot buy his way out with a bag of golden coins. Even now he plots with Kel Kelton to perform some new mischief."

"Really?" Miriam frowns. She would rather the old fellow settled down into retirement. "What is he up to now?"

"I cannot say for sure, but my agents report some unusual activity, both in London and abroad."

"And this is Cromwell's fault?" Miriam asks. She is defensive of the man she thinks of as almost a father to her and Mush.

"I think so. When was it ever not? A man disappears, or a treasured document is mislaid… and we must look to Tom Cromwell for an answer."

"Then it is better that he is living with us in the *Palais de Juis*, is it not?" Miriam says, with a certain conviction. "In this way he might not meddle in English politics overmuch. I would not have him become embroiled in the king's doings again."

"You think he does not now?" Will grins then. "I think Master Tom has a long reach, and sooner or later, his latest plot will surface, and I will have to act, one way or another."

"For or against him?" asks Miriam. "What if he acts against the king?"

"You wonder if I can ever move against a man who is like a father to me?" Will asks of her. "Then let me tell you this… I do not know, my dearest wife. I just do not know. The one thing I can say is this; Tom Cromwell loves the monarchy, even if he thinks Henry to be a fool, and he will never do it any harm."

"Then turn your thoughts to a more pleasant question, husband," Miriam says to her husband. "How shall we name our new daughter?"

"Not *Thomasina,*" Will tells her. "Let her name reflect what we wish for her… like Prudence, Faith or Charity."

"Hope," Miriam says, with sudden inspiration.

"Yes, that is it," Will says. "We wish her hope for the future… a future with out Henry in it, and a world ruled by a kinder sort of a monarch. May Edward live long, and may he prosper."

"Then there it is, we have our set," Miriam says. From now onwards, she will ensure that she never falls with child again. In her travels she has come across certain remedies from India and Cathay that will keep her childless, without denying her husband his pleasures. "Might you now consider easing up from your own punishing schedule, and spend more time with your family?"

"Why not?" Will Draper says to his wife. They are rich, the title is theirs, and they are friends with the greatest in the land. Why not step back and let others do their share? he thinks.

"Begging your pardon, sir." It is young Joe, the finder of Will's doublet and dagger, who spends his days at the door of whichever Draper house Miriam and the family happen to be occupying that day. "Only there is a smartly dressed fellow at the door, and he insists on seeing you. It seems that the king wants to see you, and no other will do."

"Then I must go," Will says, with a shrug. "Forgive me, Miriam, but who can refuse the king?"

"A good king would know when to leave a good servant be," Miriam replies, rather testily.

"Let me see what is amiss," Will tells her, "and then, I will take us all into the country for a nice break."

"Yes…some day."

Will buckles on his sword and goes down to the front door. Sir John Russell is waiting, with an anxious look on his face.

"Will, thank God… you must come at once. The king is … unwell."

"Then you must fetch a doctor."

"No, not unwell like that," Sir John Russell explains. "His Majesty is conversing with Erasmus, who has been dead these five years or more… and worse… the philosopher is mounted upon the back of a white unicorn."

"Does he complain about his leg?"

"No, not a word. I fear he is going quite mad, my friend."

"And I fear he has taken too much of his medicine," Will Draper replies, with a heavy sigh. "It will do no harm to him, unless he decides to throw Erasmus from his court, and mount the unicorn."

"Henry rules between rage and euphoria," Russell says. "Is one worse than the other?"

"Better he loves all mankind than hates it," Will tells the courtier. "Now the king has tasted blood, he will not shirk from violence from now on. I pray that Miriam's poppy juice never runs out."

"Might it be fatal in larger doses?" Sir John Russell asks, and Will gives him a strange look.

"It is a thought best pushed from your mind, sir," the King's Examiner says. "A man might lose his head for even thinking such a thing."

"I mean only that we should keep it from him, as best we can."

"Of course," Will says, with a smile.

They make their way down to the quayside, to where a fast boat awaits them. Will shall attend on the king, and sooth his wilder fantasies, but his mind will be on other things. Now Russell mentions it, the king's man cannot say if the poppy juice can be fatal or not, and it worries him.

One way or another, it seems that the Draper family holds the fate of the king in their hands.

"Whitehall," Sir John tells the boatman, "and be quick about it. The king is in great need of a friend." It is a sad irony that Henry now seeks out Will Draper to help him… yet he is the very man who causes him his worst problems.

"I doubt the unicorn will still be there," Will says.

"I seen one of them once," the boatman says. "Big, black thing, it was, with a long horn sticking out of its head. Mind you, that was after twelve pints of strong ale."

"Kings dream of white unicorns," Will says to the man. "I dare say they are of a better breed."

"Thank God I am just a boatman," the man says, with a wry chuckle. "For if Henry wishes to harness the beast to his carriage, you will have a hard time of it, General Draper."

"Yes, he changes his mind at a moment's notice," Russell says. "What will you do?"

"The same as usual," Will replies. "I shall smile and agree with him. Then hope he sees sense. If I can dissuade him from invading Scotland with too few troops, I can handle one white unicorn."

"As I say, sir… rather you than me," the man concludes. "For one day, Henry will invade Scotland, and bedamned to your advice. Why, he might even do it astride his white unicorn. He is the king, and kings can do as they like."

"Then I must hang on, and hope for the best," Will Draper says, "for I can do no other. My fate is tied to Henry's, and my future is in his hands."

"God help us all," says Russell, and the boat falls silent. The dirty water of the

Thames laps against the gunwales and the boat plows on. Will Draper thinks of the first time he made this journey, to tell Henry of the death of Cardinal Wolsey so many years before, and he wonders how long he can go on. He is weary of intrigue, and longs for the quiet life his wife wishes for them both.

One day, he muses.One day.

-end-

Book XVIII in the Tudor Crimes series '*Catherine the Quean*' is due for release in time for Christmas 2017.

Afterword

When I wrote 'Winter King' it was intended to be a single novel. Once the characters were established, I was tempted to turn it into a trilogy covering the period of Anne Boleyn's time as mistress and queen.

Now, seventeen books later, I am no nearer the end of my journey. Apart from my own fascination with history, and historical fiction, I am driven on by the generous comments, advice, and support of my readers.

Whilst the writer of historical fiction can often invent certain situations and conversations to move the story on that are only within their own imaginations, I think it is important not to alter a proven historical fact. To this end I place the various wars, rebellions and political developments mentioned within their right context and time frame.

The king's leg ulcer is well documented, although I confess that his use of opium is a fancy of mine. His wild fluctuations of temper are also a fact, and his cruelty is noted in several court papers. Being boiled alive, losing limbs and burning at the stake were all punishments handed out on a fairly regular basis, and the description of Abraham Wake's torture and subsequent hanging, drawing and quartering are taken from contemporary accounts. The death by being torn apart between horses was a French punishment, inflicted on a would be royal assassin.

Queen Catherine's foolish confession to clergymen did happen, as did her assertion that she had been raped. Had she adopted the course recommended to her by the king's advisors, she might well have escaped with divorce and banishment, much along the lines of Anne of Cleves' treatment.

Thomas Culpeper was the king's favourite for a while, but probably fell to temptation when Catherine showed interest in him. There is no evidence to support my assertion that he was a fantasist, intent on stealing the crown of England.

Whilst the fictional Will Draper faction could not displace the Duke of Norfolk in the king's affections, it is certain that, about this time, something... or someone...did. Henry's liking for Thomas Howard and his son certainly cooled from 1441 onwards, even as the Seymour brothers gained in his estimation.

Still that is for future books to explore. Yes, there are more 'Will Draper' books in the offing, and the next 'Catheryn the Quean' is due out in time for Christmas 2017/ New Year 2018. The odd spelling of both name and title is typically Tudor, and taken from a document the sixth queen signed in 1541.

I wonder if it was a jest on her part, for the word 'quean' in those times meant 'a woman of low birth, vulgar and immoral'. Whilst it is established that Catheryn was being courted by Tom Seymour prior to the king's interest, there is no evidence of sexual impropriety. She later married Seymour (her fourth husband) after the king's death.

Whilst my first love is Tudor England, I also have a soft spot for the wild and unpredictable world of the long Georgian period, particularly the reigns of the last two Georges' and the struggles of the napoleonic wars. To this end I have started to write about the period, starting in 1800, with with 'King's Quest' which introduces the reader to the infamous English master spy William McCloud, and his collection of accomplished scoundrels.

Once again, I have taken the liberty of mixing fact with fiction, and real persons with fictitious ones. Canadian backwoodsman Luke Boyd is a stone hearted killer of men who finds himself transported from Indian fighting in the wilderness, to dancing a quadrille in a Mayfair great house, whilst Lady Belinda Rourke works for William McCloud in the hope of salvaging her good name, and place in 'society' once more.

The corpulent Prince of Wales, Mad King George, Charles Fortnum, Beau Brummell,

William Pitt(the Younger), Mr Fox, Napoleon Bonaparte and his wife, Josephine, all play their parts, and a tale of politics and international intrigue is intertwined with a clever plot to… well, what exactly? William McCloud has a nose for these things, and suspects some evil deed is afoot, but what? Is he trailing the best French agent there is, or is he being trailed?

I hope you enjoy the 'taster' chapters below.

Anne Stevens
Cherry Tree Cottage, 2017.

King's Quest
by
Anne Stevens

I do hope you enjoy these two sample chapters from King's Quest; The first historical novel in my new 'Georgians' cycle. Available now in Amazon/Kindle and paperback formats.

Chapter One … The Ball

To call the ragged sprawl of Montréal a city was, Lady Belinda Rourke thought as she surveyed the panoramic view from her upper window, something of an exaggeration. The rugged French trappers and traders, who constituted two thirds of the population, were intent on raising the growing town's status to that of a city. They wished to attract outside investment, and an influx of new people; preferably French speaking.

Canada, no matter who ruled it, was ready for expansion, and the self styled *Francophones* wanted it to be both a rival to the newborn United States, and mostly French speaking. Lady Belinda Rourke knew that the British Governor General and his modest sized garrison of Redcoats disagreed, of course, and a simmering hostility lay just below the polite surface, waiting to erupt at the first wayward spark.

Lady Belinda, Irish by birth, yet thoroughly English by marriage, well understood the French point of view, but could not allow it to cloud her judgement. William McCloud, a devious gentleman of fortune, had been quite clear on that particular point. To enrol into his small army of spies, cutthroats, and secret informants had seemed like the right way to proceed, if she were ever to be able to return to England again.

He had promised that her past would be wiped out, and that any further difficulties, with the authorities in London, would dwindle away to nothing. So she accepted his offer, and here she was, a young, widowed lady of apparent wealth, pausing in Montreal, on her way to take ship for England.

    The town, which had grown up around a small French fort built in 1645, was established on a group of three low hills and quickly became a thriving trading post. Lady Belinda had listened politely to her hosts, a mixture of English gentry, and French *Bourgeoisie*, and knew that the settlement had been central to the safety of the first white settlers. Until very recently, the fort had been the military keystone that had repelled the murderous raids of the Iroquois nation, the famously treacherous Odawa, and other indigenous native tribes.

    Montréal had became a focal point for the European traders, and soon found itself the centre of a province called, rather optimistically, *New France.* In her years of mingling with the English gentry, Lady Belinda's sense of how things worked had become honed, until she could often find herself one step ahead of the political game. It was obvious that the English could not allow the French to gain a toehold in the New World, and sure enough, in the autumn of September 1760, the French forces had been confronted, and fought against, until they finally capitulated to the better led, and better armed British forces. French colonial rule was at an end.

    "The blue, or the green, milady?" Lady Belinda turned her gaze back to the young maid, loaned to her by Mr. Monk's rather dull wife. The

Monks were what passed for English gentry in the town, and Mr. Monk was constantly boasting of how he would build a stone mansion in the Outremont quarter to outdo anything ever before seen in Montréal. From now on, the biggest and the best must always be English, of course.

"The green, I think." She made her way to the little dressing table by the bed, and rummaged in her jewel box. "It will go well with my emerald necklace, Marie." The emeralds were cleverly cut green glass, and the golden mounting was nothing more than silver gilt, but one simply had to keep up appearances, and Mrs Philomena Monk, at least, was convinced of their authenticity. "What is that building over there?" She gestured towards the tallest structure on the horizon, and so Marie Dumont looked out across the town.

"*Il est l'église de Saint Gabriel, Milady,*" the pretty young girl told her, without thinking. "*Oh, Je suis trés désolé, Contesse... comment dites-vous?* ... She is the new church, built for Saint Gabriel... yes?"

"My French is excellent, Marie," Lady Belinda replied, smiling at the girl's confusion. "Now, be so kind as to dress me. I must not keep Mr and Mrs Monks' guests waiting, must I?"

The girl smiled and curtseyed at this striking young English woman, who seemed to move through life with such easy serenity. Every young man in Montréal ... and a good few of the older ones... wanted an invitation to the Monk residence, just for a chance to meet with her. Lady Belinda was the talk of *town society*, and the few hundred who could claim to be gentlefolk found her presence amongst them to be a most welcome diversion from their everyday business.

The dress, a magnificent silk affair, was one of only four she possessed, and making herself look different at each social occasion was becoming more and more difficult. The lack of funds since fleeing England has been her most difficult obstacle to overcome, and it was only Canadian society's willingness to believe in her exalted rank that had made things bearable.

"So dreary, my dear Philomena," she had told Mrs Monk at their first meeting. "One can understand the misplacing of the odd small valise, but for them to lose half of my luggage, is quite impossible!" The lie, told with practiced ease, had worked, and if anyone actually doubted that the Hudson Bay Company waggon had mislaid two of her travelling chests, they kept it to themselves.

The green gown was, compared to the town fashions, modern and eye catching, and how she filled it dispersed any negative thoughts on the matter. At twenty-five, Belinda Rourke was, quite simply, stunning. She was slim, elegant and evenly featured, and her waist length auburn hair and green eyes made grown men dry mouthed and stuttering on meeting with her for the first time. When added to the natural beauty, her various potions and powders did little more than guild the lily.

"Will I do?" She pirouetted, and the little maid clapped her hands in delight, and smiled at her temporary mistress.

"You must do *this*, Milady," Marie replied, and stabbed a slender finger at her own cheek. Lady Rourke smiled and opened the small trinket box in which she kept her most secret beauty aids. Selecting one of the small black shapes, she placed it into Marie's upturned palm.

"The heart, I think, Marie," she said, and allowed the maid to glue the small black beauty spot to her upper cheek. "Not too high, *ma chére*, or else it denotes my willingness to indulge in a romantic interlude. Just so, and it is flirtatious, rather than overtly invitational, do you see?"

"I will learn all of these clever things, Milady," Marie said, earnestly. She had served as Lady Belinda's personal maid for almost a month, and now hoped the position might become a permanent one. "When you return to *Londres*," she hazarded, "having your own personal French maid would be a most *piquant* thing, no?"

"You are not French though," Lady Belinda replied. "You are Canadian."

"And you are not an English lady," Marie told her, with a knowing smile. She may have come from a poor working class background, but she possessed enough good sense to know that the elaborate story about lost luggage, and the other tales, were just lies to make things smoother, and easier. "We would suit each other very well, I think. Perhaps if you speak with the English lord?"

"McCloud is not a lord, but an utter rogue," said Lady Belinda, "and I doubt he would pay your passage. You would do well to stay here, in Montréal."

"And have to bar my door every night against Mr. Monk when he has taken too much drink?" Marie Dumont shook her head vehemently. "No… take me with you, Milady. I am loyal, and know how to keep a secret."

"I shall ask." Belinda Rourke knew the young maid would add a certain quality to her presentation, and resolved to speak with McCloud, should he ever return from his mad jaunt into the encroaching Canadian wilderness. "Now, open the door, and let me make a grand entrance."

The Monk house was a stone and wood framed two story building that would not do for a country squire back in England, but it had a large reception room, and was deemed luxurious by Montréal standards. Belinda descended the single flight of stairs, straight into the entrance hall, where some forty guests were gathered. In one corner, a trio of musicians, made up of a violin, a viola, and a cello, were grating out a piece by some obscure Baroque period composer.

Their evening dress was as dull and

archaic as their choice of music, and Belinda felt as if she had slipped back fifty years in time to the mid seventeen fifties. If Montréal was going to become the premier city of the Americas, they would need to shape themselves, and drag the place into the nineteenth century, as soon as possible.

"Ah, Lady Belinda… we are so happy you have consented to join our little soirée this evening." Ambrose Monk was a barrel-like man, squeezed into a suit of clothing that could have done with being at least a couple of sizes bigger. His arms and legs were like great hams, and he bulged out of both coat and pants in a most alarming way. "Now, come along my dear, and let me introduce you to a few of my guests." He took her by the elbow, and steered her across the room, intent on showing her off to his main competitor in Montréal. "My dear Pierre … let me introduce you to Lady Belinda Rourke… who is our guest until the *Alice Lancaster* sails for London later in the month. Lady Belinda … this is M'sieu Pierre Monceau, who insists on trying to trade in opposition to the Hudson Bay Company. His success is only peripatetic of course, and he will always remain in second place, and not up to my own best endeavours."

"It is such a pleasure to meet you at last, my dear Lady Rourke." The tall sparsely built Frenchman spoke with an old school elegance that would charm most women. His well cut frock-coat, and lightly powdered wig, gave him the air of a comfortably off rural aristocrat, but his eyes were rather cold, too close together, and quite unwelcoming. "My people tell me that you are returning to London in a few weeks."

"That is so, sir... and pray... do call me Lady Belinda."

"It will be Montréal's great loss," Monceau said, "my dear Lady Belinda. Our society will be the worse for your leaving."

"You are well informed as to my movements, sir," Belinda replied. "I find it strange to be the centre of so much avid attention. Perhaps it is the strangeness of my dress, or the manner in which I conduct myself, that so draws people to me?"

"Or perhaps it is the company you keep madam?" Pierre Monceau cast a baleful glance around the room and then smiled at her. "I see that your mysterious Mr McCloud is absent this evening. I do hope he is keeping well."

"The gentleman is no more than a casual acquaintance, sir." Lady Belinda Rourke showed no emotion. If the Frenchman wished to know something, then he would have to quit fencing around the edges, and ask her directly.

"Yet I hear he sails on the very same ship as you do, my lady," Monceau replied, and offered her his hand. "Might I then have the pleasure of the next dance, Lady Belinda?"

"I cannot get used to such overt

informality sir," Lady Rourke told him, and moved her open fan to obscure the lower half of her face. "It seems rather odd… shocking, almost, that the ladies of Montréal do not have a dance card to be marked."

"Should you have such a thing, I believe every dance would already be taken, a dozen times over," the Frenchman said, with a curious smile on his face. "In the absence of a formal dance card, might I be so bold as to escort to you out onto the floor? See, some of these brave souls, despite the lack of formal dance cards, are already getting into formation."

"Then I believe it would be sadly remiss of me to go against the local custom, Monsieur Monceau." Lady Belinda took the proffered arm, and they joined the dozen or so other guests who had ventured out onto the small dance floor.

"It is a pity M'sieu McCloud is absent," the Frenchman told her. "I believe he was a fine dancer."

"I am a little curious to know why poor Mr McCloud and myself have been linked together, if only in the way of small talk and gossip. Perhaps you might enlighten me, sir… even as we dance?"

It became immediately apparent to Lady Belinda that the inhabitants of Montréal Society were unlikely to ever rival the gentry of either the London social circuit, or the lesser one, centred in Bath. These self-imposed exiles had no fancy for the more sociable, but rather elitist minuet, and preferred the more traditional English and French rural dances.

Country dance was the order of the evening, and a hectic reel was first on the agenda. Fortunately for Lady Belinda, she was fully conversant with such dances, which were based on the 'progressive longways' method, and usually danced in well defined parallel lines.

"Pardon me if I have offended you," the Frenchman said, as they took their place in the short line. "I meant only that it was curious to find such a diverse pair of individuals in one another's company."

"Diverse, sir?" Lady Belinda frowned at him, and tried to convey her utter inability to understand what he meant. Most men devoured her obvious beauty, and failed to understand her innate cleverness. "You speak in riddles. Is poor Mr McCloud then not of our social position?"

"Madam, you are Lady Belinda Rourke, the Countess of Arklow, and no one here… or in Montréal itself… is of your social position," Pierre Monceau told her. "You greatly honour us with your kind condescension. I meant only that your Monsieur McCloud is *not* a gentleman. I understand that the man actually works for a living!"

"I am told that is a state which many find themselves in, sir." Belinda allows her eyes to widen, and pouts to give herself a look of the inanity affected by most young women in London Society. "Do you not *do* something for your fortune?"

"I employ trappers, Lady Belinda," the elegant Frenchman replied, a little stiffly. "They produce the wealth, and I merely oversee them. The McCloud man actually soils his hands!"

"Good God above," Lady Belinda Rourke exclaimed, with a winsome smile playing about her perfectly rouged lips. "I confess that I thought him to be a disgustingly rich merchant. He dresses expensively enough, even though his taste is not out of the top drawer. What on earth does he do?" The rules of the dance sent them reeling away in opposite directions at that moment, and it was a little while before they came back to face one another again.

"He is a spy," he said.

"A spy, sir?" Lady Belinda Rourke affected an astonished look, and a tone of complete surprise. "How do you mean, Monsieur Monceau? Does he hide behind drapes, and listen into all the gossip?"

"He spies on any who he believes to be the English king's enemies, Lady Belinda," the Frenchman said. "William McCloud uses his abilities to cause unrest amongst the French Canadians in Canada. He wishes to foment a dangerous rebellion, and then arrest the ring leaders."

"Then good luck to him, sir," Lady

Belinda Rourke told him. "The French should love the king, even as we do. Would they rather have to bow down to First Consul Bonaparte, and his revolutionary thugs?"

"Bonaparte has, at least, brought peace to Europe," the Frenchman told her, coldly. "The Treaty of Amiens…"

"Will never last, or so Mr McCloud informs me." Lady Belinda Rourke replied. "He says we will be at war again… once young Mr Pitt returns to power."

"Do not misunderstand me, Lady Belinda." The dance was about to part them once more, but the Frenchman took her by the elbow, and drew her aside. The formation realigned with a few grumbles, and the wild reel went on apace. "The man is not all that he seems. He uses deception and guile to bring ruin on honest men, and I would not like you to become too heavily involved with his vile machinations."

"Machinations sir?" Lady Belinda Rourke smiled at him vacantly. "I hardly know the man, and the fact that we are to share a ship together is not at all unusual. I believe that there are only two or three crossings each month, and it would be difficult for us to avoid one another, given the severe strictures imposed by the circumstances of the voyage. Would you have me swim all the way back to England, sir?"

"Of course not, Lady Belinda, but you must understand how people might talk… if you travelled with McCloud."

"I shall be travelling with my personal maid, Monsieur Monceau, and should be adequately chaperoned during the voyage." She removed her arm gently, but firmly, from his grip, gave him a slight curtsy, and crossed the room in search of her garrulous host.

"What's this... is my French friend's company not to your liking, my lady?" Mr Monk said with obvious delight. "The French are a peculiar race, and I fear that he is an acquired taste at best."

"He seeks to blackguard poor Mr McLeod, and I cannot think why he should, for he seems to be a gentleman of rare talents, and great erudition."

"Quiet so, dear Lady Belinda," Mr Monk replied with a knowing little chuckle. "We have often shared a glass of port, and discussed the way of the world on long dark nights. William's charm and wit will be greatly missed once he is on his way back to England." The Hudson Bay manager had heard the stories of course, but had no wish to make any comment about William McCloud's rather mysterious line of business. If he was in Canada on behalf of His Britannic Majesty's government, then it was in nothing but the most clandestine way, and therefore none of his business.

"Is he a spy?" Lady Belinda asked the question in such a bright and flippant manner that any who heard her words would assume her to have a total lack of knowledge in the matter.

"I cannot possibly say madam," Monk replied, and glanced about, in case they were being listened to. "It is not a thing talked about in polite circles."

"Oh, how perfectly marvellous," she replied, and tapped Mr Monk on the upper arm with her closed fan. "A British spy, of all things. I do believe I shall be in for a most enjoyable voyage home!"

"Quite so, My Lady," Monk said, and cleared his throat gruffly. He had something to say, and was embarrassed about voicing a criticism of a member of the nobility. "My wife tells me that Marie, our maid, is talking nonsense about going to England with you. The girl is addled, of course."

"I sincerely hope not, Mr Monk." Lady Belinda Rourke gave him her most endearing smile. "For I have engaged her as my personal maid."

"I regret to inform you that such a thing cannot be, madam," Monk replied. "Marie Dumont was indentured to us four years ago. In return for bed and board, she must work for us until the contract is fulfilled."

"Oh, how bothersome!" Lady Belinda said. "How long has the indenture to run, Mr Monk?"

"Another five years, Lady Rourke,"

Monk told her. "You must see that we cannot release her, without recompense. She can buy back her indenture at any time. I am a fair man, when all is said and done."

"How much?"

"Fifty guineas," Monk said. "I doubt she can afford it."

"I see. Now, where is Mrs Monk?"

"Mrs Monk?" Monk frowned, and glanced about to make sure his wife was not in earshot. "What has it to do with her?"

"I might consider purchasing Marie's indenture," Lady Belinda told him, "but not without certain assurances."

"Assurances… what assurances?"

"Assurances of a *delicate* nature, Mr Monk." She opened her fan, and held it angled across her face, as if masking her words from the wrong ears. "I cannot take the girl if she is … well, you know … wanton."

"By God, Milady… what do you suggest?"

"Nothing, but I must know she is an honest child… if you follow my drift, sir?" Lady Belinda almost laughed at how easy it was to manipulate the man. "Perhaps your wife might know of any past … infidelities?"

"My wife?" Monk's face was slowly turning an odd shade of purple.

"Yes, or she might simply ask Marie if she has been a good child."Lady Belinda smiled then. "I am sure she has… but one never knows if some blackguard has been laying siege to the poor girl's honour."

"The girl is honest, madam," Monk said. "And to prove my faith in her, I am willing to reduce the amount required to purchase her indenture."

"From fifty guineas to … what?"

"Twenty-five?" Monk saw the look in her eyes, and reassessed. "No … ten… ten guineas."

"Very well. Marie shall become my maid, and you will pay her ten guineas, as a parting gift."

"Madam, I meant…"

"No, do not thank me, sir," Belinda concluded. "Under the circumstances, I need not bother your wife, and shall inform Marie that she is to remain discreet."

"You will make a fine companion for William McCloud, My Lady," Monk said, sharply, and left her side. Lady Belinda Rourke smiled then. Yes, she rather thought she would.

"Madam?" Marie said later, when informed her that she was going to England. "But how? Mr Monk is not that generous a man… and besides, you said M'sieu McCloud would not pay my passage."

"Mr Monk has agreed to provide the funds," Lady Belinda told her. "Please, do not let me regret my actions, Marie. The life you are choosing will be harder, and more dangerous than the one you currently lead."

"You will regret nothing, My Lady... I promise you," the girl replied. "I shall serve you well, and for that I shall see London, and get to meet the king!"

"Meet the king?" Lady Belinda Rourke laughed then, and shook her head. "Do not expect too much in that direction, girl."

"No, I will meet your famous King George," Marie insisted. "They say he is touched in the head... no?"

"My dear girl, I think we all are... if only a little."

"When do we leave, madam?" Marie asked.

"When William McCloud returns ...or rather, *if* he does. The madman has gone into the wilderness, by himself, and I doubt he will survive."

"I pray he does, My Lady," Marie said. "For I would dearly love to see London!"

Chapter Two… The Stalking

The sudden rain shower had brought a freshness to the forest glade, and something more; a distinct smell of danger. The young hunter remained crouched in the midst of his well chosen thicket, and inhaled deeply. The smell of pine cones carried on the warm afternoon breeze, filled is nostrils and made him think back to the early days on his father's homestead. Back then such smells were always with him, as he helped to fell trees and clear the land, ready for planting a crop. Now the treacherous breeze spoke of other things… dangerous things.

The stink of the Odawa war party carried on the breeze, and warned him of its close presence, well before he heard their careless sounds. When the noise did finally come, it was raucous, drunken, and unthinking. The small band, no more than seven or eight strong, were back in their own territory, and feeling quite safe from any sort of pursuit or retribution.

They were mistaken.

Luke Boyd could have slipped away, out of their path, with ease, but it was not his intention to run from this celebrating gang of murderous Odawa warriors. The small party had slipped across the invisible border between the United States and Canada, intent on raiding. They had attacked and burnt down two farmsteads, and butchered everyone they found. Four men, six women, and three small children. No, Luke Boyd's intention was not to escape from them, but to stalk them ... and then to kill them.

He glanced down at the loaded musket cradled in the crook of his left arm, and touched the fingers of his right hand to the second primed weapon lying at his feet. He must make two good shots, then rely on the knife stuck in his belt, and the short British Navy sword, known as a 'hanger' which once belonged to his father.

The first of the Odawa warriors appeared on the far side of the glade, and looked about in a cursory way. He waved for the rest to come forward, and another seven young men, drunk on stolen whisky, blood, and victory, came whooping out into the wide open space. One, grotesquely, was wearing the tattered remnants of a woman's dress.

The young Canadian held his breath, and estimated the number of paces to the leading warrior to be just under one hundred. Too far, even for his well looked after Brown Bess musket, he thought. He was a marksman of some repute in the Canadian territories, but anything over sixty paces meant chancing a fatal miss. He would wait for them to come strutting across the glade, pushing each other and passing back and forth a jug of spirits taken on their raid. Then he would begin to kill them, and not stop until the last one was dead.

"Come on, you murdering bastards," the

young Canadian murmured to himself. As if in response, the leader of the band drained the dregs of the jug, threw it aside, and started towards him. "Good lad," Boyd muttered, and eased the musket from the crook of his arm. The movement was slight, almost undetectable, but the Odawa warriors froze in their tracks, still seventy or eighty paces distant. It could not have been him they sensed, for the movement had been too slight and the noise totally inaudible.

Then the Canadian heard it too.

The sound was downwind, muffled by the density of the forest, but becoming clearer by the second. Someone was coming through the forest, singing a melancholy ballad. The Odawa warriors crouched, and reached for either bows or hatchets. The leader, a big, well muscled young buck, unslung a musket from his shoulder, and held it across his chest.

A moment later, and a stocky middle aged man came into sight, leading a well laden pack horse. He halted, not fifty paces away from the surprised warriors, and put his hands on his hips, as if in exasperation. Then he removed his broad brimmed hat, wiped his sweating brow, and replaced it on his head.

"Be Gad, but you are fine specimens," he called to them, and waved a hand in friendship. "Are you after being the accommodating type of aboriginals, or not, gentlemen?" For answer, one of the Odawa raiders drew his bow, and let loose an arrow. It sailed over the newcomer's head, missing it by a few inches. "Ah, I see that your answer is in the negative, sir," the man continued. "Then let us get down to it, shall we?"

The Odawa warriors had no English, and would not have cared to parlay anyway. A lone white man, stumbling about in their forest was an easy mark, obviously asking to be robbed and killed. Apart from the pack animal, there would be rich pickings to be had, once he was dead, and some fun in the actual killing.

Two of the Odawa screamed and rushed at the portly Englishman who, quite calmly, let go of his pack horse's tether, and pulled a long barrelled gun from the pack. He eased back the hammer, aimed, and fired, in the blink of an eye. The round lead ball hit the leading warrior in the chest, sending him staggering backwards, as if punched, and the Englishman drew a long steel bayonet. He clicked it onto the still smoking muzzle of his long barrelled gun, with a remarkable air of nonchalance, and brought it down just in time to meet the second attacker's wild rush. The Odawa had no time to stay his ill advised charge, and so rushed forward with his war axe raised, and ready to deliver a killing blow.

The older man simply lunged under the mad swing, and pushed the bayonet up into his attacker's ribs. Flesh ripped open, and the warrior screamed in agony. The Englishman twisted the eighteen inches of honed steel bayonet hard, pulled back, and allowed the skewered man to tumble down to the hard, damp ground.

Seeing this done in the space of less than twenty heart beats, Luke Boyd could only marvel at the skill, and sheer audacity of the newly arrived man. Then the remaining Odawa warriors gave a great yell, and went at the older Englishman in a rush.

The young Canadian knew he must act fast.

He let the familiar hatred of his enemies well up inside him, and gave out his own terrible roar. Most of the Odawa carried on towards the intruding Englishman, but one heard the cry, and he turned, to face this new threat. Boyd raised his musket, and fired too quickly. The lead ball hissed past the Odawa warrior's ear, and he charged at Luke, thinking him now unarmed.

Luke dropped the musket, grabbed up the second one, aimed more carefully, and fired at the screaming warrior. The range was now down to forty paces, and the lead ball struck the man in the forehead. A lump of his skull, and a spray of grey brain matter gouted upwards. He went down in a flail of arms and legs, dead before he hit the earth.

Meanwhile, the seemingly eccentric older Englishman was having a fine old time of it, explaining the art of bayonet work, even as he thrust and parried. The remaining Odawa warriors, surprised at his resistance, spread out and began to effect a wary encircling movement.

"Classic manoeuvre, you chaps," the Englishman told them, "but I'll take two or three of you dogs with me. It's all in the action, you see? Stand... thrust, twist, and out!" One of the Odawa cried out as the eighteen inches of razor sharp steel ripped across his chest, and he stepped backwards, right onto the point of Boyd's sword. The hanger was designed for hacking and stabbing in the close quarter fighting of a naval boarding action, and the swift thrust went home easily, and finished the man off.

"About time, Mr Boyd," the Englishman said, as if meeting in a country house salon. "These fellows are most bothersome!"

Boyd's rage was at its peak, and he threw himself at the remaining Odawa warriors with a passion. As he cut and hacked at them, he chanted a liturgy of wrongs to lay at their door. The warriors cowered away from him now, because they knew of him. This was the terrible *Mahigan*, the savage wolf who killed without thought, and who had plagued the tribes along the length of the St Lawrence River for the last five summers.

The legend was told around the camp fires, of a wild white man, who can become a wolf, and who rips his enemies apart without pity. It is only a legend because, in all the time he has roamed the wide forests, and scoured the river banks, not one man had survived to tell the true tale. Only the ripped and broken bodies told the story.

Mahigan ... the Wolf.

Now here he was, amongst them, snarling his rage at them, and they knew they were walking dead men. One went down under the vicious hanger, his head cleaved open, and the stout Englishman, as if enjoying a morning stroll in Hyde Park, was thrusting and stabbing his way through from the other side.

At last, all the Odawa raiders were dead, save the leader. He had fended off the older Englishman's probing bayonet thrusts, and placed himself, back against a tall tree, and with musket in hand. The Englishman retreated a dozen paces, and started to reload his gun.

"Save your powder... Mister ....?"

"McCloud," the Englishman replied. "At your service. It is no problem to reload, and dispense with this fellow. Though it does take longer to load than a good old Brown Bess."

"No, hold off...this one is mine," Luke Boyd told him. "There is either no flint, or powder in the musket, or he would have fired at me by now. "Ain't that so, *Cigosi*?" The tall Indian stiffened at the insult. It meant 'weasel', and it spoke of the utter contempt Luke Boyd felt for a tribe who thought nothing of murdering women and children, and whom he had set his heart on destroying, if possible, to the very last man. The Odawa tried to stare him down, but

Boyd just threw aside his bloodstained hanger, and pulled a knife from his belt. "Well, *Cigosi*, are you man enough to face the *Mahigan*?"

"You... *Mahigan*?" The Odawa warrior assessed his opponent, and saw only a white man; a tall, well muscled white man to be sure, but still only a white man, and so he could be killed, just like any other. "*Mahigan*?" He said it with contempt now, and drew his own knife. He had the advantage of the tree at his back, and the man who only called himself a wolf to frighten his enemy, would have to come at him, face on.

"Careful lad," the Englishman said. "I've come too far to lose you now. Let me shoot the murdering bugger, and be damned to it."

"No!" Boyd turned, just enough to break eye contact, and the warrior saw the mistake, and took his chance. He leaped forward, and aimed a killing thrust, which only cut through empty air. The *Mahigan* had dropped to one knee, and put in a return upward angled blow. His blade bit into the warrior's belly, and ripped upwards, stopping only as it bit into the heart. A huge gout of blood bathed Boyd's knife hand, and he pulled it back.

The Odawa warrior slumped back against the tree with an astonished look on his face. The light was leaving his eyes, but he was still alive as Luke Boyd pushed the knife point under his chin, and twisted it, hard. The warrior's body juddered, once, and then toppled over onto its side. Boyd stabbed the blade into the ground, and cleansed it of his enemy's blood.

"Neatly done," the heavy set Englishman said, with real respect in his voice. "I see the tales I hear of you are all true then?" William McCloud lowered his gun and surveyed the sprawl of dead and dying Odawa warriors scattered about the sunlit glade. "How many of these wicked fellows have you killed, these past five years?"

"Not enough." Boyd finished cleaning his knife blade on a handful of grass, and retrieved his bloodstained hanger from where he had cast it. "You know me, friend?"

"We have not met, sir... but I know of you," the Englishman replied. "My agents report that you are a very special sort of fellow. The sort of fellow I need. You must come and work for me, lad."

"I am my own man," Boyd said, and started back to collect his two muskets. His disinterest was only for show, and he could not help but wonder what a dandified looking Englishman wanted with him enough to brave the wilder parts of the forest. "Go home, Mister McCloud. Canada is a dangerous place for the likes of you."

"America," McCloud said to his retreating back. "You crossed the border a while back. That is against the recent treaty between His Britannic Majesty's government, and the United States."

"Perhaps the Americans should stop the

Algonquin and the Odawa from crossing their border to raid our farms, and murder innocent womenfolk and children," Boyd snapped back. "I track them, like I'd track a bear, and I kill them. A dotted ink line, scrawled on a map by some politicians, means nothing to me. It doesn't matter where they are… I find them, and I kill them."

"Oh, but it does matter, young man." William McCloud smiled and held out a package of documents, wrapped in sealskin to protect them against the worst excesses of the Canadian elements. "This is a request for your arrest, and it comes from Washington, old chap. They want you arrested, and handed over to them. It seems you also like to kill their fur traders. They claim you hanged some poor fellow from the rafters of his own barn."

"Arthur Durant deserved his fate. The bastard was selling the Indians muskets and powder, in return for pelts." Boyd eased a hand to the knife at his belt, but the sound of McCloud's gun being cocked was enough to arrest the movement. "Nice weapon you have there, Mister McCloud."

"Yes, it is one of those new-fangled rifles the Baker Gunsmith Company want us to issue to our British Redcoats. It is damned slow to load, but I can shoot a fly off a wall at two hundred paces. Please do not make me demonstrate the truth of that statement, sir."

"You'll never get me back." Luke Boyd

was not boasting. With so many miles of wilderness to traverse, McCloud would tire, close his eyes, and that would be that. Boyd knew how to be patient, and bide his time. "You would be a fool to even try, mister."

"I have absolutely no wish to deliver you up to the vagaries off American justice, Mr Boyd," the Englishman said. "All I want is for you to return with me now, to Montréal, and accept my offer of gainful employment. I see no future here for you. Every one of the six tribes have felt your terrible vengeance, and they have called on their allies for help. Come away now, before the U.S. militia start looking for you."

"Let them look."

"Are you ready to start killing innocent men, who are only serving their country?" William McCloud was a master of his art, and knew how to turn things to his advantage. "I know your story, my boy, and I think you have done enough." He has heard the tale of how Boyd had returned home, only to find his family homestead in flames, and his three brothers, father and mother, butchered by a band of raiding Indians. "Five lives, paid for by fifty ... or is it more?"

"I stopped counting." Boyd held out his hand, and McCloud handed him the brand new Baker rifle. "It's beautiful."

"Try it." The Englishman forced himself not to flinch as Boyd drew back the hammer and pointed it at him. Then, in one fluid motion, the woodsman dropped to one knee, aimed at a tree a hundred paces distant, and fired. The lead ball raised a shower of wood splinters as it struck, and he nodded his approval.

"A fine weapon," he said, and offered it back. "Only now, you are unarmed."

"Keep it. The damned thing takes too long to charge. A redcoat can reload and fire his musket three times in a minute. I fear poor Mr Baker will starve to death, for want of an order from HorseGuards."

"To be able to kill at two hundred paces would give any army an advantage," Boyd opined. "The rate of fire would slow down, of course, but the increased range, and accuracy, would kill more with each volley."

William McCloud agreed the sense of that. He went over to his pack horse, and rummaged in one of the saddle bags. He came out with a small sack of golden guineas, and held them out to Boyd. "One most excellent Baker rifle, and twenty guineas… for your signature. You can write, can you not?"

"I can write." Boyd could, by the time he was five years old, and with moving his lips, read passages from the bible, and his writing was childlike, but clearly legible. By fourteen, he had read his father's books, and would borrow from any who would lend to him. In a different world, he might have moved on to a decent university, and become a different man. "My late mother taught us all."

"Mothers, God bless them." McCloud shook the heavy sack of coins. "I am commissioned, by the highest in the land, to form a company. A special force, willing to go into enemy territory, and therein perform tasks beyond the usual scope of His Britannic Majesty's government."

"You want me to enlist, and then to fight for King George?" Luke Boyd smiled. "Against the Americans?"

"Goodness me, no!" McCloud did a very good impersonation of an effeminate dandy, but Luke Boyd has already learned not to trust his eyes and ears. The man, whatever he was, was no fop. He had just killed three Odawa Indians in close combat, after finding his way through miles of untamed forest. "I have been looking for you since Eastertide. I must admit, Montréal is full of many cut-throats, but my gut instinct told me that you were the very one for me. Had you not stepped in to my little scuffle, I would have had to attend to these fellows all by myself."

"You have been tracking me?" Luke Boyd smiled at so ridiculous a statement. He knew his own prowess, and was confident no one could trail after him, and him be unaware of it. "Since when?"

"Since yesterday." William McCloud was quite adamant about it. "You camped out by the lake, then found the trail of your quarry. I figured you would get yourself in front of them, at some point, so came on behind. Down wind of you all, of course. I found your marks going off to the east, and set myself to bring up just here."

"You could never have tracked me." Boyd thought the man was bluffing, and that their meeting must be a coincidence.

"Really? You moved fast, for fear of missing your prey. I could tell from the space between the crushed grass and broken foliage. You ran at one point, near where the stand of tall pines were. The ones so recently damaged by lightening."

"I don't believe you."

"I followed you, until you paused to eat," McCloud continued with blithe disregard for Luke Boyd's disbelief. "I could smell the beef jerky on the breeze. That is where I decided to head off at a tangent."

"What the Hell is a tangent?" Boyd demanded. It was another new word for his vocabulary, and he savoured the foreign sound of it on his tongue.

"Tangent …a different path," the Englishman explained. "The rest, you know, of course. Now I have saved you, will you return with me to Montréal?"

"Or stay here, and fight the entire American militia?" Luke Boyd asked. He looked as if he might still opt for remaining, and taking on all comers, even if it was a regiment of well armed militia men.

"What about your family, Luke?" Boyd stiffened at their mention. "Your father was still proud to be an Englishman, was he not? Fifteen years as the captain of one of His Majesty's frigates, before settling in Canada. He did it all so his boys had a chance of a decent future. You can still have that future, my dear fellow. Come back to Montréal with me, and then we can go on to England."

"Back to England?" Luke Boyd had not set foot there since he was four years old, and he thought of Canada as his home. "I was just a child when we left Cornwall. What's there for me now?"

"A well paid position, adventure, exciting prospects... and family." William McCloud, the King's finest secret agent had done his homework. "Your mother has family in Wiltshire, and your father's younger brother still lives in Devon. You have cousins, aunts and uncles."

"They do not know me." The thought of living family had never occurred to Luke, until now, and the idea was intriguing.

"Not yet." William McCloud had hung out his bait, and could do no more. He studied the tall, handsome woodsman with a careful eye, and saw in him a man who could be presented into society, but who would always retain the mind of a hardened hunter of men. "I cannot linger, Luke. Our ship sails in less than three weeks time, and I and my associates must be aboard."

"There will be other ships."

"There is talk of war again," the Englishman replied. "The French are busy swallowing up the whole of Europe just now, but soon... they will look outwards. Our king *demands* our help."

"Bugger the king." The young frontiersman had no love for some half mythical monarch, especially one rumoured to be nothing more than a simpering madman.

"Then think of your country, Luke." William McCloud considered how much to tell this dangerous young man. "When I left England, William Pitt was Prime Minister, and he was all for fighting Bonaparte before he grew too powerful. I arrived in Montréal to find out that he was forced to resign, so that a flimsy peace treaty could be signed. Now, Pitt is waiting in the wings, for when we have to fight."

"Against the French, you mean?"

"Against the French." McCloud felt a shift in the man's attitude, and pressed home his advantage. "Bonaparte means to rule the world, Luke, and that goes against the grain."

"My father fought against them as a lad."

"We have a long history... us and them," William McCloud confirmed. "Now the politicians have begged for peace. I, for one, cannot accept their glib professions of goodwill. They are two faced. I am for England, where my duty lies."

Luke Boyd collected up his muskets, and the better weapons carried by the Odawa warriors. "The decorated tomahawks fetch quite good money in Montréal."

"They will fetch an even higher price in London Society."

"I guess they will." Boyd began to load his contraband onto the packhorse. "Though I suppose there's only one way to put that notion to the test."

"Good fellow," William McCloud said, relieved at the outcome of his foray into the wilderness. "What do we do about these bodies?"

"Leave them," Luke Boyd replied. "Unless you want to scalp them. The army post pays a bounty for each one."

"I would rather not," McCloud told him. "I meant, must we bury them... that's all."

"Why?" Boyd shrugged. "The animals will eat them soon enough, so why waste your time digging?"

"Christian pity?" William McCloud offered, and Boyd just laughed, and started walking. If the Englishman wanted him to show pity and remorse, he had come to the wrong man.

"You bury them, if you want," Boyd called back, "but their friends will be looking for them soon enough, and I ain't ready to tangle with a big war party."

"I shall take your advice, Luke," McCloud said. "Besides, I forgot to bring a spade!"

Chapter Three... The Voyage

"I am bored." The prince's closest advisors made no immediate reply, so he slapped his hand, palm down, onto the very well laden breakfast table. "Bored... bored... bored, I say... you fellows!"

"There is a new play on at the..." one of them started.

"There is always some new play or other on, Bunty," the Prince of Wales snapped at the grey faced man. "I want something far, far more. Something ... interesting."

"Perhaps, Your Highness might enjoy a dalliance?" Sir Henry Bunting, known to the prince, and his coterie of hangers on as Bunty, said. "I believe there are some rather pretty new actresses performing at Astley's Amphitheatre."

"Bosh!" It was one of the prince's favourite expressions of anger, and he pronounced it like a petulant child, when told he could not have the last slice cake from the plate. "How is *he* doing then?" Bunting frowned at the discourtesy of the question, but dared not pretend to misunderstand the meaning.

"The king is coping well, Your Highness," he reported. "His physicians say that he passed a quiet night, and slept ..."

"Oh, damn his *pootling* physicians!" Prince George tried to lurch up from the table, found his stomach to be too distended with two dozen oysters, and sat back with a loud grunt. "The old fool will live for ever. What about his mind, Bunty... eh? It is weakened, you know. Why, he might become insane again at any moment. What then....hm? What?"

"The king is well... for now, sir." Sir Henry Bunting glanced across to the prince's breakfast guest for help. The young man, dressed in a beautifully fitted military uniform smiled back at him, and considered letting the fellow stew. Upsetting the prince over breakfast was not a good idea, and certainly not something George Brummell would ever have contemplated. Bunty saw himself quietly abandoned, and finished lamely. "Though the situation might well ... change... or not... and time will tell... no doubt."

"Oh, Bunty," Brummell said, softly. "Stop digging a hole for yourself, old fellow. Prinny simply wonders if he might be called upon, any time soon, to assume his place as the rightful heir to the throne. In short... will Farmer George croak this week?"

*

The full range of Tudor Crimes books are available from Amazon in e-book format, and several are now out in paperback.

Paperback versions of The Black Jigsaw and The Twice Hanged Man by Tessa Dale are also available now, with Towards Hell, The Red Maze and The Chinese Puzzle by the same author due out soon.

© TightCircle Publishing & the estate of the Author 2017

Printed in Great Britain
by Amazon